DESIRE'S FURY

"Damn it, Delia," he swore, as he swung her around to face him, "somebody's got to look after you."

"How dare you!" she snapped. "I'm more than capable of looking after myself. Now get out!"

Her anger was like a contagion. Chase tightened his hold on her arm and pulled her close.

Delia struggled uselessly with him for a moment, then looked up at him.

It was as though he'd been waiting for that, for her to gaze up at him with her eyes wide and pleading. When she did, he slowly lowered his lips to meet hers.

He wrapped his arms around her, drawing her close. His kiss was filled with a hot fury, but he knew even as he touched his lips to hers that the anger wouldn't last, that it was already being extinguished by a far more potent flame.

Delia told herself to fight him, but she couldn't. Perhaps it was the anger that had roused her passion. Perhaps it was simply the fact that she wanted him, if only for one last time, wanted to feel the way he'd made her feel o n, she was recklessly, h

SUSAN SACKETT

RECKLESS

ZEBRA BOOKS
KENSINGTON PUBLISHING CORP.

ZEBRA BOOKS are published by

Kensington Publishing Corp.
475 Park Avenue South
New York, NY 10016

First Printing: June, 1993
Printed in the United States of America

Chapter One

"Delia, *chérie,* you really charmed those British boys, didn't you? Have you no shame?"

Delia Hampton twisted around on her stool to look at the group of a half dozen artists with whom she shared the corner of the small park bordering the river. She stared for a long moment at the tall, sandy-haired man who'd spoken, then openly scowled at him. Despite her expression, she really wasn't angered by his words, and her eyes flashed with amusement when she finally answered.

"It was purely a matter of artistic talent, Claude," she replied in a primly schoolmarmish tone. Then, lest he misunderstand, she flashed him the sort of smile that was obviously intended to make him wilt. "Besides, I save my charm for more worthwhile purposes," she went on. "A half dozen British schoolboys are hardly fitting recipients for my attentions."

With that, Delia snapped closed her work case, stood, collapsed the folding stool on which she'd been sitting, and began to strap it to the side of the case. It was a tricky task to arrange the stool so that it lay flat and out of the way, but she'd done it so many times before that she hardly needed to think about it. Instead, she concentrated on the unaccustomed weight of silver coins in her skirt pocket. Before she lifted the dark brown case, she patted the pocket once to assure herself her small treasure was safe. She couldn't keep herself from smiling at the gratifying feel of the heavy lump of coins.

Despite her protestations she knew Claude had been absolutely right. She *had* charmed those British boys, and she knew that it was to that fact that she owed the extravagant number of coins now filling her pocket. Still, she felt no guilt. The boys had made it more than apparent that they had a good deal more left in their own pockets, and they'd seemed more than pleased with the silhouettes she'd made of them.

"You underestimate the value of one of your smiles, my dear Delia," the man she had addressed as Claude said. "But I must agree that your attentions are wasted on schoolboys on holiday. You deserve an older, more experienced man." He grinned, and there was a slightly lecherous spark in his dark eyes. "One like myself, perhaps?" he suggested.

"Are you offering to leave your wife and run away with me, Claude?" Delia asked, eyes wide and all innocence now.

He sighed, theatrically miming regret, but his tone, when he answered, held a hint of remorse that suggested he was more than a little serious.

"If I thought you might actually accept, *chérie*, I would be sorely tempted to do just that," he told her.

"In any case, you ought to have told those young Lotharios you were interested only in their money before you charmed it all out of their pockets," interjected a second young man, a painter who had begun to pack up his own work box, now that the afternoon sunlight was beginning to fail. "You watch, they'll be back here every afternoon for the rest of their stay, mooning around, watching you,

6

crowding away any real customers who might happen along."

Delia frowned. "I didn't take all their money," she retorted, wondering if she was insisting so strongly because she really did feel a bit guilty for having accepted as much as she had. "And I didn't cheat them or charm their money out of their pockets. Those silhouettes I made of them are as fine as any they'll find anywhere in Paris."

"Don't listen to Pierre, Delia," Claude told her. "He's jealous of the fact that those schoolboys made you laugh while he's too witless to rouse even a small smile."

"When a man tells a woman of his passion," Pierre muttered, "he doesn't want her to reply with laughter." He turned dark, soulful eyes to Delia. "You love me, Delia," he said flatly. "You just refuse to accept it."

"We'll make a pact, if you like, Pierre," Delia told him, with the same sort of melting smile she'd given Claude. "We'll meet here in twenty years and confess our passion, like Cyrano and Roxanne."

Pierre finally smiled. He put his hand to an aquiline but decidedly well-proportioned nose.

"You wound me, *chérie*," he moaned. "I've always been rather proud of my fine patrician nose. Now you compare it to Cyrano's?"

"Such a superior attitude, *ma petite*," Claude chided. "Do you really think even the smitten Pierre is willing to wait twenty years for you?"

Delia shook her head. "Certainly not," she said. "He'll have a wife and at least ten mistresses by then, I'm sure . . . not to mention a dozen children. And I'll be old and wrinkled, in any case."

"You'll never be old in some eyes, Delia," Pierre told her.

Delia smiled. Despite Claude's flippant teasing

7

and Pierre's overly intense words of pursuit, she knew both thought of her in the way they might consider a younger sister. On more occasions than she could count, they'd dealt with a drunken or lecherous tourist who'd expected her to be selling something other than the fine silhouettes she made. Those men would soon find themselves escorted from the park, pushed precariously close to the river's edge, and given a warning not to return. Claude and Pierre teased her and flirted with her and protected her when the need arose. And she loved them both dearly for all of it.

"Don't tell me you aren't going to share those ill-gotten gains of yours and buy us all a glass of Château Rive Gauche?" one of the others asked as he began to gather together the finished canvases he'd set out earlier in the hopes of selling them to a passerby. Once dusk fell, he knew, the only people walking by the river's edge would be lovers, and they would be far too busy with other matters to have an eye to buy his paintings.

This time Delia laughed out loud. "Hand me a bucket, Henri, and I'll fetch it back filled with Château Rive Gauche," she replied, and pointed to where the Seine, murky and dark, flowed sluggishly past them not thirty feet away. "The francs go for a decent dinner for my father, not to get the lot of you reprobates merry."

"Then come sit with us and drink a coffee instead," Claude suggested. He patted his pocket. It had been a profitable day for all of them, as the first sunny and pleasant afternoons always were after several miserable days of rain.

Delia shook her head. She hefted her case, turning it so that the legs of the folding stool were away from her body and unlikely to catch on her skirt.

"I've marketing to do," she said. "A woman does

8

not have the freedom to fritter away her time on the sort of self-indulgent excesses you men allow yourselves."

"We're introspective, not self-indulgent, Delia," Pierre told her. "The artistic spirit needs to be nurtured."

She grinned. "Whatever you do, indulgent or not, I wish you all a very fine evening."

With that, she started off toward the Rue Saint Jacques. When she reached the far edge of the park at the corner, she looked back and waved to the half dozen young men who were all still staring after her. Then she turned away, quickly crossing the wide street. She neatly dodged the traffic, her mind partly on the need to avoid an advancing hansom and partly on the possibilities that the handful of francs in her pocket could provide for dinner.

She'd stop by Monsieur Carbonnier's butcher shop on the way home, she decided, and surprise her father with a dinner of his favorite rare roast beef. That, she knew, would please him, for he'd never lost his taste for that typically American feast, despite the fact that he'd spent more than twenty years in France eating far more elaborate fare. It was genetic, he'd once told her, the need for a thick slab of rare roast beef, something that was bred into all Americans. He insisted that even uprooted and transplanted, they continued to yearn for it, no matter how long they were away from their native soil.

And she'd buy a bottle of really good wine, Delia thought, a rich burgundy to complement the roast. She turned onto a narrow, quieter street lined with small shops, neighborhood butchers and bakers and wine merchants, and began her marketing.

She'd buy just one bottle of wine for her father, she told herself as she opened the door to Monsieur

9

Carbonnier's shop. She hoped if he ate a good dinner, he wouldn't want any more.

Chase Sutton put his hand into his vest pocket and pulled out his watch. He opened it, glanced quickly at its face, grimaced, and then returned the timepiece to its accustomed place.

Twenty minutes, he thought, as he stared at a modest house across the street and a quarter of the distance down the block. He'd have given almost anything to learn what had been said in that house during the previous twenty minutes. He knew that in that length of time Matthew Pickering could easily plan a major art theft, and without some hint as to what it was, there would probably be no way to stop him. And at that moment, stopping Pickering was precisely what Chase was supposed to be doing.

Chase stared at the facade of the old house as though his glance could somehow give him the information he wanted. It was an ordinary enough structure for this part of the Left Bank of Paris, a bit dilapidated, the shutters drooping slightly, the fine carved door beginning to turn a sad, dull, untended gray. Once prosperous, even grand, perhaps, but now merely respectable, the house had the sort of slightly seedy air that a building takes on when its prime has passed and left it to face the onset of the final years of decay.

With his glance leveled on the house, and, most important, the front door, Chase didn't really pay much attention to the passersby on the street around him. He strolled casually to the corner, glad that particular pastime was quite common on Parisian streets and did not make him the object of any undue attention. From time to time he pretended interest in the jumbled display of small tables, teapots,

10

slightly tarnished silver, and other assorted oddments in the window of the antique shop at the corner, a fact which alternately raised and lowered the hopes of the shopkeeper who sat inside the empty shop, staring out at him.

When the door of the house opened finally, Chase was, from all appearances, deeply engrossed in consideration of the attributes of a silver flask located in the far corner of the antique shop window. Pickering stood by the door, darting a glance first down the block and then to the corner where Chase was standing. Not wishing to be noticed by the man, Chase turned quickly, hoping to avoid Pickering's attention.

His movement set in motion the sort of series of actions that would be dreaded by any normal man, let alone a private investigator hoping not to call attention to himself. His shoulder brushed against the arm of a woman walking past him, and that in turn caused her to lose her balance. He reached out to steady her, jarring her arm as he did, and this caused her to lose her grip on the packages she was carrying. They began to fall, one by one; the woman reacted by reaching for them and succeeded only in dropping the heavy leather case she had been holding in her other hand.

Her groceries landed on the thick cobblestones with a series of dull thuds. It was only through a desperate grab and a bit of luck that Chase managed to catch a bottle of wine before it met an untidy and wasteful end on the rough stones.

Chase swore under his breath as he realized that the scene could only call attention to him. His anger with himself, however, was suddenly and completely extinguished when he looked into the face of the woman to whom he'd caused so much inconvenience. He caught his breath, forgetting entirely the

11

real reason he had come to stand on that particular corner half an hour before.

She wasn't the most beautiful woman he'd ever seen, at least, not in the sense of what fashion called beauty. No little bow of a mouth, no upturned button of a nose or pale alabaster skin. Her cheeks were unabashedly healthy, bright with a flush from the brisk March wind and, most probably, from the embarrassment of the mishap as well. Her nose was decidedly straight and just a bit too long, determined rather than cute or typically pretty. Her lips were full, and they, like her cheeks, were blushed a becoming shade of pink. Looking at them, Chase could not help but wonder what they would taste like, were he to press his own to them. A mass of dark curls, mostly unruly vagrants helped by the wind with their escape from the pins that were intended to hold them neatly anchored to the back of her head, framed her face. It set off a pair of the most startling eyes he had ever seen, eyes that were slightly almond-shaped, the color of old amber flecked with burnished gold. He found himself thinking how easily a man could get lost in eyes such as hers.

"I'm sorry," he murmured, as he began to kneel to retrieve the fallen packages. Then, remembering he was in Paris and not back in London, he switched to French. *"C'était ma faute."*

"Non, non, pas du tout," Delia replied. Realizing he had spoken in English, she added, "I wasn't watching where I was going. It was my fault entirely."

She wasn't merely being polite, she realized as she joined him, kneeling and beginning to retrieve her purchases. She had been far more intent on watching the man who was exiting the house she shared with her father than she had been on the stranger

12

with whom she had collided. Now, when she looked up and watched the man starting across the street, walking briskly toward her, she was once again transfixed by him just as she had been when she'd first noticed him pulling the front door of her house closed behind him.

He was unknown to her, and that in itself was a surprise, because she thought she knew all of her father's friends. Still, it was more than that that now held her transfixed, staring up at him. It was his face, with its dark, piercing eyes and a prominent, almost hawklike nose that jutted sharply forward. Not a handsome face, certainly, but definitely not bizarre enough to cause her to stare as she was. She realized quite suddenly that it was his look of malign intelligence that mesmerized her, the sudden chilling feeling that this man could be capable of doing almost anything he set his mind to.

What, she wondered, could this man have been doing in her house? What possible business could he have had with her father?

Chase darted a quick glance up at Pickering, then hurriedly ducked his head before he could be recognized and busied himself with gathering together Delia's scattered bundles. It was only when Pickering had continued on past the two of them that he returned his glance to Delia and saw her preoccupied stare.

"Do you know that man?" he asked offhandedly.

Delia shook her head and forced herself to throw off the strange fascination that had held her interest. She returned her glance sheepishly to Chase, feeling oddly embarrassed by the fact that he'd seen her stare and not quite sure why she felt that way.

"No, and that's probably why I so clumsily bumped into you," she replied. "I can't remember the last time I saw a stranger coming out of the

13

house." She noticed the bottle where he'd set it on the sidewalk near his knee. "Oh, you are talented," she said. "You saved the wine."

She looked up at him and smiled, only then really looking at him for the first time and noticing that he was quite handsome, with sandy blond hair and intensely blue eyes. She didn't bother to consider the fact that she was pleased by the way he stared at her, his eyes seemingly glued to hers, his look pleasantly intrigued. It certainly wasn't the first time she'd seen that sort of look in a man's eyes, for she'd garnered more than her share of such stares in the previous few years, but it was, she realized, one of the few times when it didn't make her feel uncomfortable.

Chase tore his eyes from hers and stared down at the bottle. Although his interest in her was far from impersonal, he realized that her mention that Pickering had been in her house had intrigued him, especially as it was more than obvious to him at that point that he couldn't simply jump up and once again begin following the man. He lifted the bottle from its less than stable perch on the cobblestones and held it out to her, all the while thinking that perhaps she might provide him with the means of finding out how Matthew Pickering had spent the previous half hour after all.

And if he was lucky, he told himself as he glanced once again at her face, that task might very well be made decidedly enjoyable by the company of this lovely young woman.

"Purely instinctive, without any talent involved," he told her. "There's something deep inside me that refuses to be the cause of the waste of perfectly good alcohol." He looked at the label on the bottle. "And this particular alcohol is more than just adequate, I think."

She nodded. "A surprise treat for my father. In

14

celebration of this beautiful afternoon. They are far too rare."

Chase grinned at her. "You speak excellent English, for a Parisian."

Delia chuckled. "My father is American," she said. "And despite more than twenty years here, he refuses to learn to speak more than the most rudimentary French. If I speak anything but English at home, he pretends not to understand, although I'm sure he knows precisely what I'm saying."

"And so you humor him?" Chase asked with a smile.

She nodded as she tucked the bottle under her arm. "Certainly," she replied. "What else can a daughter do? And you?" she asked, considering his accent. "British?"

He nodded. "Guilty," he replied as he reached for her case. "Here," he added, "let me at least help you get all this home."

Delia pursed her lips in mock consideration, "I oughtn't," she said. "It's not considered good manners for a young woman to accept favors from strange men on the street."

Chase laughed. "The English refuse to accept the possibility that Parisians have any manners at all," he said.

Delia nodded solemnly. "And they may be right," she said, then grinned. "But Papa insisted I be raised like a proper Bostonian, and they have decidedly strict ideas of propriety."

Chase returned her grin. "In that case, necessity dictates we not be strangers. Chase Sutton," he said, and held out his hand.

Delia looked at it a second, then put her hand into his. "Delia Hampton," she introduced herself.

"There," Chase told her. "Introduced, all neat and proper, even, I believe, by the strictest of Boston

15

standards. Will you allow me to help you carry your things home now?"

Delia nodded gratefully.

"With pleasure," she told him.

He helped her to her feet, then, as Delia lifted her work case, he piled the other bundles onto his left arm and offered her his right.

"It's not far," she said, and pointed to the house he'd been watching for the previous half hour.

"Regrettably," he replied. "I haven't had the pleasure of walking along a pleasant and quaint little street in the company of a handsome woman in more time than I can remember."

Delia looked up at his blue eyes, and found herself pleased to discover that they were firmly entrenched in a consideration of her. Despite his praise of the scenery, he seemed quite oblivious to it.

"Paris is filled with pleasant little streets," she said, "a great many of them far more aesthetic than the Rue St. Clodoald." She looked up at the old buildings and sighed. She loved the ancient houses that lined the street despite their moldering walls and graying portals. "But still, this part of the city is strangely evocative. I can't imagine what it would be like to live someplace pristine and new, where there are no ghosts to entertain one, late of a rainy, windy night, where there is no feeling of the past to creep into one's dreams."

"Ghosts?" Chase asked, surprised by her words. "Surely you don't seriously believe in such things?"

He looked down at her and saw she was smiling complacently up at him. The smile and the moist, soft allure of the lips that formed it ignited a rush of disconcerting yearning within him. He was beginning to realize that he was becoming intrigued by her. He was not quite sure that was wise, especially

16

if she was involved, even indirectly, with Matthew Pickering.

Delia nodded. "I most certainly do," she insisted. "Papa tells me that a murder was committed in our house more than a hundred years ago, and it is the dead man's ghost that we hear creaking and groaning on the stairs late at night."

"More probably mice," Chase suggested.

Delia laughed. "You *are* British," she told him. "Parisians say that the British have absolutely no spark of romance in their souls." She smiled up at him. "I suppose they would rather believe in their ghosts and their passions than have good manners."

"I assure you, we British nurse our passions as thoroughly as any Frenchman," Chase told her. He was staring down at her, unable to take his eyes from her face, not wanting to consider that there might be any need, at least not just yet. "We just refuse to admit to them."

"I stand corrected," Delia murmured. "Ah, here we are."

She took her hand from Chase's arm and he watched as she put it into a copious pocket in her skirt. There was a muffled jingle of coins as she withdrew her latchkey. It was only then that he noticed she carried no purse, an object he always thought women considered indispensable. He found himself thinking how childlike of her not to carry a purse but rather to keep her coins and her key in her pocket, childlike and charming.

No sooner had she put the key to the lock when the door was pulled open. A tall, pale, thin-faced man stood beside it and stared at her through thick, round spectacles. It occurred to Chase that he must have been there in the entrance hall, waiting for her to return home, or he would not have been able to come to the door so quickly.

"Why, Papa . . ." Delia began.

He cut her off. "Delia, where have you been? You're late." He looked past her at Chase. "And who is that?"

"Papa, really!" Delia chided. This brusquely rude manner was not like him, and it startled her. She stared at him, searching for the all too familiar signs that he had spent his afternoon drinking. Happily, she found none. Reassured, she smiled and nodded toward Chase. "This is Chase Sutton, Papa, a kind gentleman who helped me carry home your dinner." She turned to Chase and completed the introduction. "Chase, this is my father, Cotter Hampton."

Chase froze with his hand half extended. He hadn't taken any special note of her name when she'd introduced herself, for Hampton certainly wasn't that unusual and he'd frankly had his attention on other things than her name. But Cotter Hampton, on the contrary, was decidedly not a common name. And as soon as he heard it, he began to have an unpleasant inkling of just why Matthew Pickering had come to this particular house that afternoon.

He forced himself to extend his right hand fully, but it was only when he felt Cotter's hand in his that he finally roused himself.

A tingle of excitement passed through him as he shook Cotter's hand. He was, he told himself, shaking hands with perhaps the finest art forger in the world.

Cotter stared at Chase suspiciously for a moment. A stranger appearing at his door after the unsettling visit he'd just had from Matthew Pickering did not sit well.

"Well, will you let us in, Papa?" Delia asked.

Cotter released Chase's hand and stepped back,

18

but did not take his eyes off the young stranger as he and Delia stepped into the house.

Delia pretended not to notice her father's preoccupation. She closed the door behind them, then put her work case down on the floor beside it.

"As you've carried home the groceries, Mr. Sutton, it would be rude of me not to extend an invitation to you to share our dinner."

"I wouldn't want to impose, Miss Sutton," Chase replied, albeit with a shade of regret.

"Oh, don't think you'd be imposing," Delia assured him as she removed her jacket and dropped it on a rather worn-looking armchair. It was, bewilderingly, the sole piece of furniture to occupy the elegant but otherwise entirely empty marble-floored entrance hall. "It would do Papa a world of good to talk to someone besides me for a change, wouldn't it, Papa?" She began to transfer her packages, one by one, from his arms to hers.

Cotter ignored the question as he stared at the heap she'd bought.

"What's all this?" he demanded.

"Fruits of a very lucrative day, Papa," Delia replied. "There was a group of rich British schoolboys, all simply dying to have me do silhouettes of them. I decided the best thing to do with all those francs was buy a decidedly opulent dinner." She smiled brightly. "A lovely beef roast, to be precise."

Cotter was unmoved by her obvious attempt to bribe him into a more effusive mood. He made no move to invite Chase beyond the entrance hall, nor did he seem even remotely pleased by the prospect of so fine a dinner. Instead, he stood and stared at Chase as though he were looking at the devil.

Chase, Delia was pleased to see, did not seem to be aware of her father's inhospitable behavior. He busied himself in the consideration of the small still life that was hung just above the dilapidated chair that served as hall tree.

"Handsome painting," he murmured.

He realized immediately it was a fine copy, knew that had it not been so obviously newly painted, it might have been taken as a minor Dutch Master by the precision of the brushwork and the richness of meticulous detail. But then he realized he would have expected no less from the hands of a genius like Cotter Hampton.

"A copy," Delia responded quickly. "Papa, why don't you show Mr. Sutton into the parlor? I'll put all this in the kitchen and fetch some tea."

Chase turned back to face her. "Please, let me help."

Delia looked up at him. He was smiling at her in a way that made her feel as though there really was nothing in the world he'd rather do. She thought fleetingly of the adoring looks the schoolboys had given her earlier that afternoon and her offhanded dismissal of them. She realized she had absolutely no desire whatsoever to be in the least offhanded in the face of Chase Sutton's smile.

She returned it as she shook her head. "No need," she insisted. "I won't be but a moment."

Cotter waited until she'd disappeared into the rear of the house. Then he turned and pulled open a pair of ornate mahogany doors at the side of the hall. He didn't offer an invitation, but Chase told himself he hadn't refused to have him follow, so that was precisely what he did.

The room he entered was large, well-proportioned and had once been quite elegant, with fine carved paneling on the walls and an ornate marble fireplace. But like the hallway just behind him, it was practically bare. The few pieces of furniture that it housed seemed to huddle forlornly in the center of

20

the room near the fireplace. A small couch, a low table and three chairs. They seemed lost in the huge space.

But if there was almost no furniture in the room, there were paintings, more than he could count, filling every available space that the paneling allowed. They were all still life paintings, like the one he'd noticed in the entrance hall, and all finely executed. And it was obvious, even to his less than expert eye, that all had been painted in the previous few years.

When he turned, he realized he had finally roused Cotter's attention.

"You have an interest in art?" Cotter asked.

Chase shrugged. "Just an amateur's fascination," he replied. "A fine collection."

"Copies, as you can clearly see," Cotter told him. "Valueless."

"If you say so," Chase said. "I really know very little about such matters."

"Don't you, Mr. Sutton?" Cotter asked. "I had quite another impression."

Chase grinned, pretending complete innocence. "I don't know why you should," he said.

"Perhaps because I've learned to identify the smell of a policeman, Mr. Sutton," Cotter said slowly, his tone soft but clearly antagonistic. "It is an odor, I might add, of which you reek."

Chase stared at him, surprised at the sudden change that had come over him, at the angered lion who had emerged from behind the mask of a peeved, impotent old man.

"You're wrong about me," he started to protest.

Cotter halted the flow of his words with a motion of his hand.

"You need not bother to sit," he said. "I'll thank you to leave my home immediately, and not return.

21

And I warn you, don't ever come near my daughter again."

Chase realized that an argument would be of no help. He'd been a fool to think he'd be able to trick a man like Cotter Hampton into telling him what he was planning with Matthew Pickering, and an even greater fool to allow himself to be charmed by Hampton's daughter.

He turned on his heel and did what Cotter had ordered him to do, walking across the empty entrance hall and slipping outside, leaving without a sound.

Chapter Two

"Papa, what have you done with Mr. Sutton?" Delia asked as she entered the parlor with a heavy tea tray in her hands. She stopped just inside the doorway and looked around to find only Cotter sitting in solitary silence, staring fixedly at the evening newspaper.

He looked up for only a second, then returned his attention to the front page of his paper.

"He asked me to convey his apologies, Delia," he muttered in reply as he began to leaf through the pages. "He remembered he had an appointment."

Delia darted a bewildered look at him, then proceeded into the room and put the tray down on the table by the couch. Her eyes narrowed as she turned to stare at her father. He'd done something, she mused silently. She could tell from the way he pretended to ignore her that he had definitely done something.

The only problem was, she couldn't imagine what that something might be and why it would precipitate Chase Sutton's sudden departure. She certainly hadn't expected that. In fact, she had been absolutely sure he'd been only too anxious to spend the evening in her company, a feeling she'd found herself warmly mirroring as she'd prepared the tea. She turned her attention to pouring the tea, thinking again of his smile and what she'd seen in those deep blue eyes of his before she'd left him alone with Cotter. No, she was sure she couldn't have been mistaken.

But as much as she didn't like to accept the fact, his disappearance made it only too obvious that she had been mistaken, completely mistaken. She tried to remember everything she'd said to him, everything she'd done, in an attempt to understand how she might have offended him. She could think of no word or action so odious that it would set a man to flight.

And yet Chase was undeniably gone. She felt a bleak wash of disappointment seep through her as she considered his desertion. The intensity of that disappointment startled her. How odd, she thought, to feel so strongly about someone she'd only just met.

Once she'd reviewed the events of the previous hour and decided that her own conscience was clear, Delia began to cast about for another explanation for Chase's departure. The only possibility, she quickly determined, was that something had happened between Chase and her father. Now that she thought of it, she realized that she didn't need all that much of an explanation from her father, after all.

Cotter had been in a strangely antagonistic mood when she and Chase had entered the house, and if she'd been less elated about the pleasant surprises with which the afternoon had presented her—both the pocketful of coins and the chance meeting with a handsome and personable man—she'd have been more attentive to his uncharacteristic behavior. She gave an evaluating glance to where he sat hiding behind his newspaper. It was enough to convince her she was right.

She had only to give Cotter a moment or two and he'd eventually tell her what had happened. For now, she'd play his game and wait for him to confess. It shouldn't take long, she assured herself. It had always been impossible for him to hide anything from her for very long, certainly not if she was determined to know what it was.

She lifted one of the filled cups and turned to offer it to him.

He was seated on the one comfortable piece of furniture in the room, an old and rather worn armchair upholstered in a faded damask. The sharp white and black of the newspaper he held up in front of him contrasted starkly with the dull green of the old fabric and the gently worn brown of his trousers, all of him that wasn't behind the page. It struck her suddenly that he was growing old. The thought was startling to her, and decidedly unpleasant. She didn't want to think of him that way, didn't want to think of what her life might be like were she ever to lose him.

Cotter gave no indication that he'd noticed either Delia or the proffered cup. He sat silent and unmoving, legs crossed in a pretense at nonchalance, staring with apparently fixed concentration at the page of the evening newspaper.

"Don't you want your tea, Papa?" Delia asked in her most simpering voice. She hoped her tone would rouse his attention.

He refused to lift his glance from the page.

"Thank you, Delia, no," he replied. "But please don't let me stop you."

Delia grimaced and returned the cup to the tray. Her patience was beginning to wear very thin, and she realized that whatever her intention had been a few moments before, she was no longer willing to sit quietly and wait for him to decide he was ready to

25

offer an explanation. She put her hands on her hips and glared at him.

"All right, Papa," she said. "Now, why don't you tell me what you've done with Mr. Sutton? And while you're about it, you might just as well explain what it is you're up to."

Still, Cotter didn't so much as lift his eyes to meet hers. He folded the paper back, then again, as though he were following an article to the bottom of the page. He shook it a bit, straightening it fastidiously. Only when he seemed satisfied with it did he finally clear his throat.

"I'm sure I don't know what you're talking about, Delia," he muttered. "Be a sweet girl and fix me a whiskey-and-soda."

"I will not," she snapped. She moved a bit closer to stand directly in front of his chair and waited a moment longer for him to look up at her. When he didn't, she put her hand on the paper and pushed it down.

"Delia!" he protested.

"Papa!" she responded.

He sighed in resignation and dropped the paper to his lap.

"I assure you I'm up to nothing whatsoever," he said evenly. "Now, will you please fetch me that drink?"

Delia didn't move. "You've been behaving very strangely from the minute I arrived home," she accused.

"For God's sake, Delia," he muttered, "must a man be completely predictable? Can't he have the privilege of being out of sorts occasionally?"

"No," she told him firmly. "Not without a reason."

They glared at one another for a moment in silence. She found his uncharacteristically persistent silence completely unnerving, and finally gave in, speaking first.

"Papa, you know I love you," she said softly.

"And I love you, Delia," he replied, as he lifted the paper once again.

"If you do, then you'll tell me what you did with Mr. Sutton," she said.

"A strapping young man like that?" he asked. "Whatever could an old man like me do with him?"

"You know what I mean, Papa," she persisted. "You sent him away, didn't you?"

Cotter only shrugged, and returned his attention to his paper.

Delia realized she was losing, and she felt her anger with him melting into frustrated bewilderment.

"Papa," she began again, this time her tone pleading rather than irate, "please tell me what's happening. There was that strange man coming out of the house before, and now you've sent Mr. Sutton away. I know something's wrong. And lest you think you can spend the evening reading that newspaper and ignoring me, I promise you, I have no intention of leaving you an instant's peace until you tell me what it is."

Cotter let the paper fall finally to the floor. He turned his eyes up to meet her gaze squarely for the first time since she'd returned to the room.

Delia realized there had been a flicker of something in his eyes when she had mentioned the stranger she'd seen on the street. That was it, she told herself. Whatever has come over him has to do with that man.

"Who was he, Papa?" she prodded. "The man who was here today?"

Cotter stared at her in silence for a moment, wondering how much he ought to tell her, how much it would be best to keep to himself. He could see she was hurt and bewildered by his evasiveness, and he understood it. They'd never kept secrets from one another, and he knew he'd feel the same way if she'd tried to keep something from him.

He also realized it was no good, that he'd never be able to sit by and watch her made miserable by his silence. The recognition of her pain generated a stab of regret in him. The last thing he wanted was to see her hurt.

That was the worst of the whole situation, he realized. There was very little chance that no matter what he decided to do with regard to dealing with Matthew Pickering, she most probably would be hurt by the outcome. He hated the feeling of impotence that came over him at the realization that he was no longer in a position to protect her as he once had been.

The pain in his chest came as a surprise to him, although if he'd thought about it, he'd have expected it. The scene with Sutton probably started it, he told himself, not that that really mattered. He ought to be used to them by now, for they came fairly often of late, too often. Soon, he realized, he'd be of even less use to her than he was now.

He grasped the arm of his chair, leaned back, and exhaled very slowly, waiting until the pain eased before he spoke, determined not to let her see what was happening to him. The sharp constriction began to ease, much to his relief.

"Delia," he said softly, "you must realize that things aren't always simple. Things happen that complicate life. Something a man does on a whim can come back to haunt him twenty years later."

Delia knelt down in front of him and put her hands on his knees.

"What are you talking about, Papa?" she asked softly.

28

The pain was gone now, although his breath was still a bit labored. He told his body to move and managed to lean forward to her. My beautiful daughter, he thought. What meager legacy will there be for you when the final pain comes to claim me?

"Only that sometimes there are things you must do, no matter how much you don't want to do them," he told her, choosing his words very carefully. "That no matter how much you want to bury the past, there's always someone who remembers and uses what he knows."

"Someone who remembers?" she mused softly. She bit her lower lip, pondering, wondering what it was he was telling her. She could see the regret in his eyes and realized that although he was now willing to talk to her, he was, in his own way, asking her to back away and not press him any further.

As much as she would have liked to honor his silent request, she realized she couldn't.

"Someone who remembers," she repeated. "That man I saw coming out of the house, Papa? Is he the one who remembers?"

"Forget you ever saw him, Delia," he told her sharply. "Forget all about him."

His defensiveness startled her.

"And Mr. Sutton?" she asked softly. "Am I to forget all about him as well?"

"Yes," he told her. "Forget both of them."

She shook her head slowly. "I can't, Papa," she said. "At least, not without an explanation."

A dull flush of anger colored his cheeks at her words.

"Damn it, Delia, why can't you simply do as you're told?"

She shrugged. "It's my life, too, Papa," she replied. "It may be your past he knows about, but I'm caught up in it, too, now."

29

Cotter swallowed, his Adam's apple bobbing uncomfortably in his throat. She was right. As much as he hated to think about it, he knew it was as much her problem as it was his.

"I suppose it's my own fault," he said. "Letting you run wild with those damned beggar artists. I ought to have seen you married to some respectable banker or lawyer and living a normal life long before this. It's unbecoming, the sort of life you lead."

Delia didn't defend herself, thoroughly aware there was no need. He was prouder of her talents and even her independence than she would ever be, and she knew it.

"You hate bankers and lawyers, Papa," she reminded him softly. "And you're hardly in a position to damn artists."

He grimaced, then pushed her hands away from his knee. There was no pain any longer, only a slight feeling of weakness. He stood abruptly, refusing to meet her eyes as he edged past her. He walked slowly to a window that overlooked the ruin of what had once been a fine garden and stood looking out at it, thinking of the time when Delia had been a child and her mother still alive. In those days there had been money to pay gardeners to keep the flower beds filled with blooms and the hedges clipped into intricate designs. In those days there had been plenty of money for everything. He sighed as he reviewed the images of the past. It had all gone so quickly, he thought, both the money and the years, like water slipping through his fingers.

For a moment he seemed overcome with bitterness over the irony of it all. As he looked back, he realized that it had all been a game to him then, and no matter how he'd played, he'd always found his pockets filled with the winnings. He wondered idly when the game had ended, wondered where the money and his youth and his love had all gone.

Delia sat on the floor and watched him, aware that it would do no good to press him now, that he would tell her when he found the words. But each second he stood silent with his back to her seemed endless to her. It must be very bad, she thought, for him to take so long to find the courage to tell her.

He didn't turn back to face her. When he finally spoke, it was as though he were simply musing aloud, or talking to the glimmer of his reflection in the window glass.

"The man who was here," he said softly. "I knew him a long time ago. His name is Matthew Pickering. He is an art dealer, a rather gifted one who has an uncanny ability to obtain especially fine and rare paintings for those clients with the pocketbook to support very refined tastes."

Delia swallowed uncomfortably. "You mean he's an art thief," she said.

"Yes," Cotter agreed. "To put it bluntly."

Delia heard her own sharply indrawn breath, audible in the silence that followed Cotter's announcement.

"You painted for him?" she asked in a hoarse whisper.

He nodded. "Just a few trifling canvases," he replied. "Nothing important. I didn't like him, and there were many far more accommodating buyers for my work. I haven't seen him in twenty years." He was silently thoughtful for an instant as he remembered opening the door and finding Pickering standing there, waiting for him, his face fixed and his lips twisted up into that unpleasant smile. "I thought I was seeing a ghost when I opened the door and first saw him, an evil, malevolent ghost."

Delia found herself brightening somewhat at this.

31

"But he can't harm you, Papa," she assured him. "He can reveal nothing about you that wouldn't implicate him as well."

Cotter turned finally to face her. "About those paintings I did for him twenty years ago, certainly," he agreed. "He probably wouldn't even be able to find anyone to listen. No one would want to admit they've accepted a forgery as genuine for more than twenty years. No, it isn't the matter of those canvases that he has to hang over my head."

"Then what else could it be, Papa?" Delia asked.

"He's a man with an extremely discriminating eye," Cotter told her slowly. "He once told me he could identify an artist's work by looking at the brushwork and nothing more. I believe him. I saw him do it a half a dozen times, and he never made a mistake, never so much as faltered."

Delia was beginning to get a sick feeling in the pit of her stomach. "And?" she asked, but even as she did, she realized she already knew.

"He spotted a small still life hanging in the Galérie des Anciens," he went on, "a canvas that bore the signature of Van Eyck. He came to tell me that he recognized the touch, to tell me that he knew it was mine."

"Oh, no!" Delia moaned softly.

Cotter struck his fist into his palm. "To think they've held the damned thing so long," he hissed. There was a slight flutter in his chest, and he forced himself to be calm, knowing he could not hide another attack from her. "Why didn't they sell it three years ago when you sold it to them?" he murmured in anguished regret.

Delia didn't try to answer his question, knew there was no answer. Her thoughts were growing muddled, clouded by a choking fear.

"What did he want?" she asked.

32

"Two paintings," Cotters said, his words pronounced very precisely. "Two Flemish still lifes. Memlings."

"Memlings," Delia said. "Impossible. They can't be copied. Memling was a master. A forgery would be spotted immediately."

"That's what I told him," Cotter said. "And he said that was why he'd come to me, that I was the only one who could do it. Then he told me to think about it, about what would happen were he to make it known that the canvases in the Galérie des Anciens were mine. And then he left."

"What will we do, Papa?" she asked.

He shook his head. "I don't know."

"You'll have to tell him," she murmured.

"No," he shouted. "You don't know him. I tell you, he wouldn't be above using what he knew. I'd sooner spend the rest of my life rotting in prison."

Not that that would be very long, he told himself. There can't be very much time left at all.

"But what else can we do?"

He paused for a moment before he answered. "We could give him what he wants," he ventured.

"No!" Delia nearly shouted. "No, Papa, we cannot," she added, in a softer tone. "There must be some other way."

"I don't know what it could be," he admitted. "I have to think. One thing's for sure, though. You stay away from strangers, and that includes that Sutton fellow."

Delia shook her head as though she were shaking away a few cobwebs inside. She was entirely baffled by the flow of his logic.

"What has he to do with any of this?" she asked.

Cotter cringed as he heard the note of disappointment in her tone. No need to bother her with that, he told himself . . . the thought of Pickering is more than enough.

"He's a stranger, Delia," he said. "Right now we can't afford to make any mistakes, can't afford to let something slip that might be repeated." He turned and faced her. "It won't be forever. Just until we have all this ironed out."

"Ironed out?" she persisted. "Just how do we iron it out?"

He shrugged. "I don't know. We both know I can't do what he asks." He stared at her a moment, then shrugged and looked away. "Maybe we could leave Paris. You'd like southern Italy. Or even Greece. There are beautiful landscapes to paint. You'd enjoy it."

"You mean run away," she said.

"Just for a while. Until Pickering loses interest."

"He won't," Delia told him. "If you thought he would, you wouldn't be so upset by all this."

Cotter's eyes once again met hers for a moment, then he tore them away and turned back to stare out the window.

"No, I suppose not," he admitted. "Perhaps all the more reason why we should leave."

"Papa," she reminded him softly, "we have no money."

She watched his reflection in the glass, saw him raise his chin sharply and stare fixedly through his spectacles at the wilderness of the garden.

"I could sell a few more paintings," he suggested cautiously.

"No, Papa!"

The sound of her words echoed loudly through the large room. Delia hadn't even realized she'd shouted until she heard them return to her, sharp and angry. She took a deep breath, trying to calm herself.

"You promised, Papa," she pleaded. "You said you wouldn't."

Cotter continued to stand with his back to her, but Delia didn't need to see his face to know what he was feeling. His shoulders fell forward, his usually proud, erect stance dropping into one that spoke unquestioningly of defeat.

She pushed herself to her feet and crossed to him, putting her hand on his shoulder to comfort him.

He reached up and patted her hand with his and pulled himself sharply erect again. He turned to face her and managed to give her a semblance of a determined grin.

"We'll try to think of something," he told her, "something legal."

"We will, Papa," she assured him. "We'll get through all this somehow."

Cotter nodded. "I have to think." He inhaled deeply, then slowly released his breath. "Damn it, Delia," he said, "I need a drink."

This time she didn't argue. She nodded, then turned and crossed to the far side of the room, to the small table that held a bottle of whiskey, a siphon, and some glasses. Her hands were shaking as she lifted the bottle and poured some of the golden amber liquid into a glass.

She replaced the bottle and took the glass, then turned and stared at her father's back. His shoulders were slumped again, and she knew his brief show of determination had been to reassure her, nothing more. Again she was struck by the thought that he seemed frail to her, suddenly very old.

She lifted the glass and sniffed the strong scent of the whiskey. This is what has done it to him, she told herself, whiskey, and her mother's death. She ought to pour the damned stuff out, ought not to give him any more of the poison that was slowly eating his life away.

Instead, she started back across the room to him. The whiskey would make him drunk, she told herself as she handed him the glass, but it wouldn't kill him, at least, not quickly.

Matthew Pickering, on the other hand, held a power over him that was a different matter altogether.

It seemed impossible to Delia that it could be such a perfectly beautiful day. After the comfortless, sleepless night she'd spent, she'd have thought the sky would be dark and bleakly gray. By all rights, she told herself, the weather ought to mirror the empty misery that was filling her soul.

But somehow it didn't. Above her was a field of solid blue, completely unblemished save for a handful of perfectly white fluffs of clouds scuttling toward the horizon. Sunshine, ordinarily a rare enough commodity in Paris, save in the summer, when there was so much of it that it set the air above the cobblestones in the streets shimmering with the heat, reflected from the old stone of the houses along the Rue St. Clodoald. It turned the usual dull gray-brown color of the stones to a beautifully warm, burnished gold. The air fairly radiated with a clear, brilliant sunshine that warmed the breeze and kissed the still bare tree limbs overhead, nudging the waiting buds and bidding them to open.

It was, Delia knew, the sort of day that would draw the rich English and Americans come to tour Paris's sights from the confines of the Louvre, Notre Dame, and Sainte-Chapelle, lure them from the comforts of the soft banquettes at Maxim's. It would take them instead for a stroll that would inevitably lead them to the small parks that bordered the

Seine. Mellowed by such pleasant weather, they'd stop to admire the work the young artists set out to sell.

The practical part of Delia's nature that so ably managed the household finances which were a mystery to her father told her that it was as perfect a day for business as she might possibly wish for. The pocketful of francs she'd earned the day before would seem paltry to what she might expect to earn on such a glorious day as this.

In short, it was a pristine early spring day, the kind that promised a pleasant and profitable afternoon, the sort that ordinarily chased away whatever cares might have plagued her in drearier weather.

The only problem was that this otherwise perfect day was marred by the realization that she could not possibly earn enough money, even were there to be a veritable mob of British schoolboys and extravagantly generous Americans, all with pockets bulging with francs and eager to buy her silhouettes, to do anything that could dispel the stormclouds generated by the revelations her father had made the evening before. She and Cotter were caught, mired by an unfortunate choice her father had made more than twenty years before.

The worst part of it was that she knew that even were Cotter to agree to give Matthew Pickering what he wanted, the problem would not disappear. She instinctively knew that Pickering would use mercilessly the ammunition he held against Cotter. She and Cotter would only become more and more deeply mired until they were both finally pulled completely under. No, giving in to Pickering would do them no good. There had to be another way.

The only problem was that she had no idea what that might possibly be.

Considering the tenor of her thoughts, it was not

especially surprising that she had little enthusiasm to hurry to her usual place at the park. The thought of all the pretense that would entail chilled her. How, she wondered, could she be expected to smile at the tourists by way of invitation to sit for her silhouettes, or banter with Claude and Pierre and the others, when she was filled with thoughts of what might happen to her father and herself if Pickering were to expose what he knew?

As many times as she told herself she ought to behave normally, ought to follow her regular routine, still she found herself unable to take her usual path to the park. Instead she found herself wandering aimlessly along the narrow, winding streets of the Left Bank, carrying her work case and stool with the reluctance she would have felt toward some odiously unpleasant burden.

Occasionally she ventured into an open courtyard and stared up at the weathered face of one old house or another, trying to pretend she was someone else, some stranger who'd never seen any of this before and was still capable of abandoning herself to the pleasure of discovery. More than anything, she wished to escape, to become someone who had nothing more pressing than the sunshine and the scenery to occupy her thoughts.

After an hour or so, though, the pretense wore too thin for her to bother with any longer. Resigned, she turned onto the Boulevard Saint Michel, found a small café and seated herself at one of the outdoor tables. She ordered *café au lait,* promising herself that once she was properly fortified, she'd do what she ought to have done an hour before, gone directly to the park and begun her day as she might any other.

But rather than quickly drinking her coffee, she found herself lingering over it, losing herself in the anonymity offered by the crowded bustle of the avenue and thinking of what it would mean were her father to break his word to her and sell some more of the paintings. Were he not caught, they'd have the money to leave, to start out someplace else anew, someplace where Cotter's past would have no meaning and hold no threat.

The prospect, she realized, rather than calming her fears, terrified her almost as much as the possibility of Pickering revealing what he knew to the police. She'd lived all her life in Paris, save for a few short trips to the south during the summers, when she'd still been a child. Her happiest and saddest memories were tied to the city. The prospect of leaving seemed to her nothing less than cutting away a part of herself.

She couldn't imagine a life were she to turn her back on all this, she told herself as she let the heat of the cup warm her hands and stared at the traffic in the street in front of her. And she knew there was little possibility that her father could long survive, were they to flee. Even if they had plenty of money, she knew he was tied to the old house and the city that surrounded it by invisible but unbreakable bonds, bonds that drew him regularly to the small cemetery behind the small Église de Saint Gérant.

That very morning Delia had heard Cotter leave the house just after dawn, and she'd known he'd gone to the cemetery to sit by her mother's grave and talk to her in the early morning quiet. Perhaps he'd wanted to discuss what had happened with her, perhaps he'd only needed to find some comfort in being near her. For nearly twelve years now he'd taken his problems to that still grave and always come away with some solution in mind. Delia prayed that there had been some answers for him that morning.

She realized she wished she could feel as he did,

wished she could feel close to the long-dead person whose remains occupied that grave. But death was something final to her, frightening and unfathomable. As much as she wished she could believe, she knew she could not. There was no such spiritual tie for her like the one Cotter had with the memory of his dead wife, only the dimming memories that slowly receded with each passing year.

One thing she did share with Cotter, however, was the knowledge that she would be breaking an umbilicus that sustained her spirit were she ever to be forced to leave. And if fleeing Paris and Pickering might save Cotter from disgrace and prosecution, she knew it would quite simply break his heart.

Surely there must be some other way to deal with Pickering. She wondered if the man could possibly be so great a monster as her father had portrayed him. Surely he could be convinced to leave them in peace if he were told the truth about Cotter.

She bit her lip and stared down at the dregs left in the bottom of her cup. Pickering was a man, she told herself, and men had weaknesses. If reason would not convince him, perhaps she could find something else that would. She was no longer a child, she told herself, and it was unfair of her to leave dealing with Pickering to her father. Perhaps it was finally time that she shouldered the responsibility of protecting Cotter rather than the other way round.

She was still staring down at the contents of her cup, but she no longer saw anything but the image of the man she'd seen leaving her house the previous afternoon. She shuddered as she recalled the vicious look she'd seen in his eyes, the look that had so repelled and fascinated her. Was this what she had waited her whole life for, she asked herself, to give herself to such a man?

For an instant Pickering's image was blotted out by another, that of Chase Sutton. Why couldn't it have been him, she wondered. With a stab of regret, she recalled her father's admonition to avoid the handsome British stranger. Hardly any need for that, she mused. He'd hardly be likely to come calling after his sudden departure the previous evening.

Her thoughts returned to Matthew Pickering, and this time when she pictured him, his sharp and vicious stare was leveled directly at her. She closed her eyes, trying to blot out the image of him, but it stayed, refusing to be banished. A tremor of fear passed through her and she nearly dropped her cup.

Her hand was shaking slightly as she set the cup down on the saucer. She had to force herself to steady it, telling herself it was not so great a sacrifice after all, reminding herself that women sold themselves every day in Paris, and most for a far smaller price. She would do whatever she had to do.

She stared down at her hand. It was steadier now. There was, it seemed, a certain amount of relief in having made a decision, determined a course.

She'd go to Pickering, she told herself, and ask him his price to leave Cotter in peace.

And whatever the price he asked, she'd pay it.

Chapter Three

Chase stood where the shadows of a shop doorway hid him from view and stared across the flow of
traffic on the Boulevard Saint Michel to watch Delia
as she sat musing over her coffee. Now, what's she
up to, he wondered? Is she waiting there to meet
Matthew Pickering?

He hadn't found it easy to keep track of her winding passage through the Latin Quarter that morning,
following her along the narrow streets and taking
pains that he not be noticed. At first he'd been confused by the apparent aimlessness of her excursion,
but finally, as it became obvious to him that she was
too lost in her own thoughts to notice either him or
even take special note of where she was going, he'd
realized that she might have simply been trying to
lose herself.

That bewildered him. It had seemed to him that
she'd appeared decidedly determined when she'd
first set out that morning. He reminded himself that
he'd been elated by his initial glimpse of her leaving
the house. She'd glanced up at the sky, then started
briskly walking along the Rue St. Clodoald as
though the glorious weather meant nothing to her,
as though its charm paled when compared to the im-
port of her errand. He'd even dared to hope that she
would lead him to Pickering.

Now, as the moments stretched on and there was

no sign of anyone approaching her table at the café, he was beginning to think he had set himself on a fool's errand. She couldn't be meeting anyone, let alone Matthew Pickering, he told himself. There was no sign that she was watching for anyone, or was growing impatient that he hadn't arrived. There was nothing about her manner that indicated she was doing anything but sipping a cup of coffee and watching the parade on the street in front of her.

He began to consider the possibility of approaching her himself. It was a risk, he realized. If Cotter had told her of his suspicions, then she would realize that Chase had probably been following her. And if she began to suspect him, then there would be absolutely no possibility that she would ever lead him to anything useful.

All in all, that would be disastrous for him, for he'd lost track of Matthew Pickering after the unfortunate mishap on the Rue St. Clodoald the previous afternoon. After being summarily ejected by Cotter, Chase had returned his attention to Pickering, only to find the art thief had checked out of his hotel and seemingly vanished. Chase had been unable to find a trace of him.

The only leads he had now were the Hamptons, father and daughter. And with Cotter suspecting him of being a policeman and on his guard, Chase's options were further limited. That left Delia. If her father was being cautious, she would be the most likely go-between in his dealings with Pickering. And assuming Cotter hadn't relayed his suspicions to her, although that might very well be assuming too much, he told himself, she would be a good deal easier to outwit.

At least, he fervently hoped she would. If she didn't lead him to Pickering soon, then he would have to admit that he'd hopelessly botched his job.

"She's all I have," he murmured softly, but not so softly that a woman staring at the display in the shop window didn't hear. She looked up at him, raised an arched brow, then turned and walked quickly away.

Her reaction turned Chase's thoughts in a different direction altogether. However appealing the thought, he didn't have Delia at all.

Not that having Delia wasn't an intriguing possibility, he thought. He stared across the street at her and let himself forget for a moment why he was there, instead losing himself in the pleasure of simply looking at her.

Her hair shone like polished ebony in the brilliant sunshine, the wisps of curls that had worked their way loose of their pins fluttering against her cheek, the pale skin of her neck, and the brim of her outmoded but oddly becoming hat. He watched as the breeze pushed a wisp of her hair onto her cheek, close to her lips, as she lifted her hand to it and negligently pushed the strands away before lifting her cup to drink. Hers was an unaffected, effortless beauty, he realized. She was probably barely conscious of it.

Chase, on the other hand, was rapidly becoming only too painfully aware of just how desirable she was. A dull yearning was slowly filling him, and he was beginning to feel more than a little uncomfortable with it. He was starting to hate the thought that she might be part of Matthew Pickering's plans. He even began to hate the necessity that had forced him to use her to get to her father and to Pickering. Perhaps, he rationalized, he could protect her, keep her from being mired in the disaster her own father was about to bring down on her.

But he quashed the growing urge he felt to shield her, telling himself that most likely she was as much

44

a part of Pickering's plans as was her forger father. As little as he might like to think of such a beauty languishing in jail, that was, most likely, where she would eventually end.

Despite his best intentions, however, Chase found that the cynic inside simply couldn't hold territory. Contrary to his own common sense, still he was mellowing and even beginning to be smothered by his desire to believe that she knew nothing of either Matthew Pickering or her own father's involvement with the art thief. He wanted to believe her innocent, he realized, wanted it perhaps a good deal more than rational consideration of the situation should let him. He had a job to do, he reminded himself, and he couldn't allow his thoughts to be clouded by a pretty face.

But he mollified his doubts by telling himself that if it was true, if she was indeed innocent, then he stood to gain a good deal from gaining her friendship. Aside from the more obvious pleasure of her company, there was always the possibility that she might let slip information about her father.

It didn't take him long to come to a decision. His desire to believe her entirely innocent of her father's association with Pickering was probably outweighing his common sense, he told himself, as he started across the street to the café.

And if, on the other hand, she really was up to her pale, lovely neck in Pickering's plans, he mused as he deftly skirted the wheels of a hansom that seemed bent on his destruction, he had no reason to feel guilty about using her.

"Surely it can't be all so terribly serious as that, Miss Hampton."

Delia had been completely lost in her thoughts.

Feeling safely alone in the midst of the crowded bustle of the street, she was startled to hear her name spoken as she did. She started, nearly sending the cup flying across the small marble tabletop as her hand knocked against it. She'd been thinking so much about Matthew Pickering that she half expected when she looked up she'd find it was him, come for her. Not yet, she prayed silently. Soon, but please, Lord, not yet.

When she gathered enough courage to turn to see who had spoken and found Chase Sutton standing beside her, however, all thoughts of Pickering miraculously disappeared.

She couldn't keep from smiling. She'd really not thought she'd ever see Chase again after his unheralded departure, and that particular loss had only intensified the misery she'd felt the previous night and all through the morning. His sandy blond hair was blowing slightly in the breeze, his dark blue eyes were shining as he stared down at her, and his lips turned up into a smile that told her only too plainly how pleased he was to see her. She decided that he looked terribly handsome.

"Mr. Sutton," she murmured. She was surprised to feel a strange fluttering inside at his sudden appearance. She was, she realized, as pleased to see him as he seemed to be to see her. "What an unexpected surprise." She smiled. *"What* can't be so terribly serious?"

Chase scanned her expression and congratulated himself, realizing his instincts had been right. She seemed surprised to see him there, just as she ought to be, and even pleased, he thought. There was nothing about her expression to indicate that she suspected him of having followed her or of being the policeman Cotter had accused him of being the previous evening.

But even as he congratulated himself on making the right decision, he realized he was forgetting that he had concrete reasons to cultivate her company. Instead, he found himself thinking of how easily he could become lost in those incredible eyes of hers. As he had the previous afternoon, he stood momentarily entranced by them, lost in a bewildered admiration, marveling at the tiny flecks of gold that shone out from the darker amber.

"Whatever it was that put that worried look into your eyes," he replied finally, when he realized she was staring up at him, waiting for an answer. "You really oughtn't to allow that to happen," he chided and smiled gently. "They are incomparably lovely eyes, and ought never to show anything but absolute happiness." He found an empty chair at the next table and pulled it close to hers. "You don't mind company, do you?" he asked as he seated himself, even though it was apparent that it was too late for her to suggest he not join her. "I pledge myself to move mountains if necessary to cheer you."

Delia laughed, and he found the sound of it delightful.

"With such extravagant promises, how can I possibly demur?" she asked.

Chase considered her smile. "Perhaps I won't need to move any mountains after all," he said.

"Perhaps not," she agreed.

"Good," he said, as he motioned to the waiter to bring two more cups of coffee. "A prospect far more appealing than setting out with a pickax and shovel occurs to me as I consider the dual perfection of the afternoon and your lovely smile."

She raised a quizzical brow.

"And that is?" she asked.

The corner of his lips turned up in a wry grin.

"Taking you for a carriage ride through the Bois

de Boulogne, buying you a magnificent lunch, and regaling you with my dry British wit."

She smiled politely at the invitation, but realized she was more than a bit baffled by it.

"After you ran away last evening," she accused softly, "I'd have thought you wouldn't want to waste so much as a hint of drollery on me."

He pretended shock. "You wound me, Miss Hampton."

She shrugged her shoulders and pursed her lips primly, falling silent as the waiter delivered the two fresh cups of coffee and cleared away her empty one. When he'd gone, she looked back up at Chase.

"Papa did explain that you suddenly remembered an appointment you'd forgotten . . ."

"Yes," he broke in, relieved that Cotter had furnished him with an excuse, however spurious. "I felt the absolute fool." He leaned toward her. "Frankly, I was so impressed with my own good luck at having chosen a lovely woman to crash into and impress with my grace and elan that I simply lost track of everything."

Delia almost managed to stifle her smile.

"You did, of course, save the wine," she reminded him.

He nodded. "And then countered my one good deed by running off like a churlish cad."

"I do hope the lady wasn't terribly angry with you for being late," she said coyly.

He shrugged. "I'd hardly call my broker a lady," he said thoughtfully. "He has whiskers that I've never thought particularly feminine. And now that you mention it, he was furious. Made me pay for the drinks."

She laughed again. "I have no sympathy for you whatsoever."

"Is there no way I can absolve myself and return

to your good graces?" he asked. "If you had some packages, I'd knock them over after I made sure I'd saved the wine."

Delia stifled a grin. "What purpose would that serve?" she asked.

He shrugged. "It worked yesterday," he reminded her. "I even dared hope you were a bit taken despite my clumsy bumbling."

"Perhaps I was," she admitted.

He shook his head in regret. "Alas, you've no packages for me to strew across the street. I have no recourse but to apologize most humbly."

"As you certainly ought," she told him. "Not even saying goodbye!"

"Let me make it up to you," he urged. "Say you'll spend the afternoon with me."

Delia raised her cup and sipped her coffee thoughtfully as she let her eyes drift to meet his.

"I oughtn't," she told him. "On an afternoon like this I can earn as much as I ordinarily would in a whole week."

No, you oughtn't, a voice inside her told her sharply. Aside from the money, she'd promised Cotter she'd stay away from strangers, and from Chase Sutton in particular.

"Really?" he asked.

She nodded. "Your fellow British must never see sunshine. On a sunny afternoon like this, they fairly swarm the quays and throw francs at the artists."

Chase considered her words with the same mock seriousness with which she'd uttered them, then looked up at the sky and stared at it with thoughtful deliberation.

"There'll be another fine day tomorrow," he announced when he'd completed his appraisal.

Delia arched a brow.

"You're certain?" she asked.

"I absolutely guarantee it." He reached across the table for her hand, and she made no attempt to keep it from him. "Work tomorrow," he urged her. "Come spend the afternoon with me."

Delia stared down at her hand where it rested in his. It seemed so small lying in his, almost dwarfed. Men are really very frightening creatures, she thought, as she looked back up at his eyes. They have so much strength in those great bodies of theirs, so much power that they must keep in check if they are to live by the laws of civilization. What a trial it must be for them.

"I shouldn't," she repeated softly.

But when he'd dropped a few coins on the table to pay for the coffee and then stood beside her, his arm extended in invitation, she found herself hushing the objecting voice of her conscience. She'd be careful, she promised herself as she turned to stare up at him. She wouldn't mention a word about Cotter or Matthew Pickering.

She stood and took his arm, bewildered by the persistent flutter his presence had roused inside her and by the ease with which she'd dismissed her promise to her father. Strange things were happening, she realized, and although she knew she ought to question them, she didn't.

A pleasant afternoon, she told herself, surely she deserved that. The matter of Pickering would still be there to be faced when the afternoon was past.

Delia lifted her wineglass and stared at the pale golden glow of the liquid inside it. A soft, mote-laden shaft of sunlight drifted from the window beside her. When she held the glass up to it, a tiny rainbow appeared in the wine.

"Is something wrong with the wine?" Chase asked. "Shall I send it back?"

Delia raised her glance to meet his and shook her head.

"Oh, no, it's fine," she assured him. "I was just wondering if there might be a treasure hidden at the end of this tiny rainbow." She held the glass up so that he might see it, too.

"Tiny rainbows have only tiny treasures," he told her.

"More's the pity," Delia murmured.

She shrugged and took a healthy swallow of the wine. It settled into her, leaving a mild warmth trailing in the wake of its passage. It occurred to her that this was her third glass, that she really oughtn't to drink so much, that however pleasant the slightly fuzzy warmth it created inside her, she wasn't really used to it.

She carefully set the glass down by her plate and started to pick up her fork, but changed her mind. She'd had her fill, she realized, Channel oysters followed by an excellent *gratin aux fruits de mer*. Besides, she reminded herself, a lady always left something remaining on her plate. Somehow it was terribly important to her to have him think well of her, to do nothing that he might find distasteful or unmannerly.

She looked up at him and realized he was watching her. She smiled at what she saw in his eyes. At the moment he appeared to find nothing in the least distasteful about her, she assured herself.

Chase reached for the bottle and lifted it to refill her glass.

Delia shook her head and put her hand over the top.

"No more, thank you," she told him. "I'm afraid I've already become a bit tipsy."

He considered her slightly flushed cheeks and grinned.

"Then perhaps there was a treasure hidden at the end of that rainbow after all," he told her.

"Am I to construe that remark as a preamble to an assault on my virtue, Mr. Sutton?"

The words were out of her mouth before she'd realized she'd spoken them. The truth was, she had absolutely no idea where such a question had come from. After all, he'd behaved the absolute gentleman throughout the whole of the ride through the Bois to this lovely *auberge,* a fact which she suddenly realized had almost disappointed her. She felt a blush creep into her cheeks as she realized what it was she was suggesting. A moment before, she'd been afraid he would not think her a lady, and now she suddenly found herself practically issuing him an invitation for seduction.

He seemed as surprised by her question as she was, but far less put off.

"Chivalry dictates I respond in the negative, Delia," he replied softly. He leaned forward and took her hand in his, then lifted it, holding it near to his lips. "But at this moment, I'm afraid honesty forces me to admit that I find it terribly difficult to be chivalrous."

He pressed his lips against her open palm.

Delia felt a tremor pass through her at the contact. The warmth of his lips seemed to seep into her hand, sending a ripple of heat that grew as it flowed upward through her arm until it finally seemed to fill her. How strange, she thought, that so small a contact could have such a devastating effect on her.

She looked down at her hand, half expecting to see it had somehow been changed by his touch. It hadn't, of course. It looked just as it had a moment before, pale and nearly dwarfed in his.

She turned then, and looked out the window at the stark ranks of the trees that edged up close to the *auberge*. They might have been miles from the city from the view she had; they might have been in the middle of an endless forest. Soon spring would bring leaves to all those huge trees, she thought, and no matter what changes might occur in her life, the flow of spring to summer and summer to fall would go on, the cycle untouched, eternal.

It was only a glance, a second in duration, but when she turned back to meet Chase's glance she knew she had come to a decision. If she was going to offer herself to Matthew Pickering, as she'd determined to do, then she had nothing to lose by giving herself first to a man she found attractive and charming. And she could not avoid the simple fact that at that moment she found herself deeply curious about what she would feel were he to wrap his arms around her. If the mere touch of his lips to her hand could have the effect it had had on her, then what would his embrace, his kiss, kindle within her?

"I'm glad," she murmured, as her eyes found his. "I think just now I'd prefer you to be honest rather than chivalrous."

He smiled that crooked smile she'd come to expect from him at her response, obviously far from displeased. Then he lifted her hand a second time, caressing it gently before he again pressed his lips to her palm. Just as it had the first time, the sweet fire radiated out from that place where his lips touched her skin, only this time far more quickly.

They sat for an endlessly long moment then, in complete silence. Delia realized they really needed no words, only the sharply electric exchange that was passing between their clasped hands, their joined gazes. She felt herself falling into the pale blue ocean of his eyes, floundering in them as though she were about to drown.

The waiter came to remove their plates, and Chase

was finally forced to release her hand. Delia drew it back slowly and put it in her lap.

She didn't move, didn't even blink as Chase turned to the waiter and asked, "You have rooms here, don't you?"

"Oui, monsieur," he said, without turning his attention away from his work for so much as an instant. There was no question but that he was quite accustomed to such requests.

When Chase returned his glance to Delia's, her eyes were waiting for his, welcoming them. He stood, moved around the table to stand behind her chair, and leaned forward to press a soft kiss to the back of her neck. Then he pulled her chair back for her and offered her his arm.

Delia stood and put her hand on his.

Delia looked around the room as Chase pushed the door closed behind them. It was small, but surprisingly luxurious, furnished with a large, shining brass bed, a lush carpet underfoot, a small, velvet-covered settee by the window, and a view of the tree branches and a pond on which swans floated in the distance. A small washstand in the corner was equipped with a handsome pitcher and bowl decorated with gilt and flowers, and towels hung ready from the rack at its side.

It was the bed, though, that dominated the room. Large, and covered with a thick, satin-covered down comforter and a heap of pillows at the head, it was unquestionably far more inviting than the narrow bed she occupied in her room at home. But despite its obvious comforts, she realized that the sight of it sent a small shiver of panic through her.

What am I doing here? a voice inside cried out to her. What do I think I'm going to do? She darted a look at Chase, his back to her as he slid the bolt on the lock. If she were to tell him she wanted to leave, she wondered, would he try to force her to stay? He suddenly seemed impossibly large to her, his broad shoulders strong and powerful. This man was a virtual stranger to her, and fool that she was, she had put herself completely in his hands.

She turned back to the bed and bit her lip. Is this the way it was to be for her, then, in a strange room with a man she hardly knew? Had she waited her whole life, imagining all sorts of magnificent, improbable seductions for her initiation, only to give herself away in this mundane manner?

"Is this all right?"

She started, startled by the sound of his voice. She moved forward, to the window, hoping he hadn't noticed.

It's no good trying to change your mind now, she told herself. It's too late for that.

"It's lovely," she told him, and stared intently out at the pond and swans that drifted along its surface with regal ease.

Chase moved up behind her and put his hands on her arms, pulling her close to him and pressing his lips to the nape of her neck. She couldn't keep herself from stiffening at his touch.

Chase felt the sudden withdrawal, the way she shrank from him. It startled him, for after his initial surprise at her apparent willingness to be with him, he'd decided she was an actress after all, an actress enlisted by her own father to seduce him and learn what she could from him. But this hesitancy didn't fit the role he'd thought she was playing, and he found he was no longer quite so sure she had an ulterior motive.

He put his hands on her arms and turned her to face him, putting his hand on her chin and lifting her face so that he could look into her eyes. And when he did, he found himself melting, found himself wanting her so much he felt the need like a physical pain.

He touched her cheek gently, stroking it with his fingers.

"Do you want to leave, Delia?" he asked her softly, wondering, even as he did, what he would do if she were to tell him yes, she did.

Delia felt suddenly weak, unsure of her own ability to stand alone. The touch of his fingers to her cheek was sending tiny ripples through her, filling her with a confusing yearning that was entirely new to her. She'd never been so lost before, never felt anything like this mix of fear and yearning. Part of her, she knew, did want to leave, wanted to flee before something irrevocable happened. But she could feel herself melting inside just being so close to him, just feeling the stroke of his fingers against her cheek.

She swallowed and let herself become lost in the warm blue ocean of his eyes.

"No," she murmured. "I don't want to leave."

He pulled her close then, pressing his lips to hers, and at the touch of them Delia realized her panic was gone, disappeared in a wave of wonder at the flood of liquid heat that swept through her. She'd been right when she'd mused that his embrace would have a shattering effect on her. She felt as though she were slowly melting inside, as though a hundred tiny fires were spontaneously igniting in her veins.

She let herself go slack, let her body soften against his. He slid his hands down her arms and then wrapped his arms around her waist, pulling her so close to him she could feel the heat of his body despite the clothing between them. How strange, she thought, as he lowered his lips from hers and moved them hungrily to her neck to find the warm spot just behind her ear, how odd that she was no longer afraid.

Because by all rights, she ought to be afraid. Nothing had changed. He was still a stranger, just a man she'd met the day before, a man about whom she knew nearly nothing, save that he was intelligent and witty. He hadn't even told her, she realized, what it was he did, or why he was in Paris. But somehow, none of that seemed to matter.

Her heart was beating wildly, as it had when she'd been small and awakened in the night with a nightmare's terrors. Surely that ought to frighten her, surely she ought to be terrified by the heat she felt growing inside herself, by the strange, throbbing, liquid sensation that was filling her. But none of it raised anything but wonder in her, wonder that it was all so pleasurable, wonder that her body had the capacity to feel this way and she'd never known it. She closed her eyes, losing herself to the surging tides that he'd awakened inside her.

When Chase released his hold on her, she opened her eyes and looked up at him. It bewildered her to see how darkly intent his expression had grown, how strangely unwavering his gaze. He seemed to be waiting for something, but she had no idea what it was he expected of her.

She raised her hands to his shoulders and then slid them to the nape of his neck, thinking as she did of the strength she felt in the hard muscles beneath the smooth wool of his waistcoat. That strength no longer frightened her. Instead, she thought only of what she felt when he'd pulled her to him, of the way it had made her heart beat. She returned his stare, not at all sure what he expected of her, knowing only that she wished he would pull her close

57

again, wished he would again put his arms around her.

"Is something wrong?" she asked softly.

The side of his mouth turned up into that strange lopsided smile of his. He shook his head.

"What could possibly be wrong?" he whispered in reply.

But it *was* wrong, a voice inside told him. It was one thing to try to get information about her father from her, but this, this was something else entirely. There might have been things he'd done in his life of which he was not entirely proud, but dishonestly using a woman had never been one of them.

But perhaps, he thought, he was being maudlin. After all, this was Paris, and she lived and worked among artists, a group notoriously lax about such matters. For all he knew, this might be nothing more than an escapade to her. Or perhaps he'd been right about her from the first: perhaps it was she who was using him.

It ate at him, the thought that she knew about her father's suspicions, that she'd known from the first that he'd been following her that morning. What if she'd turned the tables on him, intending all along to manage to cross his path, to spend the day with him? What if she were using him to gain information for her father, and not the other way round? What if *he* was the one who was being the fool?

But when he stared into her eyes, he thought suddenly how innocent she looked, how unquestioningly trusting. If those were the eyes of a wanton, he told himself, then she was not just an actress but a highly accomplished actress as well. He told himself that if he ever wanted to think again of himself as being a man of any morality, he ought leave immediately, take her home, and try to forget he'd ever touched her.

58

Instead, he raised his hands to her face, stroking the smooth skin of her cheeks and neck slowly with his thumbs as though the feel of her skin was something far more wondrous to him than it ought by rights to be, and staring insistently into her eyes. The line between right and wrong began to grow fuzzy to him. He wanted her, wanted her more than he could have imagined possible.

Delia had the strange feeling that he was asking her something with that gaze, searching for some dark secret. She knew that she would at that moment have willingly answered him if she'd had any idea of what it was he wanted to know.

Instead, she raised her lips to him in invitation.

It was all the spur that Chase needed. He lowered his lips to meet hers, his response hungry and demanding.

Chapter Four

Chase's kiss quite literally took Delia's breath away, leaving her breathless and dizzy and just a little bit lost. When she first felt the knowing probe of his tongue, she could only wonder what it was he was seeking. But she willingly parted her lips to him, too confused to do otherwise, and soon felt the sweet fires ignited by the contact. She was locked now in the circle of his arms, a willing prisoner, lost in the mystery of the flood of feeling that his touch released to sweep through her.

She hardly knew what he was doing when he lifted her and carried her to the bed. All that was real to her was the feel of his arms holding her, of his lips touching hers. And then she found herself lying back against the pillows, and his lips were moving against the flesh he bared as he unfastened the buttons of her blouse.

There was no turning back now, she realized as she snaked her fingers through his thick curls and savored the heady warmth of his lips against her naked skin. The thought was only an absent one. She no longer had any desire to run away, no longer had any desire but to go wherever it was he wanted to take her.

She let him undress her, a task she would have realized he was not entirely unused to performing, had she given the matter any consideration. There was no thought for such things, however, no thought for anything but the feel of his hands and lips against her skin, touching her in places she'd never been touched before, places she'd never thought to be touched by another.

The warm, insistent urging of his lips and hands released thick, roiling waves inside her. Nothing had prepared her for this impossible magic he was performing, the transformation his touch began as he pressed his lips to her breasts and belly and the soft, warm place between her legs. All that was real to her was the heightening need that was filling her, a yearning she did not even realize was pure animal passion, a mysterious storm that once unleashed, fed upon his touch and grew stronger and more powerful with each moment that passed.

The first sweet thrust as he entered her was like thunder being released inside her. She felt herself melting where he touched her, and it seemed to her as though she were flowing into him, becoming part of him with the joining. Nothing had prepared her for this, nothing had ever felt as this felt, nothing had ever been as shattering or as powerful or as beautiful.

When his hands urged her, she began to move, suddenly worldly, knowledgeable, as though the secret steps of this eternal dance had been buried somewhere within her and had only been waiting to be released by his touch. She no longer questioned the powerful tides that were building inside her, no longer feared where they might take her. She might be a captive in his arms, but she was a willing captive, however much it frightened her to realize the power his flesh held over her.

She pressed her body close to his, savoring the sweet fire, each shattering, blinding wave of it as it shot through her. She abandoned herself to him, pressing her hips to his, pulling him close as his lips and tongue found hers, all the while adrift in the tides he released in her, tides that grew steadily stronger and more urgent.

Nothing, she realized, could have prepared her for this, for never could she have envisioned herself feeling as she felt at that moment, joined to him, part of him, unable to distinguish where her own body ended and his began. Never could she have imagined her practical self so completely and utterly lost, so totally at the mercy of a man's touch.

When it came to her, the release was momentarily terrifying, completely beyond her comprehension of what was happening to her. She felt herself seared through by it, leaving her bathed in a pure, clean light that suddenly shattered into a million tiny bursts of fire. She clung to him, trembling and panting, nearly deafened by the sound of her own heartbeat, afraid that were she to release her hold of him, she might fade away and disappear.

Chase felt her trembling release, and the knowledge sent a warm wave of pleasure through him unlike anything he'd ever felt before. He lost himself in its wake, his control suddenly vanished, leaving him to follow her into a well of pure, sweet rapture.

Never before had it been so compelling for him, never had the release been so complete or so sweet. For an instant he told himself again that he had been wrong to use her this way, but he quickly pushed the thought aside, staring down at her, letting himself instead become lost in the golden flecks in those impossible amber eyes.

"You're smiling," she whispered, feeling suddenly very proud of herself, delighted that he seemed pleased.

"You're smiling, too," he said, as he placed his

hands to either side of her face and stared down at her. Then he lowered his lips to hers, kissing her softly now, his lips gentle and lingering, the taste of her breath sweet from the wine they'd drunk. Odd, he thought, as he finally lifted his lips from hers, how much she tastes like honey.

He lay back against the pillows, then pulled her to him, holding her close with her head resting on his chest. She was trembling, he realized, and he could feel the mingled soft thuds of both their hearts. Soon enough, he knew, he would have to find a way to get her to talk about her father and Pickering, but the thought of that was repugnant to him at that moment, and he chose not to dwell on it. Instead he wrapped his arms tightly around her, basking in the sweet warmth of her body close to his.

If he'd done something unsavory by making love to her, he swore to himself that he would not ruin the moment by dwelling on that knowledge. There would be more than enough time for him to regret his callousness . . . perhaps even the rest of his life.

Delia sighed with pure contentment. She realized she was still confused, that she really had no idea what had happened to her. All she did know was that he had changed her, and that she would never be the same as she'd been before he'd touched her. He'd somehow transformed her, completely and irrevocably. As her eyes drifted slowly closed, she told herself she would have to ponder that mystery, but she was unable to concentrate at that moment, unable to do anything but listen to the soft thud of his heartbeat.

For now, she wanted only to revel in the sweet wash of contentment that filled her. If she'd acted unwisely coming here with him, she still knew she would never regret what she'd done. She may have lost a part of herself to him, but it was far better to give it to this handsome, passionate stranger than to squander it on her father's enemy.

Delia was startled and more than a bit disoriented when she opened her eyes. She had to force herself to swallow the momentary panic that possessed her when she looked up and saw a man's face, his expression intent as he stared down at her. The panic only grew as she darted a look around the room and realized it wasn't the ceiling of her room above her nor her bed beneath her.

It took her a second or two to recognize the face as Chase's, to remember why she was waking in a strange room, in a strange bed. But once the lost feeling disappeared, she looked up at him. A tremor of warmth slipped through her as memory of what had happened between them returned to her. Wide awake and lying beside her with his head propped against a hand, he returned the smile. She lifted her hand to his face and pushed away a stray blond curl that had fallen boyishly across his brow. She thought he looked impossibly handsome.

"Have you been doing that very long?" she asked as she smoothed back the recalcitrant lock with her fingers.

"Doing what?"

"Watching me sleep."

He nodded. There was something about his smile that made her realize he was decidedly pleased with himself.

"Long enough to realize that you're incredibly beautiful," he told her.

She blushed slightly with the compliment.

"It's cruel, you know," she told him, her expression very serious. "You ought never to watch a woman sleep."

"Oh? And just why is that?" he asked. "I thought

64

it an entirely chaste and innocent pastime," he added with that lopsided grin.

"It's unfair," she said. "It ruins the mystery. Like spying on her without her corset and stays."

"Really?" He slowly ran his hand along the side of her torso, gently caressing the slope of her waist and her hip. "I do believe I've already seen you minus any accoutrements whatsoever, and the mystery is still in full force. Besides," he said, and nodded to the heap of the clothing at the foot of the bed, "I hadn't noticed any corset among your trappings." He let his hand once again drift along the length of her torso, realizing that she had no need of such paraphernalia, that her body was perfectly formed, slenderer than fashion dictated, perhaps, but lithe and supple, gently rounded and entirely to his liking. He let his hand come to rest finally on her belly, holding it there as he leaned over her and kissed her.

"It's only a manner of speaking," Delia countered, when he released her and sat up, pushing a pillow behind his back to soften the pressure of the bare wood of the headboard. "Most women don't wish to be perceived as they really are, but rather as they would like to be."

"Unlike you?" he asked, suddenly very sober as he recalled all the unanswered questions he still had about her. How would you have me think of you, Delia, he wondered, and how is that image different from reality?

Delia laughed softly as she gathered the comforter around her and sat up, too, settling herself beside him. She was suddenly deliciously awake, eager to talk, to know something about him, perhaps even to repeat the sweetly exhausting ritual to which he'd indoctrinated her.

"Oh, I am entirely as I seem," she assured him. "You are the one who's a mystery."

He grinned again. "Am I?" he asked.

She nodded. "Most decidedly."

"I think I rather like that," he said. "Chase Sutton, man of mystery. Now doesn't that have a ring to it?"

He was grinning at her, and she knew he was trying to be entertaining as he had been all that afternoon. She rewarded him with a smile.

"I know nothing at all about you," she told him.

His grin disappeared. "True," he mused thoughtfully. "For all you know, I might be Jack the Ripper, abandoning London for Paris."

"Are you?" she demanded, rolling over to lie facing him. Her expression gave no evidence that she was terrified by the possibility; she was, instead, more amused than otherwise. "Are you really a monster?"

He nodded. "But of course."

"I'd never have thought it," she said. She eyed him, doing a slow survey as though cataloging what she saw. "You have no horns, no fangs, no claws, nothing at all monstrous." She leaned forward and pressed her lips to his chest, relishing the feel of the thick, curly hairs there. "At least none that I can see," she added, as she looked back up to his face.

Chase's eyes narrowed slightly as they met hers.

"I've been told that looks are often deceiving," he said softly.

She laughed. "So I've heard, too," she agreed. "Won't you confess? I love to hear confessions."

"Like a priest?" he asked with a grin.

She shook her head. "More a voyeur, I think," she admitted with a small laugh. "Have you a highwayman's past, riddled with the bodies of seduced maidens and slain knights?"

He shrugged. "I'm afraid not. Nothing so colorful as that."

Delia was about to go on, but suddenly realized the game had turned serious for her.

"Well, then, are you at least married, with half a dozen children?" she asked, aware that she was perhaps a bit more interested in the answer to this particular question than she really had any right to be under the circumstances.

He raised his right hand. "I swear solemnly, on my honor, or what little there is of it, no wife, no children."

"Who are you, Mr. Chase Sutton?" she asked him softly.

He shrugged. "If you're sure you want the more unpleasant details . . ."

"Oh, I do," she insisted with an intent little smile. She wriggled a bit closer to him. "The more unpleasant, the better."

"Well, then, I admit to being born Charles Albert Sutton some thirty three years ago in the city of London to two very normal, middle-class parents. Charles became Chase sometime around my tenth birthday, the rechristening performed by classmates who decided Charles far too regal for a confirmed hooligan."

"You?" she asked in mock dismay. "A hooligan?"

He ignored the interruption. "My father was a lawyer who insisted I follow in his footsteps. When I suggested that the prospect of becoming a barrister was about as interesting as living one's life in a cave, he washed his hands of me. And here I stand, or rather lie, an exceedingly uninteresting man of few talents save for a rather well-cultivated taste for beauty."

He leaned forward to her and kissed her again, this time lingeringly, his tongue probing her lips and tongue.

For an instant Delia felt herself begin to melt

67

again, but she refused to be distracted. When he lifted his lips from hers, she sighed softly, then backed away from him slightly.

"But what is it you do, then," she asked, "besides seducing weak and unsuspecting women, that is?"

Chase shrugged. He certainly hadn't wanted to get into any of this, and now he realized he had no choice. Lying would only complicate matters, he told himself. Best to stay as close to the truth as possible.

"I find things," he conceded.

Delia shook her head. "I don't understand. What does that mean?"

"I find things that people lose," he said very slowly.

Delia stared at him. He was choosing his words very carefully, she thought, and that seemed strange to her, far stranger than this extraordinary vocation he was describing. What possible need would he have to be on his guard with her?

"What sorts of things?" she pressed.

"Valuable things, for the most part. I find lost valuables and return them to their rightful owners, and in return, they pay me for my efforts."

"Valuables?" Delia repeated. She was beginning to get a strange feeling in the pit of her stomach, a very uncomfortable feeling. Paintings were valuable, she told herself, some of them very valuable indeed.

"Jewelry, mostly," he went on. "Say, for instance, the Earl of Bumblefield becomes indiscreetly infatuated with the wrong woman and takes her as his mistress . . ."

"In his own bumbling way," Delia interjected with a laugh. The unpleasant feeling had disappeared with his words, and she felt ebullient now, if a bit foolish for having let her imagination run wild for the moment.

Chase nodded. "Precisely. Now, suppose our good Bumblefield, compounding this initial indiscretion when she tells him that her one dream is to wear a real lady's jewels for once in her life, brings this questionable young woman his own wife's diamond necklace to wear for an evening. To his delight, the woman is ecstatic. She entertains him that evening wearing nothing but the necklace, and sends him off too besotted to think. And when he's gone, this perfidious creature decides she'd rather like to run off and sell the bauble rather than return it to the trusting Bumblefield . . ."

"Do such things really happen?" Delia asked.

Chase nodded. "More often than you'd ever think," he told her.

"Well, in my opinion it would serve old Bumblefield right if his wife skewered him," she said with a decisive nod.

He shook his head and frowned. "Such a bloodthirsty creature you are," he chided. "I, on the other hand, abhor violence. And that is why my vocation is designed to save poor old Bumblefield from such unpleasantness. Once he finds himself in this unfortunate position, he comes to me and tells me what has happened and we eventually reach an agreement. I then locate the missing necklace before his wife discovers its absence and return it with no one the wiser." He waved his hand. "It's all very civilized, and very British," he added, as though that ought to be enough to answer any further questions she might have.

But Delia found she was suddenly not quite so amused as she ought to have been by the story.

"And what is it you've come to Paris to find?" she asked cautiously.

He shook his head and shrugged, turning away from her gaze.

"Nothing," he said. "Even the most dedicated man deserves a holiday from time to time."

Delia wondered why the unpleasant feeling had returned, why she found herself doubting him. It was a plausible enough story—a bit odd, perhaps, but certainly plausible. Still, there was something about the way he'd turned away from her that left her feeling uncomfortable. She found herself wondering if she had truly made some horrible mistake coming to this place with him. If he were in Paris to find some evidence against her father, if he'd been using her . . .

But no, she told herself, she would have known. Surely she would have known.

"No lost jewels?" she prodded. "No runaway mistress to find?"

He shook his head and turned back to face her. He put his hand in her hair, combing his fingers through it, then catching up a handful and gently pulling her to him.

"No, no jewels," he murmured. "At least I didn't come looking for any." His lips were close to hers, close enough for him to feel the warmth of them. "And even so, I've found a brilliant jewel, one far more precious than any I've ever found before."

His kiss was enough to melt Delia's misgivings, and she responded willingly, letting her body soften against his. A chance encounter with a handsome, interesting man, she mused . . . it was, after all, such an ordinary thing in Paris. And she would never forget this afternoon, not as long as she lived.

Chase released her, leaning back again and slowly trailing his fingertips along the rounded slope of her shoulders and down to her breast.

"And you?" he asked casually. "Now it's your turn."

Delia shrugged. "Me? I've already told you. I am entirely without mystery. I live with my father and make my living by inducing you rich British who come here on holiday to pay exorbitant sums for silhouettes to remind you of your walks by the Seine."

"And your father?" he went on in the same offhand tone. "Is he an artist like you?"

Delia pulled back. The unpleasant feeling was now filling her stomach, and she could find no way to counter it. Cotter's warning roared in her ears.

"Why do you ask about Papa?" she demanded.

Chase stared at her wide-eyed, with apparent innocence, all the while hating himself for lying to her.

"No reason," he told her. "I just remember all those handsome paintings I saw in your house. There were so many. I suppose I just assumed he painted them, that's all."

Delia swallowed uncomfortably. He was so full of easy words, of simple explanations. Despite them, still there was the feeling, and she no longer knew what to think.

"Papa was once a painter," she replied softly as she gathered the comforter around her and stood. "But that was a long time ago. He hasn't worked in several years. His hands are no longer steady enough to paint as he once did."

She turned away from him and walked to the window. She stood, her back to him, gazing out at the swans on the pond, their white bodies shining brightly in the afternoon sunshine.

Chase stared at her a moment, her body lost in the bulk of the comforter, her hair soft and loose down her back, dark against the white satin, shining in the sunlight. She's hiding something, he told himself, and that in itself was enough to assure him there were things Cotter didn't want known about himself. And she knows all her father's secrets . . . that's why she doesn't want to talk about him.

71

He felt a wave of smug satisfaction. It's true, then, he told himself. Cotter Hampton was going to provide Pickering with a forgery to be used in an art theft. But the knowledge raised more questions than it answered. He knew which group of paintings was the target, for, after all, he'd come to Paris to protect them while they were being transferred to the British Museum in London. But he didn't know what particular painting Pickering had decided to steal, and he had no idea when or how Pickering intended to effect the theft. Without some idea of what Pickering intended, he was as blind as he'd been when he'd first set foot in Paris four days before.

His musings were suddenly derailed when he realized his glance had drifted and he was staring at a dark red stain on the sheet beside him. All thought of Pickering and the paintings vanished. He felt a pain in his belly as deep and as sharp as a physical blow.

It hadn't occurred to him until that moment that she might have been a virgin. Living among artists as she did, and Parisian artists at that, he'd simply made assumptions. And she'd been so willing to come with him, so completely accepting when she'd been in his arms. How could he have possibly thought her innocent when she'd seemed to give herself so freely to his lovemaking?

He stood and followed her to the window, bewildered now, no longer sure what he could believe about her and what was as mistaken as his expectations of her had been. He put his arms around her waist and drew her back to him.

"Delia," he murmured as he buried his lips in the soft waves of dark curls.

Instantly Delia knew she was about to melt again, knew that the feel of his arms around her would crowd out her father's warning as it had before, would dissolve the misgivings she'd begun to feel. All Cotter's talk of Pickering and his threats had made her suspicious and fanciful, she told herself. She had nothing to fear from Chase Sutton. If she had, surely she'd know it by now.

She let her body fall back and melt against his. Surely she'd know, she told herself again, and then she banished the thought entirely.

Chase held her close, savoring the feel of her in his arms, the taste and the scent of her. He was aware of a dull wave of guilt that was beginning to gnaw at him, and he had no idea what he intended to do about it.

"Delia," he murmured softly, "why didn't you tell me?"

She turned around to face him, raising her hands to the back of his neck.

"Tell you?" she asked.

He nodded toward the bed, then looked away quickly. The dark red stain was like an accusation, and he didn't like the way it made him feel.

She was far less disturbed about the matter.

"There has to be first time for everyone," she said, and then she smiled at him. "Surely it wasn't a hardship for you, was it?"

He felt a wash of yearning sweep over him, not quite desire, exactly, although that was certainly part of it, but something more, something that wouldn't be quenched by a single act of physical intimacy. He realized that he wanted more of her, more than the few hours she'd spent in his arms, much more, just as he realized that that would never be possible. They were on opposite sides of a minor battle, he and she, and no amount of wanting things to be different would change that.

"No, it was certainly no hardship," he murmured,

remembering how he'd felt when he'd made love to her. "No hardship at all," he whispered, before he lowered his lips to meet hers.

With the memory came a wave of desire, and with the desire a new determination. He wouldn't allow himself to lose her. He put his hand beneath the comforter, stroking her back, sliding his hands slowly along the warm, satiny skin. Instantly he was caught up in the pleasure of the feel of her flesh beneath his fingers. He told himself as he lifted her into his arms that he would do whatever he had to do to protect her.

He lay her on the bed, then followed her, losing himself to the feel of her body beneath his, the hungry seeking of her lips against his. But as he began to make love to her, he grew sharply conscious of the trust she'd shown him, of the power she'd given him to do her harm. This time, he made love to her with a careful gentleness, very slowly, taking great pains to assure himself that he was bringing her pleasure. And strangely the knowledge that he was pleasing her made the act more pleasurable for him than it had ever been before.

Later, Delia lay staring up at him and listening to the sharp, staccato beating of her heart. She reached up to him, pulling his face down close to hers, She was, she realized, more bewildered and lost than she had been the first time, more confused by the long, delicious moments of ecstasy when he'd drawn her to places she'd never before dreamed of going.

"You're a magician," she whispered.

He wasn't quite sure he'd heard her correctly. His own heart was beating with the same ferocity he could feel throbbing in her.

"Magician?" he asked.

She nodded. "You've used magic on me," she told him.

74

"If there's magic," he whispered before he kissed her, "it's in you."

It was true, he thought. In the few hours they'd spent in that small room, she'd changed him completely, transformed the cynic he'd always thought himself to a man who suddenly cared about something and someone other than himself.

He *would* protect her, he swore to himself. If that meant protecting her father as well, then he would do that, too. He didn't know how, but he would find a way to deal with Pickering without letting harm come to either of them.

Delia had to force herself from the languorous drowsiness that seemed about to claim her.

"My God," she murmured, as she looked up and gazed out the window to see the daylight was gone and the sky filled with dark gray shadows. "It's late. I have to get home."

Chase reached for her, pulling her back down to him. "Surely not quite yet," he told her.

She let him kiss her, but then she pulled away, determined. She was feeling guilty now, guilty about the lies she would have to tell Cotter, guilty about having broken her promise to him.

"I have to, Chase," she told him as she stood and backed away from the bed. "You don't understand. I'm all he has left. If I'm late, he'll be horribly upset." And he'll drink, she told herself, he'll drink much too much.

He watched her find her shift among the disorganized heap of their hastily discarded clothing. Odd, he thought, how pleasant it was to watch her raise her arms and slip it on, how lovely to watch the thin fabric settle over her breasts and hips. It was hard for him to take his eyes off her.

He sighed. "If we must go," he said, as he began to climb out of the bed, too, "will you see me again tomorrow?" he asked.

She looked up at him and smiled at the prospect. But then she reminded herself that she wasn't free to do what she liked, that there was still the unpleasant matter of Pickering's threats to her father to be dealt with. She picked up her stockings and sat on the bed, her back to him, and concentrated on the task of slipping them over her legs.

"I don't know if I can, Chase," she replied finally. "Remember, you promised tomorrow will be a fine, sunny day. I have to earn my keep."

He picked up his shirt and walked around the foot of the bed as he pulled it on.

"I'll buy a dozen silhouettes," he told her. "Two dozen."

She shook her head. "I don't want your money," she said. And then she froze, suddenly realizing what his words suggested. She looked up at him. "Is that what you think of me?" she asked. A hard lump had formed in her throat, and she could barely force the words out. "That I came with you for money?"

He stood for a moment staring at her in silence. Why had she come with him? he wondered.

"No," he agreed finally. "It wasn't for money. Although if I were old Bumblefield, I'd gladly give you all my wife's jewels if you'd only allow me to run away with you."

Delia cocked her head coquettishly. "If you're as rich as your Earl Bumblefield, perhaps I'll consider it."

He shrugged. "I'm afraid I'm not, Delia."

She stood and planted a swift kiss on his cheek as she walked by him. "In that case," she said as she stepped into her skirt, "please hurry. I don't want Papa to worry."

"No, please don't get out of the carriage," Delia told him as it came to a halt in front of the house on the Rue St. Clodoald. "I'll just run in."

"Let me at least see you to the door," Chase insisted as he pushed open the carriage door.

"It's really not necessary," Delia insisted. Besides, she thought, the last thing she wanted to do was let Cotter see him with her. It was going to be difficult enough to make excuses without Chase there to complicate matters.

She pushed herself past him, quickly stepping out of the carriage, then turning to retrieve her work case from the floor.

He leaned forward, put his hands on her cheeks, and kissed her.

"Au revoir, Delia," he murmured.

"Goodbye, Chase Sutton," she replied softly.

She was terribly sad, suddenly, and there was a throbbing ache inside her as she realized that this might really be goodbye. She wondered if circumstances would allow her to see him again. Earlier she might have told herself this was simply an adventure, a compensation to take some of the foulness out of the prospect of dealing with Pickering. But now she could no longer think of the afternoon in quite such simple terms. She realized she had come to feel something for him that she'd never felt for any other man. The thought of losing that was more painful than she ever would have thought possible.

"Delia, where have you been?"

She spun around and saw Cotter leaving the house, huffing slightly as he ran toward her. He must have been waiting, she realized, staring out the window, watching for her. And drinking. That, too, was apparent. He was in his shirt sleeves, and his cheeks had grown ruddy from the alcohol.

"Oh, God, no," she murmured.

But God, it seemed, was of no mind to protect her. Cotter's face suddenly grew contorted with anger as he recognized who it was in the carriage. When she saw his expression, Delia realized there would be no easy way to calm him. She ought never to have allowed Chase to bring her all the way home. This sort of scene might even bring on one of those attacks her father had been having of late. The prospect terrified her.

"For God's sake, Delia, what have you done?" Cotter thundered.

"Papa, please," Delia begged. "Let's go inside. We'll talk about it there."

"Talk about it?" Cotter shouted. "What is there to talk about?" He turned to Chase, who had stepped out of the carriage and now stood beside Delia. "I told you to stay away from my daughter," he shouted.

"Mr. Hampton, we *do* have to talk," Chase said.

He seemed almost to have expected Cotter's rage, Delia noticed, although she hadn't mentioned her father's insistence that she promise not to see him. His relative calm surprised her and, had she had time to think about it, would have made her realize that matters were not as simple as either man pretended they were.

But she had no time to think. She was far too busy worrying about her father.

"Talk?" Cotter hissed, his cheeks becoming ruddier as his anger grew. "Is that what you did with her, *flic,* talk?"

"Flic?" Delia broke in, completely baffled now. "Papa, what are you talking about?" She darted a glance at Chase, then turned back to face her father.

"I suppose he didn't happen to mention that part, did he?" Cotter asked her through clenched teeth. "Did he bother to tell you he's police?"

At first Delia couldn't believe she'd heard him correctly, couldn't believe because she didn't want to believe. And then she remembered the questions he'd asked and the nagging, uncomfortable feeling she'd convinced herself was meaningless. It was only too clear to her now that all she'd done was turn her back on reality.

She'd know if he meant her harm, she told herself, repeating the words she'd told herself while she'd still been in the room in the *auberge* with him. But this time the words echoed back to her with a thick, cutting sarcasm. She'd known absolutely nothing. How could she have been such a naive fool?

She spun back to look at Chase and felt herself fill with a wave of sheer disgust, disgust not only with him, but with herself as well.

"Did you find what you came to Paris to find, then?" she sputtered angrily.

"Delia, you have to listen," Chase said, and reached for her arm.

But she had no intention of listening, no intention of letting him convince her again. She pulled her arm free.

"I think I've heard enough lies," she hissed. "Did it amuse you to know I accepted them so easily? Were you laughing at me the whole time?"

"No, Delia, I swear . . ."

"You disgust me," she interrupted, refusing to listen to him. "I never want to see you again."

"Delia!" Chase shouted.

But it was no good. Chase stood, helpless, and watched Cotter put his arm around her and lead her into the house.

Chapter Five

"For God's sake, Delia, how could you be such a fool? I told you to stay away from him."

Delia hardly needed Cotter's recriminations to make her feel just what he had called her, a fool, a complete fool. And her misery was only compounded by a sharp, throbbing ache inside her. As impossible as it seemed to her, she had begun to fall in love with Chase Sutton, and the hurt she felt now that she recognized he'd only used her was almost more than she could stand.

She felt the tears welling in her eyes and told herself she must not shed them, that she mustn't let Cotter see what a complete ruin she'd managed to make of matters.

"You didn't tell me he was police," she murmured.

She stared up at him, trying to muster a bit of defiance, yet all the while she knew it was useless to try to defend herself. She'd promised him, and she'd broken her promise. What she'd done was quite simply indefensible.

Cotter stopped his pacing and stood over her, staring down at her. The flush of his anger was getting deeper. He could feel the heat from the rush of blood, and after it, the sharp pounding in his heart. He tried to curb the anger, aware that it would inevitably bring on the pain and a horrible, wrenching constriction in his chest. He had to be calm enough now to think, he told himself. He could ill afford to be paralyzed by the pain.

But when he saw the glow of liquid in Delia's eyes, he found he no longer had to battle his anger with her. He could almost feel the air around her, heavy with hurt and shame. And for the first time, he realized how deep her pain was. His anger melted in a flood of pity.

He seated himself beside her on the couch, then took her hand in his.

"You didn't let him make love to you, did you, Delia?" he asked softly.

She looked away, unable to bear the pity she saw in his eyes.

"Does it matter, Papa?" she asked. "You're right. I've been a fool. Isn't that enough?"

Cotter dropped her hand and darted up again, this time ignoring his own good advice to remain calm.

"I'll kill him," he shouted. "With my bare hands, if I have to."

And then it struck him, the constriction, the sharp pain that took his breath away like a blow. It was like a hand had reached inside his chest and was squeezing his heart. He would have cried out, had he been able. He reached forward, just managing to grasp the back of his armchair and keeping himself from falling.

"Papa!"

Delia darted up and ran to him. She put her arm around his shoulders and helped him to sit.

Cotter dropped into the chair and put his hand to his chest. He could feel his whole ribcage shaking, could feel the irregular pounding beats. For a moment he thought he was going to die, but then the throbbing began to fade, not much, but enough to tell him that this attack was going to pass just as the previous ones had.

Delia needed only a glance at his pale and frightened face to know something was terribly wrong.

"I'm going for the doctor, Papa," she told him, and turned to the door.

"No." Cotter tried to shout, but the word came out as a thin gasp. He took a deep breath. This time it didn't hurt quite as much and he knew the worst was already past. "Get my pills." He pointed shakily to where he'd left his jacket lying over the arm of the sofa. "Pocket in my jacket."

Delia did as he told her, taking out the small vial of tiny pills, opening it, and shaking out two into her hand. She ran back to him and put her hand to his lips, letting the pills slip into his mouth.

"I'll get you some water," she told him, and started to back away.

Cotter put his hand on her arm and drew her back.

"No. Stay with me," he told her.

He closed his eyes and leaned his head against the back of the chair, breathing slowly and carefully, trying to edge himself past the last of the pain. Slowly the hand that had been gripping his heart began to release its hold.

"We'll find another doctor, Papa," Delia told him, staring at his drawn cheeks. "There must be some way to stop these pains."

"No," he murmured. The pain was almost gone now, leaving him feeling weak, but thankful for the reprieve. He opened his eyes to find her staring down at him. She was, quite obviously, terrified. He waved her away. "Don't fuss at me so. I'm all right."

"But there must be someone who can help."

"I've been to three doctors already, Delia," he reminded her. "They're just a waste of money." Then he added bitterly, "Better to die than to go to prison, anyway."

His words were like a knife in Delia's heart, reminding her of what she'd done, how close she'd come to endangering him. She could no longer fight the tears. They spilled over, a great, thick flood of drops that ran in wide rivulets down her cheeks.

"I'm so sorry, Papa," she sobbed. "How could I have been such a fool?"

She sank down to her knees in front of him.

Cotter immediately regretted the callousness of his words. It hurt him to see her so cowed, so utterly miserable, hurt him even more than the physical pain in his chest had hurt him. And it wasn't all her fault, he told himself. He should have told her about Sutton, should have warned her.

He put his hand on her head and stroked her hair.

"Are you in love with him?" he asked her softly.

She opened her mouth to answer, but the words stuck in her throat. Somehow, she couldn't admit that aloud. Saying the words seemed almost to make it worse. Instead, she looked down, concentrating on his knees, and nodded silently.

Her silence was all the answer Cotter needed.

"How?" he asked. "You hardly even know the man."

She shook her head. "I don't know, Papa," she murmured. "It just happened. I don't know."

Cotter sighed. It was no use pursuing this, he told himself. It was only hurting her, and in any event, talk could not change anything.

"What's done is done, Delia," he told her gently. "We have to be calm now. We have to think of what to do."

She swallowed and nodded her head. "Yes, Papa," she agreed.

"How much did you tell him? About me and the paintings?" he asked.

She looked up at him. His image seemed to sway through the wash of tears in her eyes.

"Nothing, Papa," she sobbed. "I swear. He asked, but I told him nothing."

Cotter breathed a deep sigh of relief. He was slightly surprised to realize that there was no pain in his chest when he did.

"Then no real harm's been done," he told her gently. "Except to you." He wiped away the tears on her cheeks with his fingers, then took her hands in his. "My sweet, lovely daughter. What have I done to you, letting you live this way, roaming the city with that band of brigands calling themselves artists? How could I be so weak as to sit here in this house and let you take care of me?"

"It's what I want, Papa," she assured him.

"But it's wrong," he insisted. "I never should have allowed it. Everything that's happened is my fault. I should have been protecting you from men like Sutton, and instead I hid away here, trying to find the past with whiskey." His own eyes grew moist as he gazed into hers. "And now what will happen to you?"

Delia thought her heart would break when she saw the trace of tears in his eyes.

"I'll be fine, Papa," she told him.

Cotter nodded thoughtfully.

"Yes, you will," he agreed. "You're strong, Delia, much stronger than I ever was."

"We'll both be fine," Delia went on, wanting to comfort him now, forgetting her own hurt with the recognition of his. "I'll never see him again. And you mustn't worry about Pickering. I'll take care of him, too," she added. "You'll see."

Cotter's hold on her hands grew sharp.

"What do you mean, you'll take care of Pickering?" he demanded.

"I'll go to see him," she said. "I'll convince him to leave you alone, to leave us both alone."

That was, she told herself, how this whole unfortunate episode had begun, with her determination to deal with Pickering.

Cotter's eyes grew hard. "And just how do you expect to do that?" he asked.

Delia set her jaw. "What difference does it make now?" she asked. "Any way I can."

"You'll stay away from Pickering," Cotter told her through tight lips. He put his hands on her shoulders and held her so tight his fingers dug into her flesh. "The man is a monster. You stay away from him, do you hear?"

Delia looked up at him, startled by the vehemence she heard in his tone, by the way he held her.

"Papa, you're hurting me," she whimpered.

He stared at her a second, then seemed to suddenly realize that he was, indeed, hurting her. He released his hold, then put his arms around her shoulders and cradled her gently to him.

"I'm sorry, Delia," he murmured. "But surely you understand that you mustn't go near Pickering."

"I won't, Papa," she promised.

"You must promise," he insisted, "and this time you must keep your word to me."

"Yes, Papa."

"I'll find some way to deal with him," Cotter went on. "It wouldn't do any good in any case," he added, almost absently. "He has," he hesitated a moment and looked down at her, "he has other tastes," he finished finally. "Do you understand?"

Delia returned his gaze. "Yes, Papa," she murmured.

She was a Parisian and an artist, she told herself.

She'd seen the sort of man to which her father was referring — in the coffee houses, looking for young boys, luring them with a handful of coins.

She understood only too well.

What she didn't understand was what Cotter could possibly do that she could not.

Delia looked up and made a quick survey of the sky over the Île de la Cité. A threatening wash of gray seemed to be creeping slowly over the city. It turned the ordinarily benign spires of Sainte-Chapelle and the Tour de l'Horloge into sinister, dark, knifelike spikes rising up out of the mass of rooftops beneath them.

It occurred to her that Chase Sutton's weather forecast had been equally as unreliable as everything else he'd told her, but even such an objective observation of him made her stir uncomfortably. She pushed the thought away, telling herself it was better for her not to think about Chase Sutton at all. Perhaps there would come a time when she would be able to think about him without feeling a rush of anger and a dull stab of hurt, but that would be a long time coming. For now, the only defense she had was to keep from thinking about him at all.

It was soon all too apparent to her, however, that telling herself not to think about him and banishing him from her thoughts were two entirely different matters.

She turned to the cobblestone-paved promenade bordering the quays at the Seine's edge, forcing herself to consider the foot traffic passing near the park. There were still a good number of pedestrians, she noted, but they were moving fairly briskly, as was fitting in the threatening weather. She wondered if it would be worth her while to remain in the park much longer. Her practiced eye told her there did not appear to be any likely customers. The afternoon was still reasonably warm, however; her pocket was still empty; and she was not terribly enthusiastic about returning home quite so soon. She decided to stay a bit longer on the chance that she yet might sell a silhouette that afternoon.

"Don't look so unhappy, *chérie*. The sun can't shine everyday."

She turned to find Pierre standing close to her, watching her with those huge, dark eyes of his. He'd been watching her rather more closely than usual since she'd arrived that morning, Delia thought, although she hadn't been aware of giving him any cause except, perhaps, for her vehement refusal to talk about the reasons for her absence the previous afternoon. She did not know why, but she found his attention more annoying than not, something she couldn't recall ever feeling before. Perhaps, she thought, it was because it made her feel guilty again.

"I wouldn't want it to," she told him. "Sunshine would mean we'd have to be happy, and I'm in no mood today. Besides, too much of it in Paris would make life too easy, I think."

"And none of us wants that," Claude interjected with a sharp bark of laughter.

"No," Pierre agreed with a slightly bitter grin, "the last thing any of us wants is for life to be easy. It chills me just to think of what it would be like to sell one of these paintings for a small fortune so that I might live at ease for a while."

Delia offered him a hopeful smile. Of all of them, she thought, Pierre's ego was the most fragile.

"It will come, *mon cher*," she assured him. "There will be a time when we will flock to the Académie to see your paintings, and you will be far too important to so much as admit that you once knew so raffish a group."

"And who knows, this may be your patron coming now," Claude added, nodding toward a tall man in a dark suit who had turned from the promenade onto the park walk. "Decisive-looking type, don't you think? What are the chances he might have some money to spare a starving artist?"

Delia and Pierre both darted a glance at the newcomer.

"Let us hope so," Pierre muttered, as he moved back to his own easel.

Delia hardly noticed his withdrawal. As soon as she saw the figure crossing the small plot of grass at the far side of the park, she froze. A tremor slid down her spine, although whether it was from fear or something else she was not quite sure. What she did know was that the last person she wanted to see at that moment, the very last person, was Chase Sutton.

She turned her back to him, hoping it was just a coincidence that he was walking there and that he hadn't yet seen her. She pretended to busy herself with the small display of silhouettes set out on her work box to attract business, but she hardly knew what she was doing as she shifted the lacy bits of black paper. All her attention was riveted on the staccato sound of his boots against the cobblestone walk as he approached.

It was, apparently, too much for her to hope that he would simply walk past without noticing her. When she heard the footsteps stop, she knew he was standing just behind her even before he spoke.

"I'd like a silhouette, please, miss."

She didn't bother to turn to face him.

"I'm sorry. I'm done for the day."

"It won't take but a few minutes of your time," he insisted. "It's very important to me."

"I'm sorry," she replied, making a great effort to

88

keep her tone even and impersonal. "There's an excellent cutter who usually works just at the far end of the Pont Sully. You might try him."

"I don't want him, Delia," Chase said, his voice low now, intimate. He put his hand on her arm. "I want you."

Delia told herself she ought to be revolted by his touch, or at the very least, angry that he would dare to put his hand on her. But she knew the sudden thumping of her heart was neither revulsion nor anger. She felt suddenly helpless in his presence, and filled with hurt. She tried to pull free, but when he held tight, she was forced finally to turn and face him.

When she looked up at him, she knew her eyes were beginning to fill with tears. She hated herself for the weakling she'd become, for the fact that she seemed entirely incapable of hiding her feelings from him.

"Haven't you done enough?" she demanded. "Why can't you leave me alone?"

"Just let me explain, Delia," Chase said.

"There's no need," she told him. "My father told me everything I need to know."

"He's wrong," Chase insisted. "It's true that I know about him, about the forgeries, but that's not . . ."

"What purpose can it possibly serve you to hunt him now, after all these years?" Delia broke in. "He's old and he's sick. If you had even an ounce of decency in you, you'd just go away and leave us alone."

"I'm not hunting him, Delia," he insisted. "You've got it all wrong. You have to listen to me."

"Go away!" she shouted, and jerked her arm, trying to free herself from him.

"*Ce type t'ennuye,* Delia?"

89

Delia glanced to her side. She hadn't even noticed Pierre return to her side, this time with Claude to accompany him. They were both staring at the way Chase was holding her arm. They seemed not to like it.

They'd protect her, she knew, even if it meant physically forcing Chase to leave. Logic told her that was just what she ought to do, let them force him to leave. But despite everything, still there was a part of her that did not want to see the last of him.

Uncertain for an instant, she bit her lip. Then she nodded to the two painters.

"*Oui*," she told them, as she turned her glance back to meet Chase's. "He is definitely bothering me."

"I think it would be best, *monsieur,* if you were to leave," Claude said in a tone that could not be mistaken for anything but a threat.

"This has nothing to do with you," Chase replied, without taking his eyes from Delia's face.

"The young lady is our friend," Pierre told him, "and if she tells us you are bothering her, then it has a great deal to do with us." He put his hand on Chase's arm. "Now I think it would be wise if you were to release her and leave before we are forced to become unpleasant."

Chase ignored them.

"Delia," he said, "Cotter's wrong, wrong about me, wrong about what I'm doing here, wrong about everything. Just give me a chance to explain."

"I said I think it would be wise for you to release the young lady and leave," Pierre repeated.

This time he punctuated his words by pulling Chase's arm and swinging his fist to come in contact with Chase's face.

More than anything else, Chase was perturbed by the distraction. He hadn't really paid any attention

90

to Pierre until he saw him swing his arm, and by then it was too late to entirely avoid the blow. He felt a sharp pain on the side of his cheek, but it was not so great that it kept him from answering with a swift jab to Pierre's abdomen.

Pierre exhaled with a thick *wuf*, then fell back, landing on his back on the cobblestones. He was still for a moment, obviously dazed.

Delia darted to him, falling to her knees at his side.

"Are you hurt, *mon cher?*" she asked him.

She put her hand to his cheek and stroked it softly.

Pierre smiled up at her, obviously more than willing to accept the pain in his stomach in return for the attention it had brought him.

"It's not bad," he murmured. He smiled up at her, then, when she withdrew his hand, pushed himself to his knees.

Delia looked up at Chase.

"Bully," she hissed at him. "Haven't you done enough harm?"

Chase lifted his hand to the gash on his cheek. He dabbed at the warm trickle of blood that was dripping from a narrow cut Pierre's knuckles had opened.

"It was your friend who started this, Delia," he reminded her.

"And who will happily finish it," Pierre added as he pushed himself back to his feet. Delia's attentions had apparently soothed the hurt in his stomach, at least enough to give him a fresh surge of courage.

"You don't mean that," Chase told him.

This time he took a defensive position, balling his fists and widening his stance. He wanted to make it clear that if there was going to be a fight, he had no intention of being the loser.

"Oh, yes, he does," Claude broke in.

Chase darted a glance to his side. Claude stood there, along with four others. The whole of the small community of artists had left their easels and come to defend their own. All of them seemed only too pleased to offer whatever aid Pierre might require.

"This is your idea of a fair fight?" Chase sneered. "Six against one? I don't suppose you're going to play the part of gentlemen and politely take turns?"

Claude shrugged, completely unruffled by the accusation.

"We're artists. There's no need for us to pretend to be gentlemen," he said. "Besides, there is no need for a fight. You were told to leave the young lady alone, I believe. Perhaps you might wish to reconsider your decision to insist on attention she obviously does not wish to offer you."

Chase turned to Delia. "Damn it, Delia, I'm not leaving until you let me talk to you for five minutes. Is that too much to ask, five minutes?"

She hesitated a moment, every fiber of her wanting to hear him out, wanting to believe he could explain everything, even when she knew it would only be more lies.

"Leave me alone," she murmured, and then turned her back to him.

As soon as she looked away, Pierre darted forward, more than anxious to repay Chase for the blow to his abdomen and self-esteem. This time, though, the others fell on Chase, taking hold of his arms and keeping him from defending himself.

Delia heard the dull thud of Pierre's fist and Chase's forcefully released breath. It was quickly followed by a second thud. She knew she couldn't stand to hear a third.

She turned back, running to Pierre, grabbing his

arm with both her hands to keep him from hitting Chase yet again.

"No," she begged. "Don't hurt him anymore. Just make him leave."

Pierre glanced down at her. He was breathing heavily, and Delia got a sick feeling that he was enjoying what he was doing. It was clear he didn't want to stop.

But he nodded to her.

"Comme tu veux, chérie," he replied as he lowered his fists.

"Delia," Chase said.

She looked up at him, but quickly turned away, feeling a wash of guilt for the cut she saw on the side of his cheek, for the dark red line of blood that was dripping onto his collar.

"Just go away!" she shouted, refusing to turn back to face him.

She could hear Claude, Pierre and the others as they marshaled Chase along the path leading out of the park. It wasn't her fault, she told herself. She hadn't asked him to come here. She hadn't wanted to see him.

Still, she knew if she'd given him the few moments of her time that he'd asked for, there never would have been any violence. If she'd been just a little braver, if she'd been able to listen to him without believing, none of it would ever have happened.

But she wasn't strong. Certainly not strong enough to keep herself from believing his lies. Not even strong enough to turn and watch him being pushed and prodded out of the park to the river's edge.

She put her hands to her face, closing her eyes and telling herself not to think, because if she did, she would realize how her whole world seemed suddenly to be crumbling around her.

* * *

"We won't be happy if you come back to bother the lady again," Pierre hissed through an angrily clenched jaw. He looked up quickly to see if anyone from the quay was watching. Satisfied that none of the passersby was paying the group on the small jetty below the least attention, he punctuated his words with a final sharp jab to Chase's abdomen.

Chase grunted with pain. His head fell forward, and he couldn't help but see the murky river water lapping against the side of the jetty, not ten feet from where he was standing, and the thick green slime that grew on the rutted stones of the jetty itself. A perfect place to give a man a beating, he thought, as he struggled to regain his breath. No decent citizen would think of coming down here. It might even be an adequate setting for a murder.

The thought unsettled him. He realized that he hadn't thought it would be easy getting Delia to listen to reason, but it never occurred to him that the effort would entail quite this sort of effort. He certainly hadn't planned on getting himself killed.

He looked up at Pierre.

"You're brave when you're fighting a man whose arms are being held," he snarled. Then he smiled his crooked smile. "It makes me wonder if you'd be any less of a coward if we were alone."

Pierre's cheeks flushed red and he raised his hand to strike him again.

Claude stopped him.

"Enough," he told Pierre. "He's right. I don't have much stomach for this sort of thing." He turned to Chase. "Make no mistake, though," he added. "I'll gladly swallow my objections if you don't leave Delia alone." He motioned to the others to release their hold.

Chase stood still for a moment, regaining his

94

sense of balance while the artists turned away and climbed the narrow flight of stone steps that led up from the water's edge to the quay above. So it seems I'm not to be killed after all, he thought with an odd sense of detachment as he watched them troop up the narrow stairs carved into the stone support of the quay.

He stepped gingerly forward to the steps, wondering if he ought to wait a moment or two before he attempted the climb, until the queasiness in his stomach had dissipated. He soon found the decision was to be made for him.

Pierre turned and glared down at him.

"You might do well to stay out of my path," he hissed.

Chase was angry, angry that he'd allowed himself to be beaten as he had, angry with the arrogant young man who so obviously enjoyed a certain amount of Delia's affections.

"You might do well to stay out of mine," he sneered in reply.

The challenging words were no sooner out of his mouth than Pierre kicked out at him, his boot coming in firm contact with Chase's chin.

Chase fell back onto the slimy, wet stone surface of the jetty, landing on his side, completely stunned by the blow. Pierre glared at him a moment longer.

"And stay away from Delia," the young Frenchman hissed in final warning before he turned and climbed the last of the stairs to the quay.

Chase opened his eyes. For a moment it was all he could do to lie as he was, staring at the growth of mold and slime beneath him, considering it with a dazed concentration. In a moment, though, the haze in his head began to clear. A deep breath, filled with the unpleasantly moldy smell, finally encouraged him to stir to movement. He pushed himself to his knees and then slowly to his feet.

It didn't take him long to realize that he was filthy, his jacket and shirt spotted with his own blood and all his clothing smeared with long streaks of the green slime. He found his handkerchief and wiped his face, aware the attempt did little to make him even remotely presentable. He considered the stains on the white linen of the handkerchief, dropped it with disgust, then started up the stairs.

He climbed them slowly, not quite certain about his balance, but once he was on the quay, he found he felt a good deal more settled. He crossed the quay, then stood for a moment, staring into the small park at the group of artists. They seemed to him to be acting normally enough. As though beating a man were part of their daily routine, he thought grimly.

His stride was determined as he crossed the narrow patch of grass, then proceeded onto the cobblestone path. He kept his eyes on the artists. This time, he told himself, he intended to be ready if those fools wanted to play any more games.

It was Pierre who saw him first, and Chase found he was almost happy to welcome him as he watched him dart along the path to meet him.

"I thought I told you to stay . . ."

Chase didn't wait for him to complete the expected words of challenge. He took a wide stance to steady himself, and as soon as Pierre was close enough, he leveled two quick blows at his abdomen, feeling a certain amount of satisfaction as his fists made contact. Pierre fell back, gasping and dazed.

"I think that almost makes us even," Chase told him before he continued on to where Delia stood watching.

He couldn't help but feel a pang of regret when he saw her face, pale now and frightened as she stared up at him. He saw her eyes dart to where Pierre lay on the cobblestones, but he realized that he must seem in even greater need of her sympathy, for she didn't move toward the Frenchman. Instead, her glance returned to him. He stopped when he was still a dozen paces from her.

From the corner of his eye he saw the others turn and start toward him, but he knew he still had a moment before they were close enough to be a threat.

"You'd better tell your friends to kill me this time, Delia," he told her. "Because that's the only way I'm going to disappear. They kill me, or you listen to me. Take your choice."

He didn't have to look to know he was being surrounded, but he didn't take his eyes from Delia's. Instead, he stood, his eyes fixed on hers, and waited for her to make her decision.

Chapter Six

"I told you I'd return."

Cotter stood by the door for a long moment, staring at Matthew Pickering as though he didn't recognize the man.

"You could have saved yourself the effort," he said finally. "I've already told you I can't give you what you want."

"It's really not a matter of choice," Pickering told him, assuming that Cotter's words were meant as a refusal. He darted a glance down the length of the street. "I don't think this is the sort of business to be discussed on the doorstep, do you?"

"It's not the sort of business I care to discuss anywhere," Cotter replied. He started to close the door.

Pickering, however, had no intention of allowing Cotter to dismiss him so easily. He put his hand on the door and gave it a hard shove. A powerful man, he easily forced Cotter backward. His way now clear, he stepped inside quickly and closed the door behind him. Then, without so much as turning to Cotter, he walked through the entrance hall and into the parlor, acting as if he owned the house.

Cotter felt a kind of absent numbness settle over him as he watched Pickering disappear into the next room. So it's to come now, he thought. For the previous twenty years a part of him had known that

Pickering would someday return to haunt him. The first visit had proved that premonition had been right. But that first appearance had been nothing more than a prelude, Pickering's idea of a small taunt to waken his fears and weaken his resistance. The real haunting, Cotter knew, was about to begin. He wondered if the years had made him strong enough to face up to a man who had been all too easily capable of manipulating him twenty years before. Breaking away from Pickering had cost him dearly the first time. He wondered if he would be able to do it again.

He felt his heart begin to beat more quickly, and took a deep breath, determined to calm himself and keep away the pain. He knew he could not afford to become physically ill. A show of weakness of any sort was Pickering's meat, and Cotter determined not to serve it up to him.

It gave him a real sense of triumph to find that he managed to slow the thudding in his chest before the seizure could incapacitate him. His composure returned, and he followed his unwelcome visitor into his parlor.

"You haven't learned any manners in the last twenty years, have you?" he asked offhandedly as he entered the room.

"On the contrary," Pickering told him. He was busy helping himself, uninvited, to a drink from the liquor tray. "It's not like the old, wild days. I've become quite the gentleman of late, the respected art dealer. Would you believe that the Duke of Northumberland even invites me to dinner regularly? It's really rather amusing. I must admit that I even amaze myself sometimes."

Cotter shrugged. "Nothing about you could possibly amaze me."

He felt a small satisfaction that despite the circumstances he was still managing to remain aloofly calm with the man. That was the only way to defeat him, he told himself: seem invulnerable, and he has no weapons.

He followed Pickering to the liquor tray, where he quickly half filled a tumbler with whiskey. Courage, he told himself as he watched the amber liquid flow into the glass, already anticipating the taste of it in his mouth, blessed, liquid courage.

"You shouldn't be bitter about this, Cotter," Pickering chided as he took his glass and began to walk about the room, inspecting the groupings of still lifes on a nearby wall. "Bitterness isn't becoming to you. You always had such a pleasantly optimistic view when you were young. I remember I found it quite a refreshing change from all those unsavory young men who hung about the quays. I don't mind telling you that it was my fondness for you that kept me from making your life unpleasant back then, when you decided you had no use for me."

He turned to Cotter and smiled warmly, as though that information was meant to comfort him.

"Fondness for you means stabbing a man in the belly as opposed to waiting until his back is turned," Cotter responded dryly.

He raised his glass in toast and smiled before he took the first welcome swallow. The whiskey settled into him with a much appreciated flow of comforting heat. He realized he was beginning to feel a sense of control, something that had never before happened to him when he was in Pickering's presence. There had always been fear before, a sense of being outmaneuvered, impotent. Now, however, all that was gone. Perhaps it's the years, he thought, or maybe it's simply the hovering specter of death that's empowering. Whatever it was, he was grateful for the sense of detachment it gave him.

100

He took another swallow of his whiskey, then looked up at Pickering and found he was smiling.

"I remember I liked the way you always spoke your mind," Pickering returned. "You were such a charming and witty youth, Cotter. I even found your little attempts at rebellion amusing. But then, I liked you so much more than any of the others." He turned away from the paintings, back to face Cotter. "I'm afraid it was a failing that hasn't survived the decades." His eyes narrowed as he stared at Cotter's face. "You've grown old, Cotter," he added maliciously, "old and unappealing."

Cotter nodded, completely unshaken.

"So I have," he agreed mildly. He smiled. "As have you," he added, even though he realized age had hardly diminished Matthew Pickering the way illness and the years had enfeebled him. Pickering was still decidedly robust, and the years had only added to the forcefulness of his personality.

"I suppose I have," Pickering mused. "But still, it is a shame when old affections die." He sighed, then turned back to his inspection of the paintings.

"There was never any affection between us," Cotter told him. "A morbid fascination, perhaps, but never any affection."

"Call it what you will," Pickering said. He left the group of canvases he'd been inspecting and moved on to the next. They seemed to intrigue him, for he stood a long while, staring at them thoughtfully. "You're better than ever, do you know that, Cotter?" he asked finally. "When we've finished this little bit of business we're about, you might let me take a few of these back to London for you. Just for old time's sake. I could see you hung in some of the finest houses in Mayfair."

Cotter drained his glass.

"I'd sooner be hung in Newgate," he said.

He smiled as he saw Pickering's expression lose any trace of the warmth he'd taken such pains to retain until then. He was winning, he thought with delight, as he watched Pickering's eyes narrow and grow hard. It pleased him to know that he was making the unshakable Matthew Pickering show his emotion. He knew it meant that he was chipping away at Pickering's control.

"That, too, could be arranged quite easily," Pickering hissed, his eyes grown hard now, his expression openly vicious.

Cotter didn't allow himself to be cowed by the threat. As he turned back to the liquor tray to refill his glass, he realized that he was grinning slightly. It quite amazed him to realize that he was actually enjoying baiting Pickering.

"It would seem the required pleasantries have been completed," he said as he lifted the decanter and poured. "I've already told you I can't give you what you want. Now why don't you slink away and return to the stone you live under?"

Pickering watched him return the decanter to its place on the tray.

"It's not quite that simple," he said, after what seemed a very long silence. "I need something only you can provide for me. I intend to get it."

"How?" Cotter demanded. "By threatening to arrange to have me put in prison? What good would that do you?"

"There are alternatives," Pickering sneered, "alternatives you might find unpleasant."

Cotter shook his head. "I suppose now you're going to suggest that my body might be found floating in the Seine?" he asked. He laughed. "Frankly, I find this game growing extremely boring, Matthew. I really do wish you'd leave."

Pickering smiled, but nothing warm edged its way

into his expression. Cotter realized he was re-marshaling his forces, ready for a new attack. Now, he told himself, was the time to be cautious.

"I never thought you a man without imagination," Pickering said, his tone low now and slyly insinuating. "But it seems that is precisely what you've become. I, on the other hand, am a man with a great deal of imagination. And I also know how to go about getting what I want." He smiled again. "I've learned you have a daughter."

Despite his determination to remain calm, Cotter felt a wash of fear unsettling him. His grip of his glass grew suddenly so strong his knuckles turned white.

Pickering noticed the change. It roused another smile, one of real pleasure this time.

"You really oughtn't to drink so much, Cotter," he said. "I think it's beginning to lessen your control. Your hands are shaking."

Cotter looked down at his hand and the liquid that sloshed from side to side in the glass. He'd grown accustomed to the sight of his palsied hands, but this time he knew it wasn't the liquor that was making his hands shake.

"My daughter has nothing to do with this," he hissed.

Pickering pursed his lips and shook his head. "I'm afraid she does," he countered. "She provides me with a wealth of intriguing possibilities, possibilities that give me a far greater power than even the threat of prison or death. I can not help but wonder, for instance, if it might not prove unpleasant for her were she to learn dear Papa was a forger?"

Cotter's grip on the glass softened. He let loose a loud peal of laughter.

"You're right," he replied. "Shocking. How will you do it? An anonymous letter, perhaps?"

"You find the prospect amusing?" Pickering asked.

Cotter took a healthy swallow of his whiskey.

"Decidedly," he admitted.

"It would seem I've underestimated you, Cotter," Pickering said. "But what I propose is something more public," he mused with a malign smirk. "Something that would perhaps close any chance of an entree into society to her, something that would mean she'd stand no chance of making an acceptable marriage. I could ruin her life. Is that what you want for her?"

Cotter stared at his whiskey for a moment, silently considering the choice Pickering had offered him.

"Do you really think Parisian society gives a damn for such trivialities?" Cotter asked finally. "Frankly, Matthew, I find your threats have very little currency."

"I see," Pickering mused softly. "I suppose you're right. Paris accepts minor scandals with a shrug and smirk, as though to say, What else would one expect?" He shook his head. "It's such an uncivilized city, really. Not like London. Do you remember London, Cotter? Do you remember how I taught you the ways a gentleman can sin in London?"

A dark flush crept into Cotter's cheeks. For the first time since Pickering had entered the house he began to feel a premonition of real fear. It was going wrong. He wasn't really sure how it had changed, but suddenly he had a feeling that he was about to lose the odd battle he'd been so bravely fighting. He began to wonder why he'd even made the attempt.

"It's something I've spent twenty years trying to forget," he murmured.

"Yes, I suppose it is best to leave the past buried," Pickering agreed. "Which returns us again to your daughter." Suddenly his smirk grew ominously vicious. The look sent a chill of fear through Cotter. "I have been told she is an extremely handsome young woman." He turned back to face the group of paintings on the wall. "It would be a shame were something really unpleasant to happen to her."

A sudden tide of anger welled up inside Cotter despite his certainty that it was what Pickering was looking for, that by showing it he was giving his enemy ammunition that would eventually be used against him.

"Bastard!" he shouted, and heaved his whiskey glass at Pickering.

The heavy tumbler found its mark, striking Pickering's back and leaving a wide splash of whiskey wetting his jacket. It fell to the floor, shattering on impact. Shards of crystal scattered along the pale bandings of the parquet.

Pickering obviously hadn't expected a physical attack. He was thrown off-balance by the blow and took a stumbling step forward. Then he swung around and faced Cotter and his eyes gleamed with a vicious, dark anger.

Cotter could feel the now-familiar constriction beginning to find its grip in his chest, but he didn't care. He knew that there was no way he could ever be free of Pickering. He looked at Pickering's eyes and realized that the man was capable of anything, that he would not think twice about hurting Delia if he thought it would be useful to him.

There was only one way to stop him.

Somehow finding the strength to ignore the pain in his chest, Cotter darted across the room to the fireplace. He grasped the heavy brass poker and swung it as he turned back to face Pickering.

"Well, Delia?"

Delia really didn't need the prodding. One look at Chase's bruised face and she knew she couldn't allow Claude and the others to do anything like that again.

She turned to Claude, wanting to accuse him, to tell him that she'd only wanted him to make Chase leave, not hurt him, certainly not beat him like this. But she found she couldn't accuse anyone when part of her had known that something like this would happen. Perhaps, she had to admit, however reluctantly, she'd even felt, if not exactly pleased, then satisfied that they might make Chase hurt in return for the way he'd hurt her. It was, after all, a fair and just payment.

Thirst for revenge, however, was the last thing on her mind as she looked at his bruises and the gash that slowly oozed a dark red trickle of blood down the side of his cheek. All she felt now was shame that she'd allowed any of it to happen.

"No more," she told Claude. "I don't want anyone hurt again. If all he wants is talk, then I'll talk to him."

"I'll go with you," Claude told her. He was openly glowering at Chase, obviously less than pleased at the prospect of leaving her alone with this all-too-determined Englishman.

"You don't need a bodyguard, Delia," Chase assured her. "If it makes you feel safer, I'm perfectly willing to remain someplace public. I just want to talk."

"If all you want is talk, then there's no reason I can't accompany you," Claude interjected.

"What we have to say is private," Chase said. His tone said only too clearly that he had had more than enough of her friends' interference.

However determined Claude might be, Delia realized that the last thing she wanted was an audience for this particular interview. It was quite obvious that Chase Sutton knew a good deal about her father, and the last thing she wanted was to have that information broadcast.

"It's all right, Claude," she murmured. "He won't hurt me." She darted a glance to where Pierre was slowly climbing to his knees. "Will you see to Pierre?"

Claude, too, glanced at Pierre, watching as the younger man glowered at Chase as he batted at the dust clinging to the seat of his pants. He nodded.

"I don't think much more than his pride's been hurt," he said.

"If he has any pride," Chase interjected. For the first time his eyes left Delia's as he gave Claude a meaningful glance. Claude flushed suddenly under the accusation of that stare, more than enough evidence, Chase decided, to convince him that the painter was fully aware of the way Pierre had kicked him. His point made, Chase turned back to face her. "Delia?"

She mutely nodded, then turned away from him, lifting her work case and starting off along the cobblestone path through the park. She did not so much as look back to see if Chase was following.

Chase caught up to her with a half dozen quick strides.

"I'll gladly carry your case, Delia," he offered.

She didn't bother to offer him a glance.

"I'm quite capable, thank you, Mr. Sutton," she told him.

He shrugged, deciding it wasn't worth the energy to fight about it with her. After all, she quite obviously considered him something less than human at that moment. He wasn't entirely sure he blamed her. In any case, it hardly seemed worthwhile, at least just yet, to try to make her believe him a gentleman.

She turned at the corner onto the Rue Saint Jacques with Chase walking silently at her side, letting her make the decision as to where they would stop finally, assuming she would seat herself at one of the tables of the first café they came upon.

She didn't. She strode along the sidewalk at a determined pace, as though she were late for some important appointment. She skirted the bustle of foot traffic, apparently oblivious to his presence.

When they'd gone six blocks Chase finally stopped her, putting his hand on her arm and forcing her to turn and face him.

"Is this public enough for you, Delia?" he asked.

He pointed to a small café, its handful of sidewalk tables empty, but the interior quite crowded.

She shrugged, then nodded. She turned and made her way into the small muddle of tables, finally seating herself at one near the street.

"We could go inside, Delia," Chase suggested. "It's getting cold and it looks like rain."

She finally turned to look directly at him, giving him a look that clearly said that if the weather made him uncomfortable she could not care less.

"I'm quite comfortable here," she insisted.

Chase scowled. His clothing was damp and he was beginning to feel cold. He decided, however, it was wisest to make no further protest. He seated himself across the small table from her.

"I suppose you're right," he said with a shrug as he settled himself on the stiff wrought-iron chair. He motioned to his stained and blood-spattered clothing. "So illustrious an establishment as this one would probably bar me at the door."

Delia darted a glance at the men standing drinking by the café's bar and front window. This was, she saw, a barely respectable place. Most of the patrons were decidedly shabby, with filthy, baggy pants and ragged jackets, and sporting the unshaven cheeks and hollow eyes of the poor and idle who had no place to go and nothing else to do but nurse a glass of cheap wine through the long afternoon hours.

She looked back at Chase. He was smiling at her, and she realized he was trying to be amusing. The attempt was lost on her. She didn't allow her expression to soften in the least.

Chase was not pleased to see that he was losing, that she had no intention of making it any easier for him. He reached out to take her hand with his, but as soon as he did, he knew it was a mistake. She quickly pulled her hand away from him, then rested it pointedly instead on her lap.

"Monsieur?"

There was impatience in the waiter's tone. When Chase turned to find him standing at the side of the table, he found a smirk on the man's face and realized that Delia's slight had been noticed. Chase realized he couldn't be very pleased about being forced out into the cold with only a thin white cotton jacket to ward off the damp and the chill.

"Deux cafés," Chase told him.

"None for me, thank you," Delia quickly interjected, her tone primly superior. "I've enjoyed more than enough of your hospitality, thank you, Mr. Sutton."

"Deux cafés," Chase repeated, ignoring her protest. He waved the waiter away before he could become really irked by the return of the man's smirk.

"I don't want any," Delia insisted in a tone that suggested the matter were of immense importance to her.

"Then I'll drink them both," Chase told her in equally as stubborn a tone, stopping her before she could call out to the waiter. "I could use a bit of warmth after the less than pleasant hour I've been forced to enjoy."

Delia lost some of her frost at that, his words, and the condition of his clothing, not to mention a darkening bruise and the thin line of blood on the side of his cheek, reminding her of what had happened between him and her artist friends. A flush of guilt swept over her. It was no good telling herself that he'd probably deserved what he'd gotten. She never should have let Pierre and the others beat him.

"Did they hurt you badly?" she asked, her words hushed now, her voice unsteady.

He smiled again. "My tailor will never forgive me," he said with a motion toward the filthy stains on his jacket.

This time she couldn't keep from smiling just a bit.

"There," he said with an encouraging nod. "That wasn't so terribly hard, was it?"

The smile vanished.

"I promised my father I'd never see you again," she told him. "My own wishes coincide with that request. I do not wish to be here at all. So please say whatever it is you wanted so desperately to say to me and let me leave."

"What I wanted to say is that you're wrong, that your father's wrong," Chase began. He leaned forward to her, resting his elbows on the cold marble tabletop. His expression had grown sharply intense. "I swear to you that I am not a policeman, Delia. I am not in Paris to link Cotter with any crime, ancient or otherwise."

Delia finally let herself look directly into the deep blue of his eyes. His look was so intense, so determined, she found herself wanting to believe him. She had to remind herself that he'd lied to her before,

110

that she'd be a fool to let him convince her he was telling her the truth.

"Then why *are* you here?" she demanded. "Why did you just happen to be standing on the Rue St. Clodoald two days ago, staring at our house? And please, don't insult me by telling me it was the quaint Parisian scenery that drew you."

Chase shook his head.

"No, it wasn't the scenery. I was following someone," he said flatly. "And that someone found his way into your father's parlor."

Delia couldn't keep herself from murmuring, "Pickering."

Chase nodded. "Matthew Pickering," he agreed. "What do you know about him?"

Delia drew back. "What do *you* know about him?" she countered.

Chase bowed his head. "All right, Delia," he agreed softly. "We'll do it your way. I know he's supposedly a respectable art dealer and the friend of a few minor members of the British peerage. And I also know he's an extremely accomplished art thief."

"If you know that, then why haven't you arrested him?" she demanded.

"I told you, Delia," he said, "I'm not a policeman. I can't arrest anyone. But even if I were, Pickering is good, too good ever to leave a trail that leads back to him."

The waiter appeared then. Delia sat back and stared at Chase silently as the man deposited the two cups and an extra saucer bearing a scribbled tab on the streaked marble tabletop, then stood waiting for payment so that he needn't be bothered to venture out into the cold yet a third time. Chase grimaced, but quickly reached into his pocket, withdrew a handful of coins, and dropped them onto the saucer.

When the waiter had gone, Delia realized that

111

Chase's explanation was posing more questions than it answered.

"Assuming I accept that you aren't police . . ." she began.

"I'm not," he insisted forcefully.

"Then why were you following Pickering?"

Chase silently sighed with relief. At least she was asking questions, he told himself, the right questions. At least she was listening.

"Yesterday I told you I find things for a living," he began.

"Yesterday you told me a lot of things," she snapped.

"And they were true," he insisted. "They omitted a good deal, but I swear I didn't lie to you."

Delia lifted the small spoon and began to stir her coffee. It was dark and viscous, with an unhealthy-looking oily slick floating on the top. She stared at the small whirlpool her spoon made, concentrating on it, not wanting to look up at his eyes, afraid they would make her believe when logic would tell her to doubt.

"Then what is it you failed to mention?" she asked thoughtfully.

"That I also keep things from being lost," he replied. "Or, in this case, stolen."

"Which means what?" she demanded.

"It means that I was hired by the Lloyd's Corporation to oversee the shipment of a group of privately owned works of art, Old Master paintings, to be precise, currently on display at the Louvre, and see them safely delivered to the British Museum, where they are to be shown before being returned to their owners. Just before I left London, I learned that Pickering was also on his way to Paris. It seemed obvious to me that his timing was too great a coincidence to be unimportant. Both museums have

112

excellent security, but the paintings' transport to England provides Pickering with an opportunity I don't think he can resist. I became convinced he intends to steal one or more of the paintings."

"And?"

"And when I learned he'd been to see Cotter Hampton, perhaps the finest living forger of Old Masters, I decided my suspicions weren't entirely groundless," he continued.

Delia dropped the spoon and raised her eyes once again to meet his. It sounded reasonable to her, but she wasn't sure if what she told herself was reason was really just wishful thinking.

"Let us assume I accept your story," she said slowly. "I can assure you my father would never help Matthew Pickering."

"Pickering can be an extremely convincing man, Delia," Chase told her. "He might not give Cotter any choice."

"No," she insisted. "Whatever Papa might once have done, that's all past now."

"Look, Delia," he said, once again leaning forward to her. He put his hand on her arm. "I have no designs on Cotter. It's Pickering I'm interested in, Pickering and the security of the paintings I'm being paid to protect. If you could convince your father to cooperate with me . . ."

"I told you, my father won't help him," Delia interrupted. This time her tone was sharp. She pulled her arm away from him. "Go back to watching your thief, but leave my father alone."

She started to get to her feet, but Chase grabbed her arm and this time held onto it, forcing her back into the chair. She tried to pull away from him, twisting her arm in an attempt to free herself of his hold.

"I told you, Delia," he told her, "I have no intention of involving Cotter in anything. But I need his help to get at Pickering. If I can have him caught in the act, I can see that he's put into prison for good."

Delia stopped struggling with him. Perhaps he really wasn't her father's enemy after all, she thought. Perhaps he could even help Cotter.

"How do you mean, you need Papa's help?" she asked.

"I've already told you that Pickering's good," he said. "And no security is foolproof. The transport of fifty works of art is complicated, and complications make security all the more fallible. Without knowing what it is Pickering intends to steal or how he intends to go about it, I'll stand very little hope of stopping him."

It was as though a light went on Delia's head, a light that shone through all the dusty cobwebs that had clouded her thinking in the previous days.

"So that's what yesterday was all about," she said, her tone thick with bitterness. "You want to use Papa to catch Pickering. And you intended to get to him by using me."

How could she have been such a fool as not to see it before? she asked herself. The light receded, pushed aside by a thick blanket of hurt.

Chase tightened his hold on her arm.

"No, Delia," he said, "yesterday had nothing to do with anything but you and me."

It startled Chase to hear himself speak the words so vehemently, for he knew they were partially a lie, that it had begun just as she'd said it had. But he also knew that somewhere between the moment he'd begun to follow her and that when he'd first held her in his arms, it had changed for him. Now, more than anything else, he knew he needed to make her believe that what he'd told her was true.

His grasp of her arm hurt her, but as Delia gazed

114

into his eyes, the sharp bite of his fingers seemed to fade. She wanted to believe him, she realized, wanted it desperately.

"What is it you want from Papa?" she asked him in a barely audible whisper.

Chase sighed with relief and released his hold of her arm.

"To go along with Pickering, to give him what he wants, to make whatever forgeries Pickering wants and while he's doing it, learn what he can about Pickering's plans. That way I can arrange to have him caught in the act and see he's put in prison, where he belongs."

Delia shook her head.

"Papa can't do that," she told him.

"Look, Delia, I'll guarantee he won't be involved. We can go to the police, if he likes, and have it put on record that he's cooperating with me. I'll swear that he's working for Lloyd's, sign an affidavit, if that's what he wants. Believe me, the last thing I want is to hurt your father. But I do need his help."

Delia swallowed. Her throat felt dry and her voice, when she spoke, sounded hoarse.

"He can't," she insisted. "He hasn't painted in more than five years."

Chase wanted to reach out to her, wanted to put his hand on her cheek and say something that would assuage the fear he could read only too clearly in her eyes.

"Delia, I understand your desire to protect him. He's your father. I swear to you, if there was any other way, I wouldn't ask it."

"I tell you, he can't! He can't paint anymore. He's physically incapable of giving you what you want."

Her sudden vehemence bewildered him.

"Delia," he said, his tone patient but insistent, "I was in your house. I saw the paintings on the walls.

115

Some of them were recent, with varnish that was crystal clear, without any sign of yellowing. I'm no expert, but I know enough to be certain that those paintings were less than five years old. All I'm asking is that Cotter do the same thing he's obviously done hundreds of times before, and then use his skill to age the canvases and make them look old. He's done it before, Delia. Your refusing to admit it won't change that fact."

Delia could see that he wasn't about to be dissuaded, that there was a sharp determination in his expression she would never be able to shake with a few words of protest.

"You're right," she admitted. "Those paintings you saw were all done in the last three or four years. But Papa didn't paint them."

"This isn't a game, Delia," he said softly.

She nodded. "I know," she replied. "But I swear to you, Papa didn't paint those canvases." She swallowed the lump that suddenly filled her throat. "I did," she added, fully aware that she was making an admission that could put her on the path to prison.

Chapter Seven

Cotter lunged at Pickering, swinging the poker with all his might. He gave no thought to the consequences of his act, nor did it so much as occur to him that what he was doing was attempting to commit a cold-blooded murder. Only the realization of what Pickering might do to Delia was real to him. The one thing he knew was that he could not allow this man to come into contact with his daughter.

But physically Cotter was no match for a man of Pickering's size. Pickering raised his arm defensively to ward off the blow, and as the poker came into contact with it, he twisted, turning and grabbing Cotter's wrists. He caught hold of the heavy brass shaft.

He was smiling as he wrenched the poker free from Cotter's grasp.

"Did you really think it would be that easy?" he hissed. He advanced slowly, dodging Cotter as he tried to edge backward and away from him. With each step forward, he stroked the ornate brass handle of the poker as if the tool were a beloved pet. "Did you really think you could kill me?" he asked. He leered as if to say that he was immune to those weaknesses that might plague a lesser man, that Cotter was a fool to think otherwise.

But Cotter hardly heard Pickering's words. He

saw the rage and the menace that emanated from Pickering's eyes only dimly, as though he were looking through a thick veil. He could no longer force his legs to back away. Any possibility of flight was lost to him, crushed by the growing pain in his chest. In seconds it became so strong that it was all he could do to stand, to continue to draw breath. His other senses grew pallid and distant in contrast, and Pickering's leering presence became lost in the far more immediate need to do battle with the pain.

His hands rose to his chest, as though he were trying to ward off the assault just as Pickering had done. But this blow could not be so easily parried as the one he'd leveled at Pickering. This blow was inescapable.

Pickering was either ignorant of his pain or entirely indifferent to it. He balled his hand into a fist and, with a smile of obvious satisfaction, sank it into Cotter's abdomen.

Cotter dropped to his knees, now close to being completely paralyzed by the growing hurt that was not only in his chest, but spreading to his shoulders and his arms and the back of his head. Even the stabbing jolt of hurt Pickering's fist left in his abdomen was a distant throb that faded in the wake of this agony.

Nothing had prepared him to face this sort of excruciating pain. The attacks he'd had before had been little more than mild twinges, pale preambles, compared to this. He couldn't see or hear or even breathe. The iron vise in his chest steadily tightened its hold, mercilessly squeezing his life out of him.

Pickering stood back and watched Cotter fall to his knees. He seemed entirely pleased to see Cotter take a subservient position. He assumed it had been the blow he'd delivered that so debilitated Cotter, and he stood, hovering like a bird of prey, waiting to hear the begging words that he not strike again.

After a moment, however, he realized it was something other than the blow that left Cotter shaking and caused heavy beads of perspiration to form on his forehead. He took a step back, watching, making no move to help, considering what was happening to Cotter with an intrigued detachment.

Cotter was no longer aware that he was not alone in the room. Everything receded—Pickering, even the familiar walls and furnishings of the room around him. All his existence became wrapped in the throbbing pain, and in a growing fear that his heart would burst free of his chest.

It took every vestige of his will to force his hand to move, to drop to his side and reach into his pocket, where he groped for his vial of pills. After a seeming eternity, his fingers closed around the glass vial. It grew heavy as he tried to lift it. He marshaled the last of his strength to draw it out, the act leaving him panting for breath and bathed in perspiration from the effort.

Cotter forced himself to focus on the vial, telling himself he was going to survive this attack, just as he'd survived the others, if for no other reason than that Delia was not yet ready to deal with life without him. His determination was great enough as he began to struggle with the vial's cap that it seemed to him the hurt had abated a bit.

But he was wrong. The seconds of reprieve were followed by an even sharper pain, this time too great for him to even try to battle. The vial fell out of his hand as he fell forward, facedown onto the floor, completely unaware that he was groaning and shaking spastically.

If he'd given thought to it a week before, he'd have told himself his will to live had faded, that he no longer cared what became of him. At that moment, however, as he saw his own death drawing near, he realized he still wanted life enough to fight for it.

He saw the vial lying a few feet from him and knew his one chance of surviving was inside it. He edged his arm forward, forcing himself to reach out to grasp it.

It seemed a lifetime to him before he finally felt the cold glass surface of the vial beneath his finger-tips. He was going to do it, he told himself as the sound of his own gasping breath filled his ears.

It was a shock to him when he felt Pickering's hand on his wrist, when he saw his fingers being pried open and the vial being pulled from his grasp.

"No," he gasped. "My heart . . ."

He looked up and saw Pickering kneeling beside him. For an instant he felt only confusion, wondering how this monster from his past had suddenly come back into his life. And then his thoughts cleared as he remembered. He looked at Pickering's eyes. One glance was all he needed to know that fighting was useless now, to know without question that he was staring not at a man he'd once known, but at the face of death.

Pickering lifted the glass vial of pills he now cra-dled in his hand. He stared at it for a long moment, considering what it was he held. Then he darted a vicious glance at Cotter before he dropped the vial back to the floor just beyond Cotter's reach.

"It seems matters are not to be as I would have wanted them, Cotter," he said, as he pushed himself back to his feet. "Alas, I fear they are not to be as either of us would have them. In any case, I think I must bid you *adieu,* my old friend." He smiled down at Cotter, pleased with the agonized shock he saw on Cotter's face. "No, not *adieu,* not this time. This time, I think, it is finally goodbye."

With that, he turned and started toward the door. When he'd reached it, he turned back and for a moment stood watching Cotter once again struggle to reach the vial of pills.

He strode back to where Cotter lay.

He put the tip of his boot on the glass vial, and leaned forward, crushing the glass and the pills inside it into a powder. Then he stepped back.

With the last of his strength Cotter pushed his arm forward. His hand fell into the small heap of glass slivers and white powder. It tensed spastically for a second and then went slack.

When it became apparent to him that there was nothing left for him to watch, Pickering turned away. This time he left the house without so much as a backward glance.

"You?"

Delia nodded. She continued to stir her coffee, staring into it with an apparent fascination that implied she saw something in it other than the dark brown viscous liquid and its unsavory oily slick. She wondered mutely why she was telling him these things, fully aware that she was accomplishing nothing except making herself vulnerable to him. She could find no reasonable explanation of her motivation save for the simple fact that deep inside a part of her wanted to believe she could trust him.

"Papa began drinking heavily when my mother died," she said slowly. She didn't look up at him, but continued to stare at the small whirlpool she made inside the coffee cup. "It wasn't very long before he could no longer control his hands well enough to paint."

She dropped the spoon suddenly onto the saucer and considered the oily drops that formed on the

121

surface of the coffee as soon as the small whirlpool dissipated. She finally looked up and let her eyes meet his.

"But how did you live?" Chase asked. The words were no sooner out of his mouth than he recalled the near-empty house, the shabby furnishings, and realized his question needed no answer.

"It wasn't easy at first," Delia admitted. "Papa sold things, furniture first, then pieces of my mother's jewelry. By the time there was nothing left worth selling, though, he had found we had other, unexpected assets."

"You?"

She nodded and, as though against her will, a small smile crept across her lips.

"I'd shown a bit of precocious talent when I was still quite young, while he was still able to teach me. At first we both thought it little more than amusement, but it wasn't long before I was turning out a few 'Old Masters' of my own. He aged them as he had once aged his own paintings." She looked down again. This was proving more difficult than she had thought it would when she'd begun, but she knew, much as she might wish it were otherwise, she couldn't stop now. "At first mine were very minor Old Masters, mind you, not like Papa's. And unsigned, always unsigned. He refused to allow any signatures, because that's what had gotten him in trouble in New York and London, outright signed forgeries."

"And you sold them?"

"No," she said. "Papa did. But never with any claims of authenticity. Just as old paintings he'd come across, as though he'd found them rummaging about in the attic, letting the dealers he sold them to ascribe their own lineage. They didn't bring in very much that way, but he felt I couldn't be involved as

122

long as the paintings were unsigned and he made no claims as to their authenticity."

"I can't argue with his logic," Chase agreed.

"I suppose we'd have gone on that way indefinitely if he hadn't gotten sick a few years ago. The doctors here could do nothing for him, and suggested he be sent to see some specialists in Switzerland. There simply was no money to pay for that sort of thing. And I knew it would be impossible for me to sell enough paintings at one time to raise anywhere near enough."

"And so you did what he hadn't allowed you to do before that?" he asked softly, even though he realized he already knew from her strained expression what she would say.

She nodded again. "I signed two paintings and sold them."

Chase found he could not conceal a grin.

"And just which Old Master are you?" he asked.

She looked up at him, surprised to see that he actually seemed amused by the knowledge of her crime. She ventured a small smile of her own, one that admitted a secret, perverse pride in what she'd done.

"If you're in the market," she told him, "be very careful of any Van Eycks you might consider. Of course, they'd be early works, rather less skilled than his more mature canvases." She blushed just a bit, and finally smiled at him. "Still, they aren't unrepresentative."

He laughed at her expression, at the hint of pride and the slightly guilty blush. But when the laugh faded, his grew completely sober.

"You didn't continue?" he asked.

She shook her head.

"When he returned from Switzerland and found out what I'd done to get the money to finance his

123

cure, Papa was furious. And I must admit, I was frightened. I realized that if I had been discovered, I could have been sent to prison. That's when I started doing the silhouettes. I found I could support us on what I earned," she flashed a quick smile at him, "at least as long as there were a few rich English tourists strolling the quays ready to part with a handful of francs in return for a smile and some conversation."

He nodded wryly. "We're all fools for a pretty woman," he told her with complete seriousness. "But all the paintings in your home?"

"I've continued painting," she admitted, "but we never sold another canvas. We have the house, and don't really need much, so there really hasn't been the need. The prospect of prison makes a great argument for discretion." She drew in a deep breath and released it slowly. "Not that being discreet has kept Pickering out of our lives."

"Pickering discovered what you'd done?"

She made a moue of distaste, then once again lifted the spoon and began to stir the coffee.

"It's what brought him to our house the other afternoon. He saw one of the paintings in the Galérie des Anciens and recognized what he thought was Papa's touch."

"Are you telling me Pickering is blackmailing your father into helping him?"

"Yes," she replied. "He threatened to go to the police, to see Papa imprisoned if he didn't cooperate and give him the paintings he wanted."

"And your father can't give him what he wants," Chase mused softly.

Delia shook her head. "No. It would be quite literally impossible for him to give Pickering what he wants."

"Then he and I are, however unlikely he may find it, allies in this."

"Allies?" Delia asked doubtfully.

"Your father may have information that will help me," he told her. "It only stands to reason that he'd want to see Pickering out of harm's way."

"If you can convince him, I suppose he might," she acceded.

The edge of his lips turned up into a sly smile. "I convinced you," he told her.

"Papa's a good deal more determined than I am," she replied with an answering grin. "More than likely he'll wish a pox on both your houses."

"In which case, I'll have to find other means," he mused softly. "If Cotter won't help me with the paintings . . ."

"I told you, he can't," she interrupted, this time with a hint of impatience in her tone.

Chase's eyes narrowed. "Then perhaps I can convince another Hampton," he suggested. "You've just finished telling me that you are capable of doing what your father once did," he said.

Delia's head shot up and she stared into his eyes. She went suddenly numb inside, sick at the calculating stare she thought she saw in them. After all she'd told him, after the way she'd made herself vulnerable to him, still his only interest was to use her. Her father might have been wrong about the details, but he had certainly been right about the sort of man Chase Sutton was.

She dropped the spoon. It clattered against the cold marble surface of the tabletop.

"No, I can't," she hissed angrily. "I'm not good enough to fool a real expert. And even if I could do what you ask, I wouldn't. Pickering can be dangerous to my father, and I won't help you put him in a position where he might deem it worthwhile to trade what he knows about Papa for his own freedom. If you want to catch Matthew Pickering in the act,

125

you'll have to find someone else to use. I can't and I won't."

Her anger sobered Chase, sent his thoughts chasing after hers. He realized what her confession had cost her, and knew she would never have told him all she had if she felt nothing for him. And that, he realized, was what he really wanted, more than anything else, to find himself someone she cared about. He might want to see Pickering where he belonged, but he realized he wanted Delia far more. The last thing he wanted to do was to alienate her, now that she was so close to forgiving him.

He leaned forward to her and put his hand on her arm. It tensed beneath his fingers, but she did not try to pull it away.

"I shouldn't have made the suggestion, Delia," he told her. "I'll find some other way. The last thing I want is for Pickering to come between us."

She returned his gaze in silence for a moment, wondering what it was she saw in those handsome blue eyes of his. She looked away from them, down at the stained marble of the tabletop.

"Is there an us?" she asked softly.

He put his hand under her chin and lifted it until her eyes once again met his.

"I certainly hope there will be," he told her.

Delia felt her anger melt in the heat of his stare. Her heart began to beat wildly and she could feel a pleasant throb begin to fill her. There was every possibility that she was being a complete fool, she told herself, but the thought didn't have the sobering effect it ought to have had on her. What he said he wanted was, she knew, what she wanted as well.

He leaned forward to her, and touched his lips to hers.

The first desultory raindrops began to fall, land-

126

ing with loud, wet smacking sounds as they hit the marble of the tabletop. They were a cold, sobering sprinkling that took the edge off the fire that kiss might otherwise have generated. Still, it wasn't nearly enough to cool the warmth that began to fill Delia at Chase's touch.

They pulled apart. Delia laughed, feeling suddenly slightly embarrassed and ill-at-ease, as though she'd been caught doing something vaguely inappropriate despite the fact that she knew perfectly well no one would take the effort to watch them, especially considering that the rain provided a pressing need to find shelter.

Chase looked up at a gray-covered sky.

"I don't suppose you'd object to leaving?" he asked.

"None whatsoever," she agreed.

"And would you consider it presumptuous of me to offer to share a cab?" he asked, this time with a sly grin.

"Probably," Delia replied, forcing a prim expression, but unable to mute the laughter in her eyes. He grinned in reply, and she stood and began to gather up her belongings.

Chase, though, leaned over and gathered up her work case as he stood.

"I think the moment ripe to try to convince you that I really can behave like a gentleman, Delia," he said as he tucked the case under one arm. He put his free hand on her elbow and started to guide her toward the curb. "That is, if you'll let me."

"I'd be a fool to stand and argue in the rain," she countered.

"Practical soul," he laughed. He released her arm and reached up to hail a passing cab.

He'd just handed her inside the cab when the first of the really heavy rain began to fall. Delia scooted over on the seat to leave him room and then proceeded to busy herself trying to brush away some of the wet from her coat.

"Rue St. Clodoald," Chase called up to the driver. He then climbed up and settled himself beside her once he'd placed her case on the floor beside her feet. "That's better," he muttered as he looked out the window at the growing downpour. "Nothing worse for a man's dignity than looking like a soaked dog." He turned back to face her. "What is it?" he asked when he noticed her disturbed expression.

"Perhaps you ought not to take me all the way home," she told him. "I think it might be wiser if I talked first with Papa, if I tried to convince him . . ."

"That I'm not the monster he thinks I am?" Chase finished for her.

She hesitated just an instant.

"Well, yes," she admitted. "I'm afraid he has a rather poor opinion of you just at the moment, and he may be fairly hard to persuade."

"Harder than you were?" he asked. And then, before she could answer, he asked with a chuckle, "He doesn't, by any chance, have a coterie of pugnacious young artists protecting his honor, does he?"

She blushed as she thought of all he'd been through that afternoon just to get her to agree to talk to him.

"No," she told him. "No coterie of artists, pugnacious or otherwise."

"Good," he said. "Neither my chin nor my clothing is in much of a condition to repeat this afternoon's festivities."

She looked up at him, then touched her fingers gently to his cheek beside the thin line of the cut.

"I'm sorry about what happened, Chase," she whispered.

She was, she realized. She was awash in guilt that she'd let it happen when she knew she could very well have stopped it.

He put his hand on hers, then pulled her fingers from his cheek to his lips.

"As strange as it sounds, I'm not sorry in the least," he told her. "If there had been any question in my mind about how precious you are, Delia, your friends answered it for me. And that was a valuable lesson."

"Precious?" she asked.

He nodded. "I'm a man who actively abhors discomfort," he told her. The side of his mouth turned up into a crooked grin. "Most especially my own. Do you really think I'd have come back for a second bout with your friends for anything less valuable than a truly unique work of art?"

"I'd not have thought it necessary to remind you that forgers seem to run in my family," she told him.

He shook his head, unconvinced.

"There are some things that simply can't be counterfeited," he told her.

With that, he slid his arm around her shoulders and pulled her close, pressing his lips to hers.

Delia closed her eyes and savored the feel of it, the warm, firm pressure, and the insistent throb it generated inside her. This time there was no cold spray of raindrops to force a premature end to their embrace. At that moment, she felt nothing could have forced her to tear herself from his arms.

She felt oddly safe and isolated with him inside the carriage, as though it were an island untouched by the rest of the world. Nothing, not the bumpy lurches of the wheels against the wet cobblestones, not the rumbling of thunder nor the downpour just inches away, could disturb that feeling. The scent of damp wool mingled with the taste the coffee had left on his lips, and she thought it an oddly domestic combination, homey and comforting.

The heat of his embrace, however, and the warmth that slid through her as her body awoke to the hard press of his close to her, was anything but homey or domestic. It sent a river of liquid fire through her blood, a fire that was more frightening yet more seductive than anything she'd ever known. If he asked her at that moment to go back to his room with him, she would, she realized, agree. Being alone with him was like a drug to her, and she was only too vulnerable to its narcotic lure. It made her begin to understand the hold alcohol had on her father.

But Chase did not suggest they go anywhere but to see her father. A nagging voice at the back of her conscience told her Chase Sutton was a man with a mission, and even if she refused to be a part of that mission, she would still take second place to it in his mind.

Still, when she felt the inquiring pressure of his tongue against her lips, she willingly parted them in invitation. Second place, she told herself, was better than nothing at all.

"Perhaps I should go in first and talk with him alone," Delia suggested.

Chase reluctantly released his hold of her, and sat back slightly so that he could look at her. Odd, he thought, what a pleasure it was to simply look at her.

He shook his head. Staring down at her flushed cheeks and lips, he found he earnestly regretted the ride had ended so quickly. But perhaps that was best, he told himself. If he'd gone on very much longer, holding her, kissing her, he knew he'd have wanted a good deal more.

"That's my task, Delia," he told her. "And it's one that ought to be done sooner, not later."

"He's a bit stubborn," she warned.

"A characteristic that seems to run in the Hampton family," he told her. "I suppose it's an intrinsic part of the bloodline."

"I am not stubborn," she retorted with a fair approximation of shock that he'd make such a suggestion.

"Did I fail to mention that I've come to consider it an endearing quality?" Chase asked her with a grin.

She smiled. "In that case, perhaps I am, just a bit."

He leaned forward to her and pressed one last, hasty kiss to her lips. Then he leaned down and gathered up her work box.

Delia pulled the thin curtain open and sat for an instant staring at the dark flow of the downpour outside the window. It had a dull gray cast to it, she thought, an unpleasant air that left her feeling slightly uneasy. For some reason she felt reluctant to move, to leave the warmth of the carriage and the close intimacy it provided.

"Go on," Chase told her. He pushed the door open, climbed out, and held it for her. "Run inside. I'll be right behind you."

Delia took him at his word, running the few dozen feet to the door, turning to watch him hand up the fare to the driver and then follow her only when she stood reasonably well protected from the downpour by the narrow portico.

"Ready to face the lion in his den?" she asked him when he came running up after her.

He moved into the small, sheltered space, not at all unhappy that getting out of the rain meant he had to stand very close to her.

"He's only protecting his cub," he told her. "I just

131

hope I can convince him of my entirely honorable intentions before he sinks those ferocious fangs into my neck."

"Ferocious fangs?" she repeated with a laugh.

He nodded. "Nothing more dangerous than a lion in his own den," he told her.

He leaned forward to her.

Before he could kiss her, Delia drew back slightly.

"Are your intentions really honorable, Chase?" she asked him. "Are you sure you won't press either Papa or me to help you with Pickering?"

He was slightly taken aback by her question and even more by her drawn, frightened look.

"I told you I'd find some other way, Delia," he reminded her gently. "I swear to you I am a man of my word. I won't ask you or Cotter to do anything you don't want to do."

She looked down and bit her lip.

"I didn't mean to question you," she said. She looked back up at him and when she faced him she saw her expression had become completely fixed. "I can't allow Papa to be dragged into anything that might hurt him. He's sick, his heart . . ."

Chase put his hand on her shoulder.

"I understand, Delia. You don't have to explain any more."

She nodded and offered him a slightly strained smile.

"Then perhaps it's time we went inside," she suggested.

"Better than standing out here in the rain," he agreed.

She put her hand into her pocket and drew out her latchkey as she turned to face the door. But before she inserted it into the lock, she turned back to him, stood on tiptoe, and pressed a quick kiss to his lips.

"For luck," she whispered.

Why had she said that? she wondered as she put the key into the lock and turned it. Surely Cotter would be reasonable. After all, once she and Chase explained, he'd understand that it had all been a mistake, that Chase was hardly the enemy.

But if that was true, she wondered, then why did she have a sick, unpleasant feeling in the pit of her stomach? If nothing was wrong, then why did she suddenly feel so afraid?

"Papa?"

Delia stepped into the front hallway and began to unbutton her coat, but stopped as she looked around.

"What is it?" Chase asked. He closed the door behind him and deposited the work case beside it.

Delia shrugged. "I don't know," she admitted. Ignoring the fact that she was still wearing her coat and that it was dripping a thin trail in her wake, she started across the hall. "I don't see any lamps lit. And it's cold in here. Why do you suppose Papa hasn't lit a fire?"

"It needn't be a grave mystery, you know. Perhaps he went out," Chase suggested.

"No," she replied. "He always tells me if he has any plans for the afternoon. Besides, he's always home well before dinnertime. And he hates being out in the rain. I don't think anything less than a matter of life or death could have dragged him out in a downpour like this."

She pulled open the door to the parlor and peered into the dim room.

"Look," she said as she stepped into the room. "Dark. No fire. And it's cold in here, too."

She stood in the doorway, shivering despite the warmth of her coat. It took her a moment to realize it wasn't the cold that set her teeth to chattering, but a frigid ache of unaccountable fear.

"It's more damp than cold," Chase chided gently. "Come on, we'll light a fire and wait for Cotter to come home. He's probably caught somewhere, waiting out the rain."

He started forward, toward the fireplace, but stopped when he realized she wasn't following. He turned back to her.

She was standing stock still, frozen, a look of horror on her face.

"Delia?"

But she didn't answer. She seemed oblivious of him, oblivious of everything but whatever it was she was staring at in the dim shadows at the far side of the room.

She shook herself suddenly, then darted forward, rushing past Chase to the opposite side of the room.

"Papa?"

The word sounded hoarse, as though it had barely been forced from her lips.

Chase followed after her, only now seeing what she had seen, recognizing the dark heap on the floor as having a human form.

And then Delia started to scream.

"Papa!"

The sound of her cry echoed through the still, empty house.

Chapter Eight

"I couldn't have gotten through all that without you."

It was true, Delia realized as she rested her head against Chase's shoulder. She had no idea how she would have managed to wade through all the horrible details of arranging a funeral. It had been bad enough having to remain calm as she listened to the doctor's matter-of-fact recital of the cause of her father's death, but having to choose the box in which he was to be buried, that had been nearly beyond her.

Chase wrapped his arm around her shoulders and held her gently close. He expected her to cry, to finally break down and show some of the grief he knew was tearing at her. There had been a few moments after they'd discovered Cotter's body when he'd silently prayed she wouldn't dissolve, when he dreaded the thought of being left to cope with the details of the death of a man he hardly knew. But she'd somehow managed to tunnel her feelings deep inside and bury them there, going about the unpleasant tasks she knew she had to perform with a dogged if slightly numbed demeanor.

Now, however, he was beginning to question his wisdom in having applauded her outward stoicism. He realized that she needed to cry, needed the release of giving vent to the pain she felt. But for some reason that he was incapable of fathoming, she wasn't quite ready to relinquish the tight rein she was keeping on her emotions. Even now that they were alone and there was no one from whom she need hide her grief, she stubbornly refused to release the hurt. Instead, she dropped her head against his chest and simply let it lie there as though it were too heavy for her to lift again.

"I was glad I was there," he told her. "Although you would have managed without me. You're strong, Delia, a good deal stronger than you may realize."

"Papa said something like that the other night," she murmured. "I'd told him," she hesitated a moment, then went on, "about what happened between us. He told me that I was strong, that I'd be fine, that I'd even be able to survive you."

Her words, he found, left him delving his own small well of grief. The thought that he could have hurt her as seriously as she'd obviously felt herself hurt numbed him, made him see himself in a light he found far from flattering. He told himself that the man who had seduced her as a means of getting information he wanted from her was someone else, someone who no longer existed.

He looked down at her and stroked her cheek softly with the back of his hand. Such a powerful creature, he thought, for someone whose outward appearance was all delicacy. He'd known her for what, a hundred hours, perhaps? In that time she'd managed to change a part of his nature he'd thought incapable of change. He pulled her close.

It wasn't only his regret that he'd used her badly that nudged his sense of guilt, however. Some part of him felt as though he was responsible, as though he was the cause of Cotter's death and the misery he saw when he looked into her eyes. That was nonsense, of course. Cotter had died of a heart attack, and he'd certainly had no part in that. Still, he couldn't shake the feeling that he had somehow started it all, that his following Pickering here had started events on a path they might otherwise not have taken.

"I'll repay you, Chase," she said. "I don't know when, but as soon as I can."

It was there still, he thought, the determination in her voice, the way she carefully kept it reined in, as controlled as she could make it. One last matter of business with which she had to deal on this endlessly trying day.

"There's no need for you to think about any of that now, Delia," he told her.

"Yes, yes there is," she countered. "Papa would never have accepted charity. I won't either."

"It wasn't charity," he assured her. "I wanted to help. I don't want you to give it a second thought."

"I intend to repay every *sou,*" she insisted.

Chase sighed. "We'll talk about it later," he told her. "You should sleep now."

She nodded, her face rubbing against his chest as she did.

"Yes," she agreed. "I'm so tired. I don't ever remember being this tired." The words sounded slightly muffled, spoken against his chest.

"Sleep, then," Chase told her.

"You won't leave?"

Her voice was tight, as though the prospect roused some horrible fear in her. He felt her body grow tense as she waited for him to answer.

Chase pressed his lips against the fluff of curls at the top of her head.

"Not as long as you want me here," he assured her.

She relaxed again, her body soft against his.

"Good," she murmured. "There's something we have to talk about, something wrong, something terribly wrong."

He assumed she was referring to Cotter's death. What could more terribly wrong for her than that?

"I know," he whispered gently. "Finding him like that . . ."

She shook her head again.

"No. There's something else. Like something you see out of the corner of your eye, but then, when you turn to look at it, it disappears." Her words were becoming slurred, her tongue grown dull by the events of this endlessly long day and the weariness that was finally overtaking her. "I almost had it before," she went on in a barely decipherable whisper, "when all those people were in the house, but it got away again. I can't think of it now . . ."

Her words made no sense to him, and he simply dismissed what she said as being part of her grief.

"There'll be plenty of time to talk later, Delia," he told her. "Sleep now."

She sighed, then let her eyes drift slowly closed. She could tell he was simply trying to calm her, to get her to rest, and she would have to convince him that what she had been trying to describe was not simply some sort of female hysteria. She knew for certain that there *was* something, something just at the edge of her consciousness, something that wasn't right. It had been there, haunting her with its evasiveness, but she knew it was there. Now that she was alone with Chase, perhaps it would come to her.

The image of her father's body lying on the floor floated into her mind, and she tried to chase it away, telling herself it could do no good for her to dwell on the horror of that moment. But even as she pushed aside the memory, the uncertainty bit at her. There was something, something on which she couldn't quite put her finger, something still waiting for her to discover, and it was too important for her to dismiss.

But it would wait, she told herself, wait until after the funeral tomorrow, wait until there was nothing else to fill her thoughts. For now, she was simply too tired.

And it was so pleasant to lie here, with Chase's arms around her, feeling warm, and, for the moment at least, safe from whatever it was that was lying in wait for her.

Delia stood staring down at the hole as it slowly filled with the dark clumps of damp earth that were being relentlessly shoveled into it. At first the sound of it had been awful, the thick, hollow thuds as the dirt struck the top of the coffin. But now the sound had grown more muted, and the dark, shiny wood was covered. Now it seemed almost as if someone else might be lying in that long, narrow box.

Now it seemed to her that if she turned around, she'd find her father standing there behind her, waiting to tell her it had all been some horrible mistake, waiting to take her home.

Chase put his hand on her arm.

"I really don't think you should stay here any longer, Delia," he told her. "Let me take you home."

He almost expected she'd push his hand away as she had the first time he'd made the suggestion, when the two gravediggers had first begun this gruesome part of their work. He'd stared at the two, watching their dull, bored expressions as they methodically raised and lowered the heavy shovels. Filthy men, with mud-smeared and stained clothing and eyes that had long ago grown so glazed by alcohol that they seemed more appropriate to the bodies they buried than to living creatures. He'd wondered why Delia did not seem as revolted by the sight of them doggedly throwing dirt on her father's casket as he was.

But now she'd apparently seen enough. She nodded and turned away from the grave, standing and staring at him as though she were looking at a stranger, as though she had been expecting someone else to be there.

"Delia?"

She shook herself and the disoriented look slowly left her eyes.

"Are you all right?" he asked.

She nodded. "Yes, Chase. Thank you. I'm fine."

Hardly fine, he thought. But perhaps as well as could be expected, under the circumstances. He offered her his arm and she put her own through it, willing, finally, to be taken away from the spectacle of the last of the dirt being heaped onto Cotter's coffin.

She held tight to his arm as they walked through the rows of moldering stone markers, following the path the others had taken more than a quarter of an hour before. He ought to have insisted she leave then, he thought. She was too withdrawn, and she was holding onto his arm even more tightly than even the uneven terrain underfoot required. Chase knew she was a good deal less steady than she would admit to being, and although he found he was flattered and pleased to realize that she was leaning on him for the help she needed, he was still worried about her.

"Does it seem odd to you that the sun is shining?" she asked when they were a few dozen feet away from the gravesite.

He understood what she meant, that grieving deserved the appropriate gloom of a dismal drizzle. Sunshine glinting off the first brave crocuses that had popped up here and there among the gravestones seemed somehow irreverent.

"The Arabs say sunshine makes deserts," he said.

She nodded. "I suppose that means that to some this is an awful afternoon."

"It goes to the eye of the beholder."

She nodded, and they walked on in silence for a while until they came to the gate of the graveyard.

"No, let's walk," she said, when he began to open the door of the waiting carriage. "Send it away. I can't bear to look at it."

Chase glanced up at the black crêpe-draped carriage. One glance at the driver, dressed entirely in black, his face, long and thin and gaunt and as close to a death mask as living flesh could possibly be, was more than enough to make him understand her reticence.

"As you like," he agreed.

Chase paid the driver and dismissed him, and then they turned and began to walk slowly through the pedestrian traffic on the street.

"It wasn't much of a funeral, was it?" Delia murmured softly after a while, finally breaking the silence.

"The priest didn't seem to have much to say," he admitted.

"Papa only went through the motions of converting when he and my mother married," she said. "And once it was done, he made no effort to hide that fact from Père Alphonse. If he hadn't wanted to be buried beside her . . ." Her words trailed off.

"You've done what you can, Delia," he told her. "The only thing you can do now is to let go."

She shook her head.

"You're right," she told him, "I know you're right. But something keeps bothering me and I can't make it go away."

141

"Bothering you?" he asked.

She shrugged. "I don't know what it is, actually. It's just that I can't get it out of my head, the way he looked when we found him."

"It's to be expected, Delia. It was a shock to you."

"No, it's something else," she insisted. "Maybe it's guilt, the feeling that if I'd gone home sooner he might still be alive."

"You had no way of knowing, Delia."

"No," she agreed without much conviction, "no way of knowing."

"Perhaps you should have let some of the others come back to the house with us," he said.

He wondered why he was making such a suggestion, well aware that the last thing he wanted was to share her company with the group of her artist friends, most especially the leering Pierre, who had made no effort to hide the fact that he was not pleased to see Chase standing at her side throughout the service. Still, she'd seemed comforted by their presence, much more so than by his, by the warm maternalism of Claude's wife, by the easy camaraderie she shared with the artists. He felt a wave of jealousy thinking about the fact that she was part of a community in which he was nothing more than an interloper.

And then there was the implied accusation of her words, the suggestion, unspoken but nonetheless there, that it had been his fault, that he had kept her from returning in time to save Cotter from the heart attack that had killed him. Not that Chase hadn't already thought the same thing a dozen times.

"No," she replied to his suggestion. "I don't want anyone there, not in that room." She held his arm and stared up at him. "There's something there, and I want you to help me find it."

"Find it?" he asked.

"Perhaps you'll be able to see it more clearly," she murmured.

She fell silent then, and he decided that perhaps it was better to leave the matter as it was until she deemed it time to continue with it. Instead, he concentrated on the feel of her body close to his as they walked, on the way she was keeping hold of his arm as though she never wanted to relinquish it.

Or perhaps she just needed it to steady herself, he thought. She held tight to him and stared at the ground with each step she took as though she feared it might suddenly dissolve in front of her and leave her falling into the chasm.

But Delia wasn't afraid of falling. She held his arm firmly because it was comforting to her to be close to him, because her thoughts seemed less confused when he was with her and she could concentrate rather than constantly reliving the horror she'd felt when she'd found Cotter's body. And just now she needed to concentrate, she realized, needed to think very clearly.

Because there *was* something in that room, something that was crying out to her, and she knew she wouldn't be able to live with herself until she figured out what it was.

However unpleasant it might be, she knew she had to go after this thing now, before too much time had passed and she lost any chance of finding out what it was trying to tell her.

She removed her coat and dropped it onto the chair in the hall, then stood staring at the closed door to the parlor as though it were something odious, something too distasteful to touch.

Chase put his hand on her shoulder.

"Are you sure you're all right, Delia?" he asked.

She nodded and started forward abruptly, crossing

143

the hall to the door and pushing it open with a sharp movement, almost as if she was afraid she'd lose her courage if she didn't do it quickly.

The room was sparkling bright, with a warm flood of sunshine pouring in the windows along the far wall. Chase found himself wondering how he'd thought the room shabby when he'd seen it before. The sunlight gave its proportions definition and made the fine, pale *boiserie* glow, dispelling the illusion of threadbare seediness engendered by the small cluster of furniture hovering near the hearth.

Delia had taken a half dozen steps inside and then stopped, her determination apparently lost in the wash of grief that had quite obviously overcome her as soon as she'd glimpsed the spot where Cotter's body had fallen.

"Are you sure you want to come in here?" he asked her. "There'll be time enough for this later."

"No," she told him. "There's something here. And I need you to help me find it."

"What can there be here to find?"

She looked around at the familiar sun-drenched room. It's here, she thought, just waiting for me. But what is it?

She swallowed the thick lump in her throat that formed as her glance settled on the place where Cotter's body had lain.

"I don't know," she admitted. "But it's here, I'm absolutely certain."

"It could wait," he suggested.

She shook her head. "No. It's already waited long enough."

Her reply surprised him, for he had absolutely no idea what could seem so imperative to her that she'd pursue it so soon after her father's funeral.

"Well, then?" he asked, his tone only a bit doubtful. "What are we looking for?"

144

She started forward again, only this time slowly, as though she were moving though some thick, invisible liquid. It seemed painful to her, and Chase knew it was only the force of her determination that carried her across the room. He followed just behind her.

She stopped a few feet from the wall, where a heap of crystal shards littered the floor. She knelt down beside it and touched the sharp bits with her finger, her thoughts so intense she hardly noticed when she cut it.

"Delia," Chase whispered sharply.

He reached out to her, pulling her bleeding finger away from the small heap of slivers.

She looked at the bright red drop on her finger bewilderedly, as though she'd couldn't quite understand how it had gotten there, then absently put it to her mouth and licked away the blood.

"It's here," she murmured angrily, looking around the room as she stood again. "I know it's here."

"What?" Chase asked again. "Delia, there's nothing here but a broken glass. It probably fell when Cotter had the attack."

He was becoming really worried about her, he realized. The strangely distracted expression he saw on her face was wrong, he told himself, just as wrong as the determined way she held back her tears. It seemed almost as if she was refusing to allow herself to face Cotter's death.

He stood and started toward her, but she didn't notice. She'd turned and stared at the place where they'd found the body and pointed to the small hill of amber and white dust on the floor. The amber sparkled as the sunshine hit it, giving off bright glints of refracted light.

She stood for a moment, gazing at the small pile, and the memory came back to her, clear now, more clear than it had been the countless times she'd replayed that moment in her mind, shatteringly clear. A pale thin line of parquet divided the heap of dust, and as soon as she saw it, she remembered it all as if she were seeing it for the first time.

"There," she said.

He shrugged, entirely doubtful, but he was willing to oblige her. He walked past her and knelt by the heap. He put his finger into the dust.

"Glass," he said and looked up at her. "Glass and something else."

She nodded, "Yes," she agreed. "Amber glass. My father carried his pills in a small amber vial."

"He must have tried to get his pills and dropped the vial," Chase suggested. "Someone must have stepped on it when the body was removed."

Delia shook her head, and knelt down beside him and pointed to the thin line that parted the pile of dust.

"No. Papa's hand was there when we found him," she said softly, remembering it all now, the image crystal clear in her mind. She touched her finger gingerly to the line of bare wood that pushed into the small pile. "His finger did this. He put his finger into this powder."

Chase darted a glance at her eyes. They were fixed, determined to make him see what she saw. For a moment he hesitated, wondering if she were doing nothing more than making mysteries when none existed for the simple expedient of distracting herself from thoughts she found too painful to consider. But then he told himself that perhaps he owed her this. It was, after all, little enough to give.

He stared in silence at the pile a moment longer, honestly trying to remember. Finally he nodded.

"Yes, it was," he agreed, remembering now.

"He was reaching out to the medicine," she told

146

him. "Which means the vial was already crushed when he was still alive."

"He must have dropped the vial," he said, "then accidentally stepped on it . . ."

"No," she objected, breaking in sharply. "He was very careful with those pills," she said. "Even when he'd had too much to drink, he was remarkably careful. He'd never have done this."

He looked up at her, his eyes sharp as they found hers.

"You're saying he wasn't alone," Chase ventured carefully. "That someone was with him when he had the attack."

He was wrong. Delia hadn't really known what it was she was saying. But now that he'd drawn the conclusion for her, it was as though a dam had broken inside her. It came to her in a rush that shocked her, the certainty that she knew just what it was that until that moment had eluded her, what it was that had been taunting her.

She pointed to the powder.

"That's what it is, Chase," she said. "He couldn't have been alone. Someone was with him. That someone dropped the glass that broke. And that someone made sure Papa wouldn't be able to take his pills," she murmured. She looked up at him, her eyes wide with horror and shock. "Papa was murdered!"

She put her hand to her mouth as a muffled sob seemed to be physically wrenched from her.

"Oh, God," she cried. "He was murdered!"

Chase reached out to her and put his hands on her arms, holding her firmly until she looked up at him.

"Delia, we don't know that. He could have dropped his glass when the attack started. He pulled out his vial of pills, then dropped it, too. He could have staggered forward, trying to retrieve the pills, and accidentally stepped on the vial. There's no real reason to suspect anything else."

"I just know it, Chase," she insisted. "I just know someone was here with him, and that someone made certain he couldn't take his pills to stop the attack."

"There's no proof of that," he told her firmly. "Nothing except the crushed vial even remotely suggests it, and he very well could have accidentally crushed the vial himself."

Delia pulled away from him, turning and looking wildly around the room. Her thoughts were disjointed and as spastic as her movements; they leapt from one subject to another as her eyes drifted from one object in the room to another. She was certain now that it had been Cotter's ghost that had been crying out to her, Cotter's ghost telling her what happened, Cotter's ghost begging her to set right the wrong that had been done him. And she knew she'd need Chase to believe her, knew there was nothing she could hope to do alone to avenge her father's death. But Chase could help her, if only she could convince him.

Because there was only one person who could have stood by and watched Cotter die, only one person who was capable of doing that sort of thing. She'd never met that person, but she'd seen him walking out of her house just a few days before.

And then her glance fell on something shiny glinting from beneath the skirt of her father's chair. She pushed herself to her feet and scrambled to it, kneeling and reaching her hand beneath the tattered flounce of fabric.

She pulled out a second crystal glass and held it up to the light.

"Here's your proof," she told Chase. "Two glasses. That means there were two people in this room."

148

He stood and crossed to her, taking the tumbler she held up to him and sniffing carefully at it. The scent of whiskey still clung to the glass.

"Perhaps you're right," he agreed.

It was like a great weight had been taken off her shoulders to hear him agree with her. Now whatever needed to be done would be done, she told herself. They'd go to the police. Pickering would pay for what he'd done.

She hardly noticed the wash of tears that began to stream down her cheeks. But she did notice that when she looked at the place where they'd found Cotter's body, she no longer saw it lying there.

"Oh, Papa," she murmured, and with the words came a wave of grief and loss.

Chase put his arms around her. It was almost a relief to him to be able to stand there with her, to be able to hold her, comfort her. However wrenching the sound of her sobs, he knew she needed to shed these tears, knew she needed to come to grips with Cotter's death and her grief.

He had no idea how long they stood together that way, with her in his arms. The sobs that shook her sent tremors through her, leaving her shaking and weak. Chase held her and stroked her and whispered softly, but he knew that more than anything, the release was good for her.

Delia felt as though she was dissolving with those tears. They felt hot on her cheeks and tasted salty against her lips. But for whatever reason, it felt good to her to finally shed them, for she'd felt them just beneath the surface, waiting for her to give them vent. And more than that, it felt good to her to allow herself to be weak, knowing that Chase was there to be strong for her.

Finally the flood slowed to a stream, and the stream to a trickle. She pushed herself away from

Chase, rubbing her cheeks with the heels of her palms.

"I feel so foolish," she murmured.

"No need," he assured her.

"But I've made you all wet," she said, motioning to his shirt. It was rumpled and damp.

He pushed her hands away, then put his own hands on her cheeks and wiped them dry with his thumbs. It was odd, he thought, how pleasant it was to look down into those impossibly colored eyes of hers, how much he wanted to protect her, to comfort her.

"Your monsters gone now?" he asked.

She nodded. "Yes. Now that we know what happened. Now that we can go to the police . . ."

No," he told her, cutting her off. "We've nothing to go the police with, Delia."

"But we know that Papa wasn't alone," she insisted, "that someone was here when he died."

"But we don't know who it might have been. Nor do we have any proof that whoever it was prevented Cotter from taking the pills."

Delia shook her head. "Yes, we do know," she replied. "Papa told me he was going to deal with Matthew Pickering. Well, it looks to me like he tried to do just that. And somehow it went wrong." She looked up at Chase with wide eyes, begging him to see and understand. "There's no one else who could have done such a thing, Chase. And no one else who *would* have done it. It *had* to have been Pickering."

"It may very well have been," he agreed. "But you need evidence to convict a man of murder, Delia," he told her calmly. "A second tumbler isn't enough by far to send a man to the gallows. The police won't do anything because you suspect Pickering. There's nothing they can do."

She stared up at him a moment, then backed away

from him, not wanting him to touch her, not wanting him to be able to accept so easily what she could not accept at all.

"There has to be something, some way we can prove he caused Papa's death," she cried.

"As much as I hate to say it, without proof, there's nothing we can do."

Chase watched her, watched as she seemed to change in front of him. All evidence of the grief that a few moments before seemed to consume her so totally suddenly dissolved and disappeared. Even her eyes grew sharp and hard as they returned his stare.

"Yes, there is," she insisted. "We can send him to prison." She fixed a cold, determined look at him. "What was it you wanted Papa to do to help you catch Pickering?" she asked.

"What difference does that make, Delia?" he asked. "Cotter is dead. Whatever paintings Pickering wanted his help to steal are safe now."

"And Pickering just walks away?" she cried.

"There's not much we can do to stop him," he told her.

"I don't believe that," she insisted. "And I refuse to allow it to happen. I'll do what you wanted Papa to do, give Pickering what he wants so that you can catch him trying to replace the originals with forgeries."

"You said you couldn't do it," he reminded her.

"Yes, I said that. And when I did, I didn't think I could. But things have changed now. I didn't have a real reason to hate Pickering before," she told him. She glanced back at the small pile of dust that once had been the vial of Cotter's pills. "Now I do."

Chapter Nine

Delia glanced at the exhibit catalog, quickly scanning the long list of entries.

"Papa said Pickering wanted two Memlings," she told Chase. "Specific canvases, still lifes."

"He must have a buyer with very expensive tastes and very limited morals," Chase replied. "That's the way he usually operates, finding a client first, then appropriating the precise item that client wants."

"I suppose it's safer for him that way," Delia replied. "He need have the paintings in his hands only a very short time."

Chase nodded. "It beats keeping a warehouse of stolen art and hoping someone will come along willing to buy it," he agreed.

Delia put her finger on an entry in the catalog. "Here they are," she said. "There are five Memlings, numbers sixty-seven through seventy-one. Let's see if we can figure out which are the ones that brought Matthew Pickering all the way from the other side of the Channel."

Her jaw hardened as she spoke, and her face took on an unusually set and determined expression. One glance at it and Chase knew he wouldn't like what she was thinking were he privy to her thoughts.

"I agreed to come here and see if we could figure out which canvases Pickering has his eye on, Delia," he said as they crossed the wide gallery in search of the paintings. "But that's the end of it, as far as you're concerned. Dealing with Pickering is my job, not yours. I don't want you getting involved in this."

They skirted a small group of somberly suited, top-hatted gentlemen and well-dressed women, all of whom seemed transfixed by a portrait of a very pale-faced martyr whose lack of color was doubtless due to the fact that his hands were lying on the ground in front of him while he held up revoltingly bloody stumps. His face, with a bright golden halo surrounding it, looked all the more ghastly as he was staring up to heaven with a peaceful look of serene devotion on it rather than the pain and anguish that common sense dictated ought to be there.

"You said yourself that if you knew which paintings Pickering intended to steal, it would be a good deal easier to ensure their safe transport," Delia told Chase as she darted a quick glance at the portrait that had so intrigued the group they'd passed. She made a small moue of distaste as she considered the unpleasant subject of the piece. "Di Paolo," she murmured. "His saints are always so lugubriously horrific." She sighed. "But then, fifteenth-century Italy was most likely a lugubriously horrific place for a poor artist." She turned away from the painting. "I wonder if he really did believe that martyrs died smiling beatific smiles?"

"And I've come to the decision," Chase went on, ignoring her minor excursion into the imponderable mysteries raised by religious art, "that once we determine which of the Memlings might be Pickering's targets, that ends your little venture into the world of art forgers and thieves. Pickering is dangerous, and you have no idea how to deal with a man like that."

He spoke in a hushed voice, taking pains that they

153

not be overheard. The gallery itself was fairly crowded, with twenty or more copyists diligently at work, as well as several scores of visitors milling around as they considered the paintings with varying expressions of interest and even, occasionally, abject boredom. With that much of a crowd, his words were lost in the general hum of conversation and he had little fear they might be overheard.

Delia darted a glance at him. He'd said much the same thing several times already, that he didn't want her involved any further, that Pickering was his responsibility. For a single, long, aching moment she wondered if this was simply his way of distancing himself from her, but then she quickly drew back from the possibility, telling herself he only wanted to protect her.

"I'm sorry, Chase, but it's not your decision to make," she told him flatly. "You forget, I've lived my whole life with a forger. I've even been one myself. So don't suggest that I'm an innocent. I am decidedly not." She flashed him a provocative and knowing smile. "A fact to which you, more than anyone else, can attest, I might add."

Chase couldn't stifle a small laugh.

"I warn you, Delia, anymore of those looks and you may find my resistance lacking a good deal behind good breeding," he told her with a faint smile.

"I am truly shocked," she chided, then she, too, laughed. "What a wickedly French thing for a proper Englishman to suggest. I hardly know what to say."

Chase grinned, but he refused to allow her to derail the conversation. His smile quickly vanished.

"You can't expect me to believe you know how to deal with a man like Pickering," he told her.

"I don't care what you believe," she replied. She stopped and turned to face him. Any hint of jocularity had disappeared from her expression. "Pickering killed my father," she said softly. "If I can't see him pay for that crime, then I'll have to be satisfied having him jailed for theft. But don't try to lecture me about getting involved in matters that don't involve me, Chase. Because I'm already involved. And I intend to see this through. I owe Papa that much. That much and more."

Her voice had risen with her last words, becoming loud enough to draw attention to them. Chase realized that several people in the crowded gallery had turned and were looking at them curiously.

He put his hand on Delia's arm and nudged her forward.

"We'll discuss it later, Delia," he murmured. "This is hardly the time or the place."

"We've already discussed it," she retorted. "All the way here we did nothing *but* discuss it. And all that talk did nothing to change my mind, Chase. Nor are you going to change it, so you might just as well consider the matter settled." She turned away from him and stared at the display of paintings covering the long wall. "Here we are," she said as she moved a few feet further, then finally stopped in front of a small portrait under which was hung a placard reading:

No. 67. Memling, Hans, 1430-1495(?), *Portrait of a Young Man with a Black Cape,* Flemish. Believed to be the young Duc de Jumet, circa 1460. Shown with permission of His Excellency Adrien Marie Legendre.

"Beautiful, isn't it? Monsieur Legendre has fine taste," Delia murmured as she stared at the portrait. She moved abruptly past it, before Chase had a chance to respond. "But not one of the two we're

155

interested in. Pickering told Papa still lifes."

They took a few more steps, moving a bit further along, glancing quickly at the paintings they passed.

"We're in luck," Delia said with a sigh of relief. "Five Memlings, but only two are still lifes. These have to be the paintings Pickering wanted Papa to copy."

She'd stopped in front of the two, a pair in matching ornate gold-leaf-trimmed frames. Beneath them was a neatly lettered placard:

Nos. 69 and 70. Memling, Hans, 1430-1495(?), *Still Life with Grapes* and *Still Life with Wine and Fruit*. Flemish, circa 1470-73. Shown with permission of His Excellency François Pierre Louis, Compte de Grasse.

"Damn," Delia whispered.

"What's wrong?" Chase asked, surprised by her reaction to what appeared to him to be a perfectly beautiful pair of canvases.

"They're fine paintings," she murmured.

"And that's bad?" he asked with a wan smile.

She leaned forward, standing close, examining the details.

"I'd hoped they might be early works, with enough flaws to hide my own imperfections. But they aren't. They're very fine, the style mature and detailed. Just look at the drops of condensation on the wineglass, the transparency of the ewer. They'll be very difficult."

Her evaluation left Chase smiling with obvious relief.

"All the more reason why you should consider your involvement in this little venture completed," he told her.

"I said difficult," she snapped in reply, "not im-

156

possible. Even the best forgeries aren't perfect. But then, they don't have to be. People tend to see what they expect to see."

"Delia, these paintings will be examined by curators, experts."

She flashed him a slightly malicious grin.

"Papa used to say that curators were the easiest of all to fool," she replied, and then turned her attention back to the Memlings.

She stood with her face very close to one of the paintings, staring at the minutely precise brushwork. Chase stood beside her, staring at her, torn between the desire to pull her away and the wish not to draw any more attention to her than she'd already drawn herself.

Despite Chase's wish to remain anonymous among the crowd, Delia's intense scrutiny of the paintings had not gone unnoticed. A moment later a guard strode up to them. He made a loud sound in the base of his throat in an attempt to draw Delia's attention, and when that expedient did not work, he raised his hand, extending it in front of her and making a motion to her to move away.

"Please step back from the paintings, *mademoiselle*," he said in a tone that said quite clearly this was not a request she was at liberty to ignore.

Delia glanced quickly at him, gave him an exasperated look, then continued with her examination of the painting.

"It's all right," Chase said before the guard could decide stronger measures might be required. He withdrew his wallet from his breast pocket and flipped it open, holding it up so that the guard might see. "I'm working for the Lloyd's Corporation. I'm just checking over the collection before making arrangements for their shipment to London."

The guard stared at the identification Chase showed him, his expression doubtful, though no longer quite as superior as it originally had been.

"That may be, *monsieur,* but I can't allow the paintings to be touched," he said slowly.

"Quite right," Chase quickly agreed. He put his hand on Delia's arm and tugged. "I was just about done here, in any case."

"Very good, *monsieur,*" the guard replied with a nod of entirely doubtful obsequiousness.

Chase tugged again at Delia's arm, forcing her away from the paintings. "Come along, Delia," he said firmly. "I'll buy you some tea."

"I'm not thirsty," she objected.

"Oh, yes, you are," he hissed in her ear as he pushed past her the still doubting guard.

Chase herded Delia through the museum to the tea counter. She stared at him with a defiant expression on her face as he seated himself opposite her, then the two of them silently glowered across the small marble table at one another while a waitress in black uniform and white frilly apron and cap set out tea and a plate of tiny sandwiches in front of them.

When the waitress had gone, Delia threw back her shoulders and smiled a saccharine smile.

"Shall I pour?" she asked as she lifted the pot. She filled one cup. "One lump or two, Mr. Sutton?" she asked, again flashing the falsely sweet smile as she held it out to him.

He took the cup and put it down with a slight clatter on the table.

"Look, Delia, I understand . . ."

"A sandwich?" she asked, interrupting the flow of his words as she lifted a pair of tongs and held it like a bird of prey hovering over the plate of sandwiches. "Let's see, there's cucumber and egg salad and this," she peered intently at the edges of one of the squares of bread, "looks like anchovy paste. Very British. You should enjoy them." She neatly stacked three of the small sandwiches on the side of his saucer.

Chase gritted his teeth.

"That's enough, Delia," he told her.

He put his hand on hers, keeping her from increasing the pile on his plate any further.

"You were the one who wanted tea," she insisted. She dropped the tongs, then lifted the pot again, about to fill the second cup.

Chase had to struggle to control his anger. It was beginning to seem to him that she took a perverse delight in making things difficult for him. He wondered if she was still punishing him for having lied to her at the start.

It took him by complete surprise to realize that her intractability did not put him off more than it did. In the past he'd always expected a woman to cater to him. Yet there he sat, absolutely furious with her, and all the while aware that there wasn't a woman alive he'd rather be with.

That wasn't to say, certainly, that he wouldn't at that moment have greatly appreciated just a small hint of submissiveness on her part.

"I understand how you feel, Delia," he began again, ignoring the tea and the sandwiches. "I know it can't be easy for you, coming to grips with Cotter's death."

He saw her hand begin to shake when he mentioned her father, and he found himself regretting his bluntness. If there had been any other way, he thought, any easier way, he ought to have found it. But he knew there wasn't, knew that she had to understand that what she wanted to do was dangerous, far more dangerous than she realized. And she had to know he would not allow it.

The stream of tea had begun to shake as she poured. He put his hand on hers to steady it as she returned the pot to the table.

"No, you don't know," she countered, her voice ragged.

He nodded. "You're right," he agreed slowly. "I don't know. But I do know you aren't in a position to repay Pickering for what he did to Cotter. I also know that just now it's too soon for you to be able to see things clearly, objectively. And that can only make dealing with Pickering more dangerous for you — too dangerous."

She looked up at him, her eyes growing dark and troubled as they met his.

"I don't want to be objective," she told him. "If I lose what I'm feeling now, Chase, I know I'll never again be able to feel anything, ever. Pickering can't be allowed to walk away."

"He won't be, Delia, I promise you. I won't let him. But there's no need for you to be involved."

She shook her head.

"I am involved," she told him. "Pickering involved me when he killed my father. I have to be part of it."

"Why?" he demanded. "What can you possibly gain?"

She shook her head, bewildered that he couldn't see what seemed so clear to her.

"Because I need to. Because, in a way, I'm responsible. If I'd gone home sooner . . ." Her words trailed off, and she swallowed uncomfortably. "In any case, I have to have a hand in it."

She let her glance meet Chase's, then quickly looked away, afraid that the pity she saw in his expression might lead her to think she actually deserved it.

Chase's jaw tensed. He was beginning to see her

160

insistence as a condemnation, a suggestion that he couldn't do what he promised to do.

"Can't you trust me?" he demanded. "Isn't my word good enough for you?"

He stared at her, waiting for an answer, surprised at how much it suddenly meant to him to hear her say that she did trust him and then agree to abide by his decision. But she didn't.

"Trust has nothing to do with it," she told him. She looked away, not liking the anger she saw growing in his eyes. "Besides," she added, "there isn't any time to waste dithering or feeling sorry for myself. How much longer will the exhibit remain here in Paris? Three weeks? Four? If I don't begin now, there won't be any possibility that I could copy those paintings before they're to be moved to London."

Chase pushed himself back in his chair. He didn't know what he felt more, exasperation with her, or anger or hurt. Whatever it was, it hardened into a dull ball inside him.

"Look, Delia," he told her. "I've made a decision. I'm going to go to de Grasse and try to persuade him to withdraw the two Memlings from the exhibit."

"You can't do that!" Delia cried.

"Shh!"

Delia looked around. The tearoom had become suddenly silent at her outburst and the other patrons seated near them were now staring pointedly at her. She bit her lip and lowered her glance to her teacup, waiting for the normal drone of conversation to return.

When it had, she leaned forward to Chase.

"If de Grasse withdraws the paintings," she whispered, "there's no chance of ever catching Pickering."

Chase was unconvinced.

161

"Better that than involving you any further in this mess," he told her.

"You want him to pay for what he's done," she insisted. "You want it as much as I do."

He nodded. "Yes, I do," he said slowly, "I've wanted Pickering for a long time. And this time, I almost thought I had him. But it's more important to me to know that I wasn't the instrument that led you to harm at Pickering's hands."

His words sounded so sincere to Delia that she felt a part of herself melting when she heard them. She knew that deep inside she wanted to believe herself precious enough to him that he would give up his hunt for Pickering in order to keep her safe. She stared into his eyes, wondering if she was imagining the look of tenderness she saw in them, wondering if the deep, crystalline blue was indeed a window into his heart, or just a mirror of her own desires.

But there were other matters, more pressing matters, to be dealt with, she told herself. It would be best for her to leave off trying to delve into Chase Sutton's intentions until a time when she didn't have this ragged, painful feeling of responsibility to Cotter eating at her.

"What if de Grasse refuses?" she asked finally, glad to turn her thoughts away from what it was she felt for Chase and to concentrate instead on what she owed to her father.

"He can't be so great a fool as to risk the loss of those paintings," Chase assured her. "They're worth a small fortune. Besides, I've been known to be fairly persuasive on occasion."

"But if he does?" Delia insisted. "Will you agree then to let me go to Pickering? I promise I'll do everything just as you want. I won't be foolhardy."

His expression hardened. Delia could see nothing in it that suggested he might be open to persuasion.

162

"I told you, Delia, your part in this matter is now ended," he said, his tone flat, determined. "You've provided me with the knowledge of Pickering's target. The rest is my responsibility."

"And me?" she demanded. "What about me?"

"You go back to your own life now," he told her with a shrug, "and I get on with mine."

Delia stared at him, not quite believing what she'd heard him say. His expression was so coolly distant, so unemotional. He ought to have been discussing the weather, but that was not what he was doing. What he'd said was quite plain — he was telling her he was washing his hands of her.

She couldn't believe the stab of pain his words released inside her. It was almost as though he'd physically struck her. Her father had been right about him after all, she told herself. Perhaps he'd had the details wrong, but he had been only too painfully right about the sort of man Chase Sutton was. Cotter had told her that Chase Sutton was a liar, that he only wanted to use her. And now Chase was proving him right.

A means for him to get at Pickering, she told herself, that's all she was to him, all she'd ever been. He'd gotten what he wanted, and now that there was nothing else he needed from her, he was about to turn his back on her. She'd been a fool to think the kindness he'd shown her during the previous days was anything more than a part of pursuing his job. And she was an even greater fool to let herself believe the lies he'd told her, to think he felt anything for her. But more than anything else, she was a prize fool for allowing herself to fall in love with him.

Before it could completely overcome her, she pushed back the hurt with a wave of anger with him. He had no right to treat her this way, she told herself. Whatever he thought of her, even if he consid-

163

ered himself free to use her and then walk away, still he had no right to shut her out from seeing Pickering pay for her father's death. Pickering was as much her prey as his — no, by rights, more hers than his.

And the need to see him face justice for Cotter's death was even more important to her than whatever she might or might not feel for Chase Sutton. Someday there would be time for her to come to grips with those feelings, but for now only one thing was important to her and she was not about to be cheated of it.

She stared at Chase through eyes that had grown suddenly as cold and objective as those he'd turned on her.

"You haven't answered my question," she insisted. "What will you do if de Grasse refuses?"

Chase grimaced. What she was suggesting, he realized, was more than a possibility. The remnants of the French aristocracy were famously jealous of the prerogatives their positions provided them and their smugness was legendary, even to the point of arrogance. There was no reason to expect de Grasse to accept the advice of a lowly investigator working for anything as mundane as an insurance company.

"We'll cross that bridge when we come to it," he told her. "In the meantime, drink your tea. Then I'll take you home on my way to see the Compte de Grasse.

"No," she countered, "I'm going with you. I want to know exactly what he says."

Chase scowled at her. There it was again, he realized, the suggestion that she couldn't trust him, that she had to see it all with her own eyes.

"Are you suggesting I'd lie to you?" he demanded, his tone sharp with the edge of his anger.

She heard the tone, and a felt a wave of her own

164

anger answering. He had no right to condemn her, she told herself. He was the one who'd misused her.

She pretended disinterest, shrugging her shoulders, then lifting her cup and sipping the now lukewarm tea.

"I told you," she said, her tone cold and as indifferent as she thought him, "I have a vested interest in Pickering. I have no intention of letting you or anyone else make decisions for me." She looked up at him, staring at him with determination in her eyes.

Chase returned her stare. He realized there was something in her eyes, something distant and hard he'd never seen there before.

And a voice inside him told him what he saw was distrust, deep-seated and intransigent. He answered the voice with anger tinged with regret.

"Delia," he said, reaching out for her hand, still faintly hoping he could make her understand.

She drew it away from him.

Damn, he thought, wondering what had gotten into her head now and where it was going to lead them. Whatever wall had sprung between them, he realized that she was not about to let him scale it.

"There's no time now to play games, Delia," he told her.

"I'm not playing," she told him. "You might as well resign yourself to my company. If you don't take me with you, I'll simply follow you."

Chase growled and pushed aside the cup of tea she'd poured for him. He stared at it, wishing he knew some alchemy that would allow him to transform it into whiskey. He decided he would really appreciate a stiff drink at that moment.

It was no good arguing with her, he told himself. And if she didn't trust him, there was nothing he could say that could change that.

He didn't say anything to her when she looked up

at him over the rim of her cup. There was, after all, nothing to be said.

Delia calmly sat on a small banquette covered in maroon silk and stared through the open doors to the Compte de Grasse's enormous parlor. She found she was actually quite entertained by the scurry of near frenzied activity taking place there. A small army of servants were busily rearranging furniture, fitting crystal chandeliers with dozens of fresh candles, and setting out carefully arranged bowls of flowers and enormous trays of fruits and sweetmeats.

Chase darted a glance at her. She seemed mesmerized by the activity in the next room, he realized. More than that, from what he could see, she was quite unruffled by the fact that they had been left to cool their heels in the entrance hall without anyone seeming to recognize their presence save a liveried butler who'd disappeared with Chase's card nearly a quarter of an hour before. He wished he could find some of the calm that seemed to have descended on her. He couldn't. He had gotten an unpleasant feeling the minute he'd entered de Grasse's mansion, and it was getting steadily worse with each passing minute.

"Damn," he muttered under his breath. "Who the hell does that arrogant bastard think he is?"

He must have spoken a bit louder than he thought he had, because Delia looked up at him and for an instant a slightly amused smile fluttered across her lips. Then she looked away again, back at the procession of servants into and out of the parlor, and the expression of calm detachment returned to her face.

Chase didn't have the chance to consider just what

her apparent passivity might mean, nor did he have to nurse his own impatience very much longer. When he turned away from Delia, he found the butler had finally returned.

"The *compte* wishes to convey his regrets, but he is unable to see you just now, Monsieur Sutton," the man intoned as he handed Chase his card. He moved his head an inch or so, just managing to make it clear that he was gesturing toward the activity in the parlor. "As you can see, the *compte* is entertaining this evening, and there are a great many final details to which he must attend. If you'd care to return sometime next week, perhaps he could see you then."

Delia watched as Chase's jaw set hard with anger. It was obvious he wasn't used to being treated in such an insolent manner, and equally obvious that he didn't like it.

"Did you tell the *compte* that this is a matter of extreme importance?" Chase hissed from between nearly clenched teeth. "That it concerns the works of art he has on loan to the exhibit of Old Master paintings at the Louvre?"

The butler didn't so much as blink at Chase's display of temper. He crossed the hall and then stood with his hand on the doorknob, ready to show them out.

"Indeed, *monsieur*," he replied, in a tone just slightly short of a sneer. "And he will be delighted to make the time available to discuss the matter with you one day next week." He turned the knob and pointedly pulled the door open. "Good day to you, *monsieur, mademoiselle*."

There was obviously nothing to do but leave. Delia obligingly rose and took Chase's arm. His muscles felt hard and tense beneath the fabric of his jacket, and she knew he was seething inside.

167

Chase made a point of ignoring the butler as he led her out and onto the street.

"The man's an arrogant fool," Chase muttered angrily.

"Just because he has money and position doesn't mean a man need be intelligent," she replied calmly.

"Or polite, for that matter," he added. "He deserves to lose his damned paintings."

She grinned. "But you won't let that happen, now, will you? Even if he does deserve it?"

He wouldn't, she knew. He took his damned job far too seriously even to think of letting that happen.

Chase shook his head.

"No. I may not have a title in front of my name, but I do have my plebeian sense of pride."

Is that what it is, she mused silently — pride? She'd had an entirely different word for it.

"Well, then, you have something in common with Monsieur le Compte," Delia chided. "Your plebeian pride is as strong as his patrician pride."

By way of reply, Chase made a noise that sounded suspiciously like a growl to Delia. She couldn't keep from laughing. No matter what he'd intended, he couldn't rid himself of her now.

He turned and stared at her.

"You don't seem at all disturbed by the course events have taken," he accused.

She shrugged. "I'm not," she confessed. "De Grasse can't be bothered to see you, so there's no question that he'll withdraw the paintings from the exhibit. And that means we go after Pickering directly." She was surprised at how much that fact pleased her, at how much she wanted to see Pickering pay for what he'd done. She could read the disapproval that appeared in Chase's expression as he considered what she'd said, but found she really

168

didn't care if he disapproved. She'd turned blood-thirsty, hungry for revenge, and she didn't care that the fact did not speak well of her. "Now, how do you suggest I go about getting in touch with Pickering?"

"You don't," he told her flatly. "And, however it may seem to you, nothing is settled. I haven't spoken to de Grasse yet."

"Don't be ridiculous, Chase," she returned, her tone sharp with impatience. "He made it perfectly clear he can't be bothered. With an attitude like that, you really don't think he'll remove the canvases from the exhibit, do you? He'll most likely consider himself above any threat, no matter what you tell him. In any case, we can't afford to waste a week assuming he'll go along with you. If I don't begin those paintings immediately, there's no possibility I'll be able to complete them on time."

"You take too much at face value, Delia," Chase told her. He turned and looked back at the magnificently ornate facade of the *hôtel de ville* of the Compte de Grasse. "I think His Excellency is going to have the pleasure of an unexpected guest at his little gathering this evening."

Delia raised a brow quizzically.

"You?" she asked with dry sarcasm. "The proper British gentleman? I can't believe you'd so much as suggest such a thing."

"Believe it," he told her as he took her arm. "I thought by now you'd come to the realization I don't quite fit the image you have of my more reserved countrymen." He shrugged. "Besides, if I know anything about Pickering, and I think I do, I'll wager he's gotten himself invited to the *compte's fête*. Such things amuse him. At worst, I can pick up his trail."

"Really?" Delia murmured softly.

Chase turned to the street, already lost in thought of what the evening might bring him and oblivious

169

to the interest that filled Delia's expression.

"Come along." he told her. "I'll take you home, then I have to see about getting myself outfitted with some evening clothes."

He waved a passing cab, handed her up, and climbed up beside her. Lost in his own thoughts, he didn't notice the look of determination that fixed Delia's features.

And she was certainly not about to offer the information that she had her own plans for the evening, at least not just yet . . . not until she was certain there was nothing he could do about changing them.

Chapter Ten

Delia could almost feel the eyes that followed her as she crossed the lobby of the Hôtel Saint Gerard. An unescorted woman entering a hotel at this hour of the evening, especially a hotel like this one, the sort where prosperous businessmen unencumbered by wives and families tended to stay, could only give rise to one line of speculation, and she was fully aware of what that speculation would be.

She glanced briefly at the image of a dark-haired young woman dressed in elegant if rather provocative evening clothes in a tall wall mirror as she passed it. Well, she thought, if I'm to be taken for a *poule,* at least it has to be a high-priced one. She felt a smug wave of pleasure that she'd done as well as she had in the few hours she'd had at her disposal. No one, she decided as she darted a last quick glance at her reflection, would possibly think that the dress she was wearing had lain in a trunk for the previous decade, nor that the elegantly turned out young woman wearing it was the lowly seamstress who'd spent that afternoon altering it.

Delia was not the only one who found her appearance decidedly acceptable. Bewhiskered German and British businessmen who'd resigned themselves to a dull evening with nothing more than brandy and the newspapers to occupy themselves suddenly began to consider alternative pastimes. They shifted their positions in the overstuffed chairs they occupied, sitting up straight and pulling in bellies that until that moment had seemed perfectly content to lay slack and spreading in the aftermath of an appropriately extravagant French dinner. Each one followed Delia's progress along the length of the lobby, wondering what price she might ask and if it might be possible to disguise the cost of her hire as a business expense or if it might be wiser to simply bear it himself.

The clerk who stood behind the front desk, too, found his glance riveted on her as she passed through the gauntlet of hungry eyes. He grinned broadly at her as she approached.

"Mademoiselle?" he asked in a perfectly oily, insinuating tone. *"Je suis à votre service."* He smiled. *"C'est mon plaisir de vous accommoder."*

Delia pretended to ignore his leer.

"Mr. Sutton's room number, please," she said.

She noted that her use of clipped, very upper-class British-sounding English visibly unsettled him. The French, she knew, tended to consider their sins as their own, and usually thought of the British, especially upper-class British, as totally incapable of emulating Gallic sensuality even when they tried.

"Certainement," he mumbled as he shifted his attention to his register. A splotchy red blush momentarily spotted his cheeks as he wondered how he'd made a mistake. "Monsieur Sutton's is room 210. Shall I have him sent for?"

"No, thank you," Delia replied, and just barely nodded before she turned and swept away from the desk to the winding staircase.

Once she'd started up the stairs, with her back to the trailing glance of the still befuddled clerk, she rewarded herself with a small grin. The time she'd spent talking with vacationing rich British school-

172

boys had been useful after all, she told herself. At least she could fool a Parisian desk clerk into thinking she was British.

But once she found herself in the second-floor corridor staring at the door to room 210, she began to feel a good deal less certain that what she'd decided to do was altogether wise. The smug smile that had crept to her lips as she'd climbed the stairs disappeared. An enormous butterfly was ranging around in her stomach, and nothing she could do calmed it. It was quite obvious that now that the moment had come, the prospect of being alone in a room with Chase Sutton was not to be as easily dismissed as it had been when she'd been safely alone in her own home.

She gritted her teeth, then bit her lower lip as she knocked timidly on the door. He'd used her, she reminded herself. Now she needed to use him if she was ever to see Matthew Pickering pay for what he'd done to her father. Only a coward, she told herself, would run away now. She knocked again, this time with determination.

"C'est ouverte. Entrez."

She put her hand on the knob, turned it, and pushed the door open. Chase was standing in front of a mirror at the far side of the room, struggling with his cravat. He didn't even turn around to see who it was he'd invited into his room.

"You can leave the towels on the bed," he called out without so much as glancing away from the mirror.

"Oui, monsieur," Delia murmured softly as she entered the room.

She couldn't help but grin as she watched him struggle with the bit of black silk. Her amusement faded quickly, however, as she remembered the last time she'd been alone in a hotel room with him. The

173

thought was enough to raise a flush in her cheeks and send a wash of hot shame through her, shame that she could not deny was tinged with yearning. She forced it away, reminding herself that she meant nothing to him, that she mustn't be such a fool as to let him convince her yet again that it was otherwise, or, even worse, allow herself to let him mean anything to her. She needed him to get to Pickering, and there could be nothing more between them than that.

"Damn," Chase muttered as he stared in the mirror at the crooked results of his efforts. "Do you know how to do one of these things?" he asked as he pulled it apart.

"Certainement, monsieur," Delia murmured. She moved into the room, toward him. *"Je suis à votre service,"* she murmured, repeating the words the desk clerk had spoken to her a few minutes before. *"C'est mon plaisir de vous accommoder."*

He dropped the folds of silk. In the mirror, Delia saw his expression become puzzled.

"Delia?"

He'd finally recognized her voice, and he slowly turned around to face her.

"What are you doing here?" he demanded.

"I'm afraid I'm not delivering the towels you seem to have been expecting," she told him. "I'm here to accompany you to the *fête,* of course." She pulled the ribbons that held her cape closed, then pulled off the cape and dropped it on the bed. She looked up at him. "I assume this will be acceptable?"

It didn't take clairvoyance for her to realize that he thought she was more than acceptable. His expression silently spoke volumes.

She performed a quick pirouette, then stood facing him, waiting for him to answer her.

Chase quite simply gaped for a long moment, si-

174

lently taking in the sight of her in dark rose-colored satin, sleek and tight at her waist and midriff, with an extravagance of skirt and a bodice that nearly completely bared her shoulders and neck above a very deep décolletage. She'd swept her hair up and back, and narrow ribbons of the same rose-colored satin wound through her thick curls.

"Delia, you are absolutely smashing," he told her.

She made a small moue.

"I believe that's British, meaning you find me acceptable?" she asked with an arch little smile.

He nodded slowly. "More than acceptable," he told her. "Stunning is more the word I'd have chosen."

She performed a small curtsy. "Thank you, Mr. Sutton," she replied. "You needn't sound so surprised, you know," she added with a sharp, slightly pained smile.

"You can't really blame me," he countered. "Poor, starving artists aren't supposed to be able to dress like princesses."

"It was my mother's," she explained. "Back before Papa and I were poor." She turned to the mirror and straightened the strings of pale, pearl-embellished satin roses that decorated the sleeves. "I spent the whole of the afternoon fixing the hem."

"And an excellent job you did," Chase told her. He crossed the room to her and took her hand. "I'm entranced."

"Then I can assume that you won't be ashamed to be seen with me?" she asked.

"Never," he said as he drew her to him. His hands slipped around her waist and he pressed a slow kiss to her lips. "It's a shame I have an appointment to keep this evening. I'll regret leaving you."

Delia pushed him away.

"I'm going with you."

"Impossible," he replied flatly. "I wouldn't dream of endangering your reputation by allowing you to crash the good *compte's* party."

"You'll never get in without me," she countered. "That snooty butler will have you out on your ear before you can count to ten."

"You do underestimate me, Delia."

"Look at you," she insisted. "You can't even tie a cravat properly."

"Now that you mention it," he said with a grin, "there was a chambermaid who was supposed to help me with that."

She scowled at him a moment. He was laughing at her, she could see that only too clearly. It was a game to him. Well, she told herself, she could play the same game, if that was what she needed to do.

"The chambermaid will trade her services for an evening in your company at the Compte de Grasse's," she told him.

"Is this blackmail?" he asked.

"Call it simple bargaining," she replied. "It sounds much nicer."

"Bargaining or blackmail, you extract a high price for a lowly chambermaid," he told her.

"Accept the bargain or go cravatless," she countered.

He stared down at her and the laughter left his eyes.

"If Pickering is there, you will leave," he told her.

She smiled sweetly. "Whatever you say, Chase," she agreed. "Would I do anything of which you might disapprove?"

His eyes narrowed and he sighed. "Yes," he told her, only too aware that he had no doubt but that she most certainly would. His tone deepened. "This isn't a game, Delia," he told her. "I need you to promise that you'll do as I say."

Delia nodded. She kept her eyes on his, aware that she was about to lie to him and feeling absolutely no guilt about the fact. He deserves it, she told herself. He deserves much worse.

"I promise," she said. He was, she realized, staring at her, trying to decide if he could believe her. She smiled up at him and lifted the ends of the untied cravat. "Shall I?" she asked.

His uncertainty seemed finally to vanish. He returned her smile and then lifted his hands in mock defeat.

"It would appear you have me at your mercy."

Delia nodded. "I do like a man who accepts his own failings with grace and admits when he's been bested."

"A man on his knees has little alternative but to beg for mercy," he told her. "Now, will you tie this damn thing?"

"You will take me with you?"

"Do I have any choice?"

"None whatsoever," she said firmly. "Why can't men do these simple things?" she mused as she deftly looped the black silk with perfectly measured precision. "Papa can never do his, either."

She stopped suddenly, and her hands began to shake as she realized that she'd referred to Cotter as though he were still alive, as she realized he would never again need her to perform this small service. A thick wad of hurt filled her stomach, and her throat constricted. She bit her lower lip, refusing to give in to the urge to cry, telling herself that there would be time for her to mourn when Pickering had paid for what he'd done.

Until then, weakness was a luxury she could not afford, neither weakness for her loss nor weakness for Chase Sutton. She had neither the time nor the strength to deal with the pain now. Nor was there

177

any comfort for her in the realization that it would only be the worse for her when the moment came for her to deal with it.

"Delia," Chase murmured. He raised his hand to grasp hers.

She could see that he recognized the hurt she was feeling, could see pity filling his eyes as he stared down at her. She shook away his hand, wanting his pity less than anything else in the world at that moment. She purposefully and carefully finished tying the cravat.

"There," she said when she'd done.

"I don't think you ought to go after all," he told her gently. "You're not ready for any of this."

She took a step away from him. She wanted gentleness from him as little as she wanted pity. That look of concern, the softly caressing tone of his voice, it was nothing more than a lie, she told herself, meant to make her forget who and what he really was.

"You're wrong. I am ready," she told him. She took a deep breath. "And I won't let you stop me."

He sighed, then nodded, apparently resigned. "All right," he said. "Remember your promise."

She nodded. "I remember."

Satisfied, he turned to the mirror and inspected her work.

"You are a truly talented chambermaid," he told her, his tone lightly bantering once again. He turned back to face her. "I think you deserve a reward."

"Do I?" she asked.

"Just a small one," he said as he put his arms around her and drew her close.

Delia closed her eyes and for just a moment she let herself melt from the heat of his kiss, letting it chase away any thoughts she did not want to think, letting it comfort her and rouse a pleasurable throb

178

inside her. But she pulled herself away before she could become too rapt in the possibilities that kiss engendered, before she could let herself lose sight of what she really wanted and what she knew to be true about him. It was all an act, she told herself; she ought to realize that by now. The only thing that really meant anything to him was getting what he needed. She could not allow herself to be so great a fool as to forget that yet again.

"Was that my reward, or yours?" she asked him softly, when his lips left hers.

He shrugged. "Can't it be both?" he asked.

She pushed him away, and he released his hold of her.

"I suppose we can discuss it later," she replied. "But just now we have an aristocratic party to attend. I hope you're prepared for the worst."

Delia gave no indication that she was anything but completely oblivious to Chase's restless expression. She fussed with her gloves, carefully rearranging the long row of tiny pearl buttons so they followed an absolutely straight line up the inside of her arm. Occasionally she darted a casual glance out the carriage window to the entrance to the Compte de Grasse's mansion, but beyond that she seemed entirely preoccupied in her task.

"Are you quite ready?" Chase asked finally. There was more than just a hint of impatience in his tone.

Delia had no choice but to turn to him finally, nod, and take the hand he'd been holding out to her. She let him help her out, paying less attention either to him or to the chore of climbing down from the carriage than to the fact that another carriage had just pulled up behind them. That particular noted, she flashed Chase a satisfied smile.

They started up the stone steps that fronted the

elegant townhouse, but Delia balked after only a few. She turned and stared back to the street. The air was damp and thick and made the globes of light of the gas lamps lining the street shimmer like uncertain ghosts.

"What is it now?" Chase hissed.

"I must have forgotten my fan in the coach," she told him.

He turned back, glancing down the length of the dark street and the disappearing coach that had brought them.

"I'm starting to get the feeling you are intentionally making things difficult, Delia," he said. "May I take this to mean you don't want me to talk to de Grasse?"

"Don't be ridiculous," she told him. "I wanted to come, don't you remember?"

He glanced upward as though seeking divine guidance as a source of comfort to his frayed and much abused patience.

"How can I forget?" he mused.

"Well, I can't go inside without my fan."

He stood back to let pass the group of four party guests who'd been brought by the second carriage.

"You'll just have to manage," he told her. "The carriage is gone."

Delia looked up at him, smiled, then quickly stepped behind the two couples.

"How foolish of me," she said with a purposely coquettish toss of her head as she turned to fall in with the others. "Here's my fan, right here on my wrist."

Chase narrowed his eyes suspiciously, intending to demand to know just what it was she was up to, but when he turned to face her, he found she'd already climbed the remaining steps and was walking inside along with the other guests. He took the steps two at a time to catch up to her.

He discovered Delia didn't seem to have noticed he'd not been beside her the whole of the time. She was chatting with one of the foursome she'd followed inside, a dark-haired, buxom woman, just a shade past her prime but with a stylish, if not youthful, beauty about her.

"We've nothing as nice as Worth or Doucet in London," Delia was purring. "I've gone simply mad, ruining us with my own extravagance since the moment I arrived here. But your cape is absolutely magnificent," she added with a properly breathy admiration.

The woman smiled pleasantly. *"Merci,"* she said, acknowledging the compliment. Then she returned to the weighty subject of couturiers. *"Mais, naturellement,"* she replied. *"Tout le monde* goes to them. And Pingat, course. But my favorite is Worth, and if my husband complains of the cost, I simply pout and ban him from my boudoir until he sees reason."

She laughed a tinkling little laugh, inviting Delia to join her.

Chase wasn't listening to their fashion chatter. Instead he found himself pondering the mystery of Delia's new and entirely unexpected accent. Her speech moved from English-accented French to a clipped, upper-class, very British English. Aware as he was that her French was flawless and entirely unaccented, and that as a rule she spoke English with the merest hint of a French accent, he couldn't keep himself from wondering just what it was she had in mind. She was up to something, he decided, and whatever it was, he wasn't at all sure he liked it.

He liked it even less when he saw her turn and smile up at the woman's escort as a servant helped her remove her cape. Chase could not help but notice that the meltingly saccharine smile she turned on her new acquaintance's escort was immediately rewarded with an answering smile and a decidedly interested stare.

"Such a lovely night for a *fête*, don't you think?" Delia gushed.

"Mais oui," de Grasse's guest replied. "But all evenings are fine when there is a *fête, non?"* He smiled again at Delia, then nodded briefly in Chase's direction, giving him the sort of glance he might give a dog Delia held on a leash at her side, a sort of questioning look that suggested he wondered if her pet might bite. He turned back to her. "We have met, haven't we?" he asked her, his expression mildly befuddled as he tried to place her. He held out his hand to Chase, finally willing to concede the fact of his existence. "Rémy Charpentier. My wife, Yvonne."

"Madame," Chase responded, bowing formally to Charpentier's wife before he took Charpentier's hand. "Chase Sutton." He nodded toward Delia. "And this is Delia."

Delia extended her hand, and Charpentier enthusiastically grasped it in his.

"A grèat pleasure, Madame Sutton," Charpentier said as he pressed her hand to his lips. His eyes narrowed thoughtfully as he stared down at her. "But yes, I am absolutely positive I've met you before."

Delia made no effort to disabuse him of the entirely erroneous presumption he'd made with regard to her relationship to Chase. She tilted her head and flashed him a second, unquestionably melting smile.

When he saw the smile, Chase began to seethe. He found himself trying to decide if he wanted to throttle her then and there or simply leave her alone to cope with the situation she seemed determined to create for herself.

"Why, I believe we *have* met," Delia replied to Charpentier. In fact, she remembered the occasion quite well. It had been no more than three or four months before, and she'd been forced to call Claude and Pierre to rescue her from the drunken attentions of the then less than charming Rémy Charpentier. "The opera, I think, last month," she went on, tilting her head, smiling up coquettishly at him. "The Verdi, perhaps?" She turned to Chase and made him the recipient of yet another of those unbelievably sweet smiles. "You remember, don't you, darling? The opera last month. We were with Monsieur Legendre. It was *Aïda*. You fell asleep."

The two couples laughed, and Delia's new admirer said, "You know old Legendre, eh? Adrien has always had an eye for a lovely young woman."

Delia blushed prettily. "Such a dear. We met him at the reception opening that charming exhibit at the Louvre. It won't be nearly so nice when it's sent to London, I think. There'll be a reception, of course, and Her Majesty will be there, dressed in her obligatory black and being ever so fussy. It won't be nearly as lovely as the Louvre. Here things are done with so much more elegance, so much more style." She laughed gaily. "And so much more champagne."

"Ah, I think you are a Parisian at heart, my dear," Charpentier chuckled appreciatively, "no matter where you were born."

"I like to think so, too," Delia replied, then smiled at him as she slipped her arm through Chase's.

Chase put his hand on hers, gripping her fingers tightly enough to let her know he didn't quite approve of her at that moment. She stifled her grimace before it could make a public appearance, and pretended not to notice that his fingers were digging into hers.

They both joined in the general laughter as Charpentier mentioned he was always jealous when he heard the sound of an occasional snore during the opera. He always wanted to follow suit, he said, but added mournfully that Yvonne prevented that by applying her lovely elbow to his side.

The laughter continued and the group edged through the huge entrance hall toward the doors to the parlor.

Delia found she and Chase were face-to-face with the same snooty, liveried butler they'd encountered earlier that afternoon. He was standing at regimental guard by the door, and from the look he gave Chase, Delia was quite certain he recognized them.

He stared at Chase, at first with clear suspicion and then with outright antipathy. He put out his arm, barring Chase and Delia from entering along with the others.

"Your invitation, *monsieur?*" he asked with the kind of openly superior, intimidating sneer of which, of all humanity, only Parisian butlers and concierges seem capable.

His eyes narrowed and his expression gave every indication that he relished the rare opportunity to eject an uninvited guest.

Chase scowled. The butler hadn't asked the others for their invitations, and after the flurry of conversation Delia had started, he'd almost expected to enter unchallenged. He put his hand to his breast pocket, innocently searching for the invitation that he knew wasn't there.

"I must have forgotten it," he said, "or dropped it in the carriage." He shrugged and took Delia's arm. "No matter."

"I'm afraid it is, sir," the butler insisted with a malicious smile.

Chase felt suddenly impotent. Had he been alone with the butler, he'd have been more than capable of

184

convincing the man that it would be prudent to allow him to enter the *compte's* parlor for half an hour. But Delia's connivance had made that impossible.

Luckily Delia's new friends were in no mood to be kept long from their champagne.

"Is something wrong?" Charpentier demanded. He turned his most withering glare at the butler.

"I seem to have forgotten to bring our invitation," Chase murmured, putting his hand to his breast pocket one last time and grinning shamefacedly, suddenly looking like an overgrown schoolboy who'd inadvertently performed some minor social blunder.

"No matter," Charpentier assured him with a laugh. "Any man who sleeps through *Aïa* is certainly a welcome guest."

He offered Delia his free arm, then darted a parting glare at the butler, daring him to object as the group moved forward into the crowded parlor. Properly intimidated by him, the butler stared at Chase a bit longer, but said nothing and let them pass.

If the little of the room she'd caught a glimpse of earlier that day had seemed impressive to Delia, now, filled with candlelight and glittering with the reflections of crystal and gilt and the press of magnificently dressed humanity, she realized de Grasse's parlor was truly imposing. At the far end a small orchestra played waltz music, and the center of the room was already filled with dancing couples. Their images were reflected by a row of tall mirrors set into intricately carved *boiserie* paneling that lined one long wall. The effect was to make it seem as if one were looking past a row of arched pillars into yet another glittering ballroom.

"Are you here long?" Charpentier asked her.

She had to force herself to be attentive to him, to not seem too impressed by the display of wealth that surrounded her. She was, after all, supposed to be as accustomed to such displays of excess as he was.

"Only a few weeks more," she replied, regret overflowing with her sigh.

Charpentier turned to Chase and shook his head. "Much too soon. It's criminal of you to take away this lovely jewel, *monsieur*. And I would like to become better acquainted with a man who is practical enough to sleep through the opera and the wife generous enough to leave him to his folly."

Chase needed only a glance at his expression to know that Charpentier was far more interested in exploring an acquaintance with the generous wife than one with the practical husband. He darted a slightly jaundiced stare at Delia, then shrugged in resignation.

"Alas, some matters can not be helped, sir," he replied. "However pleasant, even nuptial holidays can not be extended indefinitely. Practicality must eventually intervene." He extended a proprietary arm to his supposed bride.

Delia took Chase's arm and smiled up at him. "And I wouldn't dream of objecting," she assured Charpentier. "I am, of course, eternally dutiful," she purred.

"I'd expect nothing less," Chase added in a tone laced with sarcasm.

Delia gave no indication of noticing. She pointed to the far side of the room. "Oh, look, darling," she said brightly. "Isn't that that charming Madame LeMoine? We must say hello."

They quickly drifted off into the crowded room, leaving Charpentier and his companions to sip the glasses of champagne they were offered by a passing waiter and contend with the problem of trying to place the young couple he couldn't quite remember having met at the opera.

"You are a wonder," Chase whispered in Delia's ear.

"Yes, I am," she answered with a short giggle. She was feeling quite pleased with herself, and frankly didn't care if he knew it.

"He actually thinks he knows you."

"He was right, we have met," she whispered back. "He was very drunk at the time. He had me do his silhouette, paid me extravagantly for it, then suggested I might want to arrange something a bit more intimately artistic." She sobered. "It's lucky he didn't remember."

Chase frowned.

"Do you flirt so outrageously with every man who comes across your path?" he asked, his tone just a bit acid.

"Does it bother you?" she asked. The prospect that it did sent a warm tingle of pleasure through her.

He shrugged, apparently indifferent. "Just a matter of curiosity," he told her.

The tingle disappeared.

"Only when my personal army is nearby to guard me," she retorted.

She was, she realized, angered by his apparent indifference. She wasn't quite sure why she cared what he thought, but she was only too painfully aware that she did. He could at least pretend he felt something, she thought. Even if his only interest in her was as a path to get to Pickering.

"How could I have forgotten your private little palace guard?" he muttered at the mention of Pierre and Claude.

"And my flirting did get us in here, didn't I?" she pointed out. "Something you were about to fail at quite miserably, I might add."

"All right, I withdraw my objection," he said, his

187

disapproval wilting in the face of practicality. He looked around the glittering ballroom. He was all business, suddenly, intent on the reason they had come in the first place. "Now to find our unsuspecting host."

"I have a feeling that won't be very hard," she told him.

She nodded toward the long row of mirrors on the far side of the room. In front of them stood a tall, thin man, resplendent in pristine evening wear, a vivid flash of a paisley silk vest just visible between the black of his waistcoat and the sharp white of his starched shirt front. But it wasn't the image of the slightly dandyish *compte* that held her glance. Instead it drifted off to the far more menacing face of the man standing beside him.

It was, unmistakably, Matthew Pickering.

Chapter Eleven

Chase grabbed Delia's arm and pushed her, turning her so their backs were facing Pickering.

"You're leaving," he hissed at her sharply. "Now. Before he gets a chance to see you."

She pulled her arm away.

"Don't be ridiculous," she hissed in reply. "It doesn't matter if he sees me. He has no idea who I am."

"For God's sake, Delia. Why do I have to remind you that the man is dangerous? He killed your father!"

His eyes were blazing furiously at her, and Delia felt herself melting just a bit with the realization of the intensity of that look, with the thought that it stemmed from his desire to protect her. She had to remind herself that he had come to Paris with a single purpose — to trap Matthew Pickering. She and her father had never been anything more to him than useful pawns. He might regret Cotter's death, he might even want to save himself the guilt he might feel were the same to happen to her, but that in no way meant he felt anything beyond a begrudging sense of responsibility toward her.

And it certainly did not give him the right to tell her how she must live her life.

"Do you think I've forgotten what he did?" she demanded, her voice low and sharp. "Do you think I'll ever forget that? All the more reason for me not to run away from him. Don't you see that I can help you send him to prison? He can't think of me as a threat to him, because he has no way of knowing that I know what he did to Papa."

Chase was becoming more and more exasperated with her. "I don't want you to go near him," he growled at her.

Delia only shook her head. "You're the one who can't get near him," she told him. "And as long as Pickering is with de Grasse, you can't get near him, either." She smiled one of the same falsely sweet smiles she'd turned on Rémy Charpentier. "And lest you forget, the reason we came here was so that you could loose your much touted powers of persuasion on the good *compte*."

Chase grew visibly angrier with every word she spoke, and absolutely infuriated when she turned that false smile on him.

"Damn it, Delia, you promised me that you'd leave if Pickering was here," he reminded her through a clenched jaw that said a good deal more about his own stupidity at having believed her than it did about their earlier conversation.

"And I will," she insisted, "once you've spoken with de Grasse. But until you know that the *compte* will withdraw the canvases from the exhibition, we'd be stupid to lose track of Pickering again."

"Not *we* Delia. I told you, you have nothing to do with this matter anymore," he growled. "Pickering is *my* responsibility."

"But as long as he doesn't know who I am, he poses no danger to me," she argued. "And you can't just send me off home. Like it or not, you need me with you if you intend to pass as just another one of de Grasse's guests."

190

As though his express purpose was to prove her right, Rémy Charpentier chose to materialize at that moment directly in front of them, the buxom Yvonne firmly in tow.

"Ah, my handsome young English couple," Rémy proclaimed in a loudly jovial tone. He seemed only too delighted to be the recipient of one of the smiles that had so infuriated Chase. "Monsieur Sutton, you must give me the honor of enjoying a dance with your lovely wife. As you choose to bear her off to your drizzly island, who knows when I may again have the opportunity?"

He held out his hand to Delia, leaving Chase no choice but to murmur, "But certainly," and step aside.

Delia was perfectly content to take Charpentier's hand. Despite the expression she saw on Chase's face, the last thing she intended to do was to leave, at least, not until she'd had a chance to talk to Matthew Pickering.

Because that was precisely what she intended to do, the reason she'd decided to maneuver Chase into bringing her. The moment she'd learned about the *compte's fête,* she'd come to the conclusion that Pickering would somehow get himself invited. From what her father had told her about the man, she'd determined he was the sort who would be arrogant enough to accept the hospitality of the man from whom he planned to steal. And Chase's demand of her promise that she leave if Pickering was present had only strengthened that conviction. He'd obviously considered the possibility fairly likely, just as she had.

Now that she knew she had been right, she had no intention of allowing Chase to bully her into running away like a frightened rabbit. She had a score to settle with Matthew Pickering, and despite Chase's convictions to the contrary, she knew there was only one way he'd ever be brought to justice—and that was for her to give him the paintings he'd wanted from Cotter and

191

then see to it that he would be caught when he exchanged her fakes for the originals.

She could afford to let Chase try to convince de Grasse to withdraw the canvases if he wanted, she told herself. From what little she knew of men like de Grasse, she knew he'd never agree to withdraw the paintings from the exhibit. And no matter what Chase Sutton decided to do after that, she intended to make the acquaintance of Matthew Pickering before he could stop her. She had no intention of quietly disappearing as Chase wanted her to do and letting her father's murderer go about his life as though nothing had happened.

Chase could not help but see Delia's smugly satisfied expression as she allowed Charpentier to sweep her off onto the dance floor. He knew her well enough by now to know that the smugness came from more than the realization that her flirtations had charmed an aging lothario like Rémy Charpentier.

She was planning to do something stupid, he told himself. And with Pickering involved, "stupid" translated into "dangerous."

He was sure she was walking blindly into trouble, and it galled him to realize that she didn't trust him enough to tell him what it was she was planning, that she couldn't trust him enough to accept that he would take care of seeing Pickering brought to justice. The thought settled into him with an unpleasant lurch that he was in many ways responsible, that he'd blithely led her through the maze and put her on the path. And the realization that there was no way, short of physically restraining her, that he could stop her brought him no comfort whatsoever.

The only thing for him to do, he told himself, was to get to de Grasse as quickly as possible, and then get Delia away before she managed to get herself into something truly unsavory. A flirtatious smile might be all she needed to charm a lecherous fool like Rémy

Charpentier, but he knew Matthew Pickering was something else altogether different, even if she didn't.

He glanced across the room at de Grasse, scowling when he saw Pickering was still at his side. All he wanted to do, he realized, was talk to the *compte* and get Delia away before she got herself into some real mischief. He damned the circumstances that stood in his way.

"Your wife seems to have completely charmed my husband."

Chase had almost forgotten that Yvonne Charpentier was standing beside him. He turned to her, intending to apologize for his rudeness, but when he found that she had been watching him staring at Charpentier and Delia swirling across the dance floor, he decided to let her construe his lack of attention however she chose. He shrugged and grinned wryly at her.

She accepted his gaze for an instant, then turned to watch Charpentier and Delia just as he had been doing. A dull pain slowly filled her eyes.

"Yes," she murmured softly, "she's completely charmed him."

Chase could not ignore the hurt that had crept into her tone, nor the sadness that filled her eyes as she watched her husband hold another woman in his arms.

"So it would seem," he replied. He could think of nothing else to say.

"Rémy's always like that," she went on, her tone low and just slightly bitter, as though she didn't really want to admit, even to herself, that she cared. "He loves beautiful young women." She shook herself then, and turned back to face Chase. "And a flirtatious young bride sometimes needs a bit of time to come to accept what it means to be married," she added, the hint of hurt gone now, replaced by pity for the hurt she assumed Chase was also feeling at Delia's apparent desertion of him.

Chase swallowed uncomfortably. He didn't think he was going to like where this conversation seemed to be leading.

Yvonne apparently misinterpreted his expression. She drew close to him, putting her hand on his arm and pressing her breast against him suggestively.

"It won't last long, of course," she assured him, her tone softly comforting. "And I don't see why they should be allowed to make the two of us miserable, do you?" She looked up at him, the suggestion in her eyes clear and explicit even before she voiced it. "There's no reason why we can't find some way to amuse ourselves until they come to their senses," she added in a conspiratorial whisper.

For a moment, Chase felt seriously tempted by the invitation. After all, Yvonne Charpentier was certainly attractive enough, and the look she was leveling at him told him only too plainly that what she might have lost when the blush of her youth vanished had been amply replaced by experience and a more than willing enthusiasm.

It would serve Delia right, he told himself, if he were to leave her to deal with Rémy Charpentier without him or the members of her private army of bodyguards to defend her. It might teach her a lesson that had obviously been too long neglected.

If it had been only Charpentier that he'd be leaving her to deal with, he might have done just that. But a glance across the room at Pickering reminded him that there was more at stake than a possible assault upon her modesty. Whatever lessons Delia needed to learn, this was far from the ideal schoolroom for them.

He glowered at de Grasse, trying to will the man to move away from Pickering to someplace where he could talk to him alone. When that failed, he turned back to Yvonne, offering her a sad, slightly accepting smile.

"I am greatly flattered, *madame,* by the suggestion.

194

But it seems to me you want me a good deal less than you want to hurt your husband at the moment."

Yvonne seemed determined to convince him that he was wrong. She pressed closer to him, staring at him with wide eyes that silently spoke a world of invitation.

"You Englishmen are far too proper," she told him. "If we were alone, I'd prove to you just how mistaken you are."

"If we were alone," he told her with a boyishly gallant grin, "I doubt there'd be any need for you to prove anything. But I think you misunderstand the circumstances, as does your husband. Delia's willful, and this afternoon we had a disagreement. Flirting with your husband is simply her way of repaying me for the argument. But I know her. Flirting is as far as it will go, of that I can assure you."

Yvonne considered what he'd told her. She released her hold of his arm, taking a step back, away from him. A small smile slowly nudged at the corners of her lips.

"You're saying she'll tell him, '*Merci, chéri, mais non*?'" she asked.

Chase nodded. "That is precisely what she will tell him," he assured her. "She may choose to punctuate the refusal with a sigh of regret, but she will without question refuse him."

"But you're certain?" Yvonne demanded, her expression suddenly very intent.

He smiled wryly. "Absolutely," he told her. "This isn't the first time she's done this sort of thing." He glanced toward the dance floor, then added, "Although I think this will be the last time. As much as it pains me, I'm afraid it's time I took her in hand." He found he was rather enjoying this recounting of his fictitious life with Delia, although he couldn't imagine why this recital of imagined domesticity could seem anything but distasteful to him.

195

Yvonne was still considering the prospect of Delia refusing her husband. The thought obviously gave her a good deal of amusement.

"I should like to be there when it happens," she told Chase. A shade of malice slipped into her smile. "Poor Rémy. He does not want to think of himself growing old. I fear he will be crushed." Despite her words, she did not appear to be feeling even the slightest twinge of fear at that moment.

Chase grinned. "You could offer him some heartfelt consolation," he suggested. "I've no doubt that would cheer him."

She considered the possibility. "Perhaps," she said. "Or perhaps I may allow him his misery, just to repay him for the infidelity."

"But there will be no infidelity," Chase insisted. "At least, not with Delia."

"Well, then, for the intended infidelity," she countered. Then she laughed. "Intent is nine-tenths of the transgression, is it not?"

"I thought possession was nine-tenths of the law," he mused softly.

"Whatever," she said and added an airy wave of her hand. She laughed again, then turned her attention back to the dance floor. Whatever anger or bitterness she'd felt toward Rémy when their conversation had begun had vanished. There was tenderness in her expression now, and a comfortable look of expectancy as she watched her husband.

It struck Chase that she really loved him, that despite the hurt she felt at Rémy's sins, despite the minor peccadillos in which she might indulge by way of revenging herself upon him, still she really cared for him.

He glanced back at the dance floor to follow Delia with his eyes. Love is an unfathomable commodity, he thought, as he watched her and felt himself fill with an odd mixture of emotions. Desire and anger and tenderness and yearning and a strangely potent protectiveness all roiled up inside of him. Perhaps, he told himself as he tried unsuccessfully to free himself of the confusing onslaught, it is best to keep free of it if one cherishes one's sanity.

But Yvonne was in a perfectly happy mood now, and, feeling thankful toward him as the source of her contentment, she was not about to let the pained bewilderment she read in his expression remain there. She again grasped his arm, but this time there was none of the studied suggestiveness there had been before.

"Come," she told him. "You want to talk to our host. I'll introduce you to him."

Chase looked back down at her. He was bewildered by the flow of her logic, or rather, apparent lack of it.

"What?"

"François," she said. "De Grasse. You keep looking at him. You do want to meet him, don't you?"

"Why do you think I need an introduction?" he asked.

She shrugged and shook her head. "Just a feeling. You've never met François, have you? And you really have no invitation to be here?"

"Why would you think that?" he demanded, pretending complete innocence.

"Because I know Rémy and I didn't meet you at the opera," she replied. "Or anywhere else, for that matter." She smiled. "I'd certainly remember a man as handsome as you."

Chase considered her smile. It was warm, genuinely unforced, and quite becoming. It was a shame, he thought, she didn't allow herself to let down her defenses this way all the time.

He offered her a crooked half grin in response.

"It seems we've been discovered," he admitted, only because he was somehow sure it didn't matter to her. "Are you going to have us ejected?" he asked.

"Oh, no," she assured him. "De Grasse is a fool. There's no reason why a few strangers ought not to walk in on his *fête* and drink his champagne."

Chase took the hint, retrieving two glasses from a passing waiter's tray.

"A toast to that noble sentiment," he said as he offered her a glass.

"To François's champagne," she said, taking the glass, then raising it to touch his with a softly crystalline clink.

They both drank, Yvonne half emptying the glass quickly, then looking up at him, weighing what she saw.

"But you want more than a few glasses of wine," she went on, her tone thoughtful. "For some reason totally beyond my comprehension, you actually wish to speak to François."

"Is it really that unpleasant a task?" he asked.

She nodded. "Far greater than you could imagine," she warned. "The man is an arrogant dullard. Not that he doesn't serve excellent champagne." She drained her glass. "But if you've set your mind to it, I'd be delighted to oblige you." She took his hand and laughed. "Come along. I'll tell him we met at the opera."

Chase shook his head. "Not yet," he told her. "Not while his friend is with him."

She turned and stared at de Grasse and Pickering and an expression of mild distaste settled itself across her features.

"Oh, that horrible Englishman. They've been everywhere together the last few weeks. I don't know what it is about him, but I don't like him at all. Even as great a fool as François doesn't deserve the likes of him."

Startled by her words, Chase stiffened. He recalled all the unsavory things he'd heard about Matthew Pickering's habits.

"You mean they're friends?" he asked.

Yvonne was full of gossip, including the Compte de Grasse's personal inclinations, and only too willing to share it with him.

"Oh, more than friends, I should think," she said. "A good deal more. François is quite taken with him. I've been in their company only once, a few days ago, but it didn't take long for me to realize that François is absolutely doting on him." She glanced at Pickering and when she spoke again, her tone was thoughtful. "I don't know what it is about the Englishman. He didn't do anything that should make me take a dislike to him, but I just got an unpleasant feeling being around him."

Chase nodded. "I know what you mean," he said.

"Then you know him?" she asked.

Chase nodded. "Well enough to wish to avoid him."

Yvonne continued to stare across the room at Pickering for a long moment, then took the glass Chase was holding, quickly swallowed the wine remaining in it, and handed both her glass and his back to him.

"Give me a few minutes," she told him. She smiled slyly.

"What are you going to do?" he asked.

"Repay you for what your wife is going to say to Rémy," she said, before she started across the crowded room.

Chase stood where he was, watching her weave her way through the crowd, then approach de Grasse and Pickering. He couldn't help but smile as she pulled an obviously reluctant Pickering onto the dance floor.

He carefully deposited the glasses on a nearby table, then followed the route she had taken across the room, silently rehearsing what he was going to say to the Compte de Grasse.

Delia was surprised to see Chase approaching. At first she feared he might insist upon relieving Rémy

Charpentier of the burden of her as a partner so that he could continue their argument, but once she saw him turn toward the now solitary de Grasse, she knew precisely what he was going to do.

She kept her eyes on their faces as she danced with Charpentier, oblivious to that fact that the defection of her attentions was causing him no end of distress. She watched de Grasse's expression change as Chase spoke to him, running the gamut from initial mild interest to surprise to a look of stubborn rejection that stopped just short of outright anger. It didn't take her long to realize that de Grasse was reacting just as she'd expected he would. It was quite obvious to her that Chase was not about to persuade the arrogant *compte* to do something he was so vehemently disinclined to do. A smug little smile settled itself on her lips as she realized things were going just as she had expected them. She made no effort to banish it.

What she hadn't expected, however, was the tenacious way Chase pursued the issue, even when it was only too apparent to her that de Grasse was in no mood to continue their discussion of the matter. The *compte* was growing angry; she could see that even from a distance. She half expected de Grasse to bellow out to his servants to throw out the upstart Englishman who had crashed his party and now seemed determined to upset him with what he could only assume were wildly fantastic predictions of impending catastrophe.

Despite her expectations, de Grasse kept control of the anger that was so obviously bubbling just beneath the surface. He was apparently an accomplished and thoughtful host who did not wish to have his guests disturbed, or, perhaps more likely, did not wish to make a scene his guests might consider distasteful and would later gossip over. In any event, he kept the tone of the conversation low, for not even those standing near him and Chase turned to look at them or gave

200

any indication that something abnormal was occurring in their midst.

The debate, however, could not continue forever. De Grasse made a dismissive movement with his hand, and then nodded in the direction of the door. He was, quite obviously, suggesting in no uncertain terms that Chase take his leave before he was forced to have him ejected.

Chase turned and started toward the door. He stopped only once, to nod at Delia and glance back to see de Grasse was still watching him. He had no choice but to leave.

All of which left Delia in a quandary. She ought to excuse herself from Rémy Charpentier's arms and follow Chase, she told herself. After all, she was as much *persona non grata* as Chase was in de Grasse's home, and besides that, she was not at all sure she wanted to be alone in an environment that was just slightly beyond her grasp. Much to her surprise, she'd found Charpentier in lofty company was not a great deal different from the man who had propositioned her that afternoon in the park by the Seine. A few more glasses of champagne and she doubted she'd be able to handle him with a smile and a slightly evasive word or two.

Despite that, however, the thought of leaving without contacting Pickering was galling to her. Turning her back was like running away from her responsibility to her father, especially now that Chase had failed to convince the *compte,* and now that she knew she held the only means remaining to them to get to Matthew Pickering.

She settled her indecision quickly when she saw Pickering and Yvonne Charpentier slip to the side of the dance floor and accept glasses of champagne from a passing waiter. It needn't take her long, she told herself, and Chase needn't know what she was doing until it was already done and beyond his power to change. She didn't even glance back at him, nor did she see him idling by the entrance, his eyes firmly on her.

Luckily the waltz ended just then. She smiled up at Rémy.

"This is lovely," she purred, "but I'm terribly thirsty. I'd love a sip of wine. Could we?"

She motioned toward Pickering where he stood, a trifle disconcerted, at Charpentier's wife's side.

Rémy scowled, but he realized he really had little choice in the matter. He held out his arm for her to take.

"As you like, my dear," he said, in a voice edged with pained resignation.

Delia slipped her arm through his, gently hugged it, and smiled up at him again in a small attempt to appease him. After all, she told herself, she was using him just as Chase had used her, as a means to get at Pickering. She could at least afford to be charitable to him. Kindness would cost her nothing. It was, she told herself, a lesson that would have been useful to Chase Sutton.

Once they reached Yvonne and Pickering, however, Delia completely forgot her resolution to treat Rémy gently. She ignored him completely, willingly offering Pickering her hand as a slightly confused Yvonne began to introduce them.

Delia didn't stop to ponder Yvonne's perplexed expression. She was far more interested in Pickering's look of surprise as she interrupted Yvonne before she finished the introduction, well before she'd given Delia's presumed name, Delia Sutton.

"Oh, but I feel I already know Mr. Pickering," she purred softly, turning her glance and her attention as completely to him as she had turned it to Rémy Charpentier a few moments before. "My father has told me such a great deal about him."

"Your father?" Pickering asked, his expression, one of mere politeness a moment before, now showing a pique of curiosity.

Delia nodded. "Yes, I'm sure you must remember him," she said, keeping her eyes glued to Pickering's. "Cotter Hampton. I believe you two were friends in what he used to call his shameless, callow youth."

She had to admit that Pickering's reactions were flawless. A small tic in the muscles near his mouth was his only response to Cotter's name. And even that he quickly covered with a wide, apparently delighted smile.

"Cotter. Certainly. One of my earliest and finest discoveries. It was a shame he didn't choose to go on with his work. He could have equaled the masters, had he applied himself to his painting."

He smiled at her, a smile that could be taken as merely friendly, or, were she knowledgeable enough, as a warning. And Delia was more than knowledgeable enough to know he hardly wanted to discuss her father in front of strangers. There was only the merest hint in his expression that he was speaking circumspectly, that he would keep her father's name respectable if, in return, she gave away nothing about him.

He grasped her hand in his and brought it to his lips, then held it, pressing it between his fingers, telling her the next step was hers if she chose to take it.

She, of course, wanted nothing better.

Yvonne, however, interrupted before Delia had the chance.

"One of your discoveries?" Yvonne asked Pickering, now entirely intrigued with the mystery of what she had quite by accident begun.

"Ah, yes," Pickering replied. "Delia's father was a very talented artist. Unfortunately he decided not to continue with his work." He grinned at Delia. "Actually, I owe your father a great debt of gratitude. His were the first paintings I ever sold. He was, so to speak, the author of my career."

"A source of great pride to him, no doubt," Delia said dryly.

"I should love to see him again," Pickering ventured.

Delia caught her breath. The man is unspeakable, she thought as she firmly wished him in hell.

"I'm afraid Papa died recently," she replied once she'd resettled her composure.

"A great loss," Pickering murmured. "I'm sure he'll be in the thoughts of everyone who loved him for a long time to come."

Delia kept her eyes steadily on his.

"And I'm sure that knowing he was in your thoughts would have given him a great deal of pleasure," she said.

There was a glint of knowing respect in Pickering's eyes as he returned her gaze. He seemed to be enjoying the game they were playing.

"But I had no idea Cotter had such a lovely daughter," he went on. "I'm afraid we lost track of one another after he married and stopped painting."

"But I know he thought of you often," Delia countered.

"As I did of him," Pickering assured her. He looked up as the orchestra once again began to play and the strains of a waltz filled the room. "Would you honor me with a dance," he asked, "in memory of your father?"

He held out his hand, and Delia took it.

"In memory of my father," she murmured.

Neither of them really noticed the way the Charpentiers stared after them. Delia was too tense to think of anything but what she intended to say to Matthew Pickering. Now that the moment had come, she was terrified she would make a mistake, that she would betray something to him that would tell him she knew he had killed Cotter.

"News of Cotter's death saddens me," he said as they began to waltz.

This time Delia was prepared for the lies, for the

pretense of innocence that she knew to be false.

"I can understand that," she replied. "Especially as you were so eager for him to work for you again."

Pickering stared at her, saying nothing for a long moment. Delia felt her knees grow weak, and she wondered if she had gone about it all too bluntly, if she ought to have waited, done it more discreetly.

But before he spoke, Pickering smiled at her. It wasn't exactly an effusively warm or pleasant smile, but it did serve to calm her fears somewhat.

"I was wondering why a young woman raised in Paris spoke with a proper public school accent," he said.

She hadn't even noticed that she'd dropped the false accent, she realized, and spoken to him naturally. There was so much to think about, and she was beginning to realize what Chase had meant when he'd told her she wasn't capable of dealing with a man like Pickering. She was, she decided, lucky her slip had been a small, relatively unimportant one. She might even be able to turn it to her own advantage.

She smiled back up at Pickering and shrugged.

"It was a small ruse," she admitted, reminding herself that the truth is always better than even a plausible lie. "A way to get into the *compte's* parlor and speak to you."

He laughed, his dark eyes for the first time showing a spark of something that might have been real humor. Delia decided he might not be so great an adversary after all.

"How did you know I'd be here?" he asked.

"You forget," she said, "Papa told me a good deal about you. It just seemed likely that you'd be here." She silently added, insulting the man from whom you intend to steal.

"Really?" He arched a brow as he stared down at her, almost as though he were listening to words she'd refrained from speaking aloud. Then he smiled, reacting as though he considered the insult a compliment. "In any event, I'm flattered you'd take the effort."

"You needn't be," she replied. "After all, this is strictly a matter of business."

"You wound me, Miss Hampton," he sighed with theatrical regret. "But what business could you possibly have with me?"

The moment had come, Delia told herself. Either he believed her now, or she could forget ever seeing him arrested and put behind bars where he belonged.

"You are, I believe, searching for a pair of Old Master paintings," she murmured softly, although there was no possibility their conversation could be heard above the strains of the music. "As it happens, I can provide them for you."

Whatever hint of humor had been in Pickering's eyes disappeared. They narrowed and he looked down at her as though he were weighing something costly he planned to buy.

"Paintings?" he asked evasively.

"Memlings," Delia replied without a hint of hesitation. "Two particular Memlings, I believe — 'Still Life with Grapes' and 'Still Life with Wine and Fruit.' That is right, isn't it?"

His expression suddenly became completely blank.

"I'm afraid, Miss Hampton, I don't know what you mean."

Delia cursed herself. She'd been almost certain he'd accepted what she'd told him until that moment, and she had no idea what she'd said that had warned him off. She bit her lip, then took a deep breath. She had nothing left to lose, she told herself.

"Shall we be perfectly frank, Mr. Pickering?" she asked.

"Certainly," he replied. "There is no reason why we ought not to be, is there?"

"I hope not," she told him, speaking very slowly.

"Because if there is, I'm about to make a terrible mistake."

"Mistake?"

She nodded. "You see, Papa was unable to paint for the last several years," she told him. "When he died, he was nearly penniless."

"I'm sorry to hear that," Pickering murmured. "It is a shame to see great talent squandered. It is also a crime to think that a young woman as lovely as you might have been left destitute."

"Oh, I am far from destitute, Mr. Pickering," she assured him. "Papa may have left me without funds, but he did leave me a very valuable legacy. Actually, he'd been helping me acquire it for more than a decade."

Pickering's eyes narrowed contemplatively.

"He taught you," he mouthed slowly.

She nodded again.

"Yes, and quite well," she replied. "I believe I can say without undue immodesty that I am quite as accomplished as he once was."

Pickering considered her warily. "I would have thought I'd have come to hear of such a talent as that."

"Possibly," she agreed, "if my name was ever used. But Papa wouldn't have it. He saw to it that I was completely removed from any sales and that my name was never involved."

"Then they were your paintings I saw in the Galérie des Anciens?"

"Yes," she admitted. "Mine."

"Which leads us where?" he asked, even though it was quite obvious what she intended to suggest.

"I find myself in need of funds since Papa's death," she told him. "By protecting me, he left me in the unfortunate position of being unable to find a proper patron, one interested in the sort of work I can do." She flashed him the same overly sweet smile she'd found so effective with Rémy Charpentier.

Pickering was a good deal less malleable than Charpentier had been. He stared stonily down at her.

"I'm afraid I'm a dealer, Miss Hampton," he told her. "I lack the resources to be a patron."

"I understand that, Mr. Pickering. Which brings us to the matter of the Memlings. Before he died, Papa happened to mention that you might be willing to buy a pair of Memlings were they to come onto the market. I'd like to propose a business arrangement, Mr. Pickering. I am willing to provide the paintings for a fair price. Shall we say one thousand pounds sterling? I'm sure they're worth a good deal more."

"Perhaps, if they're of quality. But I'd be a fool to agree to purchase paintings I've not seen," he said.

"True," she agreed. "And I doubt anyone would think to call you a fool. But I assure you, you will not be disappointed. You saw my work in the Galérie des Anciens, and thought Papa had done them."

He shrugged. "I'm afraid I have only your word that he didn't."

She grinned wryly. "True," she mused softly. "May I suggest we simply come to an agreement? You hold your money until I deliver the paintings. If you don't like them, you need not accept them."

"That sounds fair enough," he agreed.

They danced a few more moments in silence, then, when the music ended, Delia took a step back from him.

Pickering held out his hand to her, and she took it.

"Thank you for the dance, Miss Hampton. I'm looking forward to another."

"Then perhaps we can celebrate the conclusion of our bargain at Fouquet's," she suggested.

"I anticipate it with great pleasure," he agreed. "About the paintings—did your father mention that I needed them quickly? I must have them in my hands in little more than three weeks' time."

She smiled at him. "Then I'd best be about it," she said as she dropped his hand. "I wouldn't want you to be less than perfectly satisfied."

"Goodbye, Miss Hampton," he said, as she turned away from him.

She looked back over her shoulder at him.

"*Au revoir,* Mr. Pickering."

With that, she moved quickly toward the door, feeling as though she'd just entered into a bargain with the devil. She could almost feel the fangs of tiny demons nipping at her heels.

Chapter Twelve

Chase seemed to appear out of nowhere just as Delia started down the front steps. She had been so deeply lost in her thoughts of Matthew Pickering that she hadn't had time to think about where he might have gone after de Grasse had so discretely shown him to the door. In fact, she'd been far too distracted to so much as give him a thought, too distracted even to notice the butler's smug expression as he hurried her unceremoniously out the door. She might have been standing on the front steps of the Compte de Grasse's mansion, but her thoughts were still firmly rooted in his front parlor, as she replayed in her mind her conversation with Matthew Pickering.

A physical presence materializing out of the darkness and firmly grabbing her arm, however, was not something that could be ignored. Startled back to reality, she quite literally jumped.

"Chase?" It took a few seconds for her to settle herself, and once she had, she realized she didn't like the look she saw in his eyes. "You frightened me," she told him, her tone firmly crisp and disapproving. She sincerely hoped decent offense was good defense under the circumstances.

Not in the mood to field complaints at that moment, he chose to simply ignore it.

"What took you so damn long?" he growled at her.

"What do you mean?" she asked, dimly hoping a bit of evasion would derail him, at least temporarily.

She knew quite well he was referring to the fact that she hadn't followed him out immediately, as he'd obviously expected her to do, but her mind was still in a muddle and she wasn't quite sure she was ready to tell him about the arrangement she'd made with Pickering—at least, not yet. She needed a few minutes to think of some way to tell him that wouldn't make him any angrier with her than he apparently already was, to think of some way to convince him to help her do something she knew he was determined to keep her from doing.

"You saw de Grasse ask me to leave," Chase insisted. "That was more than a quarter of an hour ago."

"How was I supposed to know you were going to get yourself thrown out?" she countered, even though she was perfectly aware that trying to fend off his questions with a pretense of innocence was about as useful as trying to turn away a charging lion with an admonition of, "No, bad kitty."

As she expected, he was having none of it.

"I saw you watching what was happening," he told her. "You could see very well what de Grasse was doing."

"I could see very well," she countered, "that he wasn't terribly interested in your predictions of disaster at the hands of Matthew Pickering." She freed her arm from his grasp. "It would seem your charm and powers of persuasion held little sway over the *compte*." It was a shame, she thought, that she didn't possess the same sort of invulnerability. "All things considered, I'd say you made a complete shambles of the whole evening."

"I suppose you could have done better?" he demanded.

"I would have known better than to try," she shot

211

back, feeling a touch of her own anger now, and beginning to wonder why she bothered to want to appease him.

With that, she turned her back on him and continued on down the steps. The walk in front of the *compte's* mansion was crowded with dozens of liveried men, drivers, and footmen for the long line of private carriages waiting by the curb. She knew Chase would have to hold his anger with her at least long enough to walk past them. She hoped by then some of his anger with her would have cooled and she would have thought of a way to tell him what she'd done.

She was right about Chase not wanting to share their argument with the servants of half the city's elite. He guided her in dogged silence past the long line of carriages, pretending to ignore the curious stares of the men who stood idling on the walk, all of whom seemed to have nothing better to do than stare at the pair who had been shown to the door with such relish by de Grasse's butler.

"Well?" he demanded, once they were well out of earshot of their unwanted audience.

"Can't this wait until later?" she murmured. She stared down the length of the avenue, looking for a free hansom.

He yanked on her arm, pulling her around to face him.

"No, it can't wait until later," he said. "I saw you talking with Matthew Pickering after I told you to stay away from him."

For an instant she felt a flash of guilt, but it faded behind a wave of fury with him. How dare he treat her like a blithering little fool? She'd only done what he ought to have been doing all along, arranging for Matthew Pickering to be caught. He might not agree with her, but he had no right to think he could order her about and treat her like a recalcitrant underling, no, worse, like a foolish and naughty child.

"I said not here, not now," she told him through tight lips. "It can keep for half an hour."

Chase stared at her for a long moment. In the flickering light of the gas lamps, he thought her absolutely beautiful, her skin turned a pale gold and framed by a halo of shining, dark curls. And for an instant he wanted to pull her to him, hold her close and kiss her, tell her how frightened he was for her, how much pain even the thought of losing her caused him. But one glance at the sparks of anger leaping out of those amber eyes of hers was more than enough to tell him that she wasn't interested in his fears for her, that her thoughts were firmly set on only one man, a dead man — her father.

He didn't like what he saw in her expression in the least, not the anger nor especially the return of that look of determination that had so convinced him half an hour earlier that she was about to get herself into trouble. But he knew better than to stand there in the middle of the street and try to argue the issue with someone who was making a point of refusing to be responsive.

If she was going to be a great enough fool to get herself into trouble, he told himself, he would just have to be a greater fool and get her out of it. It was either that or turn his back on her, and much as he might tell himself that was the logical, the rational thing to do, he knew it was also impossible. He didn't like it, but she wasn't giving him any other choice.

He hailed a hansom and handed her up into it. Once he'd given the driver the address on the Rue St. Clodoald and climbed up beside her, he decided he liked even less the icy anger she directed at him. The atmosphere in the cab was a good deal chillier than the weather dictated, and he doubted he could have thawed it very much even had he been of the mind to, which he decidedly was not.

213

They sat in rigid and strained silence, both trying to ignore the other as much as was possible, despite the fact that they were only inches apart. It seemed a very long ride to both of them.

When the hansom pulled to a halt in front of her house, Chase quickly paid the driver and then held out his arm to Delia to help her down from the cab. She ignored his help, climbing down without looking at him, and then walking past him to the front door.

He was beside her by the time she'd fitted the latchkey into the lock.

She finally deigned to look up at him.

"Shall I thank you for a lovely evening, Mr. Sutton?" she asked in a tone remarkable for the amount of anger it managed to convey without her uttering a single angry word.

He ignored it.

"Not until you've told me why you were talking with Pickering," he replied.

She scowled, gritted her teeth, then turned back to face the door.

"Then I suppose you'd better come inside," she told him.

She turned the key in the lock and pushed the door open, walking inside without so much as glancing back at him. Despite the fact that it had hardly been a hearty invitation, Chase followed her.

She'd left a single lamp lit in the parlor, and she crossed the dim entrance hall, going directly to it. The shadow her body cast as she held out her arms to remove the long cape turned into a tall, forbidding specter. The sight of it unsettled Chase more than he thought reasonable, and he found himself reminding himself that there really were no such things as omens or ghosts by way of dismissing the thoughts it had evoked.

He followed her into the parlor, watching her settle into the worn chair that had been Cotter's the first

214

time he'd been there. She sat and stared at the heap of dead embers that remained in the fireplace. The room was not especially cold, but he could see her shiver slightly. Again he thought of ghosts, Cotter's ghost this time, waiting in this room for her, pushing her to some foolish act that she considered justified revenge but would only end with her being hurt.

"You could fix yourself a drink," she told him, and waved a hand toward the sparse liquor tray.

He hesitated a moment, looking at her, willing her to turn and face him. When she didn't, he did as she suggested, crossing the room and lifting the single decanter from the tray, pouring a healthy portion into a glass, telling himself he certainly deserved it, already aware of what it was she had to tell him that required a drink to ease the telling. He returned the stopper, but before he put the decanter back down on the tray, he changed his mind, removed the stopper again, and poured a small tot into a second glass. Then he returned the decanter to the tray, lifted the two glasses, and crossed back to stand in front of her.

"Here," he said, holding out the glass with the smaller portion of liquor in it, "maybe this will give you enough courage to confess your sins."

She looked up at him finally.

"What makes you think I have any sins to confess?" she demanded. "And if I had, why would I confess them to you?"

She wasn't, she realized, growing any less angry with him as the moments passed. In fact, she found that every word he spoke only served to infuriate her all the more. Still, she decided he was probably right about the drink. She took the glass he offered her and quickly brought it to her lips, sipping some of the whiskey. It settled into her with a pleasant flow of warmth, forcing away the fingers of cold that had clutched at her from the moment she'd entered the house.

Chase took a swallow from his glass, then stood for a moment looking down at her, wondering just what it was he expected from her. Was it a show of humility, an acceptance that he could deal better with a situation that was beyond her experience or ability? Or was it just some salve for his male pride that he wanted, some recognition from her that confessed that she needed him? Because she did need him, and probably a good deal more than he could ever make her understand. Whether she liked it or not, she was an innocent in Matthew Pickering's world, and that was a place where innocence was not only a handicap, it was a disease that might too easily prove fatal.

Whatever he may have wanted, she gave him nothing, not even so much as a direct glance. Instead, she just stared blankly forward, as though she were looking through him. He finally gave up, turned, walked the few steps to the small sofa, and sat. He said nothing as he lifted his glass to his lips. He determined to wait her out, if need be. He continued to stare at her as he took a healthy swallow of the whiskey.

However strong his resolve, he eventually realized he wasn't prepared to wait forever. By the time he'd finished the whiskey in his glass and she'd still said nothing, he'd lost the last of his patience. He dropped his glass onto the small table beside the sofa.

"Damn it, Delia, I'm through playing this inane game. Why were you speaking with Pickering when I gave you express orders to stay away from him?"

The look she turned on him was enough to make him almost wish she were still staring blankly through him.

"Who do you think you are to give me orders, express or any other kind?" she snarled. "How dare you?"

He curled his right hand into a fist and struck the palm of his left.

"I dare because you're putting your neck into a

216

noose and you don't have enough common sense to pull it out," he told her.

"It's my neck," she countered. "And whatever I may be doing, at least I'm seeing to it that Pickering is punished for Papa's death."

Chase felt a hard thud of fear for her settle into his belly as he listened to her words. If only he had managed to avoid Pickering that time in London, if only he'd been able to remain a stranger to him. Then he could have gone back into de Grasse's parlor and forced her to leave with him, if that was what he'd had to do. And he would have done precisely that this evening, if only he could have done it without marking her in Pickering's eyes as a certain enemy.

"Just what did you do?" he asked, his voice low and tense with the control he forced on himself.

Delia looked down at the contents of her glass, then lifted it and sipped some of the whiskey. Then she turned to him.

"When I saw de Grasse wasn't about to agree to withdraw the paintings," she told him calmly, "I told Pickering that I could give him what he wanted Papa to give him."

Chase pushed himself forward to his feet and across the few steps that divided them in a single motion.

"You what?" he demanded, when he was standing over her.

She glared up at him, her eyes clearly offering no apology.

"I told him I'd sell him the forgeries he wanted from Papa."

He told himself he'd been expecting this, that it was the only thing she would have done. Still, hearing her say it and realizing that she was blindly putting herself into Pickering's hands was like an unexpected blow.

Furious, he leaned forward to her, grasping her shoulders with his hands, holding her hard enough to make her gasp from the unexpected pressure.

217

"You little fool," he hissed. "Do you know what you've gotten yourself into?"

She didn't let her stare so much as waver.

"I've done what I should have done from the start," she told him. "Instead of agreeing with you to try to get de Grasse to withdraw the canvases from the exhibition, instead of trying to force Pickering to give up the attempt to steal them, I made sure he would have what he needs to make the attempt. In short, I made sure he could be caught."

"My job is to safeguard those damn paintings."

"And I don't give a damn about your damn job," she shouted. "I intend to see that Matthew Pickering pays for my father's death. I don't care about those paintings or anything else. And what you want doesn't enter into it."

He pulled her to her feet and stood glowering at her, part of him wanting to strangle her, and part of him wanting something else altogether.

But whatever logic remained in the part of him she didn't manage to touch, told him that she was right, that this was the only way to catch Matthew Pickering for once and for all. It wasn't a conclusion he was anxious to accept, but it was undeniable.

Still, he knew it was the last thing in the world he could tell her.

Delia stood for a moment longer, still and quiet in his grasp, returning his gaze with a stolidly unflinching one of her own. The feel of his hands on her bare arms, the heat of his body filling the air between them, the sensation of those blue eyes of his tunneling inside her, it all left her feeling dizzy and slightly disoriented.

And for an instant, she found herself aching for him, wanting him to give her something she'd told herself a thousand times he didn't have to give. For a moment she wanted him to sweep her up into his arms and hold her, wanted him to swear to her that he would deal with Pickering for her sake, that he would keep her safe and protected and pledge his honor to revenge her father for her.

Tell me you love me, Chase, she prayed silently to him, tell me you love me and would die if anything happened to me. Say just that, and I'll do whatever you want of me.

When he remained silent, she became suddenly furious with herself. She told herself it was the whiskey that made her feel so weak, that she didn't give a damn what Chase Sutton thought or what he wanted. She knew what she had to do, and nothing he could do or say would change that or sway her.

She put her hands on his, pushing them away.

"I'm tired," she told him as she stepped back from him. She turned to leave the room. "Please lock the door on your way out."

Chase stood where he was, watching her back as she left, wondering why he couldn't just walk away, just let it happen the way she wanted it to happen. But he knew the answer to that question as well as he knew that Pickering wouldn't simply pay her for the paintings and be done with it. Pickering was a man who liked to use his power, liked to see other lives ruined for the simple enjoyment of exercising it. And she was completely unprepared to deal with that kind of power. Chase knew that he couldn't walk away and leave her a tempting victim to Pickering's sadism.

Worse, he knew he couldn't walk away because he was in love with her.

When he finally followed her out of the room, she was already at the top of the stairs. She didn't look down, didn't acknowledge him with so much as a word. But somehow he knew she knew he was watching her.

"Damn you, Delia," he murmured under his breath.

He started for the door, telling himself to leave, that she didn't want his help, that the mischief was already done and there was nothing he could do to change it. The best thing for him to do was leave, give himself some time to think about the logical thing to do. The best thing for him to do, he told himself, was stop thinking about her at all.

But when he reached the door and put his hand on the knob, he knew he wasn't leaving.

He threw the bolt, turned around, and strode across the hall. Then he followed her up the stairs to her bedroom.

When he opened the door to her room, he found Delia was seated in front of a small dressing table, her hair released of the pins that had held it, streaming down her back. For an instant he wished he could become invisible, wished he could just stand there and watch her without her knowing.

But that was not to be. He saw her stiffen as she looked into her mirror and saw his reflection in the glass. She hesitated before she spoke, and he saw the brush shake in her hand. He wondered what she thought she had to fear from him, why his presence could disturb her when she could contemplate becoming partners in theft with a man like Matthew Pickering without so much as blinking an eye.

"I thought you were leaving," she said as she dropped her brush onto the dressing table and stood.

She turned to face him. Chase found himself catching his breath. He was momentarily lost, just as he had been earlier that evening when she'd come to his hotel room, in the realization that she had forceful weapons at her disposal, that however much of a fool it made him, he could not fight the power she held over him.

"You're leaving Paris in the morning," he told her. "I'll find someplace safe, someplace Pickering can't find you."

It was the only thing he could think of, the only way he knew to keep her safe. He stood, his eyes on hers, watching her silently stare at him, praying she would have enough sense to let him protect her.

Finally she turned away, and began to unbutton her gown as she started across the room to the mirrored wardrobe against the far wall.

"I'm not going anywhere," she said. "And I will thank you to stop making decisions as to what I will or will not do."

As she passed him, he reached out and caught hold of her arm.

"Damn it, Delia," he swore as he swung her around to face him, "someone's got to look after you."

"How dare you presume?" she snapped angrily. She was shaking with rage, at him for thinking her a mindless child, and at herself for caring what he thought. And that rage bubbled over suddenly as she raised her hand and slapped him on the cheek. "I'm more than capable of looking after myself. Now get out."

Her anger was like a contagion. Chase found himself catching it, filling with it as it forced away any feelings of tenderness he'd felt a moment before. He could still feel the sting of her fingers against his cheek. He tightened his hold on her arm and pulled her close.

Delia caught a glimpse of the anger in his eyes, and for the first time since they'd met she found herself actually afraid of him. She tried to pull herself free, but he refused to loosen his grasp. She struggled uselessly with him for a moment, then looked up at him.

It was as though he was waiting for that, for her to look up at him with her eyes wide and pleading. When she did, he slowly lowered his lips to meet hers.

He released his hold of her, instead wrapping his arms around her body, drawing her close to him. His kiss was filled with a hot fury, but he knew even as he touched his lips to hers that the anger wouldn't last,

221

that it was already being extinguished by a far more potent flame.

He wanted her. He wanted the feel of her body in his arms, the taste of her on his lips, the warmth of her surrounding him. He wanted her as he had never wanted a woman before.

Delia told herself to fight him, not to let herself give in to him. But her own best counsel was lost on her. Perhaps it was the anger she'd felt for him during the previous hour that roused her passion, a passion that she'd kept banked but which was now released by the touch of his lips to hers. Perhaps it was simply the fact that she wanted him, if only for one last time, wanted to feel the way he'd made her feel once more.

Whatever the reason, when he pulled her to him and pressed his lips against hers, it took her breath away. And when he pressed his tongue against her lips, she parted them to him in invitation, and then raised her arms to his neck and pressed her body to his.

What began with such breathless abandon proceeded as inexorably as a locomotive on a downward grade, speeding heedlessly, headlong into the chasm below. They both realized in the same instant that the anger they'd felt only moments before was nothing in the face of a desire that increased a hundredfold each second they held one another.

Delia touched her tongue to his, tasting him, drawing the sweet fire into herself like a bee drawing nectar from a bloom. And when he put his arm beneath her and lifted her, she pressed herself close to him, grasping his shoulders and holding herself tight to him. It was as if she feared he might let her fall and if she fell, she might go on falling forever.

He crossed the room with her in his arms, then lay her on her bed. He stood over her for an instant, staring at her, wondering what insanity had made him feel as he did for a woman who so obviously was wrong for him, even as he felt the ache of yearning rising inside him.

He lowered himself to her, pressing his lips against the warm, soft flesh of her breasts that the low cut evening gown left exposed and inviting, telling himself the only thing that mattered was the way he felt about her, the way he felt when he held her in his arms. If she was obstinate about what she wanted, he would find some way to change her mind. For now, he could think of nothing beyond the heat that her body, beneath his, released within him.

Delia closed her eyes as his lips touched her. She let herself fill with the hot liquid tides his kisses sent surging inside her, let herself drown in the feel of the sweet sensation. Whatever the madness that made her love him, she knew she would rather be mad at that moment than face sanity alone and without him.

She refused to allow herself to think of what she knew to be true, that this meant nothing to him. She didn't care, she told herself as she slid her hands across the hard muscles of his shoulders and back. All she wanted was a single hour, an hour to be free of regrets and the sharply piercing ache of responsibility she felt to see Pickering pay for Cotter's death. An hour, she told herself as she felt the throbbing heat welling up inside her, an hour, and then she'd be strong again.

Chase swept her clothing away with the intense ferocity of a man dying of thirst pushing his way through desert sands to reach an oasis. She helped him, as anxious as he to feel the heat of his flesh next to hers, helping him unfasten the buttons of her gown and then turning her attention to his shirt, her fingers slyly knowing as her hands trailed against the curly hair on his chest, then turning bold as she addressed the buttons of his trousers. She had no idea what had come over her, what demon inside her directed her to perform such an act for a man. What she could see

223

was that it pleased him, and she needed no greater spur than that knowledge.

She pulled him down to her when he'd shed the last of his clothing, eager for him, almost as though she was afraid the moment might be stolen from her and lost. Chase, although he was surprised by her, more than matched the intensity of her ardor.

He leaned forward to her, pressing his lips to hers and parting her legs with his own. But he hesitated then, and held himself from her as he lifted his lips from hers and stared down at her. He might have started this, and she might have more than invited him into her bed, but still he had the strange feeling that she didn't really know what it was she was doing. Just as she had blindly gone to Pickering without stopping to think of the consequences, he had no doubt but that she was storming down another path now without a thought to where it might lead her. Unless, he thought, this was her way of convincing him that she was right about what she'd done.

She looked up at him, puzzled that he held himself from her, and he felt the desire like a knife inside him as he gazed into her eyes, a knife that cut clear to his soul.

"What is it you want, Delia?" he asked her, his voice ragged with unfulfilled want.

Her eyes grew slightly glazed.

"Only this," she murmured, and he could see the admission was painful to her, that the glaze in her eyes was a watery haze of unshed tears.

"That's all?" he asked. "Nothing more?"

It wasn't all, she knew. Deep inside she knew she wanted to be able to forget everything, to find some sort of a normal life, to be what he seemed to want her to be. Mostly she knew she wanted him. Not just for this single hour, but forever.

But none of that was possible, and she knew it, knew she could no sooner change herself than she

4 FREE BOOKS

FREE BOOK CERTIFICATE

4 FREE BOOKS

ZEBRA HOME SUBSCRIPTION SERVICE, INC.

GET
FOUR
FREE
BOOKS
(AN $18.00 VALUE)

ZEBRA HOME SUBSCRIPTION
SERVICE, INC.
120 BRIGHTON ROAD
P.O. Box 5214
CLIFTON, NEW JERSEY 07015-5214

could make him love her. And so she buried the thought, hiding it deep inside herself, not only from him, but from herself as well.

"Nothing more," she told him. She pushed aside that ache in her heart, smiling up at him with a knowingly provocative, inviting smile. "You've acted as though you were my lord and master all evening," she murmured as she pressed her lips against his neck. "Now I give you leave."

He knew she was taunting him. But a voice inside him told him that perhaps this was the way, perhaps his body could convince her where his words had been useless.

And he wanted her. How he wanted her.

He pressed himself to her, burying himself inside her, his own body echoing the tremor of aching pleasure that engulfed her at that first sweet thrust. He left himself no time to savor it, however, nor to slowly draw out the pleasure until it melted her. It was, he knew, too late for that, for he was burning with a need that had grown far too strong for him to quell.

He let the passion rule him, and the act had a strange, raw intensity it had never held for him before. He wondered how she'd managed to so completely unsettle him, how she'd robbed him of his control.

But if Chase felt his control slipping from him, Delia had lost hers entirely. Her body ached for him to fill it, and she pressed herself to him, trembling with the fearful intensity of that need, lost to the shattering release that claimed her just as he found his.

It had come so quickly, taking them both by surprise. They lay together, afraid to move, still joined. Neither wished to so much as stir the air around them for fear it would dull the echoes of what they'd felt, for fear that once parted, they would never find one another again.

Chase looked down at her, at the flushed, red-lipped face beneath him. He found himself aching with the simple admiration of her beauty, with the knowledge that she was there with him, that he held her in his arms.

But then he saw again the shadow of liquid in her eyes, and he knew, even without her uttering a word, what it was she was thinking, that it was wrong this way, without tenderness, with only the need. She was right, he realized. It was wrong. She deserved more.

He leaned forward to her, pressing his lips to her neck, wanting now to call it back, to do it as he ought to have done it from the start.

"Chase . . ." she began, but he stilled her words with a kiss, not trusting words now, wanting only to speak to her with his body, with his hands and his fingertips and his lips.

The yearning returned, rising up inside him as though they hadn't yet touched, as strong and as potent a need as he'd ever felt. But this time he kept it in rein, moving slowly inside her, pressing his lips to her breasts and her neck and her belly as he loved her, strong with the knowledge of what he was doing to her, of the way her body moved with his, of the certainty that the pleasure he felt was shared equally between them.

This time when the climax came, it was as though time stopped, an endlessly breathless moment balanced somewhere between the reality he knew and the dreams the primitive buried deep inside him from some ancient past might once have had of heaven.

Delia lay in his arms, still trembling and spent, her body damp and warm against his. It wasn't real, she knew, this strange euphoria that filled her, but she felt she would rather die at that moment than give it up.

She stared up into his eyes, telling herself that if she tried she could convince herself what she saw staring back at her was love.

She raised her fingers to his lips, afraid he might speak, afraid that if he did, the illusion might shatter and disappear, running through her fingers like quick-silver to be lost forever.

"Let's hold onto it," she murmured softly, burying her lips against his neck, breathing in the heat and the scent of his body. "Just a few hours more. Just until morning."

She'd been a fool to think she'd be content with only an hour. She wondered if she would be strong enough to face reality or if she would again beg him for a few more precious hours once the morning came.

She closed her eyes, determined to sleep, not to think, thankful for the contented weariness that filled her body. The morning would come soon enough, no matter how she might dread it. But if she closed her eyes, perhaps for a few more moments she could pretend to hold it at bay.

Chapter Thirteen

Delia's eyes were still closed, but she stirred slightly. Part of her recognized that she was awake, but another part was determined to refuse to admit the fact. She wasn't quite sure why.

It took her several seconds to remember, to realize that she wasn't alone in her bed, that a warm, muscular body, a naked body, was lying beside hers, was touching hers. Her heart began to beat faster at the recognition as the memory of the previous night returned to her.

She decided then that she most definitely wouldn't open her eyes, wouldn't admit that it was already morning—not for a while, at least. The arrival of a new day meant that she must return to sanity, must face the unpleasant realities that now filled her life. Surely, she told herself, she could be forgiven for wanting to prolong this last moment, for wanting to savor just a little longer the sensation of lying still and warm, her body, filled with a lovely languor, close to Chase's, her head on his shoulder and his arms around her. It was all far too pleasant to disturb. Once she opened her eyes it would be admitting the magic was ended. All she asked was to eke out a few more moments of pleasure before it was lost to her.

But Chase must have felt some movement, must

have noticed her stir in his arms when she first awoke. He turned on his side, facing her, and whispered, "Good morning, Delia," as he lowered his lips close to the warm hollow of her neck.

She refused to answer, hoping he would think her still asleep. The warmth of his breath on her neck was beginning to generate a pleasant flood of anticipation inside her, but she was willing to forgo even that in exchange for a few more moments of trouble-free bliss.

Chase, however, seemed to be of another mind entirely. He pressed his lips against the soft flesh behind her ear. When she couldn't hide the small tremor of pleasure that touch elicited, he chuckled softly.

"Open your eyes, Delia," he told her. "It's full light and there aren't any ogres under the bed you need hide from."

"I'm still asleep," she muttered and kept her eyes firmly closed.

"It's no good," he said and laughed. "There's a new day to be faced."

"I know," she murmured. "And I'm not ready to face it."

Her voice was filled with a deep enough regret that he couldn't ignore it. He leaned forward to her and kissed her slowly but insistently on the lips.

Defeated now, she abandoned her protestations, answering his kiss, pressing her lips to his, lifting her hands to the back of his neck. Perhaps, she thought, the world will end at this moment and we'll face eternity like this, in one another's arms. However illogical, it was an appealing thought. She kept her mind fixed on it, more than willing to find the hereafter filled with the aching bliss she felt at his kiss.

When he finally lifted his lips from hers, Chase smiled down at her.

"Now that was a proper good morning, Miss Hampton," he whispered. "May I take it you slept well?"

She nodded. She had slept well, she realized. For the first time since Cotter's death, she'd slept deeply, without dreams to haunt her and bring her to a terrified wakefulness in the dark.

And now she would give anything for Chase to repeat the kiss, for him to hold her. Her arms throbbed with the desire to pull him to her, a gnawing yearning inside her wanted her to spread herself beneath him and invite him to make love to her as he had the night before.

Instead she told herself that without love, passion waned as daylight filled the sky. Chase Sutton had other things on his mind now that it was morning, and she would be a fool to pretend it was otherwise. Better to turn aside than be sent away, she told herself. She stiffened beneath him, took her hands from his shoulders, and pushed him away.

Chase sighed, then pulled himself away from her. He settled himself with his head against the brass rails of the headboard, then turned and stared down at her. The moment had come, he realized, the moment he'd dreaded the night before. He'd spent the hours since dawn awake, looking at her, watching her sleep. Such an innocent sleep, he'd thought, her face so smooth and peaceful at rest, with none of the fears and worries she'd been carrying with her to mar the beauty of those lovely features. It roused all those feelings of protectiveness that felt so strange to him and he tried to think of some way to derail what she'd begun, some way to keep her safely shielded from harm while he dealt with Matthew Pickering. In the end, he'd succeeded only in coming to the conclusion there was none.

"We have to talk, Delia," he said.

"I know," she whispered.

She sat up, too, but found the thought of sitting next to his naked body too unnerving. She had to be rational, she told herself, had to think clearly. She could not afford to let him dictate to her, or bully her. She had to do what her conscience told her she must do. If she was ever to live with her father's ghost, she knew she had to have a hand in seeing Matthew Pickering behind bars.

She pictured in her mind the way Cotter's body had looked when they'd found it, letting her waning determination be strengthened by that image. Whatever Chase's reasons for wanting her away from Pickering, whether it be a desire to protect her or simply dismiss her, she was determined not to let it happen.

She wrapped the sheet around herself and stood, then walked to the window, surveying the untidy condition of her room. Pieces of their clothing lay scattered on the floor where they had shed them the night before, testament to what she could now only think of as the mad spell he'd cast over her. That's done with, she told herself. She had too much to worry about to waste time torturing herself with thoughts of what might have been with Chase Sutton. There was Cotter to think of now, and Matthew Pickering.

She stared out the window, watching a wagon bringing flour to the *boulangerie* at the end of the street make its plodding progress along the Rue St. Clodoald. Outside it was an ordinary morning, dull and predictable, with only the glorious bright sunshine to differentiate it from thousands of other mornings. Inside her heart, though, there was no sunshine, only a dull grayness and a feeling of unease. She knew a real storm was just about to break.

231

"This agreement you made with Pickering . . ." Chase began.

"No," she interrupted, not wanting to hear his arguments, not wanting to fight with him while she still felt the warmth of his body against her skin. "Don't try to change my mind, or tell me I have to leave Paris, or whatever else you're thinking of, Chase. Don't be logical with me, for logic has no place here. I have to do this. There's nothing else to be said. I have to see Pickering is caught, and I have to be a part of it. And if you won't help me, I'll find someone who will."

It wasn't as though her words were unexpected, or even as though he'd expected her to listen to his arguments. He'd known well enough what to anticipate from her, but that didn't ease the ache that filled him knowing what she intended to do.

He stared silently at her back for a long moment, letting his eyes caress her skin, pale and flawless and lustrous with a soft glow lit by the bright shafts of sunlight that came streaming through the window. He was filled with the desire to touch the shallow indentation of her spine at the lower part of her back, to let his hand slowly trace its progress. He felt a wave of desire, and with it came the realization that he would never be cured of it, that he would never have enough of her to fill the need.

And with that realization came another far more painful—he would never really have her as long as she was haunted by her father's ghost. Even were he somehow to force her to flee Paris and Pickering, and he knew he would have to force her to leave, for she'd never abandon her plan willingly, it would only drive her further away from him than she already was. Cotter's ghost was too deeply entrenched in her to be exorcised in any way, save by bringing Pickering to justice.

232

Unfortunately, the only certain way to catch a thief as accomplished as Pickering was to trap him, and the only way to do that was to provide him with the forged paintings he wanted.

There was no choice for him. To have her, he had to let her place herself in the center of Pickering's path and pray she wouldn't be run over before he could push her to safety.

He stood and crossed the room to her, standing behind her and putting his arm around her before he spoke.

"You don't have to find anyone else," he told her. He might be resigned to the need, he realized, but nonetheless he couldn't shake off the feeling of reluctance that settled on him as he spoke. "I've come to the unpleasant conclusion that you're going to do what you want to do, Delia, and it seems only reasonable that we work together as we both want the same thing out of this."

She turned around to face him, smiling up at him as a wave of relief swept through her. But behind the relief was an unpleasant ache of loss as an unemotional voice inside her told her that Pickering was all he wanted anyway, that nothing else really mattered to him after all.

"We'll catch him, Chase," she told him. "You'll see. You won't regret it."

"I already regret it," he replied. "But I've resigned myself to the task of making myself an invisible bodyguard. I hope in return you'll manage to follow instructions without argument for a change and realize that I know what I'm doing a little better than you might."

She nodded, and smiled. "Except in de Grasse's salon," she pointed out.

He growled, then allowed her a small grin before becoming serious again. "Matthew Pickering, despite

233

a thin veneer of polish, is not Parisian society, Delia," he told her. "You can't allow yourself to consider him anything but dangerous."

"Whatever you say," she agreed. "But there's no reason to worry about Pickering. He won't hurt me, not while I can give him something he wants."

Chase sighed. Making her understand wasn't going to be easy.

"No," he agreed, "he won't do anything as long as you can give him the paintings and as long as he considers you harmless. But he's a careful man, Delia. That's how he's managed to keep from being caught for so long. Make a slip, give him even the smallest reason to doubt you, and he'll abandon the paintings in favor of eliminating any threat he thinks you might be to him."

"I won't give him the reason," she assured him.

"Let's hope not." He hesitated for a second, wondering if it was better to frighten her or leave her with a sense of false security. He decided on the former, hoping that if she was forewarned it would mean she would proceed with some caution. "Let's also hope that once he no longer needs you, once you've given him the paintings, he doesn't decide to ensure he's left nothing behind him that might tie him to the theft."

This was not at all what Delia wanted to hear from him. She refused to allow him to frighten her enough to shake her determination.

"He didn't hurt my father all those years ago," she countered. "Why would he hurt me now if I give him no cause?"

"Because he's more cautious now," he countered. "And because this theft will probably bring him more money than anything he's ever done before. Enough money to make a murder look more like a minor inconvenience to him than a crime."

"But still . . ."

He put his fingers on her lips.

"I thought there weren't going to be any arguments," he told her. "We're doing what you want. At least do it my way."

She swallowed, suddenly afraid as she looked into his eyes and could not help but see there was real concern there. Perhaps he was right after all, she thought. Perhaps she was blindly putting her head into a noose.

"All right, Chase," she whispered. "Whatever you say."

"Good girl," he murmured.

He leaned forward to plant a chastely affectionate kiss on her forehead.

She giggled softly. "I feel like Saint George about to go forth to slay the dragon," she told him.

"Saint George with only a paintbrush for a weapon," he reminded her.

She smiled at that, but he felt no answering humor and didn't return her smile.

There was nothing for him to find amusing, he thought, about the fact that he was sending a lone lamb into a den full of lions. And it was no comfort for him to acknowledge the fact that were something to happen to this particular lamb, he might just as well rip out his own heart as face life without her.

Delia settled her easel and carefully secured the prepared canvas. Until that moment, she'd barely given a glance to the other copyists who were working in the large exhibit room, but as she settled herself on her stool and began to mix a thin wash of linseed oil and burnt umber pigment, she glanced around at the handful of diligent art students who labored, stoop-shouldered and diligent, in the gallery. She was grateful to them all, grateful that their

235

presence made her feel almost anonymous and that she would hardly be noticed by those who'd come to view the exhibit. Chase's warnings had left her with a sense of uneasiness that she'd been unable to shake all morning, and now, as she began her work, she was finally beginning to realize what it was she had gotten herself into.

And with the realization came the first doubts. What if she couldn't copy these fine paintings? What if her talents, talents she'd taken so much for granted her whole life through, were simply inadequate to the task? It was one thing to promise Matthew Pickering that she was more than up to the task, and another altogether to actually do what she'd said she would do.

She darted a glance to the far end of the gallery, where Chase, dressed in a baggy guard's uniform and wearing his hat pulled low over his eyes, appeared to be half asleep as he leaned against the door frame at the entrance. He wasn't half asleep, she knew, but at full attention, even now noticing the direction of her glance and quickly turning away from it as though he was afraid her recognition of him might somehow brand them both.

She took the hint, turning back to her work, reminding herself that she was not supposed to show any sign that she knew him while they were there, reminding herself that he'd told her Pickering would most likely come to see how her work was going. He'd told her a dozen times to pretend they were strangers, to take no notice of him at all lest Pickering appear by surprise and see her.

"He knows me, Delia," he'd told her. "I nearly caught him three years ago, and he is not likely to forget that. He has no reason to think I'm in Paris now, and unless you give him cause, he won't look twice at a museum guard."

236

She had to admit that she'd thought the warning foolish when he'd given it to her, but now she wasn't quite so sure.

Suddenly, she felt unduly exposed, the creamy white of the untouched canvas an accusation of the arrogance of which she'd been guilty in assuring Pickering of her talents. She closed her eyes for a moment, forcing away the sight of it, replaying in her mind the times her father had instructed her, listening to him say the words all over again, "It begins with a clean canvas, Delia, all very innocent, a simple student of the arts like any other learning his craft by copying the work of those who have gone before."

But it wasn't really innocent, she knew. Nothing about forgery was innocent. And before she was done, that pale, spotless canvas would not only bear the pigment reproduction of a centuries dead master, but its edges and back would have the worn, begrimed appearance it would have had, had it actually hung for centuries in rooms heated by wood fires and lit with tallow candles. She'd learned all the tricks from Cotter, yet all she'd learned hadn't hidden the fact that it all added up to one single truth.

Simply put, the truth was that what she was creating was nothing more than an outright lie.

Her hand was shaking slightly as she began to draw on her canvas the general outline of the objects in the first of the two paintings, quickly sketching the ewer and the glass of wine. She stopped and stared at the lines she'd drawn before she was half done and scowled. She'd made at least a half dozen obvious mistakes, the sort of mistakes she was long past making. If she was ever to do this, she told herself firmly, she must shake away this unsettling fear.

She took a small rag from her work box and

237

soaked it in more of the oil, then carefully began to blot out the lines until they were only pale ghosts against the white of the canvas. Then she took a deep breath, concentrated on the painting hanging on the wall in front of her, and began the process once again.

But this time she managed to ignore her fears and lose herself in the task at hand, forgetting for a time all about Pickering and even about Cotter's death, concentrating her thoughts instead only on the beautiful Memling. There was a strange joy in this for her, the joy of using a skill that came as naturally to her as breathing and knowing that when she was done, she would have created something of great beauty. For the simple truth was, there was no toil in this for her. She had inherited all her father's skills and she loved using them. As much as she might decry a work that, in the end, was of basically dishonest intent, still she could not help reveling in the fact that she possessed a nearly unique talent.

As the general outline of the ewer and wineglass began to reappear, this time as they ought to, she slowly realized that she'd lost all her feeling of fear, that a sense of mastery was quickly supplanting it. The images seemed to be there, already on the canvas, guiding her hand so that they might come to light. It was beginning to go exactly as it ought.

"You made a bit of a mistake there."

Delia nearly dropped her brush. Looking up to find Matthew Pickering's dark eyes staring at her canvas was like turning to find the Angel of Death come for an unexpected visit.

He let those dark eyes slowly survey the shadowy outlines she'd not managed to blot completely away, then turned them to meet her gaze, his sharp features turning suddenly knowing, critical. She had the distinct feeling at that moment that he knew everything, that he was telling her she was a fool to try to lie to him. A chilling tingle of fear slid down her spine and she could feel her hands begin to shake as she realized he had come up to her without her even noticing. She wondered if he could perform the same feat anytime he chose.

She covered her surprise and the discomfort it generated with a shrug and a wry smile.

"A false start," she said, hoping she sounded more at ease than she felt. "It happens sometimes."

"Not a presage of the results, I hope," Pickering murmured.

He spoke softly, smiling pleasantly at her, pretending a mildly lecherous interest in the work of a pretty young artist, something of which any Parisian might be guilty under the circumstances.

Delia dipped her brush into a small cup of solvent, then carefully wiped away the remnants of the umber pigment onto a piece of clean cloth.

"One always hopes for the best," she replied, her response coolly even, almost indifferent. "Else why begin at all?"

"I've always been amazed by the way a chosen few can turn some pigment and a bit of canvas into something ethereal," he told her. "One cannot but wonder how the muses choose the hands through which they speak." He looked down at her smeared fingers as though he almost expected to see a small angel sitting on each hand.

"That is ethereal," Delia replied, nodding toward the original hanging in front of them. "Even with a muse's guidance, I recognize that I can never aspire to produce more than a pale shadow of it."

Pickering obligingly left her side to make the expected inspection of the Memling original on the wall. His expression as he stared at it showed the proper amount of appreciative awe, Delia noted, the sort of homage that would be expected from him had he never before seen the painting. She found herself grudgingly admiring his acting skills.

When he was finished with his inspection, he turned back to face her.

"I hope you turn out to be one of those chosen few the muses decide to honor," he told her. "After all, even a shadow can oftentimes elevate the uninitiated spirit heavenward." He punctuated the words with another pleasantly impersonal smile.

"Oh, I doubt your spirit is uninitiated, *monsieur,*" she replied.

He seemed to ponder that assessment for a moment before he replied.

"I must admit that I would like to flatter myself to believe my eye capable of finding beauty whatever its guise or form." He nodded toward her canvas. "Perhaps someday soon I will find it there."

"I hope so, *monsieur,*" she said.

"As do I, *mademoiselle,*" he replied.

With that he bowed his head slightly, touched his hand to his hat, and murmured, "Good day to you, *mademoiselle,*" before he ambled off.

Delia stared after him for a moment, watching as he expertly insinuated himself into a party of slightly tipsy art fanciers come to see the exhibit after having enjoyed what must have been a most satisfying lunch. He seemed to melt into the group of strangers as if he belonged with them, nodding and laughing as one of the men made a joke, pointing at one of the canvases on the wall and making a comment that soon had the rest of them sharing a general hilarity. Then, like a sly shark hiding itself among a school of harmless fish seeking food, he moved on with the group as it passed out of the gallery. The air seemed to roil slightly in their wake before it settled into the same staid tranquility it had had before their passage.

But for Delia, there was no feeling of tranquility in the return of quiet to the gallery. For a long while after Pickering had gone, she sat numb, unable to work, feeling nothing but the dull thump of her heart beating. She closed her eyes and found Pickering's image, sharp-featured and knowing, staring at her, looking into her and telling her she had no secrets from him. Looking back at it, his pleasantly smiling manner now seemed ominous to her, for she knew it was a carefully maintained veneer, a veneer that covered a murderer's threat of violence.

She opened her eyes, forcing her attention back onto the canvas, refusing to let herself become so agitated by that short visit that she might forget who she was and what she was about. Because that was, she realized, the reason for Pickering's visit—to unsettle her, to test her, to make her believe it was futile to try to deceive or betray him.

"Are you not well, *mademoiselle?*"

It was Chase, still acting the part of the slightly bored guard, but now with a look of concern in his eyes as he gazed down at her. Of course, she told herself, he'd seen what had happened. And her reaction must have left him thinking she'd somehow betrayed herself to Pickering. Why else, she asked herself, would he have that look as he stared at her?

Well, she hadn't betrayed herself to Pickering, she thought with a sudden warm burst of satisfaction. She might have been unsettled in the aftermath of his little visit, but she'd managed to navigate her way through it without mishap. She wasn't quite as helpless as Chase Sutton seemed to think her.

She smiled up at him and found that reassuring him made her feel a good deal more pleased with herself.

"I'm fine, *merci, monsieur,*" she replied.

"Are you sure?" he persisted. "You appear pale."

She doubtless was pale, Delia thought. She realized her hands were still shaking just a bit and she could still feel the aching grasp of fear along the base of her spine. But she had made her way through Pickering's little inquisition without having made any mistakes or given anything away. And the next time she'd be better prepared, now that she knew what to expect from him. She certainly wasn't going to admit to Chase that the man had terrified her, nor was she going to give him any excuse to suggest yet again that she give up and let Pickering come to his own fate.

She smiled up at him and forced a bright smile to her lips.

"Thank you, *monsieur,* for your concern, but there is no need for it."

Chase doubted that. He'd been forced to wait until Pickering had left the gallery before going to her, but even from his place by the entrance he'd been able to see that there was fear written all over her face. Pickering's short visit had disturbed her more than she would admit to him, and he knew it.

Still, there was no point in standing there, and even some danger should Pickering choose to return for a second glimpse. There was nothing left for him to do but leave her before his interest seemed something more than the politely professional concern of a guard for the goings-on in his small domain. He touched his hand to the edge of his cap, made a cursory round of the gallery, and then returned to his post.

He spent the afternoon watching Delia as the flow of late afternoon visitors to the gallery swarmed around her, inspecting the paintings and the work of the toiling students. Some seemed to him to show an inordinate interest in Delia's emergent work, chatting with her before they passed on, leaving him in the unenviable position of wondering if Pickering might be behind the visit. It did no good for him to tell himself he must force himself to be objective, to recognize that it was only natural that an occasional admirer be drawn to her side. It was only too apparent to him that he was anything but objective when it came to Delia.

He found he couldn't keep himself from staring at her, watching her every move, even when he knew that was the last thing he ought to do. Still, she seemed entirely at her ease as the afternoon drew on, able to work despite the occasional burst of attention. But ease was the last thing Chase felt as he scanned the crowd for Pickering's unwelcome presence.

Whether Delia realized it or not, he knew there could be no moments of ease now, no relaxation of their guard. Pickering's shadow was hanging over her, and one slip, one small mistake, could very well be fatal.

Chase had taken pains, ensuring first that no one was watching the house, that there was no sign of Matthew Pickering anywhere near the Rue St. Clodoald. Then he'd quietly gone up to the door, entered using the latchkey she'd given him that morning, and slipped inside.

This evening, the far end of the parlor was ablaze with lamplight, and in the center of the circle it cast Delia stood, a small, white smocked figure dwarfed by the size of the nearly empty room, entirely rapt in her work and apparently oblivious to his presence.

It occurred to him that for all the promises she'd made to him that she'd be careful, she was still a very apt target for anyone determined to do her harm. She had absolutely none of the sixth sense he had, a feeling that warned him when he was not alone. She had never before had any reason to feel fear, and thus never learned how to be alert to possible danger. The simple fact that she had no idea he was there watching her roused a tender feeling of protectiveness in him, and along with it a sharp ache of fear, knowing that she was so vulnerable.

He started into the room, making a point of making his boots tap against the parquet floor to alert her so that he wouldn't simply appear and frighten her as Pickering had done that afternoon. She looked up from her work, smiled at him, and waved him to her side.

"It's going well," she told him.

"Is it?" he asked, thinking as he did that the painting might be progressing nicely, but nothing else was even remotely as secure as he would like it.

"No trouble coming home?" he asked, making his tone as casual as possible, asking the question he assumed she'd expect, despite the fact that he'd followed her, watching her get into the hansom that he'd had conveniently stationed at the museum gate waiting for her, knowing that the driver, a man he'd hired, would see she got safely into the house before leaving. Best not to let her know how worried he was, he thought, or how many pairs of eyes he'd hired to watch her.

"Everything was fine," she replied. "There was really no need for the cab. I could have walked."

"Delia," he said, taking no pains to keep the note of exasperation from his tone, "you agreed to do as I directed."

"I know, I know," she replied quickly. "And I will. It just seemed like a terrible waste of a lovely sunset. And I could have stopped by the park and said hello to Claude and Pierre. They'll start to worry if I don't appear soon."

Chase groaned. The last thing he wanted to think about at the moment was the appearance of her private army of bodyguards.

She laughed when she heard the groan. "I promise to keep them from attacking you," she told him.

"At least for the time being," he muttered.

She laughed again, but this time there was an ache behind the laughter. There would be time, she knew, when he'd have what he'd come to Paris for—the sight of Matthew Pickering behind bars. And then he would leave, and she'd be left with Claude and Pierre and the others, and filled with an empty ache in her heart. Perhaps the hurt would be great enough for her to turn her back on him again as she'd done that day in the park. Perhaps when that time came, the thought of seeing him hurt would seem only fair to her.

"Yes," she said slowly, "at least for the time being."

He ignored the catch in her voice and the pained look in her eyes as she stared up at him. Her thoughts were already firmly headed in another direction altogether.

"Actually, it might not be a bad idea to have them meet you when you leave the museum," he mused aloud. "A crowd is a good place to hide."

She scowled again. She was tired of being made to understand that Matthew Pickering was the central topic of his every conversation.

"Really, Chase, I think you're being overly cautious. I told you, no one, most especially not Pickering, came near me when I left."

"And there's nothing I want more just now than to maintain that particular status quo."

He had by now crossed the room to stand beside her. She looked up at him as he inspected the canvas

245

on the easel in front of her.

"Well?" she asked. "What do you think?"

He shook his head. "Remarkable," he replied.

It *was* remarkable, he realized. She had been working from memory, blocking in major areas of color, the draped fabric in the background, the basic tones of the pieces of fruit in the bowl. It was all very hazy, the forms still vague and undefined, but he could already see the Memling he'd seen in the museum starting to take form on the canvas. It was absolutely unbelievable to him that she could have accomplished so much so quickly.

"It's not really," she told him. "This is the easy part, what any art student can do. The real work will begin tomorrow." She sighed. "And then we see if I can produce something that will be able to satisfy even Pickering's discerning eye."

He could read the uncertainty in her gaze, hear it in her tone.

"His little visit really upset you this afternoon?" he asked.

She shook her head. "Not all that much," she insisted. "But there's something about the way he looked at me . . ."

"Don't let him get to you, Delia," he warned. "If you do, he'll have you blurting everything out to him before you can even think about it. You have to keep yourself under tight control with him, or you'll be lost."

"I promise, I'll be careful," she told him. She inspected the canvas with a critical eye. Then she stood back and arched her back. She was tired and sore, she realized. It seemed odd to her that she hadn't noticed the stiffness until that moment. "I've done about as much as I can do today," she added. "I'll clean up here and then we can eat. There's some bread and sausage and wine in the kitchen."

"Sumptuous," he replied dryly.

"It is to a starving artist," she chided. "You're spoiled."

He let his eyes find hers and they stood staring at one another for a moment. Chase couldn't help but think how very much he would like to spoil her for a change, how nice it would be to teach her the simple delights of a touch of real extravagance. But that, he knew, would have to wait.

Delia was the first to turn away. Odd, she thought, how unsettled those blue eyes of his left her feeling. In its way, it was almost worse than the feeling Pickering's gaze left with her. She resolutely reached for her brushes and began to clean them.

Chase watched her for a moment longer, then backed away.

"I'll see what I can find in the larder," he told her as he started for the kitchen. "Don't be too long. I'm hungry enough to eat even a starving artist's supper."

Delia tore a small piece of bread off the loaf and stared at it before she slowly brought it to her mouth. She took a bite and chewed it, her expression filled with a concentration the task hardly deserved.

"Are you sure you're all right, Delia?" Chase asked her. "It's not too late to change your mind, you know. I can still get you safely out of Paris and away from Pickering."

Delia looked across the light of the single candle between them and scowled.

"Pickering," she spat. "Can we please avoid that name, at least for the remainder of the evening? I'm sick to death of talking about him."

He seemed surprised by her outburst, and she almost wished she had enough energy to go on with it. If nothing else, she could at least still surprise him.

"As you like, Delia," he replied. He reached for

the bottle of wine and offered to refill her glass.

"No, no more," she said, and put her hand over the glass. "I've had enough."

More than enough, she thought. Two glasses, and she'd hardly eaten anything. Her head was beginning to ache and she was feeling a bit logy.

She dropped the bread still in her hand and pushed her chair back.

"Am I acting badly?" she asked.

"No," he told her. "Why do you ask?"

"Because I feel like I am." She shrugged her head. "I'm tired," she said and stood.

"You really should eat something."

She shook her head. "It's too much of an effort," she told him. "All I want to do is sleep now." She waved her hand to the clutter on the small table. "Leave this when you've done. I'll tend to it in the morning."

He pushed his chair back. "I'll see you upstairs," he said.

"No," she replied. "I can find my own bed. Finish your supper." She started toward the door, but stopped before she reached it and turned back to face him. "Will you come up later?"

Once she'd spoken she felt a vague surprise that she'd asked. The words had seemed to slip out of her before she'd had time to think. And now she fervently wished she could call them back. She couldn't afford to allow herself to become any more dependent on him than she already was. She couldn't afford to let herself love him. Despite that, she realized part of her wished fervently he would assure her he would soon follow her.

Chase stared up at her. Looking through the dim glow of the single candle, she seemed almost wraithlike, surrounded by darkness. A few minutes before, it had seemed romantic to sit in the dark room with only the light of the candle. Now it seemed almost ominous.

He didn't need to think about the ache of want he felt for her at that moment. It had been with him since he'd entered the house, since the moment he'd found himself alone with her. What he did need to think about was the far more pressing need to protect her. And that need precluded any thought he might have of spending the night in her bed.

He swallowed the lump that had suddenly formed in his throat.

"I think it best that I stay down here tonight, Delia," he told her.

It took her a moment to untangle the strange mixture of relief and disappointment those words elicited. When she had, she shrugged and turned away.

"As you like," she said as she left him and started through the darkened hall toward the stairs.

Chase sat and listened to the sound of her footsteps as they grew steadily more faint, until there was nothing left but a pale hint of a creak behind the walls that told him she was climbing the stairs. He reached for the piece of cheese still on his plate, raised it toward his mouth, but dropped it before he bit into it. His tongue felt as though it had grown a thick coating of wool, and he knew he'd lost whatever hunger he'd had. Even the last of the wine in his glass had a bitter, acid taste it hadn't had a few moments before.

He'd decided he'd had enough when he heard the scream. It was like a dagger in his belly, as painful as anything he'd ever felt in his life.

The chair fell backward, ignored, as he leaped forward, racing for the stairs.

He was terrified he'd be too late when he reached her.

Chapter Fourteen

Chase took the stairs three at a time, barely aware of the feel of them beneath his feet, oblivious to the sharp, leaden pounding of his heart in his chest. One terrifying image crowded all others from his mind, a premonition that seemed to grow more and more real as no further sound came from Delia's bedroom. For that endless moment he felt nothing but a belly-piercing fear of what he might find there, could think of nothing but his own stupidity at having let her go upstairs alone.

For if anything had happened to her, he knew he had no one to blame but himself. He certainly knew better than to make assumptions about security when he was working, yet he'd ignored his most basic rules because his thoughts were being distracted by emotions he couldn't keep from feeling when he was with her.

A wave of self-loathing swept through him as he recognized the fact that those emotions and his inability to control them might have cost Delia her life.

He heedlessly shoved the door open so that it slammed back against the wall. He was indifferent to the noise it made and even to the possibility that whoever had been in the room waiting for her, whatever the cause of her scream, might still be there, now lying in wait for him.

He felt an enormous wave of relief when he saw her standing alone in the center of the room. Her back was to him, and she was visibly shaking, but the sight of her was reassuring enough to him to let him breathe for the first time since he'd heard her scream. She was, after all, safe and alive. He would deal with whatever it was that needed to be dealt with, there was no question of that. And he vowed he wouldn't allow himself to take any chances with her life again. He'd do what he had to do, what he ought to have been doing from the beginning. One suggestion of the possible results of his own mistakes was one too many.

He ran to her, put his hands on her shoulders, and turned her to face him. He stared down at her for a long, silent moment, assuring himself that she was unhurt. Then he wrapped his arms around her and pulled her close.

"What is it, Delia?" he whispered, his lips against her ear. "What happened?"

Delia tried to speak, but words seemed beyond her power at that moment. She turned for an instant toward her bed, pointed to a dark red object lying on the pillow, then turned back to him. She was shaking as she fell against him. It seemed she wanted nothing but to have him simply hold her.

She couldn't stop trembling. She was frightened, more frightened than she remembered ever being in her life, save for the instant when she'd first glimpsed Cotter's body lying on the floor.

She'd needed only a glimpse to know who had put the thing there on her pillow. She certainly hadn't needed to touch it or read the note beneath it to know that Matthew Pickering had been there, in her house, in her bedroom. He'd stood there, by her bed, touching her pillow, leaving an elusive, malevolent spoor in the air like a trail behind him.

She shivered. What else had he touched, she wondered? Which of her belongings had he peered at, put his hands on, invaded? The thought left a sick feeling in the pit of her stomach.

She turned again and darted a glance at it. The red appeared as dark as a pool of fresh blood against the white of the lace coverlet on her bed. There was no question in her mind that the bloom had been meant as a threat thinly disguised as an offering.

It struck her suddenly that it hadn't been lying there very long. The rose was still fresh, the petals unwilted. Pickering might have been there only a short while before she'd arrived home, perhaps no more than a few moments. Or perhaps he had even been there when she'd walked in the front door.

The thought chilled her. It left her feeling even more terrified than she'd been a moment before. A thick, wrenching sob escaped her.

"He was here," she cried, her words muffled, her face against Chase's chest. "He was here and he wants me to know it."

He caressed her, staring over her head at the red rose lying on her pillow. The bloom, he knew, had been purposely chosen, the color as bright as fresh blood. The relief he'd felt to find her unhurt was dulled by anger as he imagined Pickering's sense of satisfaction as he left the small memento. He wondered if Pickering had stood by the bed and pictured how much his offering would terrify her when she found it.

"It's all right," he whispered to her. He caressed

252

her softly for a moment, gently pressing his thumbs against her shoulder blades and down the sides of her spine, instinctively massaging the tense muscles of her back as he tried to calm her. "He can't hurt you. It was just meant to frighten you."

It took her a few moments to settle herself, to realize he was right, that it was, after all, nothing more than a single flower that had sent her into this fit of terror. When she had, she looked up at him and said, "I feel like a fool, acting this way."

"Don't," he told her. "Sometimes a little fear is a good thing."

She sniffed loudly. She'd stopped crying, but her hands were still shaking.

"It doesn't feel like a good thing," she murmured.

He pulled away from her, then pushed her in front of him, forcing her into the chair by her dressing table.

"Don't move, Delia," he instructed. "Stay right there."

She nodded, completely submissive now, more than willing to do as he directed her. She was, she realized, a good deal too frightened to argue with him. He backed away from her, keeping his eyes on hers as though he was afraid she might fall apart if he turned his back on her.

But she seemed steady enough, if not precisely stoically composed, and he finally turned to make a quick survey of the room, checking the cupboard, under the bed, anywhere large enough for a man to hide. He knew it was a waste of time, a show for her more than anything else. He was certain that Pickering wouldn't have any interest in actually staying to watch the reception she would give his offering. Nonetheless the search needed to be

253

done, he realized, if only to assure her that she was safe for the night.

When he was finished, he turned back to her. He found she was staring up at him, watching every move he made, struggling with the terror that still edged her expression.

"I'm going to search the house," he told her.

"And leave me here alone?" she asked in a pained, thin voice.

He nodded. "It'll be a lot faster if I do it alone," he told her. "I don't think it's necessary, but you can lock the door behind me if it makes you feel safer."

She swallowed and let her eyes scan the room in a dazed survey.

"He isn't here, is he?" she asked. "All this is nothing more than a little game to him. He's just doing it to show me he can."

"No," he agreed, "he isn't here any longer, I'm fairly certain. But I think we'll both feel better if I take a look around."

She nodded, and he started for the door, pausing when he reached it.

"Do you want to lock it behind me?" he asked.

She shook her head. "No," she told him. "Leave it open. I want to hear you."

When he left her, he noticed her glance had returned to the blood red bloom lying on her pillow.

It didn't take Chase very long to assure himself that the house was empty, save for the two of them. If nothing else, the lack of furnishings made the search a good deal simpler than it might otherwise have been. Impoverished gentility, he mused wryly, leaves the sneak thief with as little place to hide as it gives him opportunity to steal. Not that he'd really expected to find anything out of the ordinary. Direct confrontation wasn't the way Pickering would choose to make a threat. That would be too clean and uncomplicated for a man of his far more devious tastes.

When he returned to her room, Chase found Delia still sitting as he'd left her, her eyes glued to the blood red bloom lying on her pillow.

"It's all right, Delia," he assured her. "He's long gone."

"How did he get in here?" she asked. She didn't let her glance stray from the rose.

He shook his head and shrugged, but didn't answer, not wanting to tell her how easily a determined man could enter a house, any house, no matter how well locked against intruders. Instead, he crossed to the bed and lifted the rose and the note Pickering had left for her.

"Take it away," she told him. "I can't bear to look at it."

He glanced quickly at the short note:

My dear Delia,
   I hope red is your color. This particular shade, I confess, turns my thoughts to you.

There was no signature, but neither was one needed. No one but Matthew Pickering would have dared enter her room and leave the rose on her bed that way.

Chase could almost hear Pickering's voice saying the words, could hear the taunting sarcasm that would edge them. There was no doubt in his mind but that Pickering had known precisely how Delia would react.

He crumpled the page in his fist. A surge of anger filled him as he turned to her and saw the way her eyes followed his hand with the offending bloom. He was sickened by the ease with which Pickering had violated her home and shattered her peace.

"It's nothing, Delia," he told her firmly. "You can't let him intimidate you. He just wants to frighten you, to keep you from thinking about betraying him."

"And he's succeeded," she murmured in reply. "He's frightened me to death."

Chase returned to her chair, kneeling in front of her, grasping her hands in his own and holding them, forcing her to look at him. For a moment he thought Pickering had finally frightened her enough so that she'd become reasonable and would allow him to get her safely away from Paris. For that, he found he was almost thankful.

But it took nothing more than a single glance at her eyes to convince him that there was no possibility of that. Her expression told him only too clearly that the last thing she was about to do was give up.

"You're still determined?" he asked.

He could see the movement of her jaws beneath the tightly drawn skin, could see the tenseness in her tight-lipped expression.

She nodded. "Yes," she told him, speaking so softly that he had to strain to hear her. "I'm still determined. More than determined. He killed Papa and now he's doing this to me, and for no other reason than to show me that he can do it. Well, he has no right. I will not allow him to terrify me. And I will not allow him to get away unpunished for what he did to my father."

That was the end of it as far as she was concerned. Chase knew it, could read it clearly in her eyes. There was no reason to try to argue with her. It would be nothing more than a wasted effort.

Pickering's act might have terrified her, but it had also made her resolve that much stronger. There was ice behind her eyes, and the steel of unshakable determination.

He released his hold of her hands.

"I'll be downstairs," he told her. "I won't sleep. Call for me if you need me."

She nodded, then dropped her gaze to where her hands had settled in her lap.

He remained where he was a moment longer, wondering what he'd do if she begged him to stay with her, wondering if he'd be fool enough to drop his guard long enough to make love to her.

Because that was what he wanted to do. He ached for her. His body wanted her as he'd never wanted anyone. Beyond that, there was a need inside him to hold her, to comfort her, to try to make her feel safe when her safety seemed so uncertain as long as Pickering roamed free. As foolish as he knew it to be, he offered up a silent prayer that she needed him as much as he needed her.

And for a moment it seemed to him that she would ask him to stay. She looked up at him and for an instant she seemed lost and frightened and as filled with need as he was.

That was just what Delia did feel, an aching need as strong as his, a need for him to hold her, a need to allow herself to be weak. But she pushed it angrily aside, reminding herself that Matthew Pickering was his only interest, and it needed to become her only interest as well. If she was going to be left alone when all this insanity was over, then at least she needed to know she had done what she'd sworn to do. Chase Sutton must come to mean to her exactly what she was to him—a stepping stone, a means to an end, and nothing more.

She looked back down at her hands, the fingers locked together, lying tense and nearly white in her lap. As much as she might have wanted to keep him with her, she didn't ask him to stay. She didn't say so much as a word.

Chase pushed himself to his feet, carefully burying his regret.

When he left the room, he pulled the door firmly closed behind him.

The next several days proceeded with a regularity of routine that bordered on dullness. Were it not for the constant fear that Pickering might appear at any moment, Delia might even have found some pleasure in her work on the paintings.

Unfortunately, that particular fear never left her for very long. It was always there, just beneath the surface of her every thought. The feeling that Pickering was capable of intruding into her home, into her life, whenever and wherever he chose, cast an ominous pall that demoralized and drained her.

She rose very early each morning, as soon as enough light entered her room and made objects that were dim shadows by moonlight clearly visible. There was no necessity for her to do so, for there was nothing she could accomplish until the Louvre opened its gates, but she simply had no desire to lie wakeful and worrying, alone in her bed. She hurriedly washed and dressed, almost eager to be away from the room and the nagging knowledge that Pickering had been there. Then she went down to the kitchen, where she shared with Chase a simple breakfast of coffee and fresh croissants that he bought at the *boulangerie* down the street.

Despite the domestic nature of the arrangement, they were hardly intimate. In fact, as the days passed, Delia felt herself to be drawing further and further away from him. She didn't like the feeling, but she knew it was necessary, knew that she must inure herself for the time when he would leave. It seemed odd to her that for the time being at least, it was Pickering that kept them together.

They barely spoke while they consumed their morning meal, each aware that something had happened the night of Pickering's visit to the house, each knowing that they were treading the same path in one another's company, but all the while aware that the end of that path might bring them each to an entirely different destination. When she allowed herself to think of the probable end of their adventure together, Delia felt only a dull ache and the certainty that once Pickering was caught, Chase would leave her life forever.

Nonetheless, she found she had to marvel at his fortitude. She knew he barely slept, or if he did it was very lightly, because the slightest noise she made during the night brought him at a run to the door of her room. The first time it happened, she thought he might venture inside, that he might make his way to her bed.

For that single moment she was filled with panic, fearing that the need she felt for him would overshadow her own good sense and the sure knowledge that if she let him make love to her, she would only end feeling a greater hurt than she already felt. But he never took so much as a step inside her room once he had assured himself she was indeed safe. Instead he stood there for a long, silent moment, staring in at her, and then quietly turned away. Delia swallowed her regret as she found herself lying awake and listening to his footsteps fade as he returned to the floor below.

Despite Chase's lack of sleep, each morning when she entered the kitchen and found him already involved with his rolls and coffee, he seemed clear-eyed and alert. How he managed to remain that way completely bewildered her. She herself was growing more and more hollow-eyed with each passing night.

The simple fact was that when she did finally manage to fall asleep, she slept restlessly, with nightmares filled with ghostly images of an ogre with Matthew Pickering's face chasing her around Cotter's grave and laughing at her with a vicious glee. She came almost to dread sleep, and got very little real rest, finally falling off only when exhaustion completely overcame her.

After breakfast, Delia readied her work case, checking the tubes of pigments, refilling the small tins of turpentine and linseed oil from the large bottles in her father's old studio, discarding the bits of white cloth she'd dirtied the day before with her brushes and replacing them with fresh ones. She made the effort to be very businesslike about this task, forcing herself to keep any thoughts of Cotter from her mind for fear she would dissolve into complete uselessness were she to give them free rein.

Still, Cotter's ghost filled the house for her, and she soon came to realize that she felt it the most strongly in the attic room that had once been his studio. She could almost see him standing there when she entered, a half image, not quite precisely observed, but merely a presence glimpsed out of the corner of her eye, a presence that disappeared when she turned to try to face it. It didn't frighten her, but it did disturb her. She told herself that the fact that it was there meant her father would never really be at rest until Matthew Pickering was brought to justice.

Once the preparations of her work box were complete, she hurriedly left the studio, unwilling to give Cotter's ghost any reason to think her efforts less than whole-hearted. She'd hurry down the narrow flight of stairs, don her coat, and then sit in the front hall, waiting for the hansom for which Chase had arranged to arrive and take her to the museum.

The ride was really the only peaceful part of the morning for her. Unused to the luxury of riding so short a distance on a fair day when she was perfectly capable of walking, she somehow felt pampered and secure in the dark interior of the cab. Hidden from any eyes that might care to find her, comforted by the surety that no one could hide himself from her there, she lost herself in the feel of the hard leather seat beneath her and the jostling movement as the cab traveled along the old cobblestoned streets. For those few moments she managed to suspend all the unpleasant thoughts that crowded one upon another during the rest of the day and simply let her mind empty itself to find a short period of blessed tranquility.

Once the carriage brought her safely into the courtyard of the Louvre, she dutifully followed Chase's instructions, sitting and waiting in the cab until the front doors were opened promptly at nine o'clock. If it occurred to her to wonder why the driver made no fuss about the amount of his time she wasted when he might be otherwise more gainfully employed, she did not voice her questions. She had some inkling that the driver was not an ordinary hackney, that his eyes followed her a shade too carefully when she left the hansom and entered the museum. Still, she chose not to question whatever arrangements Chase had made with him. She had come to the decision that it was more comforting than not to have the extra pair of eyes watching her, and anyway, there were things that it did no good for her to know.

She would make her way through the still nearly empty museum halls, listening to the sounds of her own feet tapping against the shiny parquet underfoot. Walking through the quiet rooms, looking at the exquisite gilded *boiserie* and the fine art that lined the walls, listening to her own footsteps against the shining parquet and marble floors, it was almost possible for her to suspend reality for a few moments, even to imagine herself there in another time, living another life in a world where Matthew Pickering did not yet exist.

She didn't allow her mind to wander for too long. A diverting imagination might be amusing for a while, but she knew it didn't change an all too unpleasant reality. Beside, she told herself with grim humor, had she walked the palace halls a century before, she would probably have been allowed there only to scrub the floors.

When she finally entered the gallery where the Memlings were hung, she gave no special notice to the guard at the door, making no gesture that might tell any curious eyes that that particular guard had slept in the same house as she had the night before and then shared her breakfast that morning. She simply nodded the same terse good

262

morning to him that she did to the other guards as she passed them.

By nine fifteen, she had her easel set, her palette readied, and her work well begun.

She worked steadily throughout the day, too intent to stop for more than a few moments when hunger drove her to the tearoom for a lunch consisting of tea and a bit of cheese and brioche, her habits as abstemious as any penniless young art student's might be. What was not typical about her, however, was the speed with which her work progressed. In less than two weeks' time all but the finest details of the Memling still life were copied with amazing accuracy. She made no fuss or celebration at its near completion, and instead began immediately on the second canvas.

During the first five of those days, there was no sign of Pickering in the gallery. Delia grew more tense as the days passed. She waited for him to appear, becoming almost anxious for his arrival for no other reason than her desire that the tension finally break. She found herself nearly jumping whenever any man approached her and inspected her work, and was often rude to those strangers in a way that no real art student, hungry for the support of a well-to-do patron, would ever dare to be.

Pickering's appearance, when it finally came, was entirely unheralded. He said nothing, just crept silently up behind her and stood watching her, waiting for her to sense his presence. And she did sense it, feeling the proximity of something evil and oppressive in the air behind her even before she turned to find him standing there, his hands clasped behind his back and a smug, sure smile turning up the corners of his lips.

Despite her expectation that it was him standing

behind her, still the sight of him so unnerved her that she nearly cried out when she turned and found him staring silently at her with those malevolent dark eyes. She barely stifled the cry, but could not entirely hide the tremble of fear that shot through her.

Pickering saw it, and he smiled.

Whatever fear she had felt, the satisfaction she saw in those eyes at her reaction was enough to rouse sufficient anger in her to allow her to force an outward calm on herself. She nodded to him and offered him a tight little smile.

"I'm so glad you've decided to return and view my progress, *monsieur*," she told him.

"Then you do remember me, *mademoiselle?*" he responded with another of those tight, mirthless smiles.

He seemed to enjoy this little game, too, she realized, pretending they were strangers, acting as though every visitor to the gallery was interested in overhearing their conversation.

"How could I forget?" she asked. She shrugged. "A man who professes an ability to search out true beauty. How could any poor student like myself forget such a man? Especially a student who hopes one day to find an appreciative audience for his labors."

Pickering moved forward and stared critically for a moment at the painting on her easel. Delia didn't need him to tell her what he was looking for—the fine brushwork, the controlled use of pigment, and the carefully detailed reproduction of the original work.

It didn't take him long to complete his appraisal. He turned and nodded to her.

"I think you will have no fear in finding a most

appreciative audience for your labors, *mademoiselle*," he told her. "In fact, your work is quite fine. It reminds me of that of an old friend of mine, a most talented man whose work has been shown in some of the city's finest galleries." He turned back to stare once more at her canvas. "This reminds me so much of his work, that it might very well be his." He grinned, and this time a hint of real mirth actually seemed to lurk behind the expression. "Or perhaps his might very well be yours."

He was, Delia knew, referring to the paintings he'd seen at the Galérie des Anciens. She silently cursed them, knowing that they were what had drawn Pickering back to plague Cotter after so many years.

"I am very much flattered by such a comparison, *monsieur*," she told him.

Pickering straightened up and took three or four steps back from Delia and the easel.

"No flattery was intended, *mademoiselle*," he assured her. "At least, not by my words."

With that he brought his hands, which he had kept behind his back throughout the whole of the interview, forward. In one of them he held a single blood red rose.

Delia swallowed uncomfortably when she saw it. He was doing it again, she knew, playing games with her, trying to keep her unsettled and unsure of herself, trying to make her afraid. He was reminding her of what he could do if and when he chose.

"But this, I must admit, was," he went on as he held out the rose to her. "When I decided to come today, I could not resist bringing you a small token of my great admiration, *mademoiselle*."

She tried to lift her eyes to meet his, but found herself incapable of moving them away from the bloom he held in his hand. For an instant she thought the room had begun to swim around her. She felt dizzy and feared she might not be able to keep on her feet. Floating in and out of her mind was the image of the first rose, the one he had left lying on her pillow, the subtle threat and demonstration of his powers.

A flower, she thought, such an innocent thing to generate such fear in her.

When she didn't move, Pickering stepped forward, coming close to her, grasping her paint-stained hand and pressing the stem into her palm.

"I shall see you again soon, *mademoiselle*," he whispered before he stepped back. Then he touched his hand to his hat. *"Adieu."*

As soon as he'd turned his back on her, Delia dropped the rose to the floor and brought her heel down on it. She was, she realized, lucky he didn't turn back to look at her again before he left the gallery.

The next several days passed in a long, painful blur. The only events that seemed to stand out in Delia's mind were Pickering's visits to the gallery. Every few days he'd appear, stand silently behind her until she finally became conscious of his presence, then proceed to inspect her work.

Save for the fact that each time he came he brought her another of the deep red roses, there was nothing at all threatening about these visits. Their exchanges were more remote, with none of the verbal interplay, and none of the veiled references to Cotter, that the previous visits had elicited. Delia realized that he was simply keeping watch over the progress of her work, to assure himself that the paintings would be completed in good time for his purposes. She began to think herself safe, now that he realized she could definitely give him what he wanted.

But Chase would not allow her to become complacent.

"He's simply concerned about his timetable, Delia," he told her several times when she protested that Pickering seemed to have grown very tame in his manner toward her. "He's behaving reasonably because he doesn't want you to be too frightened to work."

His logic seemed reasonable enough. Still, Delia was unused to being so tightly reined in her habits. As the memory of Pickering's uninvited entry to her bedroom began to fade slightly, she began to chafe under the confines Chase imposed upon her. Without enough sleep, and barred from the outlet that the normal activity of her accustomed life might have offered her, she found herself becoming edgy and irritable.

More often than not, she took out that irritability on Chase, alternately considering him a thoughtless, unfeeling cad and an aloof, single-minded despot. She fumed at him in the evenings when she returned home from the museum, and fumed again silently when he refused to allow her anger to rouse his. She wanted, she realized, to break down the armor that allowed him to keep such a tight control of himself. For some reason she didn't quite understand, she wanted desperately to know that she could at least affect him in this way, if no other. When she found she couldn't, she told herself she didn't care, didn't give a damn about him or anyone else.

She rationalized, telling herself that she was reserving what true devotion she felt for the work, the paintings that would help send Matthew Pickering to prison.

But when she was alone in her bed at night, when she had neither the distraction of the work nor the excuse that Chase was behaving unreasonably toward her, she could not escape the truth. She knew that what she really wanted was for him to come to her, for him to hold her and tell her that he loved her and wouldn't ever leave her. Because as hard as it was for her to accept, she knew she still loved him, knew that there was no way she would ever be able to totally blot out what she felt for him. She might be able to survive, might be able to face the rest of her life, somehow, alone and still endure, but she knew she would never be able to force herself to stop loving him.

She'd lie there alone in the dark and touch her body, trying to call up the memory of how his touch had made her feel. In the end, she'd succeed only in making herself feel more miserable and more alone. Her hands were no compensation for the loss of his, and her imagination was no rival for reality. As many times as she closed her eyes and imagined him whispering those three precious words to her, still she could not convince herself that it was anything more than her own wishful thinking.

More than anything else, it hurt her terribly to know that it would never really happen.

Chapter Fifteen

"That's it. They're both done."

Delia literally fell into the tattered armchair. She was completely exhausted, more worn and drained than she had ever been in her life. Always before the work had been more a game to her than anything else, a challenge to see if she could meet Cotter's exacting standards. This time, however, there was no thought in her mind that any of it might be even remotely thought of as anything but a burning compulsion.

Chase considered her drawn face for a moment before he removed the covering from the canvas. He was glad it would be over soon for her. She seemed worn thin to him, as though there was little left but an all too vulnerable shell.

He turned his thoughts to the canvas, lifting it so that the light of the oil lamp illuminated it. It was beautiful, he thought as he stared at the painting. The porcelain bowl seemed to glow, and the fruit heaped in it were all wonderfully real-looking, the surface of the grapes bright with tiny drops of moisture, the dimples of the oranges' skin and the soft surface of the peaches almost beckoning to be felt. Nothing he had seen of her work that hung on the walls of the house compared with it, and he had been highly impressed with those.

He rested the painting against the wall beside the first canvas, then turned to face her.

"None too soon," he told her. "They begin dismantling the exhibition for shipment to London at the end of the week. Pickering will be getting anxious."

Delia scowled. She'd watched him as he'd considered the painting and had really expected some small word of praise for what she'd done. He'd deemed it fit to offer none and instead thought of Pickering. She ought to have expected that, she told herself, ought to have known he had thoughts only for Matthew Pickering. That, after all, was why he'd come to Paris in the first place, and in the end, it was all he cared about.

She told herself she'd known that all along. So why, she wondered, did she continue to think she in any way competed? And why did she continue to care?

"You don't find them convincing?" she asked. She couldn't keep herself from punctuating the question with a small scowl of anger.

"Convincing?" he asked, his expression suggesting that the word was slightly foreign to him. He turned back to stare at the paintings. "They're both beautiful, Delia, but they look so *new*. I can't see how anyone would ever think they'd been painted more than four centuries ago. They're fine paintings, but they are, quite obviously, copies."

She couldn't resist smiling at that, her expression just a shade shy of wicked. It seemed there were still some subjects of which he admitted ignorance. It must be hard for him, she thought, to concede she was his superior in anything. But here he'd done it, and she relished it as her due.

"Ah, but that's the magic," she told him.

She raised her hands to her face, rubbing her eyes with the heels. She really was tired, she thought.

"Magic?" he asked.

"Well, the hard part," she told him, once she'd dropped her hands to her lap. "I'll start tomorrow." She leaned her head back and stared up at the ceiling. "Papa always helped with that part," she said softly, her voice suddenly thick with unexpected emotion. "I hope I can do it without him."

She looked lost suddenly, and Chase didn't need to ask to know what she was thinking. Her life had been so extraordinarily unusual since Cotter's death, she really hadn't had that much time to mourn him properly. It was obvious that the prospect of performing a task they had always done together was painful for her.

"And Pickering?" he asked, changing the subject abruptly. "What did he say to you when he visited you today?"

She shrugged her shoulders before she answered. "The usual. 'Lovely work, *mademoiselle*. You're very talented. I might be interested in purchasing a canvas, if you'd care to sell.' All very proper, very polite. You'd think he assumed every person in that gallery had nothing better to do than eavesdrop on his conversation."

"His caution has so far kept him from being caught, Delia," he reminded her.

"How could I have forgotten?" she asked, her voice cold with sarcasm and her eyes turning cruel. "He's even outsmarted the most astute minds in London, hasn't he? Yours included?" She smiled humorlessly. "But you'll get him this time, won't you? It's all planned."

Chase ignored her, reminding himself how difficult the situation was for her, how hard it was simply for her to deal with the reality of Cotter's death.

271

"And what did you tell him?" he asked.

She scowled again, impatient with him, tired of the same questions from him each evening after Pickering had paid her a visit, even more tired of his expectation that she was incapable of making a reasonably intelligent answer on her own, without his prior coaching.

"Just what you told me to tell him," she snapped. She pushed herself from the chair and crossed the room to Cotter's liquor tray. "That I'd be delighted to sell a canvas or two. That if he gave me an address, I'd get in touch with him when they were completed."

"You didn't tell him how long it would take you?" he insisted.

"No!" she said emphatically. She turned her back to him, lifted the decanter of whiskey, and poured a large tot into a tumbler. "Obedient puppet that I am," she went on, more calmly now, but without bothering to try to disguise the exasperation in her tone, "I mouthed the exact words you gave me—two or three days at least, probably more, I wasn't sure. Does that meet with your approval, Your Highness?"

"All right, Delia," he said calmly. He followed her across the room. "You've every right to be on edge, to be worried." He put his hand on her shoulder. "I just want to make sure you did it right."

"I did it right," she muttered. "I followed your orders to the proverbial letter."

She returned the decanter to the tray, then raised the glass and took a sip of the whiskey. She was almost surprised at the heat of the stuff as it slid from her mouth to her throat. But once it had settled into her, it seemed to calm her jittery nerves almost immediately.

"This isn't really that bad, is it?" she murmured,

272

more musing aloud to herself than speaking to him. "No wonder Papa let himself use it to keep reality at bay."

She raised her hand, about to take another sip, and found Chase's hand holding hers.

"Maybe you oughtn't to drink that," he suggested.

"And why not?" she demanded. "I think I'm beginning to like it." She swung around and stared up at him. "Why should you care, anyway? The paintings are almost finished. Pickering will have what he needs for you to catch him. What more do you want?"

Chase gritted his teeth. Her mood had been growing more and more sullen and argumentative since she'd begun the paintings, until now it seemed as if their every conversation was a fencing match. Not that he really blamed her. She certainly wasn't used to living this way, wasn't accustomed to the sort of pressure she had been under. He didn't like her antagonistic manner, but at least it made it a good deal easier for him to keep an objective distance from her than it would have been had she been sweetly dependent.

"Let's just get past all this, Delia," he said softly.

"Right," she replied as she slipped past him and returned to the chair. She took another swallow of the whiskey, this one a good deal bigger than the first, big enough to make her gasp at its unexpected potency. "Let's not ruin the plan, the precious plan. We wouldn't want the illustrious Mr. Chase Sutton's plan to go awry." She dropped into the chair again, and some of the liquor sloshed from the glass onto her hand and her skirt as she landed.

"You've made your point, Delia," he told her. "Did he give you an address?"

"Again, your precognition was impeccable," she replied. "He said to leave a message at the front desk

273

of the museum, that he would check for it and would gladly meet me at any time I asked."

Chase nodded. "It would seem greed is clouding Pickering's judgment. He's finally beginning to make mistakes."

Delia leaned her head back and stared up at him. "How do you know he's making mistakes?" she asked. "How do you know he isn't just doing what you expect him to do because he knows you're expecting it?" she added with a sly smile.

"He doesn't know I'm here," he countered.

She shrugged. "Maybe he does. Maybe he knows everything. Maybe he's trying to lull you into complacency."

"Even assuming he is," Chase replied, "it doesn't change anything. All it means is that we'll just have to provide him with a few surprises."

"And hope he doesn't expect them in the same way you seem to know what to expect from him." She laughed. "This is nothing more than an insane game between the two of you."

He stared at her, at the bitterness in her eyes. In a way, she was right, he thought. But the game was a deadly one, and she was the pawn they were using. And that made it all too real to him, regardless of what it might mean to Matthew Pickering.

"This isn't a game, Delia," he told her. "Don't ever lose sight of that fact. It's real."

She took another swallow of the liquor, then stared down at what was left in her glass.

"Deadly real," she murmured. The thought released a sick lurch inside her. Whatever comfort the whiskey had seemed to offer a moment before suddenly vanished. "And if I make the wrong move, I'll end like Papa."

Chase watched her as the anger and bravado seemed suddenly to leak out of her, leaving her look-

274

ing empty, almost deflated. He realized suddenly she had only been using them in the previous weeks to mask her fears, to keep herself from thinking about what they were planning to do. But there was no more time for hiding, and now she sat unprotected, without her armor.

At that moment he hated himself for allowing her to become involved, hated himself for having let Pickering come between the two of them. They were becoming strangers to one another, antagonistic strangers, and he was allowing it to happen because he couldn't afford to let himself become too involved with her, couldn't afford to let his thoughts of her entangle his objectivity. It was wrong, and he knew it. It might be necessary, but it was still entirely wrong.

He crossed the room to her and took the glass from her hand. This time, she didn't protest, instead simply let it slip from her fingers once he had grasped it. She watched him put it on the table beside her chair, then looked up at his face.

"I won't let that happen, Delia," he told her gently.

She nodded, outwardly accepting his promise that he would protect her. But he could see the way her lips were drawn, could see the lined tension around her mouth. She was afraid. There was no way she could disguise the fear in her eyes. For all her moodiness and needless bravado in the previous weeks, he knew she was quite simply terrified.

He knelt in front of her chair and put his arm around her waist, pulling her to him. He didn't know what to expect from her anymore, didn't know if she would try to push him away.

She did. For a moment she hesitated, then she put her hands against his chest and tried to push. But he didn't release his hold on her, not this time. It might be sheer stupidity to let his feelings for her get in the way now, but he realized he didn't care.

She didn't struggle with him for long. Because she knew, just as he had known, that she wanted to be held, that she needed to be comforted, that she was afraid enough now that the time was coming close to actually dealing with Pickering to admit that she needed his strength to get her through with what she had to do.

"What if it doesn't work?" she demanded. "What if it happens wrong? What if . . ."

He touched his fingers to her lips, stopping the flow of her words.

"I won't let it happen wrong," he told her. "I promised you I'd keep you safe."

She tried to smile, but it didn't work, and instead a small cry escaped her.

She fell against him, burying her face against his chest, closing her eyes tight enough to force away the tears she feared she might shed. It seemed so easy, she thought, to allow herself to feel safe in his arms, to forget everything else and accept the illusion, if that was all it was, even for a few hours. She told herself that what she was feeling was nothing more than foolish weakness, simple, basic fear, but she was far too tired to fight it. And she also knew she would have to fight her own inclination far more than the press of his arms drawing her close to him.

What was more, she knew she didn't want to fight it.

When she raised her face to his, his lips were waiting for hers, hungry for the taste of her. At their touch, Delia found herself forgetting everything save how much she wanted to be with him, how much she wanted him to make love to her. The warm press of his lips, the determined, knowing probe of his tongue, the feel of his body against hers, hard and solid and immutable, it seemed to her that only these things were real and all the rest was nothing more than fantasy, a desperately horrible nightmare from which his kiss was slowly awakening her.

The taste of that kiss was far more potent than the whiskey had been. The heat of it snaked through her, dulling the pain of her own fear, an addictive narcotic whose effects left her entirely defenseless. She closed her eyes and let her body drift, let herself be borne off into the realm of her own pleasure-starved senses.

As easy as it would have been to keep her eyes closed and simply let herself drift, as much as she wanted to go where he seemed willing to take her, as deafeningly insistent as was the pounding throb of her heart, still she knew it was wrong. Do this, a voice inside herself cried, and you'll spend your life hating him.

"No," she cried, as she opened her eyes and pushed him away, turning to stare at the place on the floor where Cotter's body had lain. It took only a glance, and she found there was an antidote to the narcotic after all. "No."

Chase stared at her for a moment before he released his hold on her. As much as he wanted her, he knew he couldn't ever force himself on her. There was far too much pain in her for him ever to even think of causing her more.

He dropped his hands, putting them on the arms of the chair. She was still his prisoner, locked between his arms and the chair back, suddenly small and vulnerable, and without the anger and bravado with which she'd managed to sustain herself over the previous weeks.

She stared into his eyes, and said it one last time, *"No."*

That single word was suddenly as sharp as a

blade, and just as strong a defense. He was powerless against it, and he knew it.

He drew back, then stood, swallowing the bitter taste of his own regret.

"It's late," he said, careful now to keep his voice even and impersonal.

She nodded and turned to stare at the two paintings where they were set against the wall at the side of the room.

"Yes, it's late. And there's still a good deal to be done tomorrow," she added. "And then Pickering to be faced."

She pushed herself wearily out of the chair and started for the door.

"Goodnight, Delia," he called softly after her. "Sleep well."

She stopped, but didn't turn around to face him. He thought he saw her tremble slightly.

"A demain," she murmured.

Then she left.

"How is it coming?"

Delia didn't bother to turn to face Chase as he entered the studio.

"Very well, I think," she said as she stared down at the contents of the small pot she was carefully stirring at the side of the coal stove.

At the far wall of the studio was a long work table. When he'd carried the two paintings up to the studio for her early that morning, it had been clean and empty. Now it was littered and messy, a half dozen candle stubs sitting in greasy puddles of melted tallow and beeswax. Beside them was a large porcelain plate that was filthy with a coating of dark, oily soot, and next to that were several tiny tubes of pigments in various shades of yellow.

278

The air in the room was thick and oppressively hot. It was no wonder, he thought, with the door of the stove open and the warmth of a pleasantly bright morning sun heating the roof above and churning the air in the attic studio beneath it. But it was obvious that Delia wasn't especially concerned with the heat, despite the fact that her blouse was damp and heavy tendrils of her hair clung to her face, shiny with perspiration. There were far more urgent matters to occupy her thoughts.

Chase crossed the room to her and pressed a cup of coffee into her hand.

"I thought you might appreciate this by now," he said.

She took a long swallow without taking her eyes from the contents of her pot. "You were right," she replied.

He peeked into the pot. An unpleasant odor rose from it, thick and sour.

"Witch's brew?" he asked.

She nodded. "As good a name as any," she agreed.

"I don't suppose you'd care to divulge any trade secrets?" he asked.

She finally turned to glance up at him. He was smiling pleasantly, a blank, not quite remote expression on his face. She realized he was treading carefully with her, and had been all morning. It was just as well, she thought. She wasn't at all prepared to deal with a repeat of what had happened the previous night. It had been too close, and she wasn't sure whether she would give in the next time or not.

"Not much that's secret," she assured him. "Paintings are always varnished. It seals them and protects the pigments."

He looked into the pot again.

"Doesn't look like any varnish I've ever seen," he objected.

She finally returned his smile. It was an ideal opportunity for her to impart the lessons Cotter had given her several years before, and she wasn't the least bit opposed to doing it, especially as he seemed to be asking for the instruction.

"No, I suppose not," she agreed. "But consider this: assuming there was a painting that's been hung in rooms lit with tallow candles for the last few hundred years, what would have happened to the varnish?"

"It would be dirtied by the candle soot," he replied quickly.

"Precisely. And it would also yellow somewhat with age. If those paintings you deem so horribly *new* are to appear old, they need to look as though the varnish on them has been slowly aging and soaking up candle soot for years. I'm just hurrying the process. I've melted a small bit of tallow, tinted it slightly and added a fair amount of candle soot."

"I hope you weren't planning to serve the leftovers for dinner," he interjected.

She ignored the interruption. "Now I'm mixing the concoction with the varnish, thinning it until I get what should be the right color."

"And you can tell just by looking at that mess what will be the right color?"

She grinned. "Actually it's not that difficult. The really hard part is keeping the temperature right. Varnish will burn if it gets too hot, but the tallow and soot won't mix right if it's not heated at all." She lifted her spoon, let the dirty yellow liquid slide down it and back into the pot, all the while considering the shade. "Would you pass that small tin on the table, please?"

She slowly added a thin stream of clear varnish to the pot, stirring as she did, carefully watching as the dirty yellow soup grew slightly paler.

"There," she said as she handed back the tin. "I think that's it."

"Now what?" he asked.

"Now we let the pot cool for a few minutes and then I do what every painter does, seal the canvas."

"But with a slightly unusual sort of sealer."

She nodded. "Right. I doubt that every artist would want the magnificence of his work dulled with quite so unwholesome a coat." She put the pot on the work table and continued to stir to cool the contents. "In any case, I seal the paintings, but with a varnish that's not quite like the usual sort." She lifted the spoon, touched a wary finger to its contents, then wiped her hand on a rag. "I think this should be right."

She pulled open a drawer and rummaged through it, pulling out a handful of brushes and pressing the bristles against the palm of her hand, considering the feel before she accepted or rejected it. They all looked the same to Chase, but he assumed she knew what she was doing.

She finally decided on a pair of thick brushes from a half dozen she deemed possibilities and held one out to him.

"Care to help?"

He smiled wryly. "Think I'm trustworthy?" he asked as he took one.

She scowled and then laughed. "Probably not. But you can't do much damage at this point."

He followed her to the opposite side of the room, where she'd set the two paintings on easels. She stopped and stared at them for a moment once she was standing in front of them, then shrugged and put her brush into the pot she'd carried with her. She lifted it and began to apply a neat coat of the doctored varnish to the canvas on the left.

"Do your worst," she said, nodding to the pot and the second canvas.

It didn't take long, and when they were done Chase realized the canvases already looked more like the originals in the museum. The colors were muted, slightly dulled, even though the wet varnish was still very shiny.

"Now what?" Chase asked.

"Now we move the canvases closer to the stove," she told him, "so that the varnish dries quickly. That way it will shrink as it sets, and those characteristic age cracks should appear in the surface."

"Should?" he asked as he helped her pull the easels close to the stove.

She nodded. "Let's hope so," she said as she adjusted the easels, making sure the canvases faced the heat of the stove head on. "We haven't time to repeat the process a half dozen times."

"And that's it?"

She shook her head and smiled at his naïveté. "Hardly. I still have to age the edges and backs of the canvases. It would have been a much easier job to do it before I painted, but that wasn't possible, under the circumstances."

"I suppose not," he agreed. "It wouldn't do to make it too obvious you were creating a forgery."

"Not with a detective in the employ of Lloyd's Corporation watching me the whole time," she added in a dryly sarcastic tone.

She took a few steps back, considered the easels' placement, and decided all was as it ought to be.

"Now what?" Chase asked.

Delia took a piece of clean rag, soaked it in turpentine, and began carefully to clean the brushes they'd used. A good workman, he mused as he watched her, tending to her tools.

"Now we eat a bit of lunch," she said as she

282

worked. "And then we can venture out into the garden for a handful of fresh garden dirt. And then . . ." Her voice trailed off and she shrugged. "Then we see if we can make a four-centuries-old painting."

Chase watched her expression as she finished cleaning her brushes. She was staring at the paintings, and he could only guess what she might be thinking.

Was Cotter's ghost in the studio with them now, as it had been in the night before? he wondered. Was that what she saw when she stared at those paintings she'd worked so singlemindedly to complete? And if it was, would that ghost follow the paintings when she gave them to Matthew Pickering, or would it stay here and continue to haunt her?

And if it stayed with her, would he ever find a way to free her from the hold it had on her?

Delia's hands were filthy, but she didn't seem to notice. She was absolutely intent as she carefully kneaded the clean white canvas with the mixture of dirt and candle soot she'd concocted. The effect was to leave the surface smudged, dirty gray and worn-looking — in short, old.

It was late afternoon when they'd returned to the studio. Chase had been fascinated watching her expression as she'd inspected the surface of the now set varnish. There had been nothing short of delight in her expression when she saw that it was riddled with tiny hairline cracks.

She'd looked up at him and smiled. "Perfect," she'd pronounced, and there had been the sound of real accomplishment in her tone, almost as though she was gloating just a bit that she'd actually accomplished alone what she must have had doubts she could do without Cotter. She was, he realized, quite pleased with the results.

283

"I think you're rather enjoying this," he'd accused.

The smile had quickly disappeared, and she'd shrugged.

"A workman likes to see that his labors are fruitful," she'd replied.

Then she'd removed the canvases from the easels and brought them to the work table. She'd carefully removed the stretchers, taking the frames of pale, fresh wood and dropping them to the floor. She'd held her hands tentatively over the canvases for a while, a surgeon collecting her thoughts before she made the first stroke with the scalpel. Then she'd decisively put her fingers into the bowl of dirt and melted wax she'd prepared, beginning this bizarre, slow process.

She worked very carefully, taking great pains that the stains she applied covered the whole of the surface, but did not appear too even. As she'd worked, she'd raveled the edges slightly, letting the loose threads absorb a bit more dirt than the rest of the canvas.

When she glanced at him and saw his bewildered expression, she grinned and explained, "This happens all the time. Look at the edges of any old canvas. They become worn when an old stretcher is replaced or simply from all the moving and rehanging."

He believed her. She seemed to know precisely what she was about.

The sun had long ago set, and it was growing late. Delia had been working steadily for more than six hours, and Chase thought it time he pulled her away and fed her some dinner.

He glanced at the painting lying on the work table and whistled softly. It was remarkable, he thought. Already the obviously new paintings they'd brought up to the studio that morning were something entirely different. Cotter seemed to have taught her well. Her skills were remarkable.

"Am I to take it that you're impressed, Mr. Sutton?" she asked.

He nodded. "Decidedly."

"Well, I'll have that much for my memoirs, then," she replied, her tone playful. "I once managed to impress Chase Sutton."

"You've done that quite a number of times, Delia," he told her.

She looked up at him, into the endless blue of his eyes. For a moment, her hands began to tremble. There's something there, she told herself, something real, something deep.

But she turned away, afraid that she was wrong, afraid that if she looked any further, she'd realize it had only been her imagination. She began furiously to knead the edge of canvas in her hands.

"Will it take much longer?" he asked.

She only shrugged.

"It really can't be hurried," she told him. It was easy to talk about this, she found, easy to be indifferent to him when she could think of the work instead of what she felt. "And this is probably the most important part. If my version of Memling's painting isn't exactly perfect, the errors most likely won't be noticed. But a canvas that looks too fresh is a direct giveaway. I don't think Pickering would want to take a chance with a less than perfect canvas if he's intending to make a switch that will eventually be viewed by a museum curator in London. Unless, of course, he doesn't care."

"Oh, he cares all right," he assured her. "Even if this sale nets him a fortune, even if he plans to retire and leave the country on what it brings him, still he'll need time to complete the transaction. That will mean he won't want the fakes spotted too easily."

"In that case," she said with a sigh, "it may be a very long night."

It was well past nine when Delia discarded the bit of cloth she had been using to even the dirt stains on the canvas's back. She arched her head and put her hand to her neck.

"I can't do any more tonight," she confessed.

Chase went to her and put his hands on her shoulders. He could feel the muscles, hard and tense, beneath his fingers, and he began to gently massage them.

"It'll keep until morning," he agreed. "Hungry?"

She laughed. "You've become quite domestic, haven't you?" she said. "The good nurturer, offering sustenance?"

"Just protecting my investment," he replied with an answering laugh. "We both have a lot invested in those paintings and Pickering."

She shrugged away from his hands and turned and looked up at him. He was smiling, but Delia saw he was deadly serious behind the glint of humor in his eyes. It was not as though she didn't expect it, not as though she hadn't come to accept the fact that she was nothing more to him than a means to Pickering. Still, it hurt each time he pressed the fact home, hurt more than she wanted to consider.

She felt her own expression harden. She backed away from him as though she feared he might attempt to touch her again.

She stood. "I'll bathe quickly," she told him, "and be right down."

Chase watched her leave, certain she was fleeing from him and not quite sure what he'd done to offend her this time. A few more days, he told himself, and they'd be past all this. Then, perhaps he could finally come to some understanding with her. One way or another, they would have a great deal to talk over.

In the meantime, he reminded himself, there was food to be scavenged in the kitchen, and then another long night to be gotten through. It was no good looking to the future, at least not yet. He had to take each day as it came.

He'd produced a makeshift meal of *brioches,* cold roast chicken, and *brie* when she appeared at the kitchen door. Flushed, her hair still damp from the bath, wrapped in a demure cotton dressing gown with embroidered flowers at the collar and cuffs, she looked like a little girl to him. A beautiful little girl, he amended, then told himself he'd never felt the way he did at that moment in the presence of any little girl that he remembered.

"Here," he said, and handed her a glass of white wine. "Sit down and eat. You look ravenous."

"Guilty," she agreed, as she tore off a piece of the brioche, put it in her mouth, and chewed contemplatively. "Good. I should have you cater all my meals."

"Nothing a few francs and the neighborhood *épicier* couldn't supply," he replied. He grinned at her, about to add that he could think of only a few things he'd enjoy more than seeing to the purchase of her meals in the future, when they heard a loud knock on the front door.

"What's that?" Delia asked in a sharp whisper.

Chase shook his head. "Were you expecting anyone?" he asked.

"Of course not." She looked up at him, suddenly uncertain and far from calm. "Pickering, do you think?"

He gritted his teeth. He didn't like this at all, but there really wasn't much he could do about it.

"I doubt it," he assured her. "He wouldn't bother

287

to knock. But there's only one way we'll ever find out, and that's by you answering the door."

Delia realized her hand was shaking. She put down the glass of wine.

"What do I say to him?" she asked.

"It won't be him," Chase insisted. "Don't worry, I'll be right behind you. Whoever it is, just send him away."

He followed her to the front door, checking his pistol as they walked. He stationed himself to her side, where he wouldn't be seen when she opened the door, then nodded that he was ready.

Delia took a deep breath, then pulled the door open.

"Pierre?"

It was such a relief to see the young artist standing there, and not Pickering, that she nearly laughed with relief. She let the door fall wide open, now that she realized she didn't need to defend herself against an unwanted visitor.

He was holding a bunch of violets, the sort that were sold along the quays. He held it out to her.

"Bon soir, chérie," he said with a wan smile. "I bought these for you."

Delia laughed and took them. "Thank you, Pierre," she murmured. "But what are you doing here at this hour?"

"I, uh, we," he stuttered, obviously flustered, "we've been worried about you, Claude and Henri and all the rest. None of us has seen you since the funeral. I wanted to be sure you were well."

She nodded and smiled at him, a painfully regretful smile. He seemed so shy and innocent to her suddenly, his bravado lost behind his uncertainty.

"I'm sorry I've been the cause of your concern," she replied. "But I am, as you see, fine."

"But you haven't been to the park," he reminded her.

She knew she couldn't tell him that she'd been painting forgeries, that she was trying to help catch her father's murderer. Mostly, she couldn't tell him she'd fallen in love with Chase Sutton. She knew she couldn't really tell him anything.

She shook her head. "No, no—I've been busy," she evaded.

"Can I come in, Delia?" he asked. "Just to talk for a moment."

He took a step forward, apparently assuming she'd agree, and nearly walking into her when he reached the entrance and she hadn't moved.

"I don't think that's best," she told him, trying to hold him back with her hands.

But it was too late; he'd already glanced inside and seen Chase.

His hopeful smile disappeared as he darted an angry look at Chase and then a shocked, regretful one at Delia.

"Is *he* why you've been so busy?" he demanded.

Delia was shocked by the vehemence of his tone and the intensity of the anger she felt flowing from him to Chase. It had always been a game between the two of them, she told herself, the flirting hadn't really meant anything. At least, it hadn't really meant anything to her. But she suddenly realized it had meant a good deal to Pierre.

"Please, Pierre," she begged softly, "try to understand."

Chase, realizing that he'd been seen, moved up behind her and put his hand on her waist. Let the young Frenchman tell his friends she didn't need them for protection any longer, he thought.

"I do understand," Pierre hissed angrily. "I understand only too well."

"I think you should leave now," Chase told him calmly.

"Damn you," Pierre seethed.

But Chase ignored him, pulling Delia aside and closing the door firmly in the young artist's face, then sliding the bolt shut.

Delia stood and stared at the door. She knew there was nothing else Chase could have done under the circumstances, but still she felt the weight of the hurt she'd seen in Pierre's eyes. She felt she'd just watched the door close on the last vestige of her youth.

Chase, though, saw only regret in her eyes, and that regret cut through him like a knife. For the first time he found himself wondering just what the young Frenchman might have meant to her, just what expectations she might have led him to have.

"Delia?"

She spun on her heel, turning her back to him and to the door.

"I think I'm too tired to eat," she said abruptly, and started for the stairs. "I still have a lot of work to complete tomorrow. I'll see you in the morning."

"Perhaps we should talk about your friend," he called after her.

She stopped with her hand on the railing, but didn't turn to face him.

"There's nothing to talk about," she said.

Chase watched her climb the stairs, all the time wondering why, if there really was nothing to talk about, she couldn't bring herself to so much as look at him.

Chapter Sixteen

Delia very slowly and deliberately signed her name at the bottom of the note. When she'd done, she put down the pen and stared at the neat lines of script for an instant before she lifted the sheet of stationery, folded it carefully in perfect thirds, and slipped it into the envelope Chase had given her.

She turned and briefly glanced up at him before returning her attention to the task at hand. Whatever she thought she might find in his eyes as he watched her simply wasn't there. All she saw was the same stolidly impersonal expression he'd worn for the previous few days, punctuated by an encouraging grin when she turned to him.

She bit her lower lip and told herself whatever it was she might have hoped to find in his eyes, she was a fool even to look for it. Still there was a dull feeling inside her, not a hurt, really, but an unpleasant feeling of emptiness as she took up the pen again. She had to force her hand to move, to write "Monsieur Matthew Pickering" in careful block letters on the envelope.

She stared at the outside of the envelope and for an instant she felt herself overcome by a wave of sudden panic. She didn't know why, but the letters had taken on the aura of an inscription on a tombstone. An eerie premonition of death seemed to surround her.

This is foolish, she told herself . . . I'm not the sort who believes in omens. But she did feel it, she realized, whether or not she wanted to believe it. She stared at the envelope a second longer. If it is an omen, she asked herself, whose death is it foretelling, Pickering's or my own?

She forcefully pushed the thought away, telling herself that she couldn't afford to allow herself to be afraid now. Nonetheless, once she had lifted the envelope and handed it to Chase, she found she was glad to be rid of it.

She realized she wasn't alone in feeling the unpleasant sense of foreboding. Chase took the letter gingerly, as though he were handling something that wasn't quite safe to touch. But when he spoke, his voice was calm and entirely unruffled.

"I'll have it delivered," he told her. "He should pick it up this afternoon."

"So you've told me," she murmured. She was, she realized, getting just a little bored with the fact that he was so absolutely certain of what Pickering would or would not do. She almost relished Pickering surprising Chase and doing something entirely unexpected, if only to see how he would accept the fact that he'd been wrong.

"You might get a little rest, Delia," he told her. "You look like you could use it."

She looked more than tired, more like someone who has suffered from an extended sickness and isn't yet quite recovered. It was no salve to his conscience to know that he was at least in part responsible for the sickness, that had he never come to Paris, she would never have become involved in any dealings with Matthew Pickering.

She shook her head, rejecting his suggestion. "I

can't even think of sleep now," she said. As the time grew shorter, she was growing more and more nervous about this final interview with Pickering.

"I think you should try," he insisted. "You had a pretty long night, playing with your mud and gunk."

He grinned then, a bright and unexpected grin, obviously intended to cheer her. But Delia didn't feel like being cheered.

"I'll have a lifetime to sleep when this is over," she murmured. And nothing else to do, she added silently. A long, empty lifetime without Papa to care for, and without you to love . . .

If Chase heard the hint of bitterness in her voice, he ignored it. "You have only a few hours at best," he told her. "You'll need to be alert when he gets here."

Delia wasn't all that convinced, despite his apparent certainty.

"What if he took me at my word and decides not to check for my note for another two days?" she asked. "Or what if he comes tomorrow afternoon, as the invitation suggests?"

"Oh, he'll check for word," Chase assured her. "He's a planner, and he doesn't like leaving things to the last moment. He'll want the paintings in his hands as soon as possible. And he'll come tonight, not tomorrow. He'll think it will be an advantage to catch you off-guard."

She shrugged, still not entirely convinced, but without any great desire to argue with him. It was odd how her emotions kept swinging from one extreme to the other. Two days before, she'd wanted nothing more than to bait him, to try to force him to show some vestige of human emotion, even if it was anger with her. Now, she found she'd tired of the game. She simply wanted an end to it all, to find some peace, if she was ever to have any. More than

293

anything else, she wished fervently that it was all over, and wanted to see the whole thing ended.

More than that, she wanted to see Chase go. It was torture the way it was, knowing that he would leave and being forced to wait for it to happen, being forced to anticipate the pain. She almost relished the final hurt of his leaving, for that, at least, would put the whole, miserable episode at an end.

At least then she'd be free, she told herself. Whatever freedom meant, she would have it.

She looked up at him and when her eyes found his she felt herself shiver involuntarily. He knows just what I'm thinking, she thought.

Somehow she didn't find the thought nearly as odious as she ought to have. Perhaps I've just reached the point where I simply don't care, she thought. Perhaps the part that feels has gone to sleep. Perhaps it's dead and there'll never be anything to feel again.

She realized even that prospect didn't frighten her. Nothing frightened her now, not even the thought of facing Matthew Pickering. She was nervous that she might make a mistake, but there was no real fear.

She pushed back her chair and stood.

"Perhaps I'll try to nap after all," she murmured.

"Good," he told her. "I'll arrange things in the meantime."

"Things?" she asked.

She didn't need his answer. She glanced at the two canvases, rolled into a dirty-looking cylinder that was lying where she'd dropped it on Cotter's tattered chair. He'll make sure the wares are well displayed, she thought, all the better to catch Pickering's eye. And then there's the matter of the pistol. He'll certainly take care of arranging that.

"Just try to sleep, Delia," he told her.

"Are you sure about the pistol?" she asked. "What

294

if he only intends to make an even exchange, money for the paintings? After all, that's what you want."

Chase shook his head. "And what if he has other intentions?" he asked. "It's too great a risk, Delia. At least this way we get to control the outcome."

"I still don't like doing it," she countered.

"Scruples?" he asked. "With Matthew Pickering?"

"It's not that," she said.

He raised a hand to still her objections.

"I know," he told her. "We've been over it enough. But this is the only way we can be sure. Just follow the plan."

She nodded. "Yes," she agreed finally. A wave of bitterness filled her. "We wouldn't want to deviate from the precious plan."

He put his hand on her arm.

"I'd do this if there was any way, Delia," he told her.

She nodded, then lifted her chin and pulled her arm away.

"I started this, knowing full well what he was capable of," she replied. "I told you I intended to follow it through to the end, and I meant it. I wouldn't let you do it, even if it were possible."

She backed away from him, then edged her way past him, taking care not to let herself touch him, not even brush against him. It was better that she accustom herself to being completely alone, she thought, better she learn the lesson before she was forced to face the situation unprepared.

"Miss Hampton. What a pleasure to see you again so soon!"

Delia put down the book she'd been pretending to read and looked up to find Matthew Pickering standing by the open door. He was dressed impeccably, a gentleman out for an evening at the theater or perhaps a gambling club, with pristine white linen and full evening regalia. Even his white kidskin gloves were completely unblemished.

Delia hadn't heard so much as a sound until Pickering had spoken. Somehow he'd gotten into the house without making any noise at all. He was smiling at her now, as though he enjoyed performing such acts of minor legerdemain. He was, she realized, doing exactly what Chase had told her he'd do, trying to intimidate her, to get the upper hand.

It surprised her to realize that his sudden appearance was so much less startling to her than the appearance of the first rose had been. A conjuring act that's expected, she thought, wasn't really magic after all, just a puzzlement that could be assigned to the list of other matters that would later need her attention. When she had the time, she told herself, she'd think out how he'd done it.

Just now, she was far more puzzled by the fact that she didn't feel even the smallest hint of fear. Simple logic, she told herself, dictated that she ought to be afraid.

"How did you get in?" she asked, pretending amazement, wondering if he'd reveal his little secrets to her.

He didn't. Instead, he grinned, pleased to think he'd outsmarted her.

"I thought we were past such considerations, you and I," he said.

He stared at her as he began to remove his gloves, then his hat, dropping the former into the latter.

"Ah, yes, your little present." She smiled up at him prettily. "I'd almost forgotten," she added, lying, for she had in no way forgotten her reaction to the appearance of that first rose. She hoped her act of boredom reasonably convincing. "But I wasn't

296

expecting to see you until tomorrow," she added.

"Weren't you?" he asked, his tone thoughtful. He stared at her. "I'd say you really aren't all that surprised to see me here."

She smiled, then shrugged in reply.

"Perhaps not," she agreed. "Papa did speak about you from time to time," she added, as though that were explanation enough.

"Now that, I must admit, surprises *me*," Pickering told her, as he dropped his hat and gloves on a table, then placed a heavy, gold-tipped walking stick beside them. "I had the distinct feeling when Cotter left that he never wanted to so much as think about me again. I must admit that I've always regretted that we parted on rather less than genial terms."

Delia wondered if there might be a hint of pain in his tone as he spoke those words. After all those years, did it still bother him to think both he and the life he offered had been rejected so long before? Or perhaps what she saw was simply a veneer of habitual anger, an affectation to keep others in their place. She didn't know, and she certainly didn't care to find out.

"Perhaps hate and love are closer than you think," she offered by way of explanation. "Perhaps it's only human to love, just a little, those we truly hate. Perhaps, in some ways, we even regret losing them."

That's true enough, she thought. And she had reason to know it perhaps more than most. She had been telling herself for the previous weeks that she hated Chase Sutton, and yet she knew there was a part of her that would never get over him. She would mourn his loss for the rest of her life.

She had to force herself to stop thinking of him, to keep her mind on Matthew Pickering and what was happening.

Pickering smiled. "I admit it pleases me to think

297

that in his own way, Cotter missed me," he told her. "Even if it is mere kindness of you to say so."

"Oh, it's not kindness," Delia assured him.

"No, I suppose not," he agreed. "Ours is, after all, a business relationship. That leaves little room for kindness."

"Then those roses were nothing more than business?" she asked with an arch little smile. "I'm crushed."

His eyes narrowed. "Sometimes business borders on other things," he told her.

She considered his response for an instant. "But those other things don't apply tonight?" she asked.

"I'm afraid they don't," he confessed. He let his eyes scan the room, finally letting them come to rest on the sofa. "I confess I had trouble thinking of anything besides the paintings."

"How rude of me," Delia murmured. She raised a hand and waved it in the direction of the sofa, pleased to find she hadn't had to call his attention to it first. "Please, won't you sit?"

Pickering walked past her, crossing to the worn sofa, then stood staring down at the two canvases Chase had neatly tucked over two of the cushions.

"I wouldn't dream of it," he told her, his tone slightly absent now, distracted as he considered the effect of the two completed forgeries.

Delia smiled. So far, so good, she thought.

"Then you find my choice of upholstery interesting?" she asked. "I'm afraid I wasn't all that sure. I don't think canvas quite the height of *la haute mode*. Still, I find it interesting, don't you?"

Pickering turned back to face her. She could tell from his expression that he was more than pleased with what he'd seen in that first cursory glance.

"I personally find it most intriguing," he told her. "Perhaps the idea might catch on."

She shrugged. "I'm afraid I've never been able to understand the vagaries of fashion."

Pickering smiled politely, then turned back to the paintings. Delia watched him, watched the way his hands seemed to hover over the canvases as though they had a mind of their own, as though they wanted to touch and he was forced physically to restrain them.

"May I?" he asked, still the soul of courtesy.

"Of course," she readily agreed. "I wouldn't want you to be less than certain that you're buying precisely what you were looking for."

He put his hand under a canvas and lifted it, crossing back to the table where he'd left his hat and gloves. He handled the edges carefully, letting his fingers drink in the worn feel of the canvas before he held the painting to the lamplight so that he could inspect it.

He spent several minutes silently examining it. For the first minutes, Delia sat calmly waiting. But as time began to drag on, she felt her calm slipping away. She was, she realized, growing more and more nervous.

For the first time since she'd put her brush to one of the canvases she began to seriously question the quality of her work. If Pickering didn't like the paintings, if he didn't think them good enough, she knew he'd simply walk away from them. And if he did that, all her work would have been for nothing. Without the paintings, Pickering might have to abandon his plan to steal the two Memlings, and that would doubtless please Chase Sutton, but that meant nothing to her. Unless he was caught stealing those paintings, Pickering could safely walk away from everything that had happened while he was in Paris. He'd never be caught, and there would be no way to make him pay for Cotter's death.

She began to move uncomfortably in her chair,

too nervous to sit quietly, almost ready to bolt. Before she forgot herself entirely, however, she reminded herself of the directions Chase had given her. If he was right about Pickering's intentions, then it had to go precisely as he'd planned it. There was no room for mistakes, no room for nervous errors, if she cared for her life.

She balled her hands into tight fists, and dug them into her lap in an attempt to calm her jitters. Then she pretended to stare a hole in the center of Pickering's perfectly draped back and willed him to turn and face her.

Which he eventually did, even if he wasn't guided by the projection of her will.

"I hope I haven't been rude, Miss Hampton?" he asked, his tone implying that he really didn't care. "I do tend to lose track of time when the subject matter warrants my attentions."

"Not at all," Delia assured him. "May I assume your preoccupation was caused by my humble efforts?"

"Oh, I should say your efforts are far from humble," he returned. "In fact, I'd say that they are quite remarkable." He let his gaze find hers. "You're every bit as good as Cotter ever was." He grinned slightly. "Perhaps even better."

Delia released a deep sigh of relief.

"Then you'll take the canvases?" she asked.

"Definitely," he agreed. He put his hand into his breast pocket and drew out a plain white envelope. It looked to Delia to be quite thick. "One thousand pounds was the agreed price, I believe," he said, dropping the envelope onto the table and starting back across the room to the sofa and the second canvas.

Delia kept her eyes firmly on him, watching every motion he made.

"I'm afraid that's been changed a bit," she said softly as he bent to retrieve the second canvas.

He straightened and looked around, his expression suddenly sharp.

"I believe I may have heard you incorrectly, Miss Hampton," he said.

"I'm afraid you didn't," she replied.

"We had an understanding."

"Yes," she agreed. "And I do regret that. But I've made a few discreet inquiries since last we discussed the matter. It seems that I vastly underestimated the value of those two paintings. They are, I've found, worth conservatively four times what I originally asked for them."

Pickering's eyes narrowed, and Delia thought she could almost feel the anger he leveled at her. The air was heavy with it, almost thick enough to choke her.

"You can't expect me to give you four thousand pounds for them," he hissed angrily.

"I could," Delia replied. She smiled again. "But I don't. I wouldn't want you to think me greedy, Mr. Pickering. So I've decided to be generous. You may have them for a thousand each."

"That's twice what we agreed. Do you think me a fool?" Pickering demanded sharply.

He began to raise his hand to his breast pocket a second time.

That was what Chase had told her to watch for. Delia quickly dug her hand into the side of the chair.

"I suggest you lower your hand, Mr. Pickering," she said sharply as she drew out the pistol she had been holding secreted between the folds of her skirt and the side of her chair. She held it carefully, as Chase had shown her, with both hands. "I don't think either of us wants this evening to end unpleasantly."

Pickering's expression showed only the smallest

301

hint of shock before he masked it completely.

"I must admit that you quite surprise me, Miss Hampton," he said. He smiled then, and once again the carefully fostered look of polite courtesy masked his features as he slowly lowered his hand. "I'd long ago thought a young woman incapable of surprising me. I suppose I ought to congratulate you."

"You needn't," Delia told him. "I told you before, Papa told me a good deal about you."

"I'm afraid I must tell you I think you're lying about that," he said, mouthing the words very slowly, as though he were taking great pains to make himself understood. "If Cotter had told you anything at all about me, you'd never even consider what you are doing."

"I'm doing nothing more than making a fair business arrangement, Mr. Pickering," Delia insisted. She smiled slyly at him. "Anything less than two thousand for those canvases would be allowing you to steal them from me. I should hate to be responsible for forcing the burden of such an act on your conscience."

Pickering wasn't the least amused.

"No one backs out on a deal with me," he told her, his voice sharp with anger he now made no attempt to hide.

"I'm not backing out," she insisted. "I'm simply renegotiating a more equitable arrangement." She stood, taking great pains to keep the pistol aimed at his heart. "Two thousand pounds sterling. Not a *sou* less. If you don't want them for that, I've come to understand that there are other markets for my wares."

She kept her eyes on his face, watching the way his jaw tightened, weighing his anger, and wondering just how much further she would have to push him.

He glanced at the painting in his hand and then at

302

the second, the one still lying on the sofa.

"You are putting me in an extremely unpleasant position, Miss Hampton," he said slowly. "There is no time for me to make other arrangements at this point in my venture. And frankly, even if there were, I doubt I could find anything near equal to what you have done. I need those paintings and I need them now."

She shrugged. "That is no concern of mine. I have a product, and I've named a price. If you don't want to pay for them, you're free to walk away."

He looked back at her. "I've just told you I can't do that."

"Then pay for them," she advised with a sharp, smug smile.

She watched the way he considered her expression and knew that it was the smugness that seemed to seal his anger. It would happen just as Chase had said it would, she thought. He'd known all along what Pickering would do, known just how he'd react. It was as if it had all been written in stone long before, and they were all just playing out the parts they had been chosen to play.

Pickering dropped the painting back onto the cushion. He stood staring at her for an instant before he began to move slowly toward her.

"I'm afraid you have me at a disadvantage, Miss Hampton," he told her. "I don't have another thousand pounds with me."

"No grave disadvantage, I assure you, Mr. Pickering. I'll be more than happy to wait until tomorrow if you like," she offered amiably. "I'm not without some understanding of such matters." Her eyes narrowed. "I know far better than you what it means to have no money at all."

"A situation I assume you find odious?" he asked.

"More than odious, Mr. Pickering. But thanks to

you, I believe I've learned how to overcome that particular disadvantage."

Pickering seemed more pleased by that than anything else. Perhaps greed is the only thing he can really understand, Delia thought, greed and power.

"It would seem that Cotter somehow managed to create quite a little monster, didn't he?" Pickering mused softly. "I'd never have thought he had it in him."

"Perhaps you didn't know him as well as you thought," Delia suggested.

Pickering pursed his lips and shook his head.

"Oh, no, I knew him," he told her. "Do you know you far outdistance him in almost every way? Had he ever had even half your strength and tenacity, he and I might have had a much longer, much more successful partnership."

He was continuing to move slowly closer to her. Delia pretended not to notice that the distance between them was shrinking. She *was* frightened now, she couldn't deny that. But she steadied herself with the knowledge that Chase had told her what to expect.

"This has nothing to do with Papa," she said sharply. Suddenly the thought of Pickering talking about her father had become repugnant to her, as if his words could dirty Cotter's memory. "It's simply a matter of money. I told you that his death left me in uncomfortable circumstances. I should think, under the circumstances, you'd be willing to help an old friend's orphan."

"Under what circumstances?" he asked.

He's waiting, Delia thought, waiting for me to tell him I know he killed Papa.

She didn't. "For the sake of nostalgia," she replied. "For all the memories you must have."

"But perhaps such nonsense means nothing to

me," he suggested.

Delia shrugged. "It doesn't matter," she said. "If you want the paintings, come back tomorrow with another thousand pounds and you're welcome to them, Mr. Pickering. Until then, I will thank you to leave my home."

He shook his head slowly.

"I'm afraid I can't do that, Miss Hampton," he said.

And then he lunged forward, reaching for the pistol barrel with one hand and pushing her hands upward with the other, twisting them sharply as he wrenched the pistol free of her grasp.

Delia yelped with hurt as Pickering wrested the pistol from her grip. And then there was a sharp pain in her abdomen as he struck her with his fist. She fell back, landing on the floor, too stunned by the hurt and the blow to do anything more than put her hand to the place where the pain was centered.

No, a voice cried out in her head, this isn't the way it's supposed to happen.

When the ache began to subside slightly, she collected herself enough to look up at Pickering. She was still breathing heavily, still gasping slightly from the echoes of the pain. To all appearances, he was completely oblivious to her discomfort. He stood a few feet away, staring down at her with a look of mild repugnance on his face.

But it wasn't his face at which Delia found herself staring; it was at the pistol. He was holding it casually in his hand, and it was obvious he was used to handling such things. He pointed it directly at her.

"I told you, Miss Hampton," he sneered, "no one backs out of a deal with me."

Delia looked at the barrel of the pistol and felt the dull ache in her abdomen shrink away as anticipation of a far greater hurt supplanted it.

"The thousand is enough," she agreed. "Take the paintings and just leave."

Pickering shook his head. "I'm afraid matters have gone too far for that, *Delia, my dear,*" he said. He smiled as he murmured the last three words, and his tone of intimacy sounded more intimidating than anything else. "I'm afraid they've gone much too far for that."

"What are you going to do?" she asked. Her throat had grown suddenly tight and her voice had shrunk to a hoarse whisper. She found she couldn't take her eyes off the pistol.

"Oh, I intend to take the two canvases, all right," he agreed. "But I'm afraid I now find a thousand pounds a good deal too much to pay for them, under the circumstances."

She began to edge her way backward, but before she'd moved more than a few feet, she found she'd backed into the chair she'd just vacated.

"Take them," she said. "Just take them and leave me alone."

"No, no, I can't do that either, I'm afraid," he told her. He shook his head, his expression slightly wistful for a moment, but then he quickly brightened. "I really should thank you, Delia."

That was the last thing she'd expected him to say. "Thank me?"

He nodded. "Yes. I really do revere beauty, you know," he told her. His tone grew wistful, even tender. "And you are quite beautiful." He reached out his hand as if he meant to lean forward and touch her, but he quickly drew it back. "Of course, a woman's beauty is a fleeting thing, not really something to be adored the way art can be adored. Still, I must confess that I'd begun to regret the necessity of what I'm about to do. Now, however, I find you've put yourself to the bother to make it so much easier for

306

me." He raised the pistol slightly, carefully aiming it. "You've even supplied the weapon," he said, just before he fired.

The sound of Delia's scream was muffled by the explosion, then cut suddenly short. She put her hand to her chest, then looked down as a thick stream of red began to seep through her fingers. She seemed suspended for a long moment, staring in shock at the flow of blood, then she slumped forward, against the floor, her face down. She was very still.

Pickering stood over her for only an instant, staring as the trickle of red leaked onto the floor. Sure of his aim, he didn't attempt to touch her or search for a pulse. Instead, he turned back to the sofa, dropping the pistol and taking up the two paintings. Leaving the pistol, he carried the canvases to the table where he'd left his walking stick, hat, and gloves and set them down one atop the other. Then he carefully rolled them into a neat, narrow cylinder. He lifted the heavy walking stick and unscrewed its ornate gold handle. Then he took the canvases and carefully slid them into the empty tube.

Once he had reassembled the walking stick, his thoughts returned to more mundane matters. He looked back to where Delia lay unmoving on the floor. There was no emotion in his eyes as he gazed at her still body, and he honored it with only a few seconds of his consideration.

He turned his attention back to his own belongings, carefully pulling on his gloves and tucking his hat and walking stick beneath his arm. Then he lifted the oil lamp from the table and carried it with him to the door to the room.

"It would seem I've witnessed the fall of the House of Hampton," he said with a tight, cruel laugh.

Then he heaved the lamp, watching an arc of oil

slip from it as it flew across the room. Its flight was cut short as it smashed against the far wall. Oil splattered on the wall and was ignited by the lamp's flame even before the shattered glass landed on the floor. The trailing line of lamp oil burst into flame almost immediately, and the flames quickly began to spread among the tattered furnishings of the room.

Pickering stood and watched the fire grow for a moment, apparently enjoying the unexpected spectacle of the flames as they bit into the worn upholstery of the sofa. The air began to fill with smoke and a thick, crackling sound as the blaze spread.

Pickering darted a parting glance to Delia's still body.

"I never did enjoy prolonged goodbyes," he called out to her.

Then he laughed as he turned and, putting his hat carefully on his head and hugging his walking stick to his side, he crossed the entry hall and slipped silently out of the house.

Chapter Seventeen

The moment the door closed behind Pickering, one of the long windows overlooking the garden was thrown open. Chase climbed through it, quickly clambering into the room.

As soon as he glanced around, he felt himself fill with a sick stab of terror. Flames were steadily spreading in a long line from the wall to the door and Delia lay completely motionless on the floor while a dark red puddle of blood spread out on the parquet flooring beside her.

The air in the room had already begun to grow uncomfortably hot, the flames churning it as they started to eat at the floor and furnishings. Each time he inhaled, Chase could feel it burning into his lungs along with a waft of acrid smoke.

His thoughts were too fixed on Delia's still body, however, for him to spare any for the heat or the smoke or the flames.

His conscience ate at him, and he knew it was all his fault, that the responsibility for everything that had happened lay firmly at his feet. There was no one else for him to blame, not even Pickering. If he hadn't allowed Delia to become involved, she wouldn't be lying there amidst a pool of blood and the room wouldn't be burning around her.

He skirted the blaze, racing to her side.

"Delia! For God's sake, say something."

She lifted her head slightly and peered up at him.

"Is he gone?" she asked, then punctuated the question with a thick, smoke-induced cough.

Three mundane little words, but they were powerful enough to lift away the weight of guilt that a moment before had seemed powerful enough to Chase to overwhelm him.

"Thank God," he murmured.

He reached down for her, lifting her to her feet, then wrapping his arms around her and hugging her quickly to him. A wave of warmth engulfed him, a warmth that had nothing to do with the heat of the flames. He realized then how much it meant to him to hold her, to feel her safe in his arms. Until that moment, he hadn't allowed himself to think how empty his life would be were he to be fool enough to lose her.

She was still and clinging, obviously terrified in the wake of the ugly scene with Pickering, and he wanted nothing more than to soothe away her fears. But once the relief ebbed enough to leave room for a finger of logic, he pushed her away.

"Get out of here," he ordered her sharply.

She looked at him as though he'd struck her. He returned her stare for an instant, then turned away, grabbed up a small rug from the floor, and began to use it to beat at the growing blaze.

But Delia didn't move. She stood staring at him and the flames through eyes that had become suddenly dull with disbelief.

"It wasn't supposed to happen like this," she shouted at him. She stamped her foot, lost in a wave of uncomprehending anger. "He wasn't supposed to burn the house down around me!"

Chase didn't turn back to face her. "Damn it, I know that," he shouted in terse reply.

However sharp his tone, he knew he couldn't blame her for her anger. The guilt returned, a suffocating blanket, even stronger this time. He had thought he'd worked it all out, thought he'd anticipated Pickering's every move. But it was only too obvious that he'd been wrong.

He'd known that Pickering wouldn't leave Delia alive once she'd given him the paintings. That was why he'd had her play out the little drama with the pistol. By having her force Pickering's hand, he'd thought he'd be able to control the circumstances of the violence. It had seemed simple enough — make Pickering believe he'd killed Delia, and then she'd be safe.

It had all been straightforward enough — arrange matters so that Pickering was maneuvered into shooting Delia with her own pistol, one Chase had conveniently loaded beforehand with blanks. But in his own blind arrogance, Chase had forgotten that plans sometimes don't work out entirely as they were conceived. Pickering hadn't just walked away and left Delia's body as he had left Cotter's. Instead, he'd decided to destroy it by burning the house down around it.

Chase swore at himself as he continued to beat at the flames, calling himself a fool and far worse for not having foreseen what Pickering was capable of doing. But the recriminations were of as little good as were his efforts with the fire. The blaze was spreading despite his furious attack on it, the old wood and fabric of the furniture picking up the flames even more quickly than the dry wood of the aged paneling on the walls.

Delia watched him through dull eyes for a long moment, but managed to slowly claw her way out of the daze. It was no good hiding from reality, she realized, no good crawling into some little corner of

311

her mind and refusing to see what was happening around her. As much as she might wish to pretend that she was safe and everything had gone as they had planned, she couldn't simply close her mind to escape from the blaze.

Rather than leaving, as Chase had insisted, she followed his lead, grabbing up a small, threadworn Turkish rug and using it to slap angrily at the insistent flames. The smoke had begun to sting her eyes, releasing a flood of tears to stream unheeded down her grit-smeared face. She began coughing, choking on the haze of smoke that now filled the room.

The rug Chase had been using to beat the flames had begun to smolder. It was no good, he realized. The blaze was spreading too fast for them to hope to contain it. He glanced around and realized their path to the front door was slowly being appropriated by the blaze. The thin line of flames begun by the stream of oil falling from the lamp Pickering had thrown was growing steadily. The lintel of the door was already beginning to burn, and Chase knew it wouldn't last much longer.

He dropped the smoldering rug just as it burst into flames. He was, he realized, dripping with perspiration. The room was hot, too hot. He could barely breathe. They had to leave before they were smothered by smoke.

He turned to Delia and grabbed her arm.

"We can't stop this," he told her. "We have to get out of here."

She jerked herself free of his grasp.

"I will not leave Papa's house!" she shouted in angry reply.

She was furious that he'd even suggest leaving. Ignoring him, she turned her back to him and began to beat at the licks of fire rising from the smoldering sofa. It was as though it was Pickering she was attacking, the vehemence of her anger erupting as she slapped furiously at the flames.

One look at her expression was enough to make Chase think she was willing to go on uselessly fighting the fire until the house collapsed around her.

"Delia, it's no good," he shouted at her.

"Go if you want," she replied without looking up at him.

Chase darted a second glance at the door to the room and saw the flames had now completely engulfed the lintel. A few minutes more and it would collapse. There was no more time to try to reason with her. They had to leave before they were swallowed by the blaze.

He grabbed her arms, forcing her to drop the rug. This time when she tried to pull away, he refused to release her.

"We have to go," he told her. "Now."

Delia didn't have the chance to argue. As though it was intended to punctuate Chase's words, the lintel broke with a loud *crack*. Delia turned to it just in time to watch it fall. It seemed to hang suspended in midair for an endless moment, the flames rising from it like a host of hungry mouths reaching to the walls before it finally shuddered and dropped. A shower of sparks flew into the air then drifted back downward to start tiny new blazes as they touched the wooden floor.

A thick wave of nausea filled Delia's stomach as she realized their way to the door was now completely blocked.

She swallowed, her throat dull and scratchy with smoke but not so insensitive as to obliterate the taste of remorse. The house contained the last vestiges of the whole of her life, all she had left, and it was burning down around her. She was lost and disoriented, and all she could think was that it was unfair, all of it, everything that had happened since the moment that afternoon an endless lifetime before when she'd watched Matthew Pickering step past her front door and into the street.

"Now, Delia," Chase said again, giving her no more time to think.

This time she was too dazed to argue. When he tugged at her arm, she followed him, letting him lead her to the window. Limp and compliant, she let him lift her and drop her out to the damp thicket of overgrown hedges in the bed beneath the window. She stood stock still and slightly stunned, inhaling the clean scents of greenery and damp soil as Chase dropped down beside her.

The air seemed clean to her only for a moment, in contrast to the smoke-thickened air she'd left behind. After she'd taken a few breaths, she realized it, too, was tainted and thick with the scent of smoke.

She turned then and stared in at the blaze in the room they'd just vacated. She could feel the heat in the air start to roil out into the cool night as though pursuing her. It seemed an omen of evil, a promise that she could not escape, no matter how or where she might run.

As it swept by her, the heat seemed to become more intense. She knew that it would soon be unsafe to stand even there outside the room. The flames were beginning to eat at the walls and one of the windows further along burst outward in a sharp thunder of deadly shards as the heat shattered the glass. Still she couldn't move away. Her limbs felt dead, as though she had no control of them. All she could do was stand there and stare at the growing, voracious line of flames.

Chase needed only a glance at her dull expression to know that talk was useless now. He reached out for her, and lifted her in his arms. At least she wasn't fighting him any longer, he thought as he began to tramp through the tangled, overgrown line of shrubbery. He knew she was still staring back at the house, watching in horrified fascination as the flames engulfed the walls and began quickly to rise up to the second story.

He worked his way though the jungle of growth of the untended garden, skirting the steaming bricks of the house's side wall. By the time he had carried Delia through the alleyway at the far side of the house and out to the street, the blaze had fully engulfed the structure. The light of the flames brightened the street, lighting it enough to make it seem nearly as bright as day. The sound of the roof shingles burning was unnaturally loud, the crackle and hiss an ugly, dissonant accompaniment to the destruction.

The usually quiet Rue St. Clodoald had quickly filled with activity. A pump truck had already arrived and the firemen set about their business with a remote, businesslike attitude that seemed entirely out of place after the drama of the previous hour. A swelling crowd, drawn by the spectacle, stood at the far side of the street, staring up at the fire. Their faces were filled with an awed curiosity that overlaid expressions of stifled pleasure at the unexpected diversion and a hint of relief that it was not their homes they were watching burn to the ground.

"Get out of the way," one firefighter shouted at Chase, and pushed him aside as he ran to man the forward hose from the pump.

Chase silently complied. He carried the still silent Delia across the street and then to the far edge of the crowd.

He set her down on the front steps of a house, then knelt beside her. She still seemed dazed, as though she couldn't quite understand what was happening, despite the fact that she continued to stare at

315

the fire with a rapt, unwavering attention.

He put his hands on her cheeks.

"Delia, Delia, can you hear me?" he asked her softly.

Her eyes seemed reluctant to leave the sight of the fire, but finally she tore them away. Her expression grew slightly muddled for an instant, as though she didn't quite recognize him, before it cleared and she finally looked up to meet his gaze.

"He wasn't supposed to do that," she murmured, her voice thick with a buried sob that threatened to choke her. "You didn't say he'd do that."

"No," Chase agreed. "He wasn't supposed to do that."

"I did exactly what you told me to do," she went on, her words still slightly befuddled, distant, as though she was trying in her mind to find that point when it had gone wrong, when she'd missed a cue and sent the whole course of events racing along the wrong path. "You didn't say he'd burn the house."

"No," Chase admitted. "I didn't think of that."

But he should have, he told himself, and the knowledge was followed by an agonizing stab of his conscience. He had flattered himself that he knew Pickering, that he could anticipate the way the man thought. And he had known that Pickering was careful, that he wouldn't leave Delia alive. Then why hadn't he realized that a careful man wouldn't want to leave a body behind, even if there was no obvious connection between himself and the murdered woman? Why hadn't he thought that a careful man would want to dispose of the body by burning it? He ought to have realized that Pickering would do precisely what he'd done. There was no way he could avoid both the guilt he felt and the blame he knew she directed at him.

He had done, he realized, just what he'd sworn he wouldn't do, lost his objectivity because of his feelings for Delia, and let himself be ruled by his own wishful thoughts rather than logic. That mistake had cost her her home, and might even have cost her her life.

Luckily he retained enough control to realize there was no time for nursing regrets, at least not just now.

He looked up at the crowd, scanning the faces that seemed so rapt in contemplation of the flames. There were more people than there had been only a few minutes before. The group of spectators was still steadily growing.

Anyone might be there, an inner voice shouted urgently to him. Anyone might still come. If Delia were seen alive, if Pickering were to return to watch the fire and spot her, then the whole charade would have been for nothing.

And the next time Pickering tried to kill her, if there was a next time, he'd make sure he didn't fail.

"Delia," he told her, "we have to get out of here before we're seen."

She stared up at him, recognizing the urgency not from his words but from the concern she saw in his eyes. Out of the muddle of her confused thoughts, one thing became terribly clear to her.

"Pickering?" she murmured.

She didn't need his nodded response to know that now that she was supposed to be dead, she had to stay that way. If she was to remain safe, Pickering had to think he'd succeeded in killing her. She couldn't be seen rising phoenix-like from the flames.

When Chase put his arm around her, she let him help her to her feet, wanting now only to get away from the sight of the flames, to stop thinking about what had happened.

Chase darted a glance at her bloodstained blouse and shuddered slightly. It looked all too sickeningly real. He was, he thought for an instant, staring at her dead body.

He quickly removed his jacket and wrapped it around her to hide the hideous stains. Then they both turned their backs to the fire and started to walk toward the Rue Saint Jacques.

Chase turned the room key in the lock, then pushed the door open. He stood aside to let Delia pass.

She walked into the room, and as she did she couldn't help but think of the last time she'd entered that hotel room, couldn't help but remember how determined she'd been that night, how completely sure of herself. She'd been so certain that she was going to vanquish the man who'd killed her father, that she was going to watch him forced to face justice for his act. She no longer felt determined or in the least sure of herself. At that moment she felt only empty and lost. And a sick feeling was beginning to grow inside her, a horrible doubt about whether she and Chase would succeed. She found herself wondering if perhaps Matthew Pickering was indestructible, if it was possible that he would never be caught.

She stared into the shadows that filled the corners and realized that she was afraid of what that darkness might be hiding from her. Her whole life through she'd never really been afraid, she realized, not until Cotter's death. And now every shadow, every sound seemed to fill her with terror.

Chase knew immediately from her expression just what she was thinking. He gave her arm a reassuring little squeeze.

318

"Let me turn up the lamps," he told her.

She let his jacket fall to the floor and stood staring dully at the fire that had been laid ready to be lit in the hearth while he turned up the wicks in the lamps. When the room was filled with light, she turned to face him, and as she did, she caught sight of her own reflection in the mirror on the far wall.

A small, inadvertent cry escaped her.

She couldn't take her eyes from her reflection, couldn't move it from the sight of the gruesome red stain that nearly covered the front of her blouse. She felt a shudder pass through her as she stood and stared at what might have been her own corpse.

Chase crossed the room to her and put his hands on her shoulders, forcing her to turn away.

"It's cow's blood, Delia," he reminded her. "It doesn't mean anything."

She nodded, but the dull, dazed feeling was returning, and she didn't have enough strength left to fight it off.

"I'll see to a hot bath for you," he suggested. "You'll feel better when you're clean. And then you can sleep. You haven't really slept in days."

She nodded again, recognizing the logic of his suggestion.

"Yes," she murmured, "it would be good to sleep."

He stared at her a moment, not at all sure if it was wise to leave her alone just then, then finally decided she was in no immediate danger and needed to be done with the last vestiges of the evening's events far more than she needed his company. He turned to the bathroom. Delia watched him leave, then sighed and shrugged, silently repeating to herself what she'd told him, that it would be good to sleep.

She put her hands on the buttons of her blouse and began to unfasten them. The feel of them was sticky, unpleasant, and she had to clear her mind to

319

keep from thinking what it was that had caused the feeling. Her fingers moved as though of their own volition. When she'd pulled off the filthy blouse, she lifted it close to her face and stood staring at the dull red stains for a long moment. Such an alien thing, she thought, blood, fascinating yet frightening. A disgusted shudder passed through her. She dropped the blouse to the floor.

She stripped off the remainder of her clothing methodically, her motions indifferent. It was only when she stood in nothing but her shift that she shook herself into some semblance of interest and stared down at the broken cow's bladder she'd tied beneath her breasts.

It had worked, just as Chase had promised. All she'd had to do was press against it, a single sharp pressure breaking open the line he'd cut almost all the way through, and the blood spilled out just as her own might have, had the pistol contained real bullets and not the blanks with which Chase had loaded it.

She shuddered again, remembering the feel of it as the blood seeped out and spread against her skin.

Such an ingenious deception. Yet it hadn't been enough to make Pickering simply turn and walk away. And if this part of Chase's plan had gone wrong, how much of the rest would? Perhaps Pickering really *was* indestructible. Perhaps in the end all she would gain for everything she'd lost would be a real bullet to the heart.

It had worked just as Chase had said it would, and yet she stood naked and homeless and thoroughly sickened by the smell of the blood. And afraid. She had watched herself be shot, had witnessed her own murder, and somehow Pickering's act in firing that pistol had changed her in a way she found impossible to understand.

320

She had to force her hands to untie the ribbons that held the bladder, because the last thing she wanted to touch was more blood. She looked at herself in the mirror again, at the white linen shift with its dark red stain, then at the smears on her hands. The sight of it made her sick with disgust.

"It is as it has to be," she said aloud, startled by the sound of her own voice, even more startled by the realization that her feeling of loss was slowly ebbing, that the determination was somehow starting to return. If she was to be left with nothing else, she told herself, even if it meant trading her own life to see it, she would never give up. One way or another, Pickering would pay for her father's death.

Chase heard her and appeared in the doorway.

"Delia?" he asked. "Are you all right?"

She laughed suddenly, a bitter, sharp little laugh.

"I'm fine," she replied. She looked up at him, letting her eyes find his, forcing her jaw forward. "I'm just fine."

She untied the ribbons that held the bladder and dropped it onto the pile of the rest of her ruined clothing. Then she pulled off the filthy shift and added it to the heap. Completely naked now, she marched past the disgusting pile, refusing to look down at it, and entered the bathroom, edging her way past Chase without offering him so much as a glance.

Chase silently watched her climb into the steaming tub, watched as she lowered her body into the thick cloud of scented bubbles. He felt his belly tie itself into a painful knot and knew that it was want of her that caused the ache inside him. He'd spent the previous weeks so close to her, and in all that time he'd felt her slipping away from him, growing more and more distant with each day that passed. For a few moments that evening she'd been completely dependent on him, and the recognition of that need had loosened the control to which he'd so carefully clung. He realized that he'd allowed himself to feel again all those emotions he'd been forced to keep at bay.

Now, however, as she walked resolutely past him, as he felt the sharp urgings of desire welling up inside him, he realized she was more completely clothed in her nakedness than she had been in all those days they'd spent at arms' length. The shock and despair seemed to have been filtered away, and once again he saw in her eyes a hint of that formidable determination he'd come to know only too well.

He stared at her naked body and knew she was swathed in a coat as impenetrable as any chainmail armor.

He watched her as she carefully wiped away the tiny smudges of red that her hands had left on the white porcelain sides of the tub as though she were obliterating every bit of evidence of what had happened that evening. That task completed to her satisfaction, she began to carefully scrub, washing away the dark smears that had leaked through her shift onto her midriff and down her belly. She was completely oblivious of him, intent on the task, like a child who has been warned there will be no dessert if he doesn't take exceptional care in his bath.

He wanted to stay there, to do nothing more than watch her, to stare at the warm droplets of steam that slid down her cheeks and arms, at the thick, damp tendrils of her hair that clung to her wet skin, at the way her soapy hands slid over wet skin. He wanted to let the ache inside him grow until he didn't care what it might goad him to do. He envisioned himself going to her, dipping his hands into that warm, soapy water and pressing them against her flesh.

But he knew that that was folly, that the rift between them would never be healed if he stormed at her defenses. He knew she had to come to him. If not, she would never trust him.

Delia finished washing and dropped the soap into its dish. Then she gave her body a careful survey, satisfying herself that no more blood remained anywhere on her body. Once it was done, she realized just how exhausted she was. Weariness seemed to overtake her, and she lay her head against the porcelain back of the tub and closed her eyes. The hot water tugged at her, a soothing sedative, urging her to let go, to sleep.

"I'll dispose of your clothing," Chase said suddenly, his voice sharp as he decided he could endure the torture of watching her no more. He turned his back on her, the act a real effort of his will.

"Yes," she murmured in reply. "Let's dispose of the last of the evidence. Just as you planned. Make Pickering think I'm dead. Have a nice place to hide all ready, fresh clean clothes, nothing lacking." She opened her eyes and leaned forward, staring now at his back. The exhaustion seemed secondary now, outweighed by a sudden burst of anger with him. "Only it went wrong, didn't it?" she shouted. She began to tremble and had to put her hands on the side of the tub to keep herself steady. "Can you tell me how much more of it will go wrong?"

Chase turned on his heel, facing her again, immediately finding a welled-up anger that he'd buried but not quite lost during the previous weeks. He ought to feel guilt, he told himself, ought to feel responsible. Only this time, he didn't.

He crossed the half dozen steps that divided them and stared down at her, his anger flaring up to match hers. He leaned forward to her, his face close to hers, his eyes holding hers.

"Damn it, you wanted this," he hissed at her. "You wouldn't let me do it without you. And you wouldn't let me send you away. Whether you care to be reminded or not, you were going to see Pickering punished, with or without my help."

Delia drew back and looked away, intimidated by his anger.

"I'm the one who's lost everything," she murmured.

He put his hand on her cheek and forced her to face him again.

"I told you Pickering was dangerous, but you didn't believe me," he went on. "And now that you see what can happen, you decide you don't like it. Well, I warned you. You made your decisions, Delia. Now grow up and learn to live with them."

As soon as he'd spoken the words he regretted them, wished he could call them back. They'd hurt her, and the last thing he wanted to do was add to the pain he knew she already felt. He forced himself to dismiss the regret, telling himself that he might have sworn to protect her, but that no one could or should protect her from herself.

Delia stared up at him, startled at the way he seemed determined to hurt her, to make her feel the weight of a responsibility she told herself ought to be his. But he returned the stare, his eyes unwavering, and she knew suddenly that what he'd said was true.

She *had* forced him to include her, despite the fact that he had made it clear to her that it had been against his wishes. And he'd endured her ill humor wordlessly, calmly putting up with her constant needling without rising to the bait, maintaining the calm he realized she needed if she was to complete the work on the paintings. Without him, she'd have been lost. Worse, she'd probably be dead.

It was time, she told herself, that she stopped blaming him and started accepting her own responsibility for what had happened with Pickering. If she was homeless, it was far more her own fault than Chase's. She could have turned her back on Pickering and let Chase go after him alone, as he'd wanted. But she'd chosen not to do that, stubbornly pushing her way where she knew she didn't belong.

She'd chosen; no one had forced her. She'd made her own decisions, and now she must learn to live with them.

Just as she must learn to live with Cotter's death. She'd been running away from that as much as anything else. In fact, she realized she had refused to face just about every reality since her father's death, save for her determination to see Pickering imprisoned. She'd turned her back on everything except her thirst for revenge.

And more than anything else, she'd refused to accept the simple truth that she was completely, endlessly, achingly in love with Chase Sutton.

At that moment something seemed to melt inside her, something hard and ungiving that she'd been nurturing while she told herself that she had to be strong and independent, that she had to keep herself from being hurt any more. She realized there was no escape from hurt, that by trying to seal herself off from it, she'd only succeeded in burying the pain deeper inside, in a place where it could only grow more painful with time.

"Oh, Chase!"

The words seemed to have been torn from her, a soft, urgent sob. She reached her arms up to him, not sure where she was going, but knowing that sometimes a foolish step is the first foothold on reality. She put her hands on the back of his neck and pulled him close so that his lips met hers.

Chase wrapped his arms around her, pulling her body to his, lifting her out of the warm water of the tub. The anger was gone, forgotten, and he was more than willing to dismiss it as the passion he'd not quite managed to subdue surged through him.

The touch of her lips released a painful constriction that had been slowly enveloping him since the night she'd first begun work on Pickering's forgeries. He was not so great a fool as to think everything was suddenly and totally mended between them. But he did hope that she would give him the chance to bridge the chasm that had grown between them, to tell her, if not in words, then with his body, what he felt for her.

He lifted her in his arms, oblivious to the fact that she was still dripping and slick with suds, giving as little thought to the fact that his shirt was now sodden where her body touched it. Her skin felt smooth and sleek beneath his hands, and all he wanted was to feel it once again pressed close to his own.

He carried her back to the bedroom and lay her down on the bed, following her, pressing his lips to hers, and then to her neck and breasts and belly. He wanted to touch every inch of her body, to feel her, to know her in such minute detail that there would be no part of her that would remain a mystery to him.

Delia had never felt like this before, never felt this pounding, insistent, yearning void within her, a void she knew only he could fill. She was alone now, she knew that in a visceral way that had had no meaning before that moment. The house was gone, and with it, Cotter's ghost, that insistent, nagging shadow that had seemed to hover constantly just at the edge of her line of vision. The loss struck her as something painful, and perhaps, she thought, it was the acceptance of that loss that generated this burning need inside her. Perhaps it was best that way, perhaps it was best to know she had obligations to herself as well as to her father's memory.

She pushed at Chase's clothing, tearing the buttons of his shirt in her haste to have him come to her. He needed no urging, pulling away from her for only one regretful moment as he sloughed off the damp, rumpled shirt and trousers.

And when he lowered himself once more to her, she reached up to him, her arms welcoming.

"Love me, Chase," she whispered, her words hoarse with yearning as she pulled him to her. "Just love me."

Chapter Eighteen

Delia put down the copy of the *Paris Gazette* that she'd been reading. It had seemed wonderfully decadent to her, to rise from bed and find her coffee poured, the paper set beside the cup, and an impressively sturdy breakfast ready and beckoning without her having to wash, dress, and make a morning pilgrimage to the corner *boulangerie*. But now that she'd had the opportunity to scan the paper, and one article in particular, she wasn't at all sure she was quite so thankful a recipient of the luxuries that were being so lavishly squandered on her.

She lifted her cup of *café au lait* and sipped it meditatively as she read the article for the fourth time. Then she pushed the paper across the small table to Chase.

He glanced at her expression before he accepted the gift.

"Anything wrong, Delia?"

"There's something you might find interesting," she replied slowly, trying her best to sound vaguely disinterested, taking pains to pretend she had nothing whatsoever to do with the subject of the article that had so disconcerted her.

Chase stared at the open page, quickly scanning the article that outlined the events of the preceding evening at the Rue St. Clodoald. Decimating blazes were certainly not a rarity in any large city, and Parisian buildings in the older sections of town were especially vulnerable to fires. A blaze that so totally destroyed a structure as the one that had claimed Delia's home was, however, obviously considered newsworthy.

Chase read the whole of the article before he looked up at her.

"It must be strange to read that you're presumed dead," he told her softly.

"More than strange," she admitted.

It was really a good deal worse than strange, she thought. It made her feel much as she had felt the night before when she'd seen her reflection in the mirror. It had been horrifying to see herself covered in blood, like looking at her own corpse. Reading that she was considered officially dead despite the fact that her body was yet to be found in the still smoldering ashes of her house was certainly no more pleasant a sensation. She felt disoriented, as though the world had somehow gone just a bit off kilter.

She began to wonder if she might have become mad in the preceding weeks, if Cotter's death hadn't been enough to make her so disoriented that she was imagining everything that had happened since. Certainly her life had become too impossibly fantastic to be real. Perhaps it was all some horrible nightmare. Perhaps if she waited long enough she'd waken from it and escape.

"Luckily, the papers sometimes lie," Chase said, interrupting her thoughts and making her realize that it was all real, that she hadn't imagined a thing. "I can assure you, Delia, you are most definitely alive."

Delia looked up at him. He was smiling faintly, his expression just slightly lecherous. She felt herself blush, aware he was referring to the quite uncorpselike way she'd acted in the preceding twelve hours. He reached out and grasped her hand across the table, and the lechery in his eyes disappeared to be replaced by a friendly, protective tenderness. She realized he was making an effort to reassure her that everything really wasn't as bad as it might seem.

"At least Pickering should be convinced," she told him with a game smile. "If my death is announced for all Paris to read, he won't give a thought to coming round and looking through the ashes for the corpse, just to make sure, now, will he?"

"As he believes he shot you first, I have no doubt but that he'll leave that particularly gruesome task to the officials charged with such duties," Chase agreed.

She pointed to the article. "It says it's still smoldering," she added thoughtfully, "that the fire must have been fed by the solvents in Papa's studio."

He nodded. "By the time the ashes are cool enough to be searched, Pickering and the paintings will be well on their way to London. He should be completely convinced he no longer has anything to fear from you. In fact, he should think himself completely safe. Which means that once he's left Paris, you need have no further concerns about him."

Chase had to admit that despite the unpleasant surprise Pickering had given them when he'd set the fire, as far as his plan was concerned, matters were progressing nicely. All he had to do now was keep Delia hidden away for a few days, and she would have nothing further to fear from the art thief. Moreover, she seemed to be accepting all this quite calmly now. Of course, once she had time to think, she'd probably panic again when she considered the fact that she was now homeless. But that, he thought with an inward grin, might work to his advantage. At least he hoped it would. In the meantime, it was best to simply let matters lie.

He gazed at her thoughtfully for a long moment and found he more than liked what he saw. Her face was smooth, and even the dark shadows under her eyes, which had seemed permanently etched there as the weeks of work on the forgeries had progressed, had begun to fade. For the first time in weeks she seemed calm, far more relaxed than he'd have expected after all the tension and worry. He wondered if that condition stemmed, at least in part, from their exertions the previous night and that morning.

Or perhaps, he told himself ruefully, it had nothing at all to do with their lovemaking. Perhaps it was simply due to the fact that the fear was gone, now that the worst of it was all over for her, now that she no longer had to consider herself a target for Matthew Pickering. The interpretation was a good deal less flattering to his masculine pride, and he decided to dismiss it.

He told himself there was every reason to think the tense, irritable creature might return before long, however. Sooner or later he would have to tell Delia that he intended to keep her totally incommunicado for the three days until the paintings bound for the London exhibit, and presumably Pickering as well, left Paris. As much as he might wish it were otherwise, he could not keep her occupied with lovemaking for the whole of that time. And he was under no delusion she might find the news that she was to be under virtual house arrest to her liking.

Best to leave that little piece of unwanted news until later, he thought, and enjoy this small calm before the inevitable storm it would precipitate.

Delia leaned across the table to scan the last few lines of the article one more time.

"Did you read that?" she asked, and pointed to the last paragraph.

Chase felt a twinge and with it a premonition that he wasn't going to like what was about to follow.

"It would seem there's to be a memorial service for you tomorrow," he murmured.

She nodded. "Claude and Pierre's doing, I suppose," she said. She grinned suddenly, apparently delighted at the prospect. "I can't wait to see who comes to say a few words in my memory."

Chase groaned inwardly, told himself that he had to have been deranged to think there might be a day or two without fireworks between the two of them, then nodded.

"Shame you'll have to miss it," he told her.

Delia dropped her cup into its saucer. Some of it sloshed out and propelled itself over the rim of the saucer and onto the white linen cloth, but she didn't even notice.

"I have absolutely no intention of missing it," she insisted. "I can't let them go on thinking I'm dead."

"That was the general idea, Delia," he reminded her. "You're supposed to be dead. Or have you forgotten? You're only safe as long as Pickering thinks he's already killed you."

She shrugged, dismissing his argument. "But that has nothing to do with Claude or Pierre," she insisted. "I can't let *them* think I'm dead. That would be cruel."

"You don't have any choice," he told her, his tone sharp and commanding. "As far as the world is concerned, Delia Hampton died in that fire last night. If your friends choose to honor your memory, so much the better. And a tear or two shed in the course of the event is more than welcome. It makes your death that much more convincing."

She pulled her hand away from his.

"You aren't serious," she insisted.

"I most certainly am," he replied.

She shook her head. "Well, I don't care what you say. I intend to go and tell them I'm not dead."

Chase glowered at her. "And tell Matthew Picker-

332

ing at the same time," he said. "Why don't you just send him a personal note? While you're at it, you might add the name and room number of the hotel. That way he'll be able to come after you at his leisure."

"Claude and Pierre won't tell Pickering anything," she insisted. "They have no reason not to keep a secret if I ask them to. Besides, they don't even know who Pickering is."

"And what if he decides to pay his respects?" Chase demanded. "He's arrogant enough to go to his victim's funeral."

Delia thought for a moment. He was right, and she knew it. Still, it seemed cruel to her to have people mourn her when there was no need.

"I can wear a dark veil," she suggested. "People wear dark veils on such occasions. No one will notice me."

"People don't usually have to avoid the man who thinks he's murdered them," Chase countered. "And don't underestimate Pickering. He's capable of a great deal more than you think."

"And apparently a great deal more than you, even with your touted knowledge of him, think," she shot back. "You didn't anticipate he'd set the fire."

"Damn it," he hissed angrily, "no, I didn't. All the more reason to be wary of him. There's no reason on earth to take the risk of going to that service."

"There is," she insisted.

"For God's sake, what?"

She paused for a moment, wondering just why she was so determined. Then it struck her, the image of Pierre's face as he'd looked the last time she'd seen him, standing on her doorstep, staring at her in disbelief when he saw Chase there with her.

"I owe something to Pierre," she said softly.

She did, she realized. It was an obligation she'd incurred the night he'd come to her house. She'd hurt him then, and now it pained her to think that she was hurting him again.

"Really?" Chase asked. "Just what is it you owe him that would make you want to risk your life to tell him you're alive?"

He stared at her, watching the way she turned her glance away from his as though the prospect of answering made her uncomfortable.

"I owe him the kindness of not causing him anymore pain," she shot back, suddenly angry with him, hating him for forcing her to defend herself. "But then, kindness isn't something you'd know about, is it? You know about the sort of motives a man like Pickering has, motives that can be translated into coin of the realm, but simple kindness doesn't work that way, does it?"

She regretted the words almost as soon as they were out of her mouth, for she was more than aware that Chase could be kind. But she didn't try to apologize for them, or say she hadn't meant them. Her life had fallen into a shambles from the moment he'd entered it. When the time came for him to leave, she knew she'd have nothing left. He had no right to question what she knew she must do to salvage what little was left to her. It might not be right, but some part of her wanted to hurt him, to make him pay for the hurt he would leave behind in her when he left. As petty as that feeling was, still she couldn't completely rid herself of it.

But Delia had no idea of the effects her defense of Pierre engendered in Chase. His eyes narrowed and he felt a wave of jealousy wash over him and leave him with a thick knot in his belly. Her mention of Pierre had set loose a monster inside him, and he couldn't ignore the unpleasant things it was whispering to him.

"Unless you forgot to mention that you're in love with him?" he said angrily.

Delia was shocked by his suggestion. It wasn't love for Pierre that was driving her. Whatever it was she felt for the young artist, it was far closer to pity than love. How much easier it would be for her if she were in love with Pierre, how much less painful to know that the man she loved cared for her as she now realized Pierre cared for her. But instead of loving Pierre, she loved Chase, and Chase, she was only too painfully aware, cared only for his own interests. She might be a temporary part of his life, but she wasn't so great a fool as to allow herself to think she was anything more than temporary.

Then why his unexpected show of jealousy? she wondered. Unless, she thought, it simply piqued his pride to think he wasn't the sole proprietor of his temporary conquest.

And now she was furious with him. He had no right to question her about Pierre or anyone else. He had no rights with regard to her whatsoever. And if his masculine pride made him think he did, he was wrong.

"I haven't forgotten to mention anything," she hissed. "And what I feel for Pierre—or anyone else, for that matter—is none of your affair. The only thing that is of your concern is making sure we send Matthew Pickering to prison."

The knot in Chase's belly tightened. He'd been a fool to think that she might have left Cotter's ghost back in the ashes of the house on the Rue St. Clodoald. And he was an even greater fool to think he'd ever be able to find his way past the walls she didn't even realize that ghost was building around her.

Cotter's ghost and her French puppy were pushing their way between the two of them, and what hurt him the most was that she seemed only too content to let it happen.

He stood and dropped his napkin onto the table.

"You are, as ever, quite right, Miss Hampton," he

told her. "And to that end, I have work to do. In the meantime, you will occupy yourself here."

She arched her brow as she looked up at him.

"Am I to suppose you consider yourself my lord and master and those are orders?"

Her tone was taunting, and he couldn't miss it. She was pushing him away with both hands. Now that they were finally close to catching Matthew Pickering, she seemed determined to let him know she no longer needed him.

"You can consider whatever you damn well please," he replied. "But if you want to live long enough to see Pickering punished, you'll do as I tell you."

He stalked past her, picking up his jacket from the chair where he'd dropped it before breakfast and pulling it on as he walked to the door.

Delia made no attempt to stop him. Nor did she so much as turn to watch him leave. But she couldn't help but be aware of his angry departure. He slammed the door so hard on his way out that the walls fairly shook and her cup shivered noisily in its saucer.

It had been a tense evening and an even worse morning. Delia was heartily pleased that she'd managed to weather them without initiating yet another unpleasant scene with Chase. The truth was, she was thoroughly tired and bored with being told what to do, and even more tired of his expectation that he had every right to issue edicts to her and expect her to obey them.

But she had managed to hold her tongue. Despite the fact that she found living in the same few rooms with a man she wasn't speaking to harder than she'd ever imagined, the long, painful hours had passed without further incident. Not that it had been easy. Keeping her intentions from him, even though they weren't talking, had been an exercise in control. She'd been on edge all morning, waiting for him to finally decide it was time for him to leave and be about the task he'd supposedly come to Paris to do, oversee the shipment of paintings to London.

And now, she hoped she wasn't too late. She had a distinct impression Chase had purposely stayed with her as long as he had just to make certain she'd given up the idea of going to the memorial service. Logic told her that he should have gone off to the museum to oversee the crating of the paintings early in the morning, as he had done the previous day. Logic, however, at least what Delia deemed logic, seemed to have little to do with the workings of Chase Sutton's mind.

But now she was free. She realized that spending the previous afternoon alone indoors, followed by an evening and morning taking pains to ignore Chase, only served to increase the pleasure she felt to be outdoors amid the pleasantly noisy bustle of a Parisian street. It was an incredibly beautiful afternoon, the sky brilliantly clear without so much as a hint of a cloud, the air warm and brightly sunny with just enough breeze to keep it from becoming uncomfortable. In short, it was the sort of spring afternoon that was all too rare in Paris, and the more intensely embraced because of its rarity.

It occurred to her that she couldn't possibly have asked for a more pleasant afternoon on which to hold her funeral.

She didn't linger on the street, despite the glory of the day, but instead hailed a cab quickly, wary of those around her. She climbed inside, not feeling comfortable until she was safely hidden. Once she'd recognized it, she found herself considering the uneasiness she'd been unable to shake during the previous weeks, wondering why she could not shake it. She asked herself where her innocence had gone.

Over and over, she told herself that she had nothing to fear any longer, that she ought to be able to regain her former sense of ease and feel carefree once again on the streets of a city that had always been beautiful and nurturing to her. The words didn't change how she felt, however, and she realized she was unable to dismiss completely Chase's warnings as overly cautious nonsense. Not that Pickering would be likely to come searching for her, she assured herself. Even if he wasn't completely convinced he'd killed her, still he'd have no way of finding her. The chance that he might have come to this particular street out of all those in Paris at the precise moment she appeared was so slim as to be ridiculous.

Still, the preceding weeks had taught her a measure of caution, if nothing else. She did not like the fact, but she could not entirely dismiss the fears that seemed to have become a permanent part of her life.

She settled back against the dark leather of the seat, darting careful glances at the pedestrians on the street as the cab lurched forward and joined the flow of traffic, searching among the blur of faces for the one she feared to find there.

Pickering, however he might haunt her, was nowhere to be seen. She slowly relaxed and tried to convince herself she was being as foolish as Chase with his misguided cautions. This was her city, she told herself firmly, and she would not allow it to be taken from her along with everything else. She peered out the window, drinking in the sight of the familiar streets as the hansom made its journey through the hectic traffic across the Pont Neuf to the part of the city that had been, until two nights before, her home.

When the hansom came to a halt after the short ride, Delia carefully adjusted her veil, then climbed out. She paid the driver and then, feeling unpleasantly exposed, walked quickly into the small church.

It was dim and cool inside, and the service had already begun. Delia scanned the small crowd in the pews, surprised to see how many people had come. An excellent turnout, she thought with an amused sense of smug satisfaction, noting the dozens of street artists, the hawkers of books and flowers who had so often shared with her the walk at the edge of the small park to sell their wares, and the neighbors from Rue St. Clodoald who had come to bid her a final farewell. Perhaps she wasn't quite so alone or unloved as she had supposed, after all.

She silently took a seat in a pew to the rear, feeling an odd sense of merriment at the bizarre circumstances. It wasn't long, however, before her amusement vanished. The hard seat and Père Alphonse's droning voice were more than enough to sober her.

She began to make a slow survey of the occupants of the pews in front of her, looking at their profiles when they turned to whisper to a neighbor, telling herself it was merely a professional interest, that of a maker of silhouettes. But even as she rationalized her interest to herself, she realized there was a darker reason pushing her: she knew she was really looking for one particular face among the mourners. But when she did not immediately see him, she relaxed and began to plot how she would make the unlikely announcement that she wasn't really dead.

It was strange to her, she realized, to see Pierre and Claude and Henri and the others, ordinarily quite a raucous group, so quiet and subdued. Claude's wife was sniffing softly and dabbing at her eyes with a richly embroidered handkerchief as Père Alphonse spoke in his droning, pedantic way. Delia couldn't help wondering if it was loss that caused the tears, or simply frustration with the monotony of the priest's oration.

Delia decided she might begin to shed a few tears herself if it continued much longer. She fidgeted uncomfortably and told herself she had inherited her father's lack of reverence for Père Alphonse and the ritual of the Church in general. After a few moments, however, she realized that the discomfort wasn't entirely due to the hard wood seat or the dull, droning sound of the priest's voice.

Sitting there and staring at all those slightly bowed heads in front of her was disorienting, and it was making her extremely self-conscious. Delia found herself struck with the sudden desire to stand up and shout that everyone could go home, that the effort they were taking, although kind and appreciated, was wasted.

But the inclination was thoroughly quashed when she saw a man sitting four rows in front of her turn and reply to the whispered words of regret murmured in his ear by the woman seated at his side.

There was no possibility that she could mistake the profile of that hawklike nose. She stiffened, her whole body suddenly taut with fear and surprise.

Unquestionably the man was Matthew Pickering.

She felt as though she had been submerged in ice. Chase had been right, she realized. He'd told her that Pickering was enough of a villain to gloat over the body of his victim. She'd thought he meant only to frighten her, to keep her docile and willing to follow his orders. But he'd been right, and she'd been a fool not to listen.

She should never have come. And now she was doomed to sit there until the end of the service, or until there was some opportunity to get away without calling attention to herself. She began to pray, as fervently as she had ever prayed in her life, that Pickering wouldn't decide to turn around and look at her.

Every move Pickering made left her trembling. If

340

he turned and saw her, he would be able to see through the veil, she told herself. It wouldn't surprise her to learn that he was able to see through a brick wall.

Père Alphonse spoke for perhaps half an hour more, not long, really, but to Delia it was a lifetime. Finally he stood aside, his ponderous body wavering as though he was reluctant to give up this opportunity to instill the good word in a captive flock. Delia breathed a heavy sigh of relief that it was all over and darted a hopeful glance toward the thick old church doors.

She waited, expecting people to begin to stir and make ready to leave. They didn't. Instead, Pierre strode up to the pulpit.

Delia watched his mournful progress, unable to take her eyes off him even to dart a watchful glance at Pickering. With his plain black suit and stiff white collar, Pierre looked more uncomfortable than she had ever seen him. Once in the pulpit, he grasped the carved stone with both hands, steadying himself before he cleared his throat and looked out at the small congregation with wide, sorrowful eyes. Delia amended her evaluation of his state. He wasn't just uncomfortable, she realized. He was openly and unabashedly miserable.

He didn't say much, just a few words about the times they had all spent together, comrades in the arts, trying to make a life in an unsympathetic world. His final words were, "I think I can speak for us all when I say that we will dearly miss her, that we loved her." He paused, and then burst out, his voice loud enough to startle those listening, "I know I loved her."

He hurried down the steps from the pulpit, almost running, nearly tripping in his haste to be away. But he didn't return to his place in the front pew. As though fleeing the sympathetic whispers, he ran down the central aisle and out of the church.

There was a small confusion of talk after that as people turned to one another, voicing their surprise at the unexpected intensity of Pierre's words and his flight. Père Alphonse returned to his place in the pulpit and motioned to the organ loft, gesturing to the organist to play, in hopes that music might calm the unseemly agitation and return his small realm to a more appropriate demeanor.

Taking advantage of the confusion, Delia slipped quickly out the door. The sound of the slightly out-of-tune organ drifted out of the old church after her as though it was following her.

Returning to the brilliant sunlight after the hour inside the dark of the church, she was stunned, for an instant nearly blinded by the brightness. When her vision cleared, she looked around, searching for Pierre, feeling as though she were personally responsible for the misery to which he had given vent in those few moments when he'd spoken.

He wasn't hard to find, a tall, stiff, black clad figure trying to lose himself in the flow of foot traffic, but unable to keep himself from staring dolefully at the cemetery to the far side of the church. He stopped as he approached it and stared through the ornate grillwork of the gate, searching among the tombstones for the burial site of his lost love.

Delia hurried after him, unsure as to what she would say to him, knowing only that she couldn't leave him alone with such a weight of misery burdening him. She knew Chase would be furious with her, worse than furious, for what she was about to do, but she also knew she couldn't do otherwise.

"Pierre," she murmured as she strode up behind him.

He stiffened, his back straightening sharply before he spun around. And then he stood and stared at her, wide-eyed with disbelief, and he slowly began to shake his head as though he were trying to settle whatever had suddenly gone wrong inside it.

"Delia?"

He reached out and touched her, the gesture tentative, almost as though he expected her to disappear before his eyes. Instead, his fingers found a firm arm covered by equally as real black linen. He gasped and pulled his hand away.

"You're dead," he mouthed in a stunned whisper.

Delia grasped his hand in hers.

"Listen to me, Pierre," she told him. "I'm quite real, decidedly alive still. But if you love me, you must not tell anyone."

He shook his head again, then lifted the hand she held and stared at her gloved fingers as though he'd never seen such things before. His eyes narrowed as the meaning of what she'd told him sank into him. He lifted his gaze to find hers.

"Why are you doing this?" he asked her, his voice ragged with hurt. He stared at her with angry accusation in his eyes, implying that what she'd done had had the sole intention of dealing him the aching hurt he'd felt for the previous two days. "The fire. Your neighbor swears he saw you inside, silhouetted by the flames. They said no one came out. But you did." There was a hint of wonder in his tone now, as though her escape had the markings of the supernatural about it. "Why didn't you tell anyone?" he demanded. Then, remembering his own hurt, he added, "How could you let me think you were dead?"

Delia ached with guilt.

"Please, Pierre," she begged softly. "Please believe me. It wasn't meant to hurt you."

He dropped her hand, pulling his own away with a gesture that said only too clearly she'd sinned against him in doing what she had done.

"What was it meant to do?" he demanded.

Delia bit her lower lip before she answered. She could see he wanted an explanation, that he would be satisfied with nothing less, and knew she could give him none.

"I can't tell you, Pierre," she murmured.

It obviously wasn't a sufficient response.

"You let me believe you died, Delia," he said sharply. "You broke my heart, and now you tell me it wasn't real, just a game?" His voice broke and he seemed nearly to choke. "But you can't tell me why," he went on. "Did you tell your Englishman why?" He waited an instant, and when she didn't respond, he grasped her wrists and pulled her close. "He's part of this, isn't he?" he demanded. "It's that damned Englishman who's gotten you into this, this insanity."

"Please, Pierre, you don't understand . . ." Delia began.

"Then make me understand," he broke in. "Tell me what it is you're doing, Delia." The anger leaked away from his features. "If you're in trouble, then let me help you. You know I'd do anything for you."

"There's nothing you can do," she told him softly.

"But there is something the Englishman can do," he suggested, his voice once again growing angry and a bit sly. "He's gotten you into something, and you're so in love with him you're willing to let him use you this way. What is he doing, trying to defraud insurance? Is that what this is about?"

Delia sighed. There was nothing she could tell him, nothing that would make enough sense to satisfy him.

"No, Pierre," she insisted, "it's not like that. He's not using me." She swallowed uncomfortably. Chase *was* using her, of that she was only too painfully aware. Pierre might have the details wrong, but he was also right in many ways, too. "There's just

344

something I have to do, something that must be kept secret."

"And so you pretend to be dead?" he asked sharply. "Why?"

"I can't explain, Pierre," she told him, her voice thick with regret. "If I could, I swear, I would."

"But the Englishman, *he* knows," he shot back. He pulled away from her again, this time making a gesture of dismissal. "Then why are you here?" he demanded. "Why did you speak to me? Why not let me go on thinking you dead?"

She was suddenly confused by the intensity of his anger.

"Because I felt guilty," she murmured. "I saw you were hurt and I felt guilty."

"You should have saved your guilt, Delia," he hissed. "It would have been kinder of you to let me think you dead. That way, I might have gotten over you. I might even have somehow erased from my mind the memory that he was in your house alone with you that night, that you let him touch you."

"I never meant to hurt you, Pierre," she said softly. "Please, believe at least that."

"Go away, Delia," he said as he took a step back, away from her. "Go away and let me bury you again."

If she'd felt guilty and ashamed when she'd first seen Pierre's grief, Delia now felt a hundred times worse. Chase had been right, she realized — she ought never to have come. His reasons had had nothing to do with Pierre, but he'd been right just the same.

Thoughts of Chase reminded her of just how foolishly dangerous her gesture had been.

"You won't tell anyone you've seen me?" she asked him, her voice tentative, regretful, for she hated to ask anything of him now.

He shook his head.

"How could I have seen you when you're dead?" he muttered angrily.

Then he turned on his heel and strode quickly away from her as though he was afraid that any further contact might prove dangerous to him.

Delia watched him for a moment and thought of how clumsy and stupid she'd been, how completely she'd ruined things. It took her a long moment to still the recriminatory voices that were shouting silently at her before she turned and hailed a passing hansom.

If she hurried, she told herself, she still could return to the hotel before Chase did. At least she might salvage the uneasy peace between them. It was all she had left to hope for after a day that was nothing short of disastrous.

Her thoughts were so completely centered on Pierre that Delia didn't notice the tall figure that had emerged from the church and stood staring at her as she climbed into the hansom, then set out after Pierre. If she had, she'd have realized that Chase's warning had been even more prophetic than she'd thought it to be.

Chapter Nineteen

"What the hell are you doing here?"

Delia swallowed uncomfortably. She hadn't been idiot enough to expect Chase to be exactly pleased to see her, but then again, she really hadn't been prepared to face the sort of fury she'd seen in his eyes, fury that was leveled directly at her. The guard apparently saw it, too, for he took advantage of Chase's preoccupation with her to slip back to his post on the platform. There would, she realized, be no help from that front. She'd have to just brave it out alone.

"I presented myself to the guard at the entry of the track platform and told him you were expecting me," she said, taking what she hoped would be the easiest course, outright evasion. "He was most accommodating. He most courteously escorted me to the car."

Actually, she thought, that part had been quite easy, far easier than making her way through the bustle of the Gare Saint-Lazare. In fact, gaining access to what was supposed to be a closed platform and into a car that was supposed to be sealed to find a man who was not supposed to be there had required little more than a few words and a smile.

Chase, however, wasn't the least pleased with her

347

feat. He scowled, balled his right hand into a fist, and before Delia could consider the possibility that he was actually angry enough to consider using it on her, struck the palm of his left.

"Damn it, I'll have to have the fool fired. And as for you, Delia, this is no time for jokes, however amusing," he growled. He fixed a steely glance on her, expecting, she assumed, to intimidate her with it. "What are you doing *here?* I told you to stay in the hotel and out of sight for the next few days, until I sent word that everything was settled."

Delia swallowed again, but she refused to let him cow her, refused even to let that coldly uncompromising stare of his unsettle her. She wasn't about to be sent off like a wayward puppy with her tail between her legs. In fact, she was completely fed up with repentance.

She'd been more than repentant enough about her previous unauthorized outing and her abortive meeting with Pierre, she reminded herself. In fact, she'd been so repentant that she'd spent the previous thirty-six hours being unnaturally accommodating to him. But behaving sweetly had been more than trying, after a day she had already tired of being meek and smiling in response to his every word. She was not about to repeat the act, especially in atonement for something she'd had a perfect right to do.

From the very first she'd been determined to be present when Chase caught Matthew Pickering. That was the reason she'd begun the whole unpleasant episode in the first place, to see Pickering pay for Cotter's death. After everything she'd been through, she had no intention of allowing Chase to cheat her out of that satisfaction now.

That was all she had left, she told herself. After all, there wasn't going to be anything else for her. Her father was dead, her home destroyed, and Chase Sutton would soon be nothing more to her than a painful memory. At least she deserved to see Pickering's expression when he realized he'd finally been caught. It was small enough payment for all she'd lost.

"Yes," she agreed, her tone bright and completely disinterested. "I believe I do recall that you did say something like that."

Her manner, she realized, wasn't exactly endearing her to him.

Chase gritted his teeth.

"Then perhaps you'd care to tell me why you're here, rather than there?"

Here. Delia looked around her as though she wasn't quite sure how to answer. After all, this was hardly what she'd expected.

From the outside, the car, when the guard had brought her to it, had seemed like any freight car, flat-paneled and windowless. But now that she was inside, she realized this was unlike the usual car that carried crates of potatoes and cheap wine from the Continent to England. For one thing, it was divided. The portion she and Chase now stood in was virtually empty, with only the neatly marked crates of paintings against the side walls, securely fastened with special braces to keep them from being jarred loose by the train's motion. The remainder of the section of the car, which was really most of the area, for the crates occupied only a fraction of the space, was comfortably furnished with a table, chairs, and a small sofa, presumably set aside for the guards who were to remain with the valuable shipment throughout its journey. Delia began to wonder if perhaps the arrangements weren't too snugly secure, to wonder if Pickering, once he saw the care that was being taken with the shipment of the paintings, would abandon his plan to make the exchange, at least on this portion of the trip.

"Well?"

Delia started. She had almost forgotten that Chase was staring at her with that inquisitorial look in his eye. The look, though, was hardly enough to shake her resolution to keep him from sending her away. She turned back to him, taking pains to make her expression as determined as his.

"I came here because I intend to see the look on Matthew Pickering's face when you catch him," she told him. "I want him to see me, to know that I helped put him in prison."

Chase sighed and shook his head.

"Delia, we've been over this before," he reminded her. "There's no need for you to put yourself in any further danger. I have a dozen guards on board the train, all with very precise orders. You've done your part. Now let me do mine."

"And I told you," she replied, "that I want Pickering to know that killing Papa was the biggest mistake of his life."

Chase was getting steadily more exasperated. It took a resolute act of will for him to go on with the discussion.

"He will, Delia," he assured her for what he was sure must be the hundredth time. "It will all happen. Pickering will be brought to trial. I'll see to it that you can testify against him to satisfy your need for personal vengeance. But if you're here, if he chances to see you too soon, he's sure to know something's afoot. If that happens, he'll back off and we'll lose him entirely. Haven't you been through too much to chance losing him now?"

"He won't see me," she insisted. "I'll stay out of sight, here with you. He won't see me until it's too late."

"Damn it, Delia, you'll just be underfoot here."

"Then you can walk around me," she snapped.

Chase gritted his teeth. "I don't want you here," he hissed.

350

"And I don't give a damn what you do or don't want," she retorted.

Chase released a thick sigh of resignation. He wasn't happy about what he was going to have to do, but he realized she wasn't giving him much choice.

"You don't give up, do you?" he asked.

"If you were in my position, would you?" she replied. "I've given up everything I had left to be here. I won't let you take that from me."

"You're still alive, Delia," he told her. "You still have that. But if you stay, Pickering might terminate that condition, this time for real. I can't allow that to happen. And I can't be sure I'll be able to protect you here."

His argument didn't sway her.

"I don't need your protection," she shot back. "And I'm not leaving."

Chase growled in exasperation. Arguing with her, he'd long before realized, was nothing more than an exercise in futility. And this argument seemed more fruitless than all those that had preceded it. There was only one way to handle her. However much he might regret it, his conscience was clear. She had driven him to it.

"Fortunately, it is not a matter of your choosing," he told her firmly. He put his hand on her arm. "I haven't any more time to argue with you now, Delia. The platform is about to be opened to passengers and the train will begin to board them any time now. I will not allow you to be here when Pickering arrives."

With that he began to half urge, half push her toward the door. His hold on her wasn't exactly gentle, but he told himself he couldn't do otherwise.

Delia, however, wasn't about to allow herself to be simply ejected. She balked, locking her knees and refusing to move. She tried to pull herself free of his grasp, but Chase held firm. He had no intention of releasing her and losing what little advantage he had.

"What are you doing?" she fumed.

"I'm going to present you to the guard who so stupidly allowed you on the train, offer him my compliments, and let him know just what a grievous error he made in allowing himself to be duped by a pretty smile. Then I will instruct him that you are to be escorted back to the Hôtel Saint Gerard and kept there, under lock and key, if necessary."

"Let go of me," she hissed. "I am not leaving and I am not going back to the hotel."

"Oh, yes, you are," he said as he reached for the latch on the door and pushed it open. "I've been accepting and accommodating about everything because I recognize how difficult it's been for you since Cotter's death, but I simply have no time for those niceties now. When this is over and done with, we can have whatever kind of fight you want to have, and when that's finished and settled, you can agree to marry me. But for now, all that will have to keep."

Delia stiffened and stopped struggling. A sudden flush of confusion swept over her. She must have heard wrong, she told herself. Certainly he hadn't said what she thought she'd heard.

"What did you say?" she asked softly.

He grinned, perfectly aware of what she was asking, but determined to draw it out as long as he could.

"I said we can fight later," he replied.

She shook her head. "No, not that. The other part," she insisted.

He pulled the door open a few inches and stared through the opening at the first few passengers who had begun to trickle onto the platform and approach the train.

352

"You mean the part about you agreeing to marry me?" he asked while he cautiously scanned the faces of the passersby.

Delia put her hand against the door and pushed it shut.

"Yes," she said. "That part."

He was just trying to confuse her, she thought, just trying to keep her from becoming too much of a bother, now that his thoughts were occupied with catching Matthew Pickering. But she wasn't a total idiot to be fooled like a child with a few words, she told herself. He was just trying to manipulate her, to use her the way he'd used her all along. And she had no intention of letting him get away with it.

He turned back to face her. "Well, if you do it quickly, I suppose there's enough time for you to say yes now."

The man is without conscience, she thought. And arrogant. And unspeakably cruel, to play this sort of game with her.

"What makes you think I'll say yes now or ever?" she demanded.

"Because you're alone and homeless," he told her.

"You arrogant, self-absorbed, insolent," she sputtered, and shook her head when she couldn't find the proper descriptive and finally had to settle for, "male."

"You can do better than that, Delia," he told her with a grin. "I know for a fact you can insult a man quite fluently in two languages."

She ignored him. "If I'm alone and homeless, it's your fault. This whole thing is your fault. You've used me and manipulated me and . . ."

"I hope you'll excuse me if I interrupt before you say something you'll regret, Delia," he told her as he pulled her close.

"I will not regret it," she muttered angrily.

"Yes, you will," he insisted. "Because there's one other reason for you to say yes."

He was smiling as he wrapped his arms around her. Delia felt a trail of warmth spread through her as his body pressed close to hers. She oughtn't to let him do this to her, she told herself. It wasn't as if she didn't know what he was doing. She ought to stop it before he made things even more difficult for her than they already were.

But before she could muster enough resolve to push him away, she found herself staring up into his eyes and wondering if perhaps he wasn't lying, wondering if the unwavering gaze of those deep blue eyes was something more than artful deception.

Could anyone be so gifted at lying that he could meet her glance that way? she wondered. Was it possible that he could say those words and look at her that way without flinching, without betraying the least hint of guilt?

She heard a voice, a hoarse, uncertain whisper that seemed almost distant, and only after reflection did she realize it was her own voice she heard asking, "One other reason?"

He nodded. "Yes, one other reason," he insisted.

"Which is?"

He grinned slyly. "Because you love me."

He kissed her then, his lips warm and knowing against hers. And as much as Delia told herself that this was only a game to him, that she was letting him do what he'd set out to do, still she found herself kissing him back.

His arms tightened, pulling her so close she wasn't sure if she could breathe, at least not apart from the breath he shared with her. And at that moment she realized she wanted nothing more than to believe him, if only for a second or two, so that she might guiltlessly feel the sweet, hot flow that that kiss released inside her. What would it matter if she suspended reality for just an instant? she asked herself. Surely there was no real crime in believing a lie if it comforted her, if it made her feel like this.

She wrapped her arms around his neck and abandoned herself to his kiss, parting her lips to him, welcoming the coursing heat that surged through her veins, losing herself to the feel of his body, hard and lean, pressed close to hers. She closed her eyes and pretended the moment would never end. She almost wished she might die, so that she need never have to face grim reality again.

When he finally lifted his lips from hers, Delia saw he was smiling. Now, she told herself, now he's going to tell me to go off and behave and do as he says. That's what that smug smile means, that he's won. And all the rest, that meant nothing.

Worse than nothing, she amended. He'd told her she loved him, but had said nothing about his feelings for her. It wasn't fair, she thought, the way he could look into her heart and coldly use the weakness he found there. It was nothing less than cruel, nothing less than a man who felt nothing might do.

Chase *was* feeling smug, but not for the reasons Delia thought. Her moodiness, the arguments, the fits of ill temper, he told himself they were all understandable, considering what she'd been through, and he was more than willing to forgive them. As for his own questions about her painter friend, he told himself they meant nothing. Surely she wouldn't have kissed him the way she had if she'd been thinking about another man.

Now he knew he had nothing to fear as far as her feelings for Pierre were concerned. He told himself he had only to end this matter with Pickering and get back to Paris, to her. Then he could take up this moment and lead it to a more satisfying conclusion. Unfortunately, he had no time for that now. However much he might wish matters were different, he

355

had business to finish, business even more pressing than the desire that welled inside him the instant he'd taken her into his arms.

He loosened his hold of her, but did not release her.

"Now that that little matter is settled, I think it's best you leave before it's too late," he told her.

Delia felt her veins suddenly fill with ice. She told herself she expected it, but still it wasn't a very comfortable feeling. She pulled herself away, telling herself as she did that games were played by two, that he couldn't hurt her unless she let him.

"Nothing is settled, and I have absolutely no intention of leaving," she told him in her primmest tone.

Chase's smile vanished.

"Damn it, Delia, this isn't the time to behave like a mule. You leave *now*. That's an order."

"I'm not taking any more orders, Mr. Sutton," she replied, "not from you or anyone else. As you so succinctly pointed out to me, I'm alone now. That puts me in a unique position for a woman, one that I suddenly realize is not without advantages — I have no one to answer to but myself."

Chase's jaw hardened with a sudden jolt of anger. He grasped her wrist firmly, not really caring that he held it a bit tighter than he'd intended and she emitted a small squeal of pain. He pulled the door open once again and called out to the uniformed guard who was standing on the platform, surveying the growing stream of passengers passing by on the way to board the cars further along the train.

Delia saw the guard turn and face him. She recognized the man immediately as the guard who had been so sweetly cooperative when she'd appeared at the station side of the platform with her story that she had an appointment to see the Lloyd's Corporation representative. She smiled at him now and he returned the favor, then blushed. She saw him dart a confused glance to the obviously less than tender hand that Chase held clenched to her wrist.

"Oui, monsieur?" he asked, as he approached them. *"Qu'est-ce qu'il y a?"*

"You will take this young woman to the office of security and hold her there until the train leaves," Chase instructed him. "Then you will escort her to the street, hire a cab, and accompany her . . ."

He stopped suddenly. "Damn," he hissed through tight lips. He stepped back and roughly pushed Delia to the side, away from the opened door and out of the view of any curious bystander on the platform.

The guard, puzzled by Chase's brusque action, stepped inside the car and stared at the two of them, wondering if he ought to defend what he assumed was a woman in trouble or if it would be wiser to blindly follow the orders of the man he knew wielded enough influence to see him out on the street and without a job. Instinct and chivalry, at least at the first blow, won out over self-interest and greed.

"Monsieur," he said in a tight croak, "I think it would be best were you to release the young lady."

Chase leveled a furious glance at him.

"Get out," he ordered. "Get back to doing whatever you were hired to do. And should anyone care to inquire about the possibility, you never brought a woman onto the train. Do you understand?"

The guard hesitated for a moment, then shrugged his shoulders.

"Oui, monsieur," he murmured.

The woman didn't seem frightened, he muttered to himself. And there was no need to play the defending knight to a woman who had never asked for protection, especially if there was nothing to be gained by the act.

"Then do it," Chase ordered.

The guard backed out of the car and obediently returned to his post on the platform. Chase followed him to the door and quickly swung it nearly closed.

Delia watched him with a feeling of triumph liberally mixed with confusion. She realized he was not about to banish her after all, but she had no idea what had changed his mind.

"It would seem you've had a change of heart, Mr. Sutton," she purred in a saccharine tone. "And here I've wronged you and thought you without a heart altogether."

Chase darted her a glance filled with daggers, enough to make her wish she'd dispensed with the sarcasm entirely.

"I had it changed for me," he said. "And before you start to preen, let me inform you that it wasn't changed by you."

He took a step back, then motioned her to the narrow crack he'd left the door open.

Delia edged toward the door and stared out the narrow slit. A second later she felt herself involuntarily draw in her breath, then quickly turn away. She pressed herself against the side wall of the car as though she hoped it might somehow absorb her and make her invisible.

"At least you've got enough common sense to be afraid of him," Chase told her. He pushed the door closed and threw the bolt. "Well, it seems you are to have your way, after all, Delia," he said. "There's no way you can get off the train and past them without being seen."

Delia nodded and slowly pushed herself away from the wall, moving further into the car and away from the door, away from any prying eyes that might roam in their direction. It seemed a bit odd to her that it was Pickering who was forcing Chase to give her what she'd wanted, odd and a bit frightening, but that was exactly what he was doing.

For what she'd seen when she'd taken that quick glance outside the car was Pickering and the dapper Compte de Grasse standing on the platform only a few yards away. They both seemed quite merry, affably greeting and chatting with a dozen or so of de Grasse's friends who had decided to accompany the *compte's* art treasures across the Channel and into the wilds of London.

Not that she doubted for an instant that Pickering's attention wasn't really firmly planted on the freight car, measuring, calculating, making his plans. For the moment at least, she realized, it was the quarry that was holding the hunters at bay.

"Here."

Delia stirred. The car, for all its apparent amenities, was after all still a freight car, she'd discovered. Without windows out of which she might look at the passing landscape, the motion of the train soon became an opiate, deadening her senses and making her feel dull and listless. Even though she hadn't really been sleeping, she had to force her eyes to fully open and focus.

It seemed to take an enormous effort for her to concentrate on the face of the man standing in front of her. Rather dull after all that work, she thought, just Chase holding out a piece of baguette and a mug to her. But the bouquet of strong coffee filtered from the mug and soon filled her nostrils. She found herself salivating for a taste of it.

"How hospitable of you, Mr. Sutton," she said as she shifted herself stiffly erect. She reached eagerly for the mug.

"Hospitality has nothing to do with it," he growled as he handed it to her. "I'd simply rather forgo the honor of having you add starving you to the long list of my sins you've no doubt carefully compiled."

The sound of a not quite entirely stifled chuckle made Delia look up to the two uniformed guards, the official accompaniment to the shipment of art, who were seated at the table. They were both happily sipping from mugs of their own and devouring huge pieces of the same bread Chase was offering her. However official their function, it seemed that forfeiting a meal was not an inconvenience to be tolerated in the course of its completion.

The younger of the two men, one Jean Gautier by name, was the guard who had earlier challenged Chase's treatment of her. He'd obviously overcome his reservations about the tenor of their relationship, for he now seemed, if anything, more amused by Chase's remark than his companion.

The second, older man had entered the car just as the train began to leave the station. He'd flashed an impressive looking badge, introduced himself to her as Charles Rampeau, Préfet de la Sûreté, and then waited to make sure she'd been sufficiently impressed by that title before he'd loosened his tie and settled himself at the table to read the newspapers he'd brought with him. His uniform, unlike the conservative dark gray of the railroad guard's, was a deep, rich blue, a color that was not at all becoming to either his extraordinarily flushed features or his decidedly rotund form, and he seemed happy to shed the jacket and sit comfortably in his shirtsleeves. Delia decided that he'd obviously not recovered any need to reestablish any great formality, for his jacket remained draped, like a huge bird with drooping wings, over the back of the chair.

Delia eyed the impressive amount of food that had been set out on the table — a heavy tin carafe, presumably the source of the coffee, and two unlabeled bottles of red table wine, as well as a considerable array of bread, *brie,* and fruit. She had little doubt that anyone might starve on this particular journey, especially not Rampeau, who seemed to find even more to hold his interest in the food than he had previously found in his newspapers.

She sipped the hot coffee, savoring its warmth and the sharp mild chicory bite of its taste, and then stood and stretched. The small sofa, for all its appearance of luxury amidst the bleakness of its freightcar surroundings, was lumpy and hard. The small of her back ached and the stretch did little to ease the condition.

But it wasn't a hurt great enough, she found, to dissipate her hunger. She accepted the piece of baguette from Chase and took a healthy bite of it as she transferred herself to the free chair beside the table.

The bread, she realized, had been liberally anointed with warm, runny *brie.* The sharp, slightly ammonia taste of it seemed unreasonably good to her. She chewed the bite thoughtfully and then swallowed, letting it settle into her stomach with a comforting solidity before reaching once more for the mug of coffee.

"How long before we reach Cherbourg?" she asked, after she'd swallowed.

"Not until six tomorrow morning," Chase told her. "That leaves plenty of time for our friend to make his attempt for an exchange."

Delia glanced at the three men sitting at the table, then shook her head. "I don't see how he would even consider it," she said. "If you'll excuse the criticism, I think the paintings are too well guarded."

Rampeau obviously took her words to mean that his presence was more than enough to frighten away even the most dedicated thief. His wide chest swelled a bit and he straightened up in his chair.

"I agree, *mademoiselle,*" he told her. "There will

be no attempt to steal these great French treasures. Certainly not while they are on French soil and under the protection of the Sûreté."

Delia thought it unnecessary at that moment to point out to him that Pickering was expected to steal works by a Flemish artist, not a French one. His point, if a bit skewed, seemed more than valid enough to her.

But Chase was not quite as impressed with the power of the presence of the Sûreté.

"Oh, he'll do it in France, all right," he said. "Either that or when we're crossing the Channel. He won't want to get his hands dirty on home soil."

"But surely he won't walk in here with Monsieur Rampeau and Monsieur Gautier sitting here waiting for him," Delia insisted. She smiled tartly. "Your presence could do nothing other than send cold chills of abject fear down his spine." His only response to her provocation was a raised brow and a scowl. "And you said you had other guards on the train as well," she added.

Chase chose to ignore her defamatory comment.

"The others Pickering shouldn't recognize, as they are in mufti, masquerading as ordinary passengers," he said. "And like you, I am an unheralded passenger here; Pickering should have no hint of my presence. He should expect the paintings to be protected only by the ordinary train guard and the special agent sent from the Sûreté." He nodded pleasantly at Rampeau, assuring him that nothing disparaging was intended by his words. "And I have no doubt but that he'll find some plausible way to dislodge them before he makes his attempt."

"And whatever his ruse, *mademoiselle,*" Gautier added, "we will make every appearance of accommodating him."

"Then we stand here and wait for him?" she pressed.

362

He shook his head. "We hide," he said, pointing to the partition that separated this part of the car from the rest, which supposedly contained more ordinary freight. "And wait until he's played his hand."

"After which we appear and proceed with the arrest," Rampeau assured her.

"And the paintings continue on to London unharmed," the railroad guard added.

Delia shrugged. It all seemed plausible enough to her, but still she had an itch of doubt that things weren't going to happen quite as Chase and the policemen seemed to think they would.

"In any event, *mademoiselle*," Rampeau added, reaching across the table to pat her hand, "you need have no fear about the safety of these treasures."

Delia smiled weakly at him. His huge ham of a hand was damp and hot and felt entirely unpleasant. She carefully extricated her hand, reaching instead for the coffee mug, hoping he'd accept the excuse without taking undue offense. Then she diplomatically took a sip of coffee, glancing one after another at the faces of the three men. The two uniformed men seemed complacent, almost bored with the proceedings. She decided it would be best to refrain from telling them that it was Pickering she was interested in and that she didn't give a damn about the safety of the paintings.

She glanced once again at Chase and saw his eyes had narrowed and he was staring at her. She knew that he knew exactly what it was she was thinking.

Chase reached across the table, touching his fingers to those of her hand that still held the coffee mug.

"We've only three of these, Miss Hampton," he told her. "You were, after all, an unexpected addition to the party."

"However delightful," Rampeau interjected.

"However delightful," Chase repeated with dry resignation. "There are only three mugs. I hope you have no objection to sharing."

"No," she replied as she released the mug to him.

He lifted it and sipped a bit of the coffee. But Delia knew it wasn't coffee that he was talking about when he spoke of sharing, it was the satisfaction of seeing Pickering brought to justice. After all, she thought bitterly, there was nothing left for them to share but that.

Chapter Twenty

·Delia was stiff and bored and uncomfortable. It didn't make her feel any better to realize that during the previous hours her nerves had been growing steadily more ragged. She was more on edge now than she had been during those long, hot weeks when she'd been working on the paintings and waiting for Pickering to suddenly appear.

She was, she realized, once again waiting for Pickering's appearance, only this time not to be frightened and threatened by him. This time she wouldn't need to pretend with him that she knew nothing of his part in her father's death. This time she would finally have the opportunity to say to him what she'd been waiting to say since the moment she'd realized he'd killed Cotter.

Strangely, waiting for this meeting was proving to be much harder for her than all the past waiting had been, even worse than waiting for the visit that she knew was to end in her own faked death. She found herself straining to hear some strange sound, anything that might be the diversion Chase had said would precede Pickering's entry, the cue that she and ·Chase were to hide and lie in wait. But there was no sound, no outcry, nothing except the steady grind of the train's wheels against the tracks. And with each passing hour, she grew more and more afraid Pickering might have changed his mind.

It was odd, she mused . . . she was feeling the sort of anticipation to finally confront Pickering that she assumed women usually reserved for the times spent waiting for lovers to appear, a feeling of mixed elation and anticipation, a deep, urgent longing for the moment to finally arrive. She realized that before the day both Chase and Pickering had walked into her life, she'd neither loved nor hated. In the weeks since, she'd learned to do both, and neither, she'd found, would leave her the better for the lesson.

She wondered if this strange anticipation meant she had grown as deeply involved with her hatred of Pickering as she was with her love for Chase. It frightened her to think that once Pickering was caught she might feel the same sense of loss she knew she would feel when Chase had disappeared from her life. Perhaps losing an object of love and an object of hate were not so greatly different. Perhaps emotions as strong as love and hate were much closer than she'd ever thought opposites could be. Still, it terrified her to think that she was so empty that she might be left to mourn the loss of a man she hated.

In any case, she knew she was tired of waiting. She wanted the moment to come, wanted the whole horrible experience to end, finally. Then, she told herself, she could turn her back on both love and hatred. Better to be empty than to live with the pain they had brought her.

She felt cramped and hot. The air in the car was close, far too warm. A warm drip of perspiration was slowly slipping down the small of her back, leaving her sticky and uncomfortable in its wake. She wished for the luxury of a long, relaxing bath followed by a real, restful sleep.

She stood up and stretched, wondering if the three men had known they were not losing much when they'd gallantly given up the sofa for her use. She stared at them, Rampeau and Gautier sprawled over the table, their heads on their arms, the sparse remnants of their picnic meal, crumbs and peelings and the empty wine bottles, crowded into the center between them. The sharp sound of thickly indrawn breath followed by low, nasal snores emanated from them both, Rampeau's deep and sonorous, Gautier's higher, the sounds short and sharp.

The ever vigilant guards, she thought as she stared at them. With such as these, it was obvious why Pickering had no fear of the authorities. She wondered what would happen if Pickering were to burst into the car at that moment, if they'd even waken, or if they'd continue to snore as he calmly stole the paintings.

The Memlings, however, were not without protection. Chase, unlike the other two, was fully awake. He was sitting soberly erect, his back pressed against the comfortless wooden chair, his eyes focused straight ahead at the single entrance to the car. When she stood, he looked up at her and nodded.

Delia approached him, treading carefully, not wishing to waken the two sleeping men whose job it was to alertly guard the works of art.

"What time is it?" she whispered when she stood beside him.

He silently put his fingers into his vest pocket and withdrew a heavy gold watch. He clicked open the cover and held the watch face up to her so that she might see.

"Five-thirty," she murmured as she glanced at the hands. "So late?"

He shrugged. "So early, you mean," he corrected. "About dawn."

She scowled at the implied criticism. He was still taking pains to make it plain to her that he wasn't pleased she was there. The night before, each small pique had dug a tiny hurt inside her, until now she was left with a dull ache. It would be so much easier, she thought, if they could at least make peace.

"We should reach Cherbourg soon," she ventured.

He nodded. "The train's already begun to slow a bit. It must be ahead of schedule."

"And no sign of Pickering," she murmured, aware that the realization left her with an aching feeling of regret. It was wrong, she thought, but still she could not deny it.

"And no sign of Pickering," Chase repeated, his tone empty of any sign of emotion whatever.

Delia finally allowed herself to give voice to the fear that it might all have been for nothing.

"Do you think he's given it up?" she asked.

Chase shook his head. "No. He's given up nothing. He's waiting to do it on the trip across the Channel."

She stared at his fixed expression. He seemed so certain, so sure of what would and wouldn't happen. Pickering will do this, we'll do that. But it was a pretense, she knew, that image of certainty. He hadn't thought Pickering would burn her house down around her. And he really couldn't know what Pickering would do now, either.

Perhaps, she thought, Pickering will wait until the paintings are in the museum in London. Perhaps he'll wait until the exhibit is over and they're being returned to France. Perhaps he's devised some plan so improbable no one can anticipate it.

And a mean voice inside her said perhaps he'll get away with it.

The possibility was physically painful to her, leaving her with a thick ball of anger inside her, big enough, it seemed, to choke her. The thought that Pickering might actually go unpunished for what he'd done to Cotter, for what he'd tried to do to her, filled her with a sense of impotent rage that left her ragged with anger and indignation at life's unfairness.

Worse, she knew it wasn't a remote possibility, but one that was very real. Chase had told her that a thief had to be caught in the act or else with the stolen

368

goods in his possession for there to be any certainty of conviction. Unless Pickering attempted the robbery while the paintings were being transferred to London and Chase caught him, there was very little chance he'd ever face trial. He was far too careful and he'd succeeded too many times in the past to make the sort of mistake that would lead to his arrest unless he walked into their trap.

"And what if he doesn't?" she muttered.

Her tone had been sharp, she realized, although her anger could hardly be directed at Chase for the fact that Pickering had yet to make his attempt. She realized she wanted Chase to assure her that he wouldn't give up, that he'd keep after Pickering for the rest of his life, if need be.

He didn't.

He looked up at her, his eyes narrow, and she felt as if he were looking through her, searching for something inside she knew wasn't there. Or perhaps it was there, she amended. Perhaps it was there but kept so carefully guarded that he couldn't find it. If its loss disappointed him, she told herself she didn't care. She must guard herself, muster her defenses against him. It was, she knew, the only way she'd ever survive.

Chase returned his glance to the door as if it might draw Pickering to them then and there.

"He will," he told her. "For whatever reason, he's decided to wait until we're crossing the Channel. Perhaps he thinks the guards will be too tired to think straight then." He nodded toward Rampeau and Gautier and grinned suddenly, a wry, humorless grin. "He's probably right. I doubt even he'd imagine our fearless security force would be quite so relaxed in the pursuit of their task as they now are."

"But if he doesn't, can't we have him arrested for trying to kill me? For burning down my house?"

Chase shrugged. "You were the one who first

brought out the pistol," he reminded her. "And he could say the fire was an accident. It might be hard to convince a jury otherwise. Our word against his." He shook his head. "No, it has to be this." He looked up at her again. "But don't worry. He's in too far. He won't give it up."

"I wish it were over," she said with an empty little sigh. "I don't think I've ever been so tired in the whole of my life just waiting for something to happen."

He looked at her in silence for a moment. It was, Delia found, suddenly hard for her to bear that searching glance. She'd had enough of those looks of his, enough of those secret, knowing stares.

She stepped back, almost afraid that if she didn't, he would somehow trap her with his stare. But he seemed unwilling to let her escape. He stood and casually arched his back to stretch, pretending that was his only reason for moving. Then he watched her take another step away from him and she could see he was weighing his choices before he decided what he was going to do.

He hesitated for an instant, then put his hands on her arms, holding her firmly so that she couldn't repeat her small retreat. For an instant she was afraid he was going to kiss her, afraid he was trying to repeat the futile little scene they'd had before the train had left Paris. But then she realized it wasn't a suggestive gesture, that he was holding her in a different way now. She looked up at him, wondering why her heart suddenly felt as if it might break inside her, and found he was staring down at her, waiting patiently for her to offer him her full attention.

"I want you to remain on the train, Delia," he told her softly. "I want you to go back to Paris where you'll be safe. I want you far enough away so Pickering can't touch you."

He wasn't ordering her, Delia realized, but begging, or as close to begging as he would ever bring himself.

370

And, much against her will, she found herself weakening, found herself wondering if he might actually be sincere. His unwavering glance, the supplicating way he held her arms, it was far more convincing to her than the impassioned embrace had been, far easier to believe than the lie about his wanting her to marry him.

But still it wasn't nearly enough to make her believe she'd ever be able to live with Cotter's ghost were she to turn her back on Pickering now.

She shook her head. "You know that's impossible," she told him.

"Damn it, Delia, it's for your own good," he insisted. His grasp of her arms tightened and he pulled her close to him. "I don't want to have to live with the memory of you being hurt, or worse," he said. "I don't think I could live with that."

The words seemed almost torn from him, as though he spoke them against his will, and his stare could only be described as haunted. She thought him tortured, almost as tortured as she felt at that moment, as torn between what she wanted and what she knew must be. As she looked up at him for that endless moment, Delia found herself pressing close to him, found herself wishing that he'd lower his lips the few inches that divided them from hers, found herself wanting to be swept to a place where she did not need to force herself to think, where both of them could lose their pain.

How easy it would be, she thought, to give in to him, to abandon herself to him and leave behind her the fear and the hurt that had been stalking her since Cotter's death. She felt the warmth of his breath against her cheek and she parted her lips to it, wondering if she might draw part of him into her for one last time with each intake of his breath.

And then the train lurched and slowed sharply. The jolt caused Rampeau to come to a grudging wakefulness, grumbling incoherently and emitting a low belch as he sat up. He looked around, getting his bearings, realizing with obvious difficulty where he was. He looked up at Chase, and his flushed cheeks grew just a bit redder as he realized that Chase must know he'd been asleep.

He nudged Gautier's arm, hissing, *"Reveillez-vous, cochon paresseux,"* by way of waking the younger man and vindicating his own laziness.

Chase, however, wasn't at that moment interested in Rampeau's dereliction of duty. He released his hold of Delia's arms, quickly turning away. His movements were sharp, almost awkward, as though he was ashamed of his confession of weakness, of his momentary lack of proper British restraint.

Delia followed him with her eyes as he walked the length of the car, staring at his back and wondering what it had cost him to make such a confession. An avowal of passion, a smoldering embrace, that might mean nothing to him, just words a man would use to buy what he wanted. But a confession that he contemplated her loss with pain, that was something else again. Perhaps she'd been wrong all along, she thought. Perhaps she'd simply been too afraid that he'd hurt her to allow herself to believe what he'd said was true.

But there was no chance then to contemplate possibilities of their future or the complete impossibility of it. Rampeau was grumpily arranging himself inside his castoff jacket and Gautier, roused from sleep, immediately stood and busied himself marching along the line of crates, checking that they were all secure. The motions were intended more to salve the hurt of Rampeau's insults than to serve any practical purpose, but they nonetheless left Delia with a sense of urgency, a feeling that something was finally about to happen.

Chase threw the door bolt, edged the door open a

few inches, and looked out into the pale morning light. He stood staring at the passing countryside that was quickly changing into the outskirts of the city as the train sped through it. He inhaled a deep breath of the salty sea air, filling his lungs with it before he pushed the door closed and turned back to face Delia.

"Cherbourg," he announced.

Then he grimly turned his attention to the crates of paintings, quickly touching his right hand to the pistol that was holstered beneath his left arm, assuring himself that he was prepared to face whatever necessities fate and the coming hours might dictate.

They waited in the freight car until the passengers had all left the train and gone in to the morning buffet being served in the ornate, gingerbread-embellished building that served as railroad station and transfer house to those passengers continuing on across the Channel. Rampeau made a quick foray, returning after a few moments to assure Chase that Pickering, de Grasse, and the group of their friends were all completely engrossed with the effort of appeasing their morning appetites with a breakfast of ham, eggs, and champagne. Rampeau's manner suggested that he could make good use of similar endeavors himself.

Only then did Chase and Delia, now both disguised in porters' uniforms Chase had commandeered and bearing an appropriate burden of luggage, venture from the confines of the freightcar. They melted into a line of porters laden with luggage to be stowed in the hold of the Channel steamer.

The passengers might have the leisure to spend the hours between the train's arrival in Cherbourg and the steamer's departure from it eating, drinking, and entertaining themselves, but the porters had a far more rigorous time of it. They sweated in the early morning sunshine, grunting with the weight of their burdens, transferring crates of freight as well as the large trunks and luggage of the passengers from the train to the steamer's hold. If the work was not enough to plague them, Rampeau and Gautier made themselves extremely visible overseeing the transfer of the precious crates of artwork. The porters darted angry glances at them while they lifted and carried and stowed, thinking their own private thoughts about the added attention of the railroad security and the man from the Sûreté.

"I told you no sane man would dare put a finger on the shipment while it was on French soil," Rampeau told Chase, once the crates had been brought on board the steamer and carefully secured.

Chase grinned wryly. "Pickering isn't especially sane," he muttered.

Rampeau turned to Delia, smiling smugly, implying that it was his presence that had a deterrent effect on the thief even the Lloyd's Corporation feared.

"A few hours more," he told Chase, "and you and your Scotland Yard friends will have the full responsibility to see they are equally safe in England."

"First there is the Channel to cross," Chase reminded him.

"And then I can turn my back on you with good conscience," Rampeau told him.

Chase offered no reply. He knew that beneath the bluster, Rampeau was afraid. Were any of the paintings to be stolen while they were in his jurisdiction, his career would be ruined. Chase couldn't blame him for being anxious to turn over his responsibility to his counterpart from Scotland Yard, who would meet the steamer once it docked in Southampton and return to the safety and comfort of his desk at the offices of the Sûreté in Paris.

Delia ignored them both, wandering along the rows

of freight stacked in the hold and finding a place to seat herself on a large leather-covered trunk. She removed her porter's cap, releasing the hair that had been piled beneath it, then pulled her legs up onto the trunk, wrapped her arms around them, and dropped her head onto her knees.

This part of the steamer, the upper hold, intended for passengers' luggage and valuable cargo, was just below the passenger deck and was relatively light and airy and far less dank than the lower hold, where more mundane cargo was stored. Still, it was hot and close enough to make her uncomfortable. Already the motion of the steamer as waves hit its side was starting to rouse something unpleasant in her stomach. She wondered how horrible the feeling would become once they were out on the Channel.

Chase took one glance at her and realized what was happening.

"I don't think you'll make a good sailor, Delia," he told her.

"I suppose not," she agreed.

"Perhaps you might care to change your mind?" he suggested. "You can still go back to Paris."

She shook her head.

"I wouldn't give you the satisfaction of saying I told you so," she told him with an arch smile.

He scowled but said nothing more, apparently resigned to her presence, if not exactly pleased. He made a point of ignoring Gautier's halfhearted attempt to stifle his laughter, aware that the guard had completely changed his opinion regarding Delia's need for protection from him.

Rampeau, himself a veteran of what Delia was beginning to feel, was more sympathetic. He held out to her the contents of a tin of mints with which he'd thoughtfully armed himself in anticipation of this portion of the trip.

"The singular blessing, mademoiselle," he told her

as he popped one into his own mouth by way of demonstration, "is that it does not last very long."

She thanked him with a wan smile, then turned to stare out the salt-smeared porthole, watching the procession of feet on the pier as passengers began to board.

"Two pair," Gautier announced, as he spread his hand and lay the cards down for Rampeau to inspect. He was smiling, more than delighted that he was winning and able to get his own back at the Sûreté man. Neither Rampeau's rank nor his superior manner seemed to be serving him very well when it came to cards.

Rampeau dropped his cards, muttered a string of indecipherable swearwords that ended with an emphatic *"Merde."* Then he darted a look at Delia and murmured, *"Pardon, mademoiselle."* Had he not suggested the game of cards in the first place, he'd have pled that poker had never been his game and begged off. As it was, he'd trapped himself, and there was nothing he could do but sit and take his own medicine.

Chase, who had joined them but done little more than ante and then pass each hand, smiled to himself. He knew that being beaten by a man he considered an inferior was galling to Rampeau, the indignity almost more painful than the loss of his francs.

Delia pointedly ignored the whole of the proceedings. Instead, she kept her eyes fixed on the stenciled markings of the crates of paintings. She was afraid that if she let them stray to the porthole and the sight of the ceaseless movement of the waves, she would be unable to control any longer the unpleasant drifting feeling inside her stomach.

The steamer had left Cherbourg less than an hour before and already Delia was sick, sicker than she could have imagined herself becoming in so short a time. The knowledge that there was nothing she could do about it only added to her misery. The only comfort she had was the fact that she'd eaten nothing that morning, and therefore had been saved the indignity of emptying her stomach in front of Chase and the others. Still, it was an empty satisfaction when compared to the heaving misery in her belly, a misery she knew would continue for several hours longer.

The droning thump of the steam engines filled the hold, reverberating through her head, an echo of the dull throbbing waves of nausea that filled her stomach. It seemed to Delia that she had traded the discomfort and boredom of the train for more discomfort and boredom on the steamer, only this time she had the added misery of seasickness. She told herself it was one last not inconsiderable item she must add to the list of her reasons to hate Pickering.

Again she found herself listening, just as she had on the train, praying for some sign that Pickering was finally about to make his move. But when it came, her discomfort was great enough, and the sound of the engines loud enough, so that she hardly differentiated the loud crash from the regular beat of the steamer's metal heart.

The three men, however, noticed it immediately. Even muffled by the echo of the engines, it was more than loud enough to make them all drop their cards. Chase darted up, and Gautier followed.

"What was that?" the railroad guard demanded, turning to Chase and Rampeau as though his position of least importance provided him with a valid excuse to plead ignorance.

"It might not have been anything," Chase suggested. "Or perhaps it was the first of Pickering's smokescreen."

"It sounded like an explosion," Rampeau muttered. He turned to Chase. "No one sets off an explosion on a ship at sea. Not if he's on it, he doesn't."

"And that was no normal engine sound," Gautier insisted. "I've made this trip a hundred times. I've never heard anything like that."

Rampeau seemed willing to be convinced by the railroad guard's words of experience. "Perhaps we've hit something," he offered, and he began to push his pudgy body through the stacks of trunks and crates so that he could get a look out the porthole.

Gautier shook his head. "No," he said. "No, we've hit nothing. It sounded like it came from in here, not outside." He looked up to Chase in sudden panic. "What if it was an explosion in the boiler room?"

As though its express purpose were to lend credence to Gautier's suggestion, the ship's klaxon sounded.

Gautier's face drained of color at the sound.

"That's the fire alarm," he whispered in obvious terror. "It *was* an explosion. There's a fire." His voice rose in panic. "We're all going to drown."

"Don't be a fool," Chase hissed angrily. "We're not going to drown. What we are going to do is wait here and find out what's happened. This is probably Pickering's diversion."

"No," the guard insisted. "No one in his right mind starts a fire on a ship at sea. This has nothing to do with your thief."

"We operate under the assumption that it *is* Pickering," Chase ordered. "You know what you're supposed to do."

Gautier, however, was too frightened even to listen to him.

"I have to go to my emergency station," he insisted. "I have orders to follow in case of emergency, a post to take in the event the klaxon sounds." He deigned not to add that his post was to oversee the loading of passengers into the lifeboats, a task that, at that moment, sounded more and more appealing to him as he contemplated the alternative of being left on board a sinking steamer.

His words were punctuated by the dull thudding noise of running feet on the deck above and the muffled sound of a bullhorn shouting that all crew must take emergency stations.

"Excuse me, *monsieur*," he said to Chase, his tone making it plain that his polite words were not to be mistaken as a sign he would do otherwise, "but I must leave."

With that he darted for the heavy door that sealed this part of the hold, pulling it open and darting through it without a backward glance. It was obvious that he was not interested in waiting for Chase's permission. He was far too terrified by the thought of a fire at sea to be interested in any interpretation other than his own and far too eager to be up on deck and near a lifeboat.

Rampeau turned to Chase.

"What do you think?" he asked.

"It's Pickering," Chase said, his tone flat and without question. "He's given us a diversion, all right. He'll assume that no one would bother guarding some bits of canvas if they think the boat might sink."

"But he wouldn't risk his own life?" Rampeau insisted.

Chase shook his head. "No, nor would he risk the paintings. There's no fire. Or at least, not a dangerous one. He just wants to make sure we're looking someplace else while he takes what he wants."

"And I?" the Sûreté man asked.

"You pretend to be part of the panic," Chase instructed. "Give him at least ten minutes down here before you return. We don't want to interrupt him prematurely."

Rampeau nodded, then quickly removed himself from the hold, following after Gautier. His exit, Chase noted, was rather a good deal faster than his entrance had been, a hint that he wasn't entirely convinced that Pickering, and not a dangerous fire, had been the cause of the alarm.

Chase turned to Delia and quickly dragged her off her perch on the trunk.

"What do we do now?" she whispered in a frightened voice.

He glanced down at her, noting that her eyes were wide with fear, just as Gautier's had been.

"You could go out on deck," he suggested. "If you keep your porter's hat low, no one should look twice at you. Stay among the other passengers and you should be safe enough."

She shook her head. "No," she insisted. "You said it was Pickering. I believe you."

She might be frightened, she thought, but she wasn't about to turn tail and run.

"What you mean is, you're more stubborn than you are afraid," Chase interpreted.

Delia bit her lip. He was right and she knew it.

"All right," she said, "I'm more stubborn than afraid. Whatever the reason, I'm staying."

Chase pushed her along the rows of piled luggage.

"Then what you do is hide," he told her, his tone sharp. "You keep your head down and your mouth closed. Not a sound out of you."

With that he pushed her into a narrow space between two tall piles of trunks, and slid in beside her.

"Now what?" she whispered.

He put his hand on the top of her head and forced her down.

"You keep low," he hissed. "And quiet, damn it."

Delia obediently crouched down, too flustered now to think about the unpleasant lurching in her stomach or even that the space in which he'd chosen to hide was cramped and uncomfortable, with the sharp corners of trunks in front and behind her waiting for the slightest movement to make themselves felt. She wondered how long she would be able to crouch there before her legs grew uncomfortably strained, for it was an awkward position.

She oughtn't to have worried. They were hardly settled before the heavy door to the hold was swung slowly inward. The metal hinges squealed slightly, and then Delia heard the door quickly closed. It clanged shut with a metallic bang.

She dared to shift herself slightly, moving a bit to the side until she found a narrow but clear glimpse through the piles of luggage and freight at the place where the crates of paintings were stowed. A tall, dark-haired man was standing in front of the crates, reading the neatly stenciled markings on their fronts.

There was no question who it was. Delia knew she would never forget that particular profile, nor would she ever mistake it for anyone else.

His movements were carefully measured, made without undue haste that would indicate he was afraid or in any way agitated. Whatever was happening on deck, he seemed to have very little concern that he might be trapped belowdecks by a fire.

Delia pulled herself back, crouching down, trying to make herself as small as she possibly could. The last thing she wanted was to be seen. Her heart began to pound in her chest, and she knew the moment had finally come.

Chase had been right. There was no fire, no real danger for the steamer.

Pickering had come to steal the paintings after all.

Chapter Twenty-one

Pickering stood for a few moments, apparently puzzling over the coded markings stenciled on the sides of the crates of paintings. But he must have known what he was looking for, because he seemed quite certain when he located the specific crate for which he'd been searching. He moved quickly to it and set his walking stick down by his feet, then pulled out a small, ornately jacketed pocketknife. He flicked the knife open and slid the blade carefully beneath the edge of the crate's lid.

Even to Delia's untrained eye, it was obvious that he knew what he was about. Using the blade as a pry, he gave it one swift blow. The lid edged up sufficiently for him to slip his fingers into the gap and pull to free it. He'd obviously performed the task many times before. He calmly leaned over the crate and slowly began to inspect the paintings inside it.

Delia was shocked by his manner, by the matter-of-fact way he went about his business, as though stealing priceless paintings was some ordinary task that he performed daily. There were no furtive glances, no sign that he was afraid that the guards might appear suddenly and catch him. The man has no nerves, she thought with amazement and not a little awe.

Unlike Pickering, her own nerves were worn ragged. She could feel her heart thumping wildly. The moment had finally come when Pickering was about to learn that he would be made to pay for what he'd done. Her taste of satisfaction was like honey, thick and sweet on her tongue.

She darted a glance at Chase. Like her, he was watching Pickering intently. But he also seemed bewildered, as though he'd seen something he didn't quite understand. She had no idea what could possibly be so confusing to him. The purpose of Pickering's actions seemed only too clear to her—he was searching through the crate for the specific paintings he was going to steal.

Pickering allowed himself a moment to admire the half dozen paintings in the crate as he rifled though them for the two that interested him. He paused for a few seconds over each, staring, touching his fingers to the surface. It was almost as though he regretted the necessity of leaving it behind, as though he wished he could steal them all.

The frames were all heavily padded, of course, to keep the paintings safe during shipment. They made virtually no sound as Pickering shifted them, none whatsoever when compared to the sporadic dull thumping noise of feet running along the deck above. In the hold it was quiet enough for Delia to think the sound of her pounding heart might actually be audible to Pickering. She began to fear it might even be loud enough to give her and Chase away.

Despite her fears, however, Pickering gave no indication that he knew he was being watched. He found what he wanted and pulled two frames from the crate. He set them aside, then retrieved his walking stick from where he'd dropped it by his feet.

If Delia hadn't recognized the cane immediately as the one Pickering had been carrying the night he'd come to the house on the Rue Saint-Clodoald, she could not mistake it once he twisted off the ornate gold handle. She watched him pull out the tightly

383

rolled canvases, her forgeries of the Memlings. He smoothed them out, laying them on the top of the crate beside him. Delia stared at them as if she'd never seen them before. From where she watched, they looked identical to the originals.

It was more than obvious now what Pickering was about to do — substitute her forgeries for the genuine canvases and then return the frames to the crate. It was such a simple plan, almost foolproof. No one would even know that the genuine Memlings had been stolen, at least not unless they were examined by an expert. If and when that happened, he would have long since sold the paintings. There would be nothing left to tie him to the theft.

Now, she thought, was the time to arrest him. She glanced at the door, wondering what was taking Rampeau so long, wondering why he didn't appear as he was supposed to.

She turned to Chase, not quite believing that he had remained so calm. She wondered why he wasn't doing anything, why he was just watching. Surely they'd seen enough now, she thought, surely there could be no question, even to the most dull-witted jury, of what Pickering was about to do.

But Chase didn't move. He stood watching, waiting. In those incredibly long moments, Delia found her thoughts began to shoot off at odd tangents, wondering first why no one had ever noticed that Pickering's cane was a good deal thicker than the usual sort, then musing over what he really thought of de Grasse, the man he'd befriended so that he might more conveniently steal from him. Meanwhile, Pickering had removed the Memlings from their frames and begun to pry off the tiny tacks that held them to their stretchers.

Chase chose that moment to make his presence known. He removed his pistol from its shoulder holster, then slipped out from their hiding place. He straightened and took a few steps forward, moving silently toward the place where Pickering was busily intent on his task. When he was still perhaps ten paces away, he stopped.

"It would seem you've finally made a mistake, Pickering," he said softly. "A very serious mistake."

Pickering spun around on his heel to face Chase. He stared at him for a long moment, then smiled, as if he were bidding Chase welcome.

"So it's you," he said, his tone implying he'd expected no less. "Sutton, isn't it?"

Chase grinned crookedly.

"I'm flattered," he replied.

"You needn't be," Pickering told him. "After that last time, when you got close . . ."

"Not close enough, unfortunately," Chase interrupted. "Those paintings you stole were insured for a hundred and fifty thousand pounds."

"So much?" Pickering asked. He pursed his lips. "I only got a hundred for them. I should have charged my client more."

"A hundred thousand—not a bad profit," Chase chided.

"I suppose you're right," Pickering conceded. "Greed is such an uncultured emotion."

"And we wouldn't want to make it general knowledge just how base you are, now, would we?" Chase returned. "The fine Mayfair gentleman. It wouldn't do to let people know you were really born on a Shropshire farm and raised with dirt under your fingernails."

Pickering's eyes grew sharp as he stared at Chase. He pretended he hadn't heard a word, but there was pure hatred now in his glance.

"In any event, after our last skirmish, I decided I'd be best served to know my enemy. I made a few discreet inquiries." He arched his brow. "The talk is you're supposed to be good."

385

Chase grinned again.

"Good enough to catch you," he said.

"Odd we've never run into one another socially," Pickering mused. "We do, I believe, travel in the same circles."

Chase shook his head.

"Hardly," Chase said. "I try to keep my private life free of the stink of thieves. But if it pleases you to be formally introduced to the man who'll see you spend the next twenty years of your life in prison, I see no reason to fault you."

Pickering scowled. "Perhaps you're not the sort I'd meet, after all," he hissed.

"Perhaps not," Chase conceded. He motioned with the pistol. "Now, if you're quite sure that the niceties have been satisfied, drop your toys, if you please. I wouldn't want you to get any wild ideas that might force me to shoot you. The thought of you rotting in Newgate is far too appealing."

Pickering silently did as he was told, setting the canvas down and dropping the knife he'd been using to remove the small tacks.

"You *are* good, you know?" he said. "I was resigned to reluctantly bidding these beauties a very sad *adieu* when the lovely Miss Hampton conveniently appeared to offer her services. I don't suppose it was your deft hand behind that clever maneuver?" he asked.

Chase shook his head. "I'm afraid the idea was all hers," he replied as he slowly took another step toward Pickering. He put his free hand into his pocket, withdrew a pair of handcuffs, and tossed them the short distance that divided them. They landed with a clatter on the top of the crate closest to Pickering. "If you would be so kind?" he said, and motioned to the cuffs with his pistol.

Pickering scowled, but reached for the cuffs. "I do so hate these plebeian gestures," he said as he lifted them. "I don't suppose we could dispense with these? We are, after all, both gentlemen."

"No, I'm afraid we can't," Chase replied. "And we're not gentlemen, not me and certainly not you."

Pickering's face grew sharply colored. It was obvious that Chase's manner was angering him, but he controlled himself, slipping his left wrist into one side of the handcuffs and snapping it shut.

"And that little scene at the end," he went on, apparently eager to satisfy his curiosity about the events that had led to his capture. "Miss Hampton was a surprisingly adept actress," he mused as he fingered the handcuffs. "I really thought I'd killed her. Foolish of me not to have administered a *coup de grâce,* but with all that show of blood and the fire, I made the normal assumptions." He turned to glance back at Chase. "I don't suppose you're completely innocent of that small subterfuge, either? I must admit, now that I think back on it, the scene was quite convincingly staged."

Chase's expression grew sharp.

"Scene? What scene?"

"Come, come, Sutton," Pickering chided. "There's no need to pretend any longer. I know she's alive. That fool of a painter friend of hers told me the whole of it, or at least what little he knew. It wasn't hard to reason out the rest."

Chase felt a sudden sick feeling in the pit of his stomach, a premonition that it had all been too easy, that something was going to go terribly wrong.

"Painter friend?" he asked, even though he knew perfectly well Pickering must be referring to Pierre.

Pickering sensed his discomfort and seemed pleased by it. He grinned.

"You mean you didn't know she went to him?" he asked. "Such a touching scene, the dead coming back to life at her own funeral."

"The little fool," Chase muttered under his breath.

Pickering heard. "No, of course you didn't know," he said. He shook his head. "It would seem you've made mistakes, Sutton. Perhaps I've given you too much credit. Perhaps you're just luckier than the others, not smarter, after all." He laughed quietly.

Chase was startled by the sound of that laughter. The sick feeling in his stomach grew worse, much worse.

"Competent or lucky," he said, "whatever the reason, I've still caught you."

"So it would seem," Pickering agreed. "Oh, if it sets your mind at ease, you needn't worry that Pierre fellow will go spreading stories about your little failings," he added in a conspiratorial whisper. "No one will hear of your mistakes from him. I saw to it that he'll be silent. Eternally silent, you might say."

Delia had been listening intently, waiting until Chase told her it was safe for her to show herself, safe for her to say what she'd been waiting all those long weeks to say to Pickering. But his remark about Pierre startled her. Eternally silent, she thought, and her mind suddenly tumbled into a confused panic. She stood up, all caution completely forgotten.

"Pierre?" she cried out softly.

Pickering transferred his glance from Chase to her, and then he smiled.

"Ah, I was wondering where you were keeping yourself, my dear," he said. His expression grew smug. "Somehow, I knew you wouldn't allow yourself to miss this opportunity to see me one last time." He grinned. "It's odd, this attraction between us, don't you think?"

Delia ignored him.

"What did you do to Pierre?" she demanded.

She slipped out from her hiding place among the trunks and started to move forward, toward Pickering. Chase reached out and grabbed her arm, keeping her a safe distance away.

"The other bracelet, Pickering," he directed, and motioned with his pistol.

Pickering scowled with distaste, but made no other objection as he placed his second wrist into the handcuff and clicked it shut.

Delia pulled herself free of Chase's grasp. Her attention was fixed on Pickering, and she had no thoughts that he might still be dangerous.

"What did you do to Pierre?" she demanded a second time.

Pickering had been considering the unpleasant condition of his wrists. Now he looked back up at her.

"I did you a favor, my dear," he told her, his tone oily and mean. "Such a childishly brash and irrational young man. Able to hold neither his liquor nor his tongue. And jealous, decidedly jealous. A man like that is no asset, I assure you. You really ought to have chosen your companions more carefully."

Delia felt her blood pounding in her ears. He's killed Pierre, she thought. And it's all my fault. As much as it would be if I'd put a pistol to his head, it's all my fault.

"What happened?" she cried, terrified, but still needing to know.

Pickering was apparently determined to torture her a bit longer, determined to draw out the story and tell it in his own way.

"I must admit he did startle me when he confided to me that you were still alive," he said. "But once he'd planted the seed, I realized it wasn't such a great impossibility after all. That little scene you staged was nicely performed, but still, a bit too pat. A bit melodramatic, actually." He turned slightly and bowed to Chase. "No doubt of your direction."

His evasions were making Delia frantic.

"What did you do to him?" she shouted.

Pickering's eyes narrowed. There was no question but that he was enjoying the pain he was causing her. He shrugged.

"I did nothing to him," he replied. His expression grew vicious as he anticipated the hurt he was about to cause her. "Absolutely nothing," he went on. "I can hardly be blamed if he allowed himself to become drunk enough to stumble into the river. As I said, a childish, foolish young man. Hardly a suitable match for you. You're well rid of him."

Delia gasped. She couldn't believe he was standing there, calmly dismissing a death he had caused. She could believe even less that he was enjoying the retelling of it.

"You monster," she hissed. "You pushed him into the Seine and then walked away. You left him to drown."

Pickering shook his head. "I assure you, my dear, I did not push him into the Seine or anywhere else. He was so drunk he simply fell."

"And you were the one who gave him the liquor to get him that drunk," she said, knowing it was so. "You got him drunk and then you turned your back on him and let him die."

"He was a fool," Pickering sneered. "And he met a fitting fool's end."

Delia opened her mouth to speak, but suddenly realized words failed her. She was momentarily stunned, awed by the complete lack of concern Pickering displayed. It was as though Pierre had been nothing more than an insect, something so small and inconsequential, it was beneath Pickering even to consider him. And suddenly she was overcome with anger, not only with what Pickering had done, but with his complete lack of remorse or humanity. She began to shake with rage.

"You killed him," she shouted, "just like you killed my father!"

Her display of passion only made Pickering that much colder.

"I'm afraid you're disturbed, my dear," he said, "totally delusional. I had nothing whatsoever to do with Cotter's attack. I didn't so much as touch him."

Delia had expected none of this. All the times she'd thought of this moment when she would finally see Pickering learning he would face justice, she'd expected to feel a great release, to feel a cleansing sense of satisfaction that she'd finally appeased Cotter's ghost. But her father's spirit had abandoned her, and all she felt at that moment was disgust and even a hint of shame that she was honoring Pickering's sickness by listening to his words. She'd long before come to think of him as a villain, but now she realized he was much worse than a thief, much worse even than a murderer. She could see now he was without conscience, without honor. He was nothing less than a beast masquerading in a man's body.

"You took away his pills," she said. "You as good as killed him."

She had no idea why she kept on. Accusing him, showing him her impotent fury, only seemed to feed the evil sickness inside him. But still part of her expected to see him cringe, to see him show some sign of regret, even if it was only for the fact that he had finally been caught.

He didn't.

"I did you a favor," Pickering hissed at her in reply. "He was turning himself into an invalid, letting his intellect and talents be rotted away by alcohol. I confess, it was a great disappointment to me to see him that way. Such promising youth turning to such useless and pathetic wretchedness. But he wasn't a man any longer. He was a parasite, living off your talents."

Delia was stunned, overwhelmed by his words, shocked by the magnitude of his sheer callousness.

"He was my father," she shouted.

Pickering ignored her interruption.

"He would have drained you dry," he went on, his tone lecturing now, pedantic. "You should thank me for saving you."

The fury was suddenly gone from her, drained away in a wash of complete incomprehension. There was no way she would ever understand Pickering or his motives, no way she could ever find reason, however warped, in what he was saying.

"You are a monster," she whispered. "An insane monster."

Chase, too, was disgusted. And he knew that he could not let Pickering go on any longer, if only for Delia's sake.

"Enough, Pickering," he shouted. "It's over. You can keep the rest of your filthy thoughts to yourself."

"Over?" Pickering asked softly. He smiled, first at Chase, then at Delia. "Do you really think you've caught me, you young fools? Do you think I'm nothing more than a common second-story man, too stupid and incompetent to keep himself from falling into your tawdry little trap?"

Chase ignored him, looking up to see the hold door being pushed open once again and finding Rampeau, pistol in hand, entering.

"I see you've completed the formalities without me," the Sûreté man said to Chase, as he noticed Pickering's wrists were already handcuffed. "All according to plan."

"Here's your art thief, Préfet," Chase told him. As Rampeau was armed, he returned his own pistol to its holster. "I'm only too delighted to wash my hands of him. You can throw him in the bilge, for all I care. It might serve to wash away some of his stink."

Rampeau glanced at Pickering and smiled. "A great pleasure, *monsieur*," he said.

Pickering turned to face him and scowled.

"Don't just stand there, you idiot," he snarled. "Shoot him!"

An obedient servant, Rampeau turned his pistol on Chase and fired.

"No!"

Delia hardly knew she'd screamed. Her cry was nearly lost in the sound of the shot being fired. All she heard was the blast, the sound of it reverberating through the metal sides of the hold. The noise kept on, echoing inside her head, leaving her frozen and numb.

She felt rooted, unable to move, her limbs numb with disbelief. She stood and watched Chase crumble and fall backward, and the shock inside her grew as she saw a thick red gush of blood seep over his white shirtfront. He's dead, a voice inside her shouted. You've killed him just as you killed Pierre.

She wanted to deny it, wanted to tell herself she wasn't to blame, but she knew she couldn't. If she hadn't gone to that memorial service, if she hadn't spoken to Pierre, Pickering would have gone on thinking her dead and himself secure. If she hadn't alerted him, Pickering would never have thought to enlist the Sûreté man, would certainly never have killed either Pierre or Chase.

But if there was guilt, then surely she had every right to share it. She suddenly filled with an animal fury, an indescribable anger that turned her fear to rage and sent her charging blindly at Pickering. He'd done unspeakable things, and he felt nothing. The boiling fury inside her told her he must be made to pay.

At that moment she had no thought of what might happen to her, no care that she would be the next target. At that moment, feeling that she had been the cause of Chase's death, she could even welcome a similar fate if first she could see Pickering suffer. All she wanted was to reach Pickering, to rake her fingernails on his face, to feel his blood wetting her hands and know that she had caused him to finally feel pain.

But however great her rage, it didn't make her strong enough to overcome Pickering. As she reached out to claw at him, he raised his handcuffed hands and brought them down hard on the side of her head.

She fell. It seemed to her that she fell endlessly, that a great chasm had opened up beneath her and swallowed her. Her head and neck were filled with a thick, shooting pain, a pain that spread slowly through her to her arms and her legs, until she felt it wouldn't matter if she ever reached the bottom of the chasm for she'd never feel herself landing, never feel anything but the reverberations of that blow.

A haze filled her mind. It wasn't a total darkness, a complete oblivion that might mercifully end the hurt. Instead, it was as though she was surrounded by a thick mist, with light and sounds drifting slowly through it until they seemed distorted and distant.

There were voices, men's voices, speaking, and she strained to listen. But it was like listening to a foreign language, one whose words she had learned, but not so well as not to require her puzzling over them before they had meaning.

She had to force herself to concentrate, to make sense of the words. Some small part of her that had not yet given up hope told her she must listen if she was to survive.

"The key. In his pocket. Get the damned key to these things. There isn't that much more time."

It was Pickering's voice, ordering Rampeau, shouting at him in the sort of tone he might use to order a dog to heel.

The pain was slowly ebbing, easing into a constant, aching throb. Delia found she could see now, and

394

Pickering's words were less strange, easier to understand. But she was still numb, and even though she tried to move her arms and legs, they refused to respond. For a moment, she thought she might already be dead. Then she told herself it was impossible to be dead and still feel pain.

She saw Rampeau cross to Chase and lean over his still body. She wanted to shout at him to keep his filthy hands away, but something held her back, something told her she must not move, must not make a sound.

Rampeau found the key to the handcuffs and quickly returned to release Pickering.

"What about the girl?" he asked as he fumbled with the lock. "What do we do with her?"

The lock finally popped open and Pickering dropped the handcuffs. They fell, landing noisily against the metal flooring.

"The same as you do with him," Pickering snapped. "Put them both in the trunk and lock it. They'll suffocate long before anyone finds them."

Rampeau didn't seem pleased with the idea.

"You didn't say anything about killing a woman," he argued. "That wasn't part of our bargain, and I don't like it. It's bad luck to kill a woman."

"Idiot," Pickering sneered, as he pushed Rampeau out of his way. "You weren't thinking about bad luck when you accepted my offer, and I'm paying you enough to make you forget about bad luck. Now get about it. I haven't the time to argue with you." He fixed the *préfet* with a steely, emotionless stare. "Unless you have changed your mind and suddenly decided you're willing to retire on the pittance the French government allots persons of your ilk."

Rampeau swallowed uncomfortably. He might not like what Pickering was telling him to do, but he liked even less the prospect of living out his retirement in near poverty.

"No," he muttered. "I haven't changed my mind," he said.

"Then get about it," Pickering hissed.

Delia lay very still. Despite the desperation of her situation, hope was beginning to grow inside her. Perhaps Chase isn't dead, she thought. He couldn't be dead, she thought, not without her telling him that he had been right, that she did love him. And that seemed only logical to her, that no fate would be so cruel as to let it end like this, without the words being spoken, without her saying those three small words that her pride had refused to allow her to say before. Suddenly pride seemed meaningless to her. Suddenly all that was left was the hope that Chase was still alive and that there might be some way for her to tell him what she ought to have told him long ago.

If they think I'm dead, she told herself, perhaps I can find some way to get help. Chase isn't dead. I know he isn't dead. If I can fool Pickering, perhaps I can save him, save us both.

And what hope had initiated, stubbornness made stronger. She was not going to give Pickering the satisfaction of simply giving up. She was not going to let him kill her without a fight.

Her first thought was to scream, to cry out for help. But before she did, she realized that it would be a mistake, most probably a fatal mistake. No one would hear, no one except Pickering and Rampeau. The whole of the crew and all the passengers were up on deck, preparing to board lifeboats if the explosion in the boiler room proved to have dealt the steamer a mortal blow. After all, if there had been someone nearby, surely they would have come to investigate the sound of the shot that had felled Chase.

So she lay there, silent, her eyes just barely open so she could watch, hoping she'd be able to recognize the chance when it came. Rampeau pulled a large trunk out and placed it near where Chase lay. He snapped back the locks and he pulled the sides apart, settling it like an enormous open, pageless book. Then he grasped Chase beneath the arms and began to pull.

As soon as he touched Chase, he was rewarded with the sound of a low moan. Rampeau dropped him, and stepped back.

"He's still alive," he said. There was no special emotion in his words, just a statement, like a comment on the weather.

But his words, to Delia, were what a life preserver is to a drowning man. They sang through her heart, and she clung to them, nourishing herself on them. They chased away the pain in her head and the numbness in her limbs, and she felt herself grow stronger each time she silently repeated them to herself.

But Rampeau's next words sent a deathly chill through her: "Should I finish him off?"

Now, Delia told herself, do something now, don't let him kill Chase. She had no idea what she could do, but she did know she couldn't lie there and let him shoot Chase again.

It was Pickering, though, who stopped Rampeau.

"It doesn't matter," he said. "We don't need to risk another shot. Put him in the trunk. He'll have bled to death long before anyone thinks to open an unclaimed trunk left in Victoria Station."

"As you say, then," Rampeau replied. Once again he began to heave Chase, huffing and groaning as he pushed the dead weight of his limp body into one side of the open chest.

Pickering, still busy with the paintings, glanced up when he heard Rampeau make one final, thick grunt of effort.

"The girl next," he directed. "Then mop up the blood. The fewer suspicions roused, the better," he added, before he turned back to his own task.

Rampeau lumbered over to Delia and stood above

397

her, staring down at her still form. She held her breath, hoping he wouldn't realize she was conscious, afraid he might decide to silence her once and for all. Chase is still alive, she thought, holding onto that, feeding on it to give her strength.

Then Rampeau inhaled deeply, preparing himself for the effort, knelt, and lifted her in his arms. She let her head loll and her body go limp.

"I still don't like this," he said as he carried her to the trunk. "I think it should cost you more."

Pickering turned and stared at him.

"Cost me more?" he asked in a low tone. There was no sign he was angry, just surprised, as though the thought would never have occurred to him.

Rampeau dropped Delia. She choked away the grunt of hurt that sprang to her lips as she came in contact with the hard decking, forcing herself to remain still. Rampeau got clumsily down to his knees and began to fold her limbs, trying to press her limply uncooperative body into the trunk.

"I'm going to have to explain their disappearance," he went on as he neatly pushed Delia's limp arms inside the trunk and arranged her hands primly in her lap.

"I have great confidence in your talents," Pickering assured him.

"It won't be easy," Rampeau insisted. "I should be paid for the effort. Maybe ten thousand francs more." He bent Delia's knees and pressed her legs up. Still kneeling, he turned his head to look up at Pickering. "Not so much, ten thousand."

"Perhaps not," Pickering agreed. His hand slipped into his jacket pocket. "But still more than you're worth."

He withdrew his hand from his pocket and, with one fluid motion, pointed it at Rampeau and fired.

* * *

Delia had thought she'd become numbed to the enormity of Pickering's villainy, but once again she found herself overwhelmed with the shock of what she'd seen him do. The last thing she'd expected was for him to shoot his own hireling. He'd used Rampeau and now he disposed of him, doing both with equal contempt.

She knew she had no time to ponder. Rampeau's body fell forward, landing beside her, splattering her with his blood. The feel of it was repulsive, but she didn't allow herself to think of it. Now was her chance, she told herself. Now was her only chance.

Pickering was approaching her, and there was a grimness in his expression that told her he was determined to finish up what had begun so badly. His right hand, in which he held the pistol, was lowered to his side.

An instant, she thought, that's all it would give her. She had nothing else beside that instant, save for the fact that he thought her still unconscious.

Moving with a speed and a strength she'd never thought she possessed, she pushed herself forward, flinging the weight of her body against Pickering's legs. Her body struck them with a startling force, strong enough to send a wave of hurt through her shoulders and spine.

Disoriented by the unexpected attack, Pickering stumbled and fell back. The pistol dropped from his hand and struck the hard metal floor, then skidded dizzily away.

Delia knew she had no time to consider the throbbing hurt the contact had released in her. Guided more by some instinct rather than by conscious thought, she pushed herself, forcing her body to roll away from Pickering and toward where the pistol had settled. She knew she had to reach it before Pickering regained his senses. If she didn't manage to reach it before he did, she and Chase would certainly be dead.

Unfortunately, it took Pickering only an instant to realize that she'd only pretended to be unconscious. Anger bubbled up inside him as he realized she'd tricked him. He didn't like to be made a fool of, and this was the second time she'd done just that.

He lunged forward, determined to reach the pistol before Delia did.

For the fleeting instant when Delia felt the hard metal of the pistol in her hand and as she slipped her finger onto the trigger, she thought she had won. But before she could turn and aim it at Pickering, he slid on top of her. She flailed wildly, twisting, trying to free herself of him, but it was useless. His hand reached forward and grasped hers, pressing it, harder and harder.

She refused to let it go, refused to allow herself to feel the pain of his fingers digging into the soft skin of her wrist. But she was not strong enough to keep him from twisting her arm until the pistol, with her own finger still on the trigger, was pointed at her head.

"It would seem that the sleeping beauty wasn't really asleep after all," Pickering said. He smiled maliciously down at her.

Delia said nothing. She was occupied with the effort of trying to keep control of the pistol, panting with the pain in her wrist and the weight of his body on hers.

He pressed his fingers a bit harder, hoping to force her to release her hold of the pistol. She didn't.

"Damn you," he muttered. "Then kill yourself, just like your fool of a friend did. And this time, I promise you, you won't rise from the dead."

He put his hand on top of the finger she had on the trigger. Delia had only to glance at the vicious look in his eyes to know he was about to force her to shoot herself.

Chapter Twenty-two

"Drop the pistol, Pickering, and get away from her."

Chase's voice was shaking, but there was still more than enough force in it to make Pickering hesitate, then turn and stare at him. And much to his obvious displeasure, Chase was very much alive. He was holding his pistol and aiming it directly at Pickering's head.

A low, angry growl escaped Pickering's lips. He loosened his hold on Delia's hand slightly, but he didn't release it. Nor did he move.

"Put it down, Sutton," he hissed sharply at Chase. "You can't hope to beat me. You were a fool even to try."

Chase wasn't moved by the command in Pickering's tone. He knew that were he to give up the pistol, Pickering would waste no time in killing Delia and then turning his own weapon on Chase. His only chance, Delia's only chance, was to outbluff Pickering.

And he was not about to give up. He could feel the sticky warmth of his own blood slowly seeping down his chest, he was breathing heavily, and he had to fight a searing pain in his shoulder, but still, he was not ready to accept his own or Delia's death. More than that, there was an angry stubbornness inside him that refused to admit that Pickering had won. Chase might be dying, but he hadn't yet given up fighting.

"I may be a fool, Pickering, but not so great a fool as that," he said. "I drop the pistol and you'll kill her and then you'll kill me. I, on the other hand, am a man of my word. Release her now and I'll let you live."

"I could kill her before you had the chance to fire."

"Perhaps you can," he admitted. "But don't think you'll live long enough to gloat over the fact. I swear I'll splatter your filthy brains all over this place unless you get away from her. You have three seconds to release her, or I'll fire. Three seconds, Pickering. Starting now!"

Chase shouted the last two words, shouted them loudly enough and sharply enough to make Pickering react. He dropped his hand away from Delia's and pushed himself to his knees.

"Wise choice," Chase told him.

He motioned with the pistol, keeping the movement short and tight, afraid that if he moved too much he'd betray just how much pain he was in. He knew Pickering would take advantage of any sign of weakness.

"That fool of a policeman should have emptied your holster," Pickering hissed.

"Don't blame the hired help, Pickering," Chase told him. "He probably thought I wouldn't live to use it again."

"A shame he was wrong," Pickering said with a sadistic smile.

"It's a pleasure to disappoint you," Chase replied. "Now move away from her."

Pickering eyed him for a moment, aware that Chase's hand was less than perfectly steady, that his face was drained and pale. Considering the amount of blood he saw seeped onto Chase's clothing, he realized he'd probably have made the same assumption Rampeau had.

But he decided there was very little need for him to be concerned. He could see that Chase could not hold on much longer. In only a short while, Chase would be unable to aim the pistol at all, let alone aim and fire it. He could afford to give in, at least for the moment. He had nothing to lose except a little time.

He arched his brows and scowled.

"As you like," he muttered as he pushed himself slowly aside, freeing Delia.

As soon as he did, Delia slid away from him, scuttling backward on all fours, too eager to be away from him to take the time to get to her feet first. She was, she realized, still holding the pistol unsteadily in her hand, her finger still on the trigger. She pulled it away gingerly. The thought of how close that finger had come to squeezing the trigger and sending a bullet into her brain left her weak and visibly shaking.

"Come here, Delia," Chase directed her. "Keep your eyes on him, and slowly back away."

She did as he directed, steadying herself enough so that she could get to her feet. Then, with the pistol held in both hands and aimed at Pickering, she backed away until she was standing at Chase's side.

One glance at him and she saw what Pickering had seen, that he was in far worse condition than his confident words a moment before had made him seem. Although he'd managed to push his legs out from the trunk, he had not been able to completely extricate himself. He was now sprawled with his back still supported by the thick leather case. His face was deadly pale, his right arm hung limp by his side, and his shoulder showed a gory hole where Rampeau's bullet had struck him. The most frightening thing to Delia, though, was the sight of all the blood. There was an ugly, dark red stain emanating from the wound and spreading down the front of his shirt, steadily growing larger.

Despite the fact that she was no student of human anatomy, and although it was clear the bullet was well above Chase's heart, Delia was still certain he could not go on much longer bleeding as profusely as he was now. She glanced quickly at Pickering and saw he was grinning at her. She could see that he was telling her he knew what she knew, that Chase would not continue to be a threat to him much longer. He was telling her that he still intended to kill her.

She turned away from him, refusing to accept her fate, and Chase's, as already sealed.

"Chase," she murmured.

She began to kneel at his side, ignoring Pickering's malicious grin. All that mattered, she told herself, was that Chase not die, that he get the help he so obviously needed. The pistol she'd fought so violently to keep from Pickering fell to the metal planking at her side.

"No," Chase ordered. "Get the pistol, and keep it aimed at him. Don't take your eyes off him." When she hesitated, when he saw she was still staring at the gore Rampeau's bullet had left in his shoulder, his voice grew sharp. "Do it!"

The vehemence in his words startled her. She grasped the pistol, then lifted it until it was once again pointed directly at Pickering.

"Chase, you need help," she murmured.

"She's right, Sutton," Pickering agreed pleasantly. "I can assure you that you're bleeding to death. You won't last much longer."

Chase ignored him, addressing Delia when he spoke.

"It looks worse than it is," he told her. "The only help you can give me just now is with him," he added,

404

with a weak nod in Pickering's direction. "We have to hold him here until someone comes looking for us."

Delia bit her lip. She didn't doubt that the wound was far more serious than he'd admit. But it was also clear that they could not trust Pickering, nor could she leave him unguarded and go search for help. Still, even knowing how dangerous the man was, she had to force her attention away from Chase and back to Pickering.

Pickering, although unarmed, was still far from weaponless. For half a century he'd used words to frighten people, to bully and intimidate. And he was not about to be silent when he knew how effective a weapon he still had in his possession.

"How long do you think you can keep this up, Sutton?" he asked sharply. "Ten minutes? Fifteen? You're bleeding to death. You're just too stubborn to recognize the fact."

"It won't have to be much longer," Chase said. "I assume that explosion of yours in the boiler room, that wasn't much more than noise and smoke, now, was it? You should be congratulated. It was a perfect subterfuge to get you in here unseen. Who watches a man go off into a hold when everyone is concerned that they're about to be drowned?"

Pickering nodded in recognition of the compliment.

"It was really a small enough matter to arrange," he said modestly. "Actually, the whole plan was quite simple. I like to keep things that way. There's less to go wrong."

"But something *did* go wrong this time, didn't it?" Chase prodded.

"Unfortunately," Pickering agreed with a resigned shrug. "If you'd had the good sense to die when Rampeau shot you, I'd be out of here by now, and soon to be a very, very rich man."

405

He'd watched Chase as he spoke, watched his hand shake and his grasp of his pistol grow unsteady. And Chase returned his stare. He was forced to grit his teeth to hold back the pain. Still, he managed to settle himself before Pickering thought to take advantage of the spasm.

"Sorry to ruin your plans," he said.

Pickering grinned. "Oh, you haven't ruined them," he assured Chase. "Even if the fools running this tin can realize soon that there's no real danger, it won't do you any good." He pointed to Chase's hand. "You can hardly hold that pistol now," he said. "You won't have the strength to do even that in a few more minutes."

"Won't I?" Chase countered. "Let's wait and see, shall we?"

Pickering settled himself on top of a crate, sitting with his knees wide and his hands hanging lazily between them.

"Admit it, Sutton, you're getting weaker," he said.

Delia was disgusted by Pickering's satisfied smile and smug manner. But mostly she was revolted by the ghoulish way he stared at Chase as though he enjoyed the spectacle of watching a man bleed to death there in front of him.

"Stop it," she hissed angrily.

Pickering's brow rose in mock surprise. "Stop what?" he asked. "I've done nothing."

"Nothing?" she hissed angrily. "You monster. Perhaps it would be wisest for me to just shoot you now. No need to waste the time and expense of a trial. And no question about a fit punishment."

The pistol seemed to come alive in her hands at the thought. She could pull the trigger now. It would finally be settled and over and she would be free. Cotter's ghost would have no further claim on her. And for a long, painful moment the temptation to give in

406

to her hatred of Pickering was incredibly seductive, a hot, throbbing hunger in her blood.

Pickering let his glance slowly meet hers, as though he'd forgotten her and was trying to figure out just how she'd gotten there in the first place. It made Delia shiver, the knowing way he smiled as he watched her, as if he was silently saying, We're not so very much different after all, you and I.

She felt invaded, forcibly penetrated by the implied intimacy of that look. And it was obvious from Pickering's pleased expression that he knew what she felt. His glance fell for an instant to the pistol, then returned to meet hers. Once again he smiled, still smug and sure of himself, despite his position.

That smile sent a chill through Delia, a chill strong enough to make her shiver. Despite the pistol in her hand, she was still afraid of him.

No, a voice inside her cried out, I am a civilized human being. I am not like him. And I will not be ruled by hatred.

Again Pickering seemed able to read her thoughts. "You couldn't shoot me in Paris," he told her softly, his tone even and completely confident. "We both know you won't do any better now. You have doubts and you have a conscience. And that is your fatal weakness."

Delia felt a bitter wash of rage. The pistol began to shake in her hands and she felt her finger trembling as she placed it on the trigger. She bit her lip, hard enough to steady her unsettled nerves and keep her focus on Pickering.

"That was a game back in Paris, Pickering," she told him. "But I'm not playing anymore. You killed Papa and Pierre." Now it was her turn to smile, and it gave her an odd sense of satisfaction to see that just as Pickering's smile had frightened her, hers had an unsettling effect on him. "Killing might be a sin, but

407

justice is something else. And God knows, you deserve to die."

"And you'd kill me in cold blood?" he asked. He swallowed uneasily, then laughed suddenly, telling her that he refused to be intimidated by her threat. "If God holds no sway with you, perhaps consideration of the law does. I'm an unarmed man, Miss Hampton. Shoot me and I assure you, you'll end up on the gallows."

But Delia found that she, too, seemed to have shed her fear.

"It would be worth it," she hissed, "to see you dead."

"There's no need," Chase broke in. "Rampeau's dead body. Me shot. You won't walk away from this, Pickering."

Pickering's expression didn't change.

"It does look unpleasant, doesn't it?" he mused. "Still, where there's a will . . ."

His words trailed off and he smiled again, turning his glance from Chase back to Delia.

And as he did, the door to the hold swung open.

"I knew you'd come to save my paintings, Matthew," de Grasse exclaimed. "But there's no need. It was a false alarm." His words slowed and his effusive manner abruptly sobered as he looked around. "It was all an unpleasant mistake."

Delia, Chase, and Pickering had all turned to stare at de Grasse as he slowly entered. He was silent now, and his eyes were wide with disbelief as they settled on Rampeau's still form and the spatterings of blood, then shifted to Chase and Delia, both with pistols in their hands.

He trembled and seemed about to turn tail and flee.

Pickering's voice, however, halted him.

"Thank God you've come, François," Pickering shouted to him. "With you here, they'll have to give themselves up. They won't dare harm you. They must know there's no way they could escape if they killed you, too."

Delia heard this, but told herself that she must have heard it wrong, that what he'd said was meaningless nonsense. Chase simply ignored him.

"Go after the guards, de Grasse," he ordered. "Bring them down here."

But de Grasse didn't move. He stood, completely numb, with his mouth agape. He turned to Pickering, silently asking for an explanation.

"No, don't leave," Pickering begged. For the first time, his tone had turned supplicating, pathetically pleading, as if he was begging for his life. "If you leave, they'll shoot me, just as they shot that poor policeman."

It was then that Delia realized he was trying to get de Grasse confused enough to believe that he was the victim, that she and Chase were the thieves and had shot Rampeau. He was convincing, she realized, and more than that, de Grasse's sympathies were with him.

"That's a lie," she shouted. "It was him. He shot Rampeau. He was trying to steal the Memlings."

Where there had been only fear in de Grasse's expression a moment before, now there was fear mingled with complete bewilderment. He stared at Delia for a moment as if he thought her deranged, then turned his glance back to Pickering.

"What is that woman saying, Matthew?" he asked.

"She's trying to confuse you," Pickering told him. "Just look. They have the weapons. I'm unarmed. How could I be anything but an unsuspecting victim here?"

409

"And I suppose you're going to add that I shot myself?" Chase suggested, in a tone that was laden with sarcasm.

De Grasse's eyes narrowed as his confusion grew. It was obvious that he wanted to believe Pickering, that their friendship colored his judgment and the way he perceived what he saw. But he could not argue with the wound he saw in Chase's shoulder and all the blood.

"What happened here, Matthew?" he demanded.

Pickering shook his head. "I don't know," he lied in an extraordinarily convincing tone of innocence. "I can only surmise that these two were in the midst of stealing your paintings when the policeman came in. The two men must have scuffled and shot one another. Unfortunately, the wrong man died."

"That's all lies," Delia burst out. She was awash in anger. She couldn't believe that de Grasse could be so stupid as not to see what Pickering was trying to do.

"Damn it, go for the guards," Chase ordered.

He tried to straighten himself up and only succeeded in slumping further against the side of the trunk. The pistol grew a bit more unsteady in his hand.

"Yes," Pickering agreed. "We'll both go."

"No, just the Compte," Chase shouted. He fought to steady the pistol. He was breathing heavily, and it was obvious that the effort of holding the weapon was becoming more laborious for him. "Just bring the guards down here," he told de Grasse. "Let them work it out."

De Grasse nodded, apparently accepting the wisdom of Chase's suggestion. He turned and began to walk to the door.

But as he passed, Pickering reached for him, grabbing his arm and refusing to let him go.

"Don't leave me alone with them, François," he

410

begged. "I won't live long enough for the guards to get here. They'll make up some insane story and I'll be dead."

Delia told herself this couldn't go on much longer. If Pickering confused de Grasse enough, if he muddied the waters enough, he might actually go free.

"Just look," she insisted. She pointed to the paintings Pickering had been in the act of switching. "He was exchanging them with forgeries."

She took a half dozen steps forward to the open crate and the two canvases that were lying without stretchers beside the pair that were set, as yet unpinned, into the ornate gilt frames. She lifted one of the canvases to show it to de Grasse.

The Compte was intrigued enough by the glimpse f the forgeries to edge his way to the side of the crate.

"My beautiful paintings," he moaned softly.

He was suddenly plunged into total misery. Pickering and Rampeau's body and even Chase's pistol pointed at his friend seemed momentarily forgotten in the enormity of the crime that had been committed against his precious property.

"You can't believe her," Pickering sputtered. "François, you know me. You can't believe that lying nobody." His voice rose in morally offended innocence. "Ask her who painted those forgeries," he shouted. "She did, François. Ask her. She's the thief."

De Grasse turned a questioning glance at Delia.

"Well?" he demanded. "Is that true?"

Delia gritted her teeth. It seemed that Pickering had a ready lie for everything. She was shaking with rage inside, aware of what he was doing and knowing that the truth would hardly help her now.

"I painted them," she admitted reluctantly. "For him, so he could steal the originals. And he tried to kill me in payment."

411

"Can't you see the girl's deranged, François?" Pickering insisted. "Or a consummate liar. Either way, we must stop them."

Delia was in torment. The longer the argument went on, she thought, the greater the chance that Pickering would somehow win. She glanced back at Chase. His eyelids were drooping and the hand that held the pistol had gone slack. He'd exhausted what little strength he'd had and now it seemed it was all he could do to breathe.

"For God's sake," she cried. She pointed to Chase. "Can't you see he's bleeding to death? Go find the guards. They can settle this."

De Grasse turned to Pickering. "That does sound reasonable, Matthew," he said.

"I tell you, they'll kill me," Pickering shouted.

De Grasse shook his head and nodded toward Chase. "He's not going to kill anyone," he said. "Look at him."

"Then she will," Pickering shouted. He pointed his finger at Delia. "That crazed woman will shoot me!"

And then he leaped forward.

It happened almost too quickly for Delia to realize what he was doing until it was too late. Pickering reached de Grasse's side and his hand snaked out, grasping the knife that was lying beside the canvases, the knife he'd used to pry the original canvases free of their stretchers. He grabbed it up, and then he lunged forward, toward Delia.

The knife came precariously close to her chest. She screamed and jumped back just in time to avoid the blade. And as she did, Pickering grabbed the pistol's barrel and twisted it sharply.

Startled, Delia hardly knew what had happened until she realized he'd wrenched the pistol from her hand.

She cried out more with surprise than from any real

412

hurt that he'd done her. But then her surprise turned to fright and the fright to anger. She knew she couldn't allow Pickering to keep the weapon.

She didn't stop to consider what the blade could do to her, what use Pickering might put it to were she to give him the opportunity. She knew only that she had to get the pistol back before he had the chance to take it by the stock and point it at her. If she didn't, he'd kill her, then he'd kill Chase, and probably even de Grasse as well.

And somehow she knew that once he'd done, he'd go about stealing the paintings as if nothing had happened, oblivious to the charnel house around him. Then he'd walk away, just as he'd walked away from Cotter's dying body, just as he'd walked away and left her in a burning house, without so much as a twinge of remorse. And if by chance he was ever to be questioned about it, he'd manage to invent a convincing enough lie to get away with it all.

She darted forward, throwing her body across the crate as she reached for the pistol with both hands. She somehow managed to catch hold of it, and she continued to hold it tight even as Pickering slashed angrily at her with the knife.

There was a sudden tingling sensation in her forearm, and then a wave of heat followed by a sharp, biting hurt. She screamed in pain.

"Mon Dieu, Matthew, what are you doing?" de Grasse cried. His face was filled with shock, and it was obvious he didn't believe what he saw happening. But he collected his wits enough to reach for the pistol, grasping it in the center of the barrel and pulling hard.

Delia felt the stock slip from fingers that had become wet with the perspiration of fear, and she knew she couldn't keep her hold of it. But it didn't seem to matter now, because she realized that Pickering's

413

hold, too, had faltered, and de Grasse taken possession of the pistol. She fell back, putting her hand over the slash in her arm and eyeing the slow seep of red that appeared between her fingers for a moment before she looked up to watch the unexpected drama that was unfolding between the two men.

Pickering was staring at de Grasse's hand, looking hungrily at the pistol. And as he did, Delia could almost see him making his choices, deciding which tack he would take, which lie would seem the most convincing.

She had only one thought, to give de Grasse a warning, to cry out to him, "Don't listen to him. Don't give him the pistol. He'll use it to kill us all!"

De Grasse turned and glanced at her and she knew immediately she'd made a mistake. His expression said only too clearly that her outburst had sounded insane to him, that it had convinced him that she was as deluded as Pickering had said she was.

Pickering saw it, too. His eyes grew sharp and bright with the expectation of winning after all, of turning what had seemed moments before like sure disaster to yet another triumph.

"Thank God you got it away from her," he said to de Grasse. "I shudder to think what she might have done with it. Now give it to me, and you can go for the guards."

But de Grasse didn't move. His glance had fallen to Pickering's hand and now his eyes were glued to the knife that Pickering was still holding. The blade was wet, red with Delia's blood.

"I don't think so, *mon vieux*," he whispered through tight lips.

"But, but why?" Pickering sputtered.

De Grasse pointed the pistol at Pickering's hand.

"The blade," he said. He inhaled deeply, as if he were trying to store enough breath to ask the question

414

he knew he must ask, however reluctantly. "Why was that knife there, lying beside my paintings and those forgeries?"

"It's hers." Pickering was nearly shouting now, a hint of desperation beginning to edge his words. It was becoming clear to him that despite everything he'd done, still it was not going to go as he'd hoped. "She was using it to take the pins from the frames. I told you she was trying to steal your paintings."

De Grasse shook his head.

"No," he said, "no, that knife is yours." His voice was low, a near moan of pain as he finally began to realize that Pickering had befriended him only to betray him. "That is your knife. I've seen it lying on your dresser at night." He grew suddenly pale, as though he'd been struck and he were in agony.

"It was her," Pickering cried. "She took it."

But de Grasse was no longer listening. He was filled with his own special pain as awareness began to slowly awaken in him, an awareness that he was unable to turn away from no matter how much he would have liked to.

"I thought you were my friend," he gasped. "I welcomed you into my home. I opened my heart to you. And now I see you did it only to betray me."

Pickering's eyes narrowed and grew hard as he returned de Grasse's stare. And then his lips curled up into a vicious sneer. It was clear there was no longer any need for him to act, and he seemed glad to finally abandon the farce.

"Stop whining, you witless, self-indulgent fool," he snarled. "You opened nothing to me. All you wanted was someone to admire your home and your antiques and your precious paintings. I paid for whatever little hospitality you showed me, paid for it by flattering you and telling you just what you wanted to hear. With your title and your inherited mansion and the money that you never had to work a day in your life to earn, what did you think you deserved?"

De Grasse looked as if he had been whipped. His face had drained of color and in his eyes was the shocked expression of a man on a battlefield who looks down to find his legs have been shot from beneath him. He raised his hands, as though they could protect him from the flow of Pickering's words.

But it wasn't words that he had to fear, it was the knife in Pickering's hands, the same ornate pocket-knife that had started him on his unpleasant journey of discovery. Now that he'd learned what Pickering really was, he had made himself as much an enemy to the art thief as were Delia and Chase.

It had finally become only too clear to Pickering that he never should have gotten involved in the theft of those particular paintings. He ought to have simply walked away from the commission when he saw how complicated it had all become, when he realized the number of bodies he was forced to leave behind him had grown large enough to arouse suspicion. But he had no choice now; there was no way he could possibly turn back. He had to silence three more accusing voices if he was to walk away unscathed. Logic said he had to kill not only Delia and Chase, but de Grasse as well.

As the Compte tortured himself with his regrets and his tattered self-esteem, Pickering went about his business with a sickeningly calm objectivity. He grasped his knife firmly and then he lunged.

"Shoot!" Delia shouted as Pickering slashed out with the knife.

But de Grasse was too shocked to move. He stood statue-still and stunned as the blade struck his hand and sent the pistol flying.

Delia flung herself forward, ignoring the pain in her hurt arm as she grasped for the pistol that Chase had let fall. She snatched it up and turned to aim it at Pickering.

For just an instant Pickering's smug smile ran through her thoughts, the look he'd given her when she'd held the pistol on him and threatened to shoot. She swept it forcefully away. This wasn't an act of hatred, she told herself. It wasn't even an act of vengeance, although God alone knew how much she wanted Pickering to pay for what he'd done to Cotter and Pierre, and now to Chase.

This is self-preservation, pure and simple, she told herself as she put her finger on the trigger. This is to save Chase's life and my own.

Just as Pickering raised his arm to dispatch the still frozen de Grasse, she closed her eyes and squeezed the trigger. The pistol seemed alive in her hand, bucking back like an angry horse and making her arm ache. The report was sharp and explosive, abnormally loud in her ears.

I've killed a man, she thought. Fear settled through her, not satisfaction, but a cold, numbing fear of what she was capable of doing. She had to force herself to look up and see what had happened.

Pickering had fallen back and was slumped against the crate of paintings. The knife was still in his hand, but he seemed unaware of it, unaware of everything save the seeping red wound in his side. He stared down at it in disbelief, as if he'd never contemplated this, never considered the possibility of his own life being threatened. He put his hand on top of it, as though to make sure he wasn't imagining the blood.

That seemed strange to Delia. Surely, she thought, he'd taken more than enough lives to know his own was not inviolate. Perhaps that was how he killed so calmly, she thought. Perhaps the fact that he had never imagined his own pain made him oblivious to the pain of others.

Pickering looked up at de Grasse.

"She's shot me," he said, his words filled more with surprise than any sign of pain.

His words seemed to waken de Grasse. The *compte* shook himself and looked down at the cut Pickering's knife had slashed on his own hand. Then he turned his gaze to meet Pickering's. The shock drained slowly away and his expression filled with anger and undisguised contempt. He had been used and betrayed by a man he'd thought was his friend. This was not a sin he would easily forgive.

He continued to stare at Pickering as he knelt and retrieved the pistol he'd dropped.

"Get away from my paintings," he hissed at Pickering as he straightened up. He pointed the pistol, suddenly menacing now that his opponent seemed no longer capable of threatening him any longer.

Pickering stared at him with eyes that grew round with terror.

"She's shot me, François," he said again, but this time the surprise in his tone had been replaced by fear.

De Grasse ignored him. "Away from my paintings!" he repeated, shouting hysterically, as though he feared Pickering's presence might somehow contaminate his valuable works of art.

Pickering seemed not to have heard the *compte's* order. He held up his hands, staring at the stain of his blood on his fingers. He still grasped the knife, but he seemed oblivious to it, seemed oblivious to everything save the fact that he had been wounded. He looked out to de Grasse to find himself met only with the *compte's* icy stare in return.

He raised his hands, displaying the red stains, desperately determined to prove to de Grasse the extent of his injury.

But de Grasse saw nothing but the knife Pickering still held limply in his extended hand. He raised the pistol and fired.

Delia screamed. It was clear that de Grasse's bullet, fired at a range of only a few feet directly at Pickering's heart, had dealt Pickering a fatal blow. His body arched at the impact, then fell.

After all she'd seen in the preceding hours, still Delia was shocked by de Grasse's action. She had to force herself to look at its results. Pickering lay slumped across a crate. He was completely still.

De Grasse glanced at her briefly before he turned his attention to his paintings. He seemed not to notice the presence of Pickering's body a few feet away.

"He had the knife," he said. "He would have used it again."

Delia gulped for air and tried to swallow the thick lump that filled her throat. But she knew enough to say nothing.

Instead, she edged her way to Chase's side. She reached out for him, desperate to feel a pulse, to know he was still alive.

"He had the knife."

She looked up to find de Grasse had followed her. He was standing, staring down at her, still insisting that what he'd done was justified. At the moment, Delia realized she didn't care.

"Go for help," she screamed at him. "Find the other guards. Find a doctor!"

Stripped of his arrogance and his anger, the *compte* was docile now, even willing to be ordered about like a common messenger. He nodded, and started out of the hold at a run.

Delia put her hand on Chase's cheek and stroked it gently.

"Don't die," she whispered, suddenly angry with him, angry with herself for letting it all become so twisted and wrong between them, angry with the fate that had not given her the chance to make it right. "Damn you, Chase, don't you die now."

Chapter Twenty-three

Delia sat numb and motionless. She stared unblinkingly at the doctor, who was bandaging the hole in Chase's shoulder. All around them milled the guards who had been stationed on the steamer to protect the shipment of artwork, the half dozen special guards who, in the end, had never appeared when they'd been the most needed.

They were busy enough now, however, covering over and removing Pickering's and Rampeau's bodies, taking statements from de Grasse about how he'd been forced to kill a dangerous man, a man who he'd thought was his friend and who had betrayed and almost killed him.

Delia remained stoic and silent through all of it. None of the guards seemed especially interested in asking her any questions, at least not just yet, and for that she was thankful. She certainly was not in the mood to answer any questions, not in the mood to think about the things that had happened during the previous hour. She had one and only one interest at that moment, and that was Chase's still body lying stretched out on the floor.

From time to time she would glance up at the grim expression on the face of the doctor who was busy trying to stem the bleeding and keep Chase alive. Luckily he'd been among the passengers, for the steamer had no medical facilities, and had willingly offered his services. He was young and earnest and, from what Delia could see, he was doing all that could be done with the limited resources of his small black bag. He had not yet reached a point where he was able to hide his thoughts, however, and maintain an air of confident authority. His doubts were only too clearly mirrored by his expression. And each time she looked at him, Delia became painfully aware that there was no comfort for her in what she saw in his face.

She wished she was more devout, wished she had some confidence that the silent prayers she was desperately offering up would be heard and answered. All those years of listening to Père Alphonse's dull, droning sermons had never inspired more than a nodding acceptance of ritual in her, and now she was left bereft, wishing there had been something more, something that would make her really believe God would intervene and save Chase's life.

"Drink this, *ma'amselle*."

She looked up. Jean Gautier was standing beside her, holding out a chipped mug to her. The look in the young railroad guard's eyes as he stared down at her was heavy with remorse and pity. She knew he must deeply regret that he'd fled when his duty had been to stay with her and Chase, when his presence might possibly have saved some of the blood that had been so indiscriminately shed in the past hour.

Delia eyed the mug quickly, then shook her head. If he'd come to her looking for absolution, she thought, she would be forced to disappoint him. She simply had none to give.

"I can't," she told him.

He knelt down beside her, lifted her hand with his, and pressed the mug into it.

"Drink it," he told her. "It will do you some good."

She stared at him for an instant and realized he seemed genuinely concerned about her. That was foolish, she thought, and she glanced once again at Chase. She wasn't the one in need of anyone's concern. Still, his interest made him hard simply to dismiss.

She glanced into the mug and sniffed its contents. He had, she realized, poured a healthy tot of strong brandy into it, although she had no idea where he could have found the stuff on the steamer. She took a small sip, hoping it would satisfy him so that he'd leave her alone. But she found the liquor sent an unexpectedly comforting warmth radiating through her and even seemed to steady her shaking hands. She drank a bit more.

"Merci," she said as she handed the mug back to him.

He didn't take it. "Perhaps a bit more?" he suggested.

She shook her head and glanced again at Chase. *"Non, merci,"* she told him. "I think it best to keep my wits about me." Again she offered the mug back to him.

"You must not worry so," he told her as he took it from her. "We dock in a few minutes, and they will take him to the hospital immediately. The British may know nothing about food or women, but they have excellent doctors and hospitals."

He was grinning foolishly at her, and Delia could see how desperately he was trying to comfort her. She rewarded his effort with a weak smile.

"I'll try to remember," she promised.

"Your arm is in much pain?" he asked.

She glanced at her forearm. Someone, perhaps it had even been Gautier, had torn away the sleeve of her blouse and clumsily wrapped a thick bandage around her arm. The slash had begun to ache, but until he'd mentioned it, she'd hardly paid any attention to that. She had other, far more pressing hurts to nurse at that moment and little thought to give to it.

"It's fine," she assured him.

He nodded. "Not like the scratch on the *compte's* hand, eh?" he asked. He lowered his voice. "He's demanding a surgeon as soon as we arrive in Southampton," he confided. He smiled again, this time his expression suggesting a good deal about the *compte* that he wouldn't dare voice aloud.

Delia could not muster the interest he seemed to expect from her, and she only nodded. She didn't care about de Grasse's demands, nor about the fact that he was once again the superior aristocrat, now that the danger was past. She was well aware the man was a fool and had completely lost interest in him. She didn't care to think about him or anything else except Chase.

Still, she couldn't help but notice the small commotion de Grasse was creating as he stood and held up the paintings that had been removed from their stretchers. He explained how he'd interrupted Pickering during the theft, then began to expound on how Pickering had been about to switch the forgeries for his masterpieces, placing them on the stretchers and in the frames, and then making away with the original masterpieces.

He's got it slightly askew, she thought absently. She was absolutely sure that Pickering had already exchanged her forgeries for the originals before de Grasse appeared. She remembered distinctly that Pickering had already begun to secure the forgeries to the stretchers when Chase had interrupted him. And he'd worked for a while after that, she remembered, at least long enough to finish putting them on the stretchers and settling them in the frames before Rampeau had foolishly forced his attention to other matters. So it had to be the real Memlings that were lying limp and looking like nothing more than dirty bits of canvas while her forgeries were set luxuriously into the ornate gilt frames.

The thought was a distant one, not important enough for her to bother herself to correct the lecture, even had she not been far more interested in Chase's condition than in the way de Grasse was exaggerating his role in the affair. It would all eventually be straightened out anyway, she told herself. The curators at the museum in London could deal with it. She wanted only to wash her hands of the whole ghastly episode.

But she could not help but be roused by the end of de Grasse's performance. He grabbed up the knife, Pickering's ornately handled pocketknife that had been left behind in the confusion.

"And lest any other thief think he can succeed with such a plan, I say this to him," de Grasse cried as he raised the knife over the two paintings.

"No," Delia screamed, roused from her lethargy and aghast to realize that de Grasse was about to destroy the two masterpieces. "Don't do that!"

De Grasse turned a wilting stare toward her. He was no longer the whimpering weakling he had been half an hour before when he'd tried to justify her shooting Pickering, no longer the eager messenger she'd sent off to bring back help. He was once again the arrogant French aristocrat, and he was not about to allow his veneer to be pulled away again, certainly not in front of so large an audience as he now had.

"What is this?" he sneered at Delia.

She pointed to the two canvases. "Those are the original Memlings," she told him. "The forgeries are in the frames."

De Grasse's cheeks grew vivid.

"Do you think me a fool that I can not recognize

425

my own property?" he bellowed. "Of course these are the forgeries."

And with that, he brought his hand down, thrusting the knife through the two paintings and pulling it to tear viciously at the old, fragile squares of canvas.

Delia sat completely stunned as de Grasse dropped the torn masterpieces like so much trash to the floor. Then he imperiously ordered the guards to return the two framed paintings to the crates, secure them and see they were well guarded on the remainder of the trip to London. He made a point of completely ignoring her.

"I will not have these precious paintings threatened any further," he shouted as he marched out of the hold, nearly pushing over the steward who had come to announce that the steamer was at dock in Southampton.

Delia dismissed the *compte* and his precious paintings, telling herself that he deserved to lose them, and perhaps even that the paintings themselves deserved to be destroyed. They'd cost four lives already, her father's, Pierre's, and now Rampeau's and Pickering's. She could only pray that they would not claim Chase's life as well.

As Gautier had promised, an ambulance arrived almost immediately. She walked beside the stretcher on which they carried Chase and then found herself being handed up into the ambulance once the stretcher had been secured inside.

She didn't give either de Grasse or his paintings another thought after that. She simply didn't have the time or the energy to waste on what had become mere trivialities.

They'd taken Chase away, telling Delia the bullet had to be removed from his shoulder and that the op-

426

eration wouldn't take all that long. She mustn't worry, they'd told her, she must think about her own wounded arm. Then they'd ushered her off to a white tiled room, stripped off her blood-spattered blouse and the bandage on her arm, and proceeded to clean and sew the ugly gash.

She began to feel like an object, a mindless creature to be sutured and bandaged and then shunted between operatory and dreary hospital room. It seemed to her that by placing herself in their hands she had lost all her rights and abilities to think or function on her own. While a part of her relished the prospect of being taken care of, of giving up the need to think or make decisions and letting herself simply escape in sleep, still she felt that allowing herself such weakness was nothing better than turning her back on Chase.

Her continued questions about him were all met with absent, meaningless admonitions not to worry. And that, of course, only made her more frantic to see him. Finally, when they tried to give her a medication to make her sleep, she balked. She refused both the medication and the hospital bed, demanding instead to be left at Chase's bedside when he was brought out of surgery.

It was obvious they weren't pleased either by her manner or her demands, but she was adamant, refusing to allow herself to be bullied any longer, even if they insisted it was for her own good. She knew far better than they that she had to see Chase, had to be with him. All the doctors and nurses in England could not persuade her otherwise.

Not that she found much comfort in sitting beside him, watching his still, pale face, staring at the mass of bandages that swathed his shoulder and chest. Nor were the words of the doctor who told her the bullet had only barely missed his lung and that he'd lost a good deal of blood destined to lessen the ache inside her. If she'd been waiting for assurances that he'd be fine, she received none, neither from the doctor nor from Chase himself.

There was nothing for her to do but hold his hand and whisper to him the words she wished so vehemently she'd not refused to say before. She said it now, over and over, "I love you, Chase. Don't leave me," praying that some part of him could hear and would fight to come back to her.

Twice that night they came to her and offered the medicine, telling her she ought to sleep, that her body needed to rest. Both times she refused. She was too afraid to sleep, too terrified that if she did, Chase might die and leave her without ever giving her the chance to tell him how much she loved him. She even welcomed the throbbing ache in her arm because it kept her so sharply awake through that seemingly endless night.

When the first glimmer of dawn began to light the sky, she stood and stretched and went to the window to stare at the world beginning again for another day.

"Darkness to light," she murmured softly as she watched the sky to the east slowly brighten and fill with a soft, pale glow. However ordinary, that first glimmer of daylight woke something inside her, something that she'd nearly lost through the long hours of darkness. Those first pale fingers of dawn reminded her that some things are immutable, that what seems weak and ineffectual can be more solid than a wall of rock. Love might seem ephemeral and unsubstantial, like those first pale shafts of daylight, but if it was powerful enough to humble her pride, then perhaps it might be strong enough to return Chase to her.

She felt an odd sense of peace settle over her. In some ways, she told herself, there was proportion in life, a balancing of the scales that had tipped too much to one side. And at that moment, the ache inside her began to ease. Chase would recover, she knew that now. As bad as it seemed at that moment, still he would live. He had to, if only for the simple reason that the scale had been weighted too far against them for much too long.

Just as she turned back to the bed, a slim line of morning sunlight slid through the window and crept to the bed. When it reached Chase's face, his eyes slowly opened.

She stood beside the bed, leaning forward to him, reaching for his hand.

"Chase?"

He stared up at her silently for a moment, his expression confused and lost. But the confusion lasted only an instant, then a weak smile turned up the edge of his mouth.

"Am I dead, then?" he asked in a hoarse, low voice. "Are you an angel?"

She grasped his hand, more thankful for those foolishly inane questions than she had ever been for anything in her life.

"No," she told him. "You are still very much alive. And I assure you, no one has ever so much as suggested I might be an angel, or ever become one."

He shook his head slightly, then winced from the effort. She put her hand out to quiet him, but he pushed it away.

"If you're not an angel, why do you have a halo?" he demanded.

He reached up for her, touching her hair. With the light coming in from the window behind her, her dark hair was framed in a pale, golden glow. And the hospital robe they'd given her to wear was white and large, flowing softly around her. Given a pair of wings, he thought, she might really be an angel, or at least as close an approximation of one as he ever expected to see.

She reclaimed his hand, grasping it in hers and bringing it to her lips. She pressed first one gentle kiss against the palm and then another and another.

He smiled again, this time crookedly.

"You're beginning to convince me I really am alive," he told her. He moved slightly, reaching for her, and winced again with pain. "Shame on you, Delia. You are tempting a gravely injured man."

She paled as she realized he might be causing himself serious hurt. She put his hand back onto the bed by his side.

"I'll have them find the doctor," she told him. "Try not to move."

But before she could turn away, he reached for her hand and stopped her.

"No, not yet," he told her.

He coughed, and motioned for a drink. She quickly filled the glass on his bedside table, and held it to his lips. He drank greedily, as though nothing had ever tasted quite so good to him as that water.

"Better?" she asked when he'd done.

He nodded. "Much better," he said, in a voice that was nearly normal. He watched her as she returned the glass to the table. "You'd better be careful, Delia," he told her with a sly grin, "I might grow to like this sort of devoted care you're showering on me. Then what will you do?"

She smiled gently and shrugged. "I suppose I'd have to go on giving it to you," she replied. "That is, if you're sure it's not your weakened condition that's making you so vulnerable."

"Vulnerable, am I?"

"Aren't you?" she insisted.

"I suppose I am," he agreed. His grin disappeared,

430

and he became suddenly very serious. "I've been vulnerable from the first moment I saw you."

A lump materialized in her throat, and she had to force it away.

"Sprawled on the sidewalk with my scattered, fallen marketing?" she asked.

"I don't remember you sprawling," he said. "And as I recall, I was the cause of the disaster."

"Still, it was hardly graceful," she insisted.

He grinned again.

"What could be more appealing to a man than a woman in distress?"

"You did save the wine," she reminded him.

"Thus proving my mastery over gravity." He sobered. "It's a shame I never could find an equal mastery over you."

"Is that really necessary," she asked, "mastery?"

"Isn't it?"

She shook her head. "I hardly think so."

His eyes narrowed as he stared up at her.

"Have they told you I'm going to die?" he demanded suddenly.

She was taken aback by the question.

"No," she hurriedly answered. "No, of course not."

"Then why else would you be behaving this way?" he asked. "We've been talking for fully five minutes, and you've been nothing but sweet and accommodating. You haven't started a single argument."

She scowled. "I am not argumentative," she insisted.

"Then prove it," he said. "Be agreeable."

"I am agreeable."

"Agree to marry me."

She took a deep breath. This wasn't exactly the sort of conversation she'd expected to have with him at that moment. She swallowed, but the lump had returned to her throat and now refused to disappear.

"Marry you?" she asked, in a tone so tentative that he had to strain to hear it.

"It isn't that complicated," he insisted. "We've even discussed it before, if you will remember. Before we left Paris."

"Then you weren't just trying to get me to do what you wanted me to do, to leave the train?" she demanded. "You really meant it?"

His expression filled with surprise.

"Of course I meant it," he said. He became genuinely perplexed. "Why, in God's good name, would a sane man joke about such a thing? What would he do if the woman took him at his word?"

That hadn't ever occurred to her, the thought that generally men so abhorred the thought of losing their freedom that they'd never utter those particular words in anything but deadly seriousness.

"What, indeed?" she agreed with a soft laugh.

"Assuming I'm sane," he muttered.

She nodded and laughed again. "Perhaps a rash assumption?" she asked.

"No doubt," he grumbled. "You've done just about everything you could to make a man wonder if he'd become unbalanced."

She meekly accepted the rebuke.

"I have behaved badly at times," she admitted.

"At times? Incessantly is more like it."

He stared up at her, watching her scowl at that, sure she would finally rebel. But she didn't, instead murmuring, "Perhaps you're right, Chase."

She was far too accommodating, he thought, and he wondered just how seriously he'd been injured. For that was the only explanation he could think of for the change that had come over her, the expectation that he would die. And he did hurt, his whole body ached in ways he'd never thought possible. Still, he was sure he'd know if he was facing death, and he was very sure he was nowhere near the brink.

He decided he'd be a fool not to take advantage of the situation.

"Well?" he demanded.

"Well what?"

"Are you finally willing to admit you're in love with me?"

She nodded. She'd spent the whole night admitting that she loved him. She wasn't about to deny it now.

"I suppose I am," she said softly.

"About time," he muttered. "I expect it won't require my getting myself shot again before you're induced to say it?"

"I love you," she said.

"And you'll marry me?"

She nodded. "If you still want me after all the trouble I've caused."

He slid his hand up her arm, then to the back of her head.

"Come here and let me show you just how much I still want you," he whispered, as he pulled her down so that her lips met his.

Chase stirred and woke. Delia waited a moment before she went to him, wanting to see what his mood would be before she spoke to him. Now that he was better, he was proving to be an absolutely abominable patient, anxious to be up and about despite the doctor's admonitions that he was not yet well enough healed.

He looked up at her and growled, "Hullo."

She smiled. "Hello, grumpy. Did you have a pleasant dream?"

"It was a nightmare," he replied. "I dreamt they kept me here for years, torturing me with their horrible food and constant suggestions that I might want

433

to use the bedpan." He stirred, trying to find a comfortable way to settle his bandaged shoulder. "And you weren't much help," he went on. "You kept promising to come to bed with me, but only when the doctors allowed it. I grew old waiting."

She stifled a laugh and nodded with a politic show of sympathy.

"No wonder you're in a bad mood," she agreed.

"I don't suppose the doctor happened to stop by and agree to release me from this glorified prison?" he demanded.

She shook her head. "I'm afraid not. But the nurse did bring this." She held up a small brown box with both their names neatly printed on the top. "I waited until you woke to open it." She frowned slightly. "Nobody knows I'm here," she muttered.

"Perhaps it's from the Lloyd's Corporation," he suggested. "An offering to ease their guilty corporate conscience. Or maybe they're just hoping I'm so badly wounded, I'll forget about sending them my bill for saving them the expense of de Grasse's paintings."

Delia swallowed uncomfortably. It would seem the moment had finally arrived to tell him a few of the things she'd not wanted to tell him. She was not at all happy that she would have to tell him he hadn't saved de Grasse's paintings after all.

"They may choose not to honor that bill, Chase," she said. She swallowed once again, then told herself the only way to say it was simply to say it. "The Memlings were destroyed."

Chase pushed himself up to his elbow, wincing as his injury objected to the sudden movement.

"What are you talking about?" he demanded, as he slowly lowered himself back to rest against the heap of pillows. "They're in London, safe and secure."

"I'm afraid there was a small misunderstanding,"

434

she said. "I tried to stop him, honestly."

"Stop who?" he demanded.

She told him the whole thing then, describing what de Grasse had done, how he'd taken the knife and slashed his own paintings, determined that her forgeries were authentic.

To her surprise, Chase heard her out without so much as a groan of disgust or a word of anger. And then, when she'd done, he put his head back and began to laugh.

"That arrogant fool," he crowed.

"But it's horrible," she insisted. "Those paintings were irreplaceable."

"Not to de Grasse," he said. "Your forgeries seem to be more than adequate replacements to him." The thought set him off into another peal of laughter.

His mirth was contagious. Delia began to laugh as well.

"I can just see him now," she said, "pointing out his fine possessions to his friends, telling them how he singlehandedly outsmarted a vicious art thief." She laughed some more, laughed hard, until her sides began to ache.

Chase shook his head. "You mean a ring of art thieves," he corrected. "I'm sure in the telling it will become at least ten or fifteen murderous villains."

Delia sobered suddenly.

"One villain was more than enough," she said, thinking of all the misery Pickering had caused.

Chase, too, sobered at her words. "It's incredible that one man could ruin so many lives," he said. He let his glance find hers. "I intend to spend my life being thankful that he didn't succeed in ruining ours."

"He very nearly did," she reminded him.

He nodded and held out his hand to her. Delia went to him, sitting on the side of the bed, taking his hand in hers.

435

"We're very lucky," she murmured.

He raised a doubtful brow. "Lucky?" he asked. He put his hand lightly on the arm Pickering had slashed. "Is this lucky?" he asked. He touched his own bandaged shoulder. "Or this?"

"Yes, lucky," she insisted. "We got a second chance, Chase. Not everyone's given a second chance in life."

He grinned. "All right," he agreed. "But this time I'm going to see to it that you have no chance to get away," he told her.

"This time," she said, "I don't want to get away." She leaned forward and kissed his forehead. "Your fever's down," she told him.

"You've become such a diligent nurse," he said.

"Haven't I, though?" she asked, and laughed, a small, low, slightly lecherous laugh.

He put his hand on her chin, holding it as he pulled her to him until her lips met his. It set her on fire, that long, slow, sweetly provocative kiss. It left her breathless and hungry for more.

"Mmm," he whispered, when finally their lips parted. "That is my idea of absolutely first-class nursing. It is all the medicine I need."

"I'll be sure to mention that to the doctor," she promised.

"Don't," he warned. "We're in England now, and such excesses are hardly condoned."

"I forgot," she mused. "You British are far too civilized for passion."

He nodded. "Even purely medicinal passion," he agreed.

She smiled. "I'm not British, Chase," she reminded him. "I hope we won't prove to be incompatible."

He smiled lecherously. "Wait until your wedding night, Miss Hampton," he told her. "I'll entertain no complaints until after that."

436

"I'm not sure I can wait," she said as she forcefully turned her attention to the box, lifting it from where she'd dropped it at his side. "Well, should I open it?" she asked.

He shrugged his unwounded shoulder.

"I suppose so."

She pulled away the strings, pulled the top off the box, and looked inside.

"I don't believe it," she murmured.

"What is it?" he asked.

She pulled the two Memling paintings from the box and handed them to him. Each had three long tears radiating from their centers.

He stared at them for a long moment, then looked up at her.

"These are the real ones?" he asked.

She gently touched the surface of one of the canvases. "Yes," she said softly, "they're the originals."

"You're absolutely positive?"

She nodded. "Yes."

He stared at the paintings for a moment longer, then looked back up at her.

"Who sent them to us?"

She shook her head, as bewildered as he was, then looked back in the box. A piece of cheap notepaper lay on the bottom.

"Let's see if this solves the mystery," she said, as she drew it out and unfolded it. "As Monsieur le Compte has no need for these, I believe they rightly belong to you," she read. "I'm sure you will know how to deal with them. With my compliments, Jean Gautier."

"The railroad guard," Chase murmured. "How did he get them?"

Delia felt the laughter begin to bubble up inside her again.

"De Grasse left them in the hold," she told him.

"He dropped them like so much refuse. Gautier must have retrieved them."

He raised a wary brow. "And sent them to us?"

"Our first wedding gift," she chided. "You should be appreciative."

"Torn canvases?"

"You don't understand," she told him. "I can mend them. You'll see. They'll be lovely. No longer priceless, but certainly beautiful."

He smiled. "It seems you have a wealth of talents," he said.

"Talents?"

He nodded. "And at the moment, I think I have need of your special nursing talents. Don't you think you'd better check my temperature again?"

She laughed.

"If you insist," she said. Then she leaned forward and kissed him.

Chapter Twenty-four

Delia stood in the entry and stared around the crowded gallery. There were a great deal more people there than she'd expected.

"Perhaps this isn't such a good idea," she told Chase. "Perhaps we ought to come back some other time."

"No time like the present," he insisted, and started forward.

"But with such a press, someone might bump into you . . ."

He turned back to find she hadn't moved.

"Delia, stop making excuses," he told her. "My shoulder is nearly healed, and even if it weren't, no one is going to purposely come plowing into a man wearing a sling. Now come along."

She watched as he adjusted the sling that held his injured arm immobile, shrugging against the dark fabric. She knew he was trying to be discreet about easing the insistent itching his healing wound left in his shoulder. That was the worst of it now, he'd assured her, the fact that it constantly itched.

She hesitated, wondering why the prospect of seeing her paintings again seemed so odious to her. Perhaps it was just that she didn't want to think about everything that had happened and she knew the sight of them would bring it all back.

Chase held out his arm to her. She finally took a tentative step forward, grasping his arm as though she feared without the contact she might fall through the floor and into a bottomless abyss.

"Brave girl," he told her as he tucked her hand into the crook of his arm. "You'll see, there really aren't any monsters here. Nothing to be afraid of."

"I know there aren't any monsters," she countered. "And I'm not afraid. It . . . it just seems so strange, that's all."

Indeed, everything did seem strange to her since Chase had been released from the hospital four weeks before. It seemed unendingly strange suddenly to find herself married and living in London, a proper lady, after all. It had been decidedly strange to discover that Chase's house faced fashionable Green Park and was quite a good deal larger and more luxurious than her old house on Rue St. Clodoald had been. And it was wonderfully strange to realize that she was going to have a baby. But mostly, it felt strange to her to be so unquestionably happy.

"Strange or not, I still have my doubts," he told her. "I want to see your proof for myself."

She scowled, but realized that further objections wouldn't help and so resigned herself to the inevitable.

"Well, just be careful of your shoulder."

"Damn it, Delia, I'm not an invalid," he told her.

She sighed softly, and looked up at him and flashed a come-hither smile.

"You certainly didn't behave like one last night," she agreed.

He smiled his crooked smile. "Didn't I?"

She pretended not to notice the smile. "Or maybe it wasn't you. It was dark, after all." She lowered her voice. "Anyone could have slipped into my bed. Probably wasn't an Englishman. He was very passionate."

"Unless there were three of us there, you'll have to accept the fact that not all Englishmen are made of stone."

"Well, this one wasn't," she mused softly. "Of course, there was a certain obeliscal appendage . . ."

He laughed out loud. "Delia, you spent too many of your formative years in Paris," he told her. "You are going to scandalize London society."

She smiled seraphically up at him, eyes wide and innocent.

"Have I said something scandalous?" she asked.

"You know damn well you have," he told her. "And it's not going to work. You're not going to make me leave without seeing those paintings."

She shrugged, admitting final defeat. "Very well," she said. She glanced quickly at the exhibit catalog. "They've arranged them differently from the order they were in at the Louvre." After locating the entries in question, she glanced at the numbers beside the painting closest to them, then motioned to the far side of the long gallery. "They should be back there somewhere."

They crossed the gallery slowly, Delia grasping Chase's good arm firmly, almost afraid to let go. She found herself staring at the paintings on the walls as if she'd never seen them before. In a way, they were all new to her, despite the fact that they were the same paintings she'd seen every day during those long weeks she had spent in the Louvre making the copies for Pickering.

That whole episode seemed impossibly distant to her now, as though it had been another person

441

who'd done those things, someone she'd once known but who'd left long ago. Indeed, she was a different person now. The numbing fear and the haunting accusation of Cotter's ghost had finally disappeared, and she found she could hardly remember what it had been like to be so obsessed by them. Her memories of her father were friendly and comforting now, and she knew that had Cotter lived, he'd be happy for her.

She touched her belly, wondering how long it would be before she would feel movement there. That would have pleased Cotter, too, she thought, the knowledge that there would soon be another child to teach to paint.

"Here," Chase said, stopping and turning her attention to two paintings in ornate gold frames.

An elderly woman wearing an enormous hat covered with bizarrely colored feathers was standing in front of them. "Lovely," she exclaimed as she stared at them. She adjusted her spectacles and leaned forward, then turned and faced Delia. "Aren't they simply extraordinary?"

Delia cleared her throat, then smiled weakly at the woman. "Yes," she murmured, "I suppose they are."

Her lack of enthusiasm seemed to offend the woman, for she made a loud noise in the back of her throat that sounded something like "Hrumph," then turned away.

"She has no idea just how extraordinary they truly are," Chase murmured with a soft chuckle.

She was growing more and more uncomfortable and would very much have liked to leave. But she had no excuse to pull Chase away. They stood there several moments longer, staring at the paintings. Slowly Delia felt a strange sense of detachment creeping over her, an odd awareness that it was her hands that fashioned what all the world now accepted as genuine. And then, suddenly, she began to laugh.

Chase turned to her. "Delia?"

She smiled up at him. "I was just wondering what Papa would have thought of this," she said.

He grinned again. "A professional and a master in his own right," he told her. "He would have been proud."

She nodded. "Yes," she agreed, "I think he would have been."

Chase leaned back against the leather back of the coach seat and groaned softly. Delia turned to him, surprised and concerned at his open display of discomfort. If anything, he'd been far too stoic about his pain.

"My poor darling," she murmured. "I should never have let you talk me into going into that crowded gallery."

He closed his eyes and touched his left hand to his injured shoulder.

"Maybe you were right," he agreed.

"We'll send for the doctor immediately when we get home," she told him.

"I don't think it's really that bad, Delia," he said.

"But you're in pain," she objected.

"I'm sure I'll be fine, if you just help me to bed."

He waited an instant, then opened one eye. He found she was staring at him with slightly narrowed, knowing eyes. He opened his other eye and grinned.

"Are you terribly uncomfortable?" she purred softly, sure now that he was thinking of something entirely different from his wounded shoulder when he suggested she help him to bed.

He nodded as he put his arm around her.

"Horribly," he told her.

Then he pulled her close and kissed her. It was a long, slow, knowing kiss, the sort that speaks of banked passion held just in check and promises to lead to a great deal more. It left Delia flushed and breathless and liquid inside.

"I think you have a fever, Chase," she whispered.

"I think you're right," he agreed as he nibbled gently on her ear. "And I wouldn't be surprised if I was in desperate need of some very special nursing quite soon."

"That was part of the promise, wasn't it?" she asked softly. "Back in the hospital."

He pulled away suddenly and stared at her.

"Any regrets, Delia?" he asked.

"Only one," she replied as she glanced out the window of the coach. She grinned mischievously at him. "That we're still so far from home."

He returned her smile, then put his hand on the back of her neck, pulling her gently to him.

"Some hungers are better sated when they're honed by anticipation," he said softly.

It was true, he thought. He had certainly waited a long time for her. Or perhaps it wasn't really that long. Perhaps it had only been the fear of losing her that had made it seem that way.

He only knew that he loved her more than he'd ever thought he could love another human being. And he yearned for her, ached for her, every hour of every day.

She shook her head slowly, as though with deep regret.

"You're far too stoic, my love," she said before

she leaned forward to him and pressed her lips against his neck. She could feel his body heat and the thick beating of his heart and she knew all too well that he was as anxious as she.

Chase leaned his head back and let the sweet ache of want fill him as he felt the touch of her lips against his flesh. He would never have enough of this, he knew, never be tired of the wonder of it. Even if he made love to her every moment for a lifetime, still there would not be enough.

"We have all the time in the world," he murmured softly.

He put his hand on her cheek and raised her face until her eyes found his. He stared into her eyes, thinking, as he had the very first time he saw her, that he could easily lose himself in those strangely mesmerizing amber eyes. That was precisely what he'd done, he realized, lost himself in those eyes, and he knew he had absolutely no regrets.

Delia smiled softly, and nodded.

"A lifetime," she agreed as she wrapped her arms around his neck, pressed herself close to him, and proceeded to start that lifetime with a kiss.

DISCOVER DEANA JAMES!

FEEL THE FIRE IN CAROL FINCH'S ROMANCES!

BELOVED BETRAYAL (2346, $3.95)

Sabrina Spencer donned a gray wig and veiled hat before blackmailing rugged Ridge Tanner into guiding her to Fort Canby. But the costume soon became her prison—the beauty had fallen head over heels in love!

LOVE'S HIDDEN TREASURE (2980, $4.50)

Shandra d'Evereux felt her heart throb beneath the stolen map she'd hidden in her bodice when Nolan Elliot swept her out onto the veranda. It was hard to concentrate on her mission with that wily rogue around!

MONTANA MOONFIRE (3263, $4.95)

Just as debutante Victoria Flemming-Cassidy was about to marry an oh-so-suitable mate, the towering preacher, Dru Sullivan flung her over his shoulder and headed West! Suddenly, Tori realized she had been given the best present for a bride: a night of passion with a real man!

THUNDER'S TENDER TOUCH (2809, $4.50)

Refined Piper Malone needed bounty-hunter, Vince Logan to recover her swindled inheritance. She thought she could coolly dismiss him after he did the job, but she never counted on the hot flood of desire she felt whenever he was near!